MW01047295

The Brittle Riders

Book One

Bill McCormick

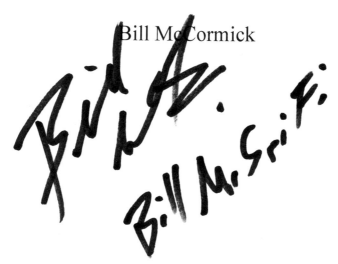

Azoth Khem Publishing
July 2017
Rocky Mount, Virginia

AN AZOTH KHEM PUBLISHING PUBLICATION

Copyright © 2016 Bill McCormick
Copyright © 2016 Azoth Khem Publishing
All rights reserved.

3rd Edition (revised)

ISBN: 1-945987-04-9
ISBN-13: 978-1-945987-04-5

All rights reserved. No part of this publication may be reproduced,
distributed, or transmitted in any form or by any means, including
photocopying, recording, or other electronic or mechanical methods,
without the prior written permission of the publisher, except in the case
of brief quotations embodied in critical reviews and certain other
noncommercial uses permitted by copyright law.
For permission requests, write to the publisher, addressed
"Attention: Permissions Coordinator," at the address below.

Azoth Khem Publishing
70 Foxwood Drive
Rocky Mount, Virginia   24151
Tel: (540) 352-8457

www.azothkhempublishing.com

Ordering Information:
Quantity sales and special discounts are available on quantity purchases by
U.S. and International trade bookstores and wholesalers. For details,
contact the publisher at the address above.

Printed in the United States of America

To Bayla Kompel for believing in me when I no longer
believed in myself.

CREDITS

Character Design: **Brian "Bigger Lion" Daniel**
Twitter.com/Biggerlionart

Cover Logo: **Nick Holmes**
RemixedByNick.com

Cover Art: **Brhi Stokes**
brhistokes.com

Editor: **Warren Belfield**
warrenbelfield.com

Writing Spaces
The Chicago Public Library's Logan Square Branch, The
Levee Bar, The Two Way Lounge,
and The New Wave Café.

Wi-Fi, Caffeine, and Alcohol Are Musts When Writing.

Greetings:

There are too many people to thank for this. Those in the know, know who they are. Also, there are those who would prefer to keep their association with me a dirty little secret. Given my history I can, certainly, sympathize.

The Brittle Riders has, twice, been a labor of love. First, in the late 80's, and early 90's, when I was inspired by a toxic mix of illegal chemicals, long trips on tour busses, and alcohol bearing groupies, to write a story about revolting farm animals. I mean "revolting" as in "disgusting." The basic idea came from driving past an infinite number of farms and being too wired to sleep through it.

After I straightened up, a little, I took all my notes and began banging everything out on the fastest 486 processor the world had to offer at the time. I slaved, sweated, typed, and hammered out an epic (FUCKING AWESOME, DUDE!) masterpiece. It was over fifteen hundred pages and had everything you'd want in a fucking awesome epic. It had the Sword of Truth, the Shield of Valor, and pretty much any other cliché I happened to find lying around.

I called it *The Brittle Riders*, printed it out, and set about making the very minor edits it might have needed before it made me the zillionaire I so richly deserved to be.

Spielberg was set to direct the film adaptation. At least in my mind.

As I read it I came to the slow realization it might be a touch less than epic. Something just shy of fucking awesome. Godawful would be the term you were looking for. If you were being kind.

At one point, and I offer this as a warning to other writers, I, may God have mercy on my fetid soul, had a character say "The yielding shall never commence!!!"

Yeah, it was that bad.

It was exactly the kind of thing paper shredders

were invented for.

Flash forward to 2010. I'd lost my job, my wife, and was on the verge of losing my apartment. So, to protect my sanity, I started writing fiction. I'd already been writing non-fiction for a while. I started with little things like short stories, flash fiction, pieces for various and sundry blogs, and so on.

The first piece of fiction I had published was a short story called "And the Beat Goes Phut" about a DJ watching the apocalypse unfold around him. While the story was, and is, funny, the story behind it is even funnier. It was due to be released on September 11, 2011. Kind of a famous anniversary here in America. I thought the publisher had a wicked sense of humor. After all, the antagonist in the story was of Middle Eastern descent.

Instead, it turned out that no one made the connection until almost the day it was due to be posted. So they pushed it back to November and breathed a sigh of relief. Me? I still wish it had come out as planned. It would have been one hell of a first release.

Oh well.

During that time, I found my notes on *The Brittle Riders*. As I re-read them, now more than two decades' drug free, I found kernels in there that, I felt, might be worth salvaging. I kept the five titular characters, whittled the villains down from thirteen to one, crafted a story arc, and set about writing a nice novella. I was pretty sure I'd be lucky to get twenty thousand words out of it.

You may not have noticed but I'm wrong a lot.

So this bad boy cranked in around three hundred thousand words when it was done. That happened because I have one rule when it comes to writing. I refuse to write a character into a scene just to advance the plot and have them disappear. When the story called for someone to interact with the characters I already had I'd craft the new character a back story and get them involved, even at a minimal level, in the plot.

Another thing that happened was the characters forced me to throw out my original story arc. They didn't like it. Not one bit. I'm grateful I listened to them.

When I finished up Book I the characters informed me there was more to tell. So I wrote a second book. And then a third. And that, finally, concluded their story. It truly is one linear story, with lots of asides to keep it pumping along.

I suppose I should thank Nancy and Kasey for signing me to their fun publishing house and not trying to force me to tone this bitch down or add "a perky teen" to make it appeal to the Y/A market, as others had. Don't get me wrong, I like a lot of young adult fiction. I just didn't write any in this book. Any attempt to retrofit the putative perky teen into this book would have resulted in my being charged with pedophilia, cruelty to minors, or both.

At best I would have been called tacky.

Now that you've read this far you may as well read the rest. In for an inch, in for a mile, I always say. I hope you enjoy reading it as much as I enjoy telling people how good it is.

My best to you always,

Bill McCormick

WELCOME TO ARRETI

NOTE: *This appendix contains all the brands which will appear over the course of the trilogy so some may not be represented in the book you are reading. You can skip this if you hate appendixes and just start with the preamble. You'll probably regret it, but you can always come back.*

All brands are human hybrids and omnivores. They were designed to be low maintenance slave labor for a depleted human population. While many brands were designed to perform specific tasks, ranging from dangerous to tedious, others were simply aesthetically pleasing and were created as toys or living statues.

All brands, however, were designed for speech so they don't have long snouts or beaks and, instead, have mouths that, more or less, look human.

All brands were given enhanced immune systems as well as the ability to create embryonic stem cells in a specially designed organ that also provided an unending supply of Telomerase enzymes to keep their bodies in peak condition. All brands had a built in bio-bomb which would kill them ten years after decanting so that Rohta could continue to restock the same orders over and over. Their immune systems overcame the bio-bombs and the brands called their triggering the "ten-year flu."

THE REGIONS

Children of the Waters – A collection of amphibian races who reside primarily on the west coast of the old United States. They also have crossed the Pacific to live on many islands. The most populous of the brand alliances, they adhere to a modified form of Buddhism. While not completely pacifists, they go out of their way to avoid conflict.

Dwellers of the Plains – A loose collection of brands who populate the area from east of the Mississippi River to Lake Michigan and from about middle Arkansas to the Canadian border. After the Gen-O-Pod war, they renounced technology and developed an agrarian lifestyle. Each brand had its own military presence but they had very few disputes between brands so they were more ornamental than effective. There are some brands who believe in a deity but only in a casual manner.

Eastern Warrens – A diverse collection of brands who live from the Smokey Mountains to the Atlantic Ocean. They inhabit territory as far south as Miami and as far north as Newfoundland. After the Gen-O-Pod war, they picked and chose what technologies they wished to keep. While, in the main, they adopted an agrarian lifestyle, they kept a standing military and armed it with weapons made by the makers, or weapons adapted from those to fit special needs. Their southern clans tend to be followers of Islam, but the rest take a more casual, slightly Gnostic, approach to God.

Kalindor – A collection of reptiloid brands united under a single ruler called The Exalted. They live south of the Rio Grande all the way to Antarctica. They want all the technology the world has to offer but were bred in such a way that imaginative thought eludes them. Once something is explained to them they understand it readily enough, but nothing comes to them originally. In order to get what they want their Exalteds have forced them to wage war, unsuccessfully, against the realm of Lord Südermann and the *Children of the Waters* for hundreds of suns. Their belief system is essentially neo-pagan. Their book of the five gods is part mysticism and part, ecologically friendly, instruction manual.

Realm of Lord Südermann – A collection of insectoid races who live in the southern Mid-West of the old United States. Their territory covers from near the Rocky Mountains to the Mississippi River. By far the most technologically advanced brand alliance they salvaged as much infrastructure as they could after the Gen-O-Pod war and built on it. They adhere to a modified form of Christianity. They have a defined military with an elite guard, a regular army, and one militia sworn to Lord Südermann. Their policy for dealing with trespassers, until the final war with Xhaknar, was to put them to death and destroy the body.

THE BRANDS

Ant Person – Part fire ant, they average around 4½ feet in height and were bred to be desert espionage specialists. Unlike ants, they do not have mandibles, but they do have very sensitive, silica based, body hair that they can use to propel their bodies while prone or sense changes in the atmosphere that elude others. They also have multifaceted, insect-like, eyes and can see in near darkness and in multiple, simultaneous, directions. After the Gen-O-Pod war, they became severe isolationists who only would work with the *Periplaneta* brand (see below). They prefer to wear full body uniforms of nondescript colors.

Athabascae Warrior – Part buffalo, they were made by the New Sons of Freedom Militia to help protect their mountain compounds before the Gen-O-Pod war. They have shaggy body hair and tend toward dark colorings. They prefer clothing made from natural materials and tend to favor buck skins. They live close to nature and are excellent healers.

BadgeBeth – Part various species of badger, they average around 5 feet in height or less. They have a mixed black and white coloring and are covered with light fur. They were designed to work exclusively with soil and were engineered to repel or attract the basic molecular structure of the natural ground. They have razor sharp talons and fear almost nothing. However, they were forced to live underground, or far from civilization, when Xhaknar attacked. They tend to favor simple clothing decorated with small pieces of jewelry.

Chaldean – Part cow, they average around 5½ feet in height. They tend to have blotchy reddish brown colorings with no fur. They were bred to be corporate functionaries but took up an agrarian lifestyle after the Gen-O-Pod war. Even so, they do keep a small militia that serves the clan. They became followers of Allah prior to the Gen-O-Pod war and have retained that faith throughout, albeit with some discrepancies to take into account their genetic differences and fallacies told to them by their makers.

Columba – Part pigeon, they average a little over 5 feet in height. They are gray with touches of white. They were designed to be messengers, despite all of the high tech capabilities of the makers, and they were a popular item purchased by wealthy people who felt that they added the perfect level of secrecy to their long distance conversations. Their heads bob when they walk, but they are almost matchless in the air.

Cudas – Part barracuda, approximately 5 ½ feet tall, a mix of mottled brown and black coloring they have small mouths with blade sharp teeth. They were designed to be aqua assassins, and tend to be very self-contained, to the point of annoyance, but are rabid believers in the ideals, if not always the practicalities, of the *Children of the Waters*.

Cyclops – Pure mutant, they average around 7 feet in height, have bright yellow skin (which is mildly phosphorescent) and just one eye. Their eye can see the complete spectrum from X-rays to Infra-Red. They were built to work in dangerous mining situations and handle heavy objects with ease. A quirk in their design gave them eidetic memories and a deeply philosophical bend. Their philosophy includes the phrase: "Love everyone until they cross you, then kill them."

Din-La – Part rodent, probably rat, they average around 4½ feet in height and are usually portly in adulthood. They are lightly furred, usually gray, and slightly nervous. They wear a uniform of a purple jacket and yellow pants, though they've never explained why. They are very good at keeping secrets and have a global subculture / trading network, which keeps them in the good graces of brands that would otherwise exterminate them.

Fierstan – Pure mutants, they were designed to be simple laborers. They have four, powerful, arms and well-muscled bodies. They average around 5½ feet in height and have bright red skin with dark patches under their eyes. Despite their intended breeding, they have keen intelligence and salvaged what technology they could after the Gen-O-Pod war. They built a powerful city within a fortress after the war and were the acknowledged leaders of the plains until Xhaknar came.

Grindle – Not an actual brand, but a creature created by Rohta for amusement. Part lizard, part bat, it has native intelligence and the ability to speak. While not intended by its makers, they developed sapience and can develop loyalties.

Haliaeetus – Part eagle, they were made by the New Sons of Freedom Militia to help protect their mountain compounds before the Gen-O-Pod war. They average around 5½ in height and are covered with white and brown feathers. They have large wings and can fly faster and farther than their genetic predecessors. They have keen eyesight and talons for fingers and toes. After the Gen-O-Pod war, they retreated to the mountains to live a primarily agrarian lifestyle.

Horun – Part falcon. They average around 3 ½ feet in height, are thin with very agile wings. They have 200/20 eyesight and were bred to be airborne spies. They were also quite facile at micro-processing and micro-manufacturing. They have talons instead of fingernails and they can use those for very delicate operations. They are uniformly ebony colored with blood red wings and some red markings around their wrists and ankles. They have light down around their eyes which stretch across their necks and hides their ears. They tend to wear dark colored clothing and prefer lighter fabrics so they can be dressed while flying.

Human – Not technically a brand they were the creators, or "makers," of all the brands. A race that was genetic cousins to apes and other primates, they lived on Earth and ruled over it due to their native intelligence and supposed superiority for approximately 12,000 years. When finally, aware that they were to be denied travel amongst the stars, the race began to die off. It was this lack of human labor combined with the need to keep up a certain lifestyle that led them to create genetic hybrids to do the work and/or fighting for them. They called these hybrids Gen-O-Pods and divided them into trademarked brands.

Kgul – Pure mutant, inspired by the ancient tale of the Gollum, they are large, clay based, creatures and were designed to provide manual labor for extended periods of time. Due to the fact that they were difficult to make they were created with the ability to survive almost any injury and to be able to regenerate body parts as needed. They are smarter and more resourceful than they look and are fiercely devoted to the *Rangka* (see below).

Kleknar – Pure mutant. No one has any idea what their inspiration was. They average around 3 feet tall, are pure white and are almost perfectly round. They were designed to get into small places in mines and can swim surprisingly well. Developed with an ability to control autism they have keen senses that they can enhance at will and are deadly shots. If they open their senses up too much they enter a sort of null state and need care for the rest of their lives. They also have a twisted sense of humor and the ability to turn almost anything into an explosive.

Koi-San – Part koi, they were bred to be decorative additions to large homes with pools or fountains. They average just under 5 feet tall and are covered with translucent scales of many colors which cover pale skin. They tend to be the more thoughtful members of the *Children of the Waters*. While they did fight in the Gen-O-Pod war they've never taken up arms again.

Kwini-Laku – Part seal, they were the first brand ever made by Edward Q. Rohta. They were designed for underwater research and to be able to go into areas that would be lethal to human divers. Averaging just over 5 feet in height, they are powerfully muscled and intelligent. After the Gen-O-Pod war, they joined the *Children of the Waters* and set up small island communities around the Pacific Ocean.

LGX-117 – Part broad snouted caiman, they average barely five feet in height and have greenish, scaled, skin with pale eyes. They were designed to survive in jungle environments and handle any task they were assigned no matter the heat or the humidity. Physically strong, they are smart enough for many tasks but lack any originality.

Llamia– Part horse, part steer, part armadillo, they average 7 feet in height and weigh around ½ a ton. They have the torso of a human, the body of a horse, with the cloven hoofs of a steer that have razor sharp points and armadillo-esque armor that starts in the middle of their backs and then covers their entire rear loins and rump. They were designed to be a warrior brand that could haul supplies, fight close battles and survive harsh environments. Their skin color is as varied as the humans that were used for genetic source material and they each have a mane that stretches down the middle of their torsos to the tip of their backs. Bred for intelligence and the ability to utilize many weapons, they were a major factor in the success of the Gen-O-Pod war. They wear clothing when they are in social situations or in battle. Otherwise, they prefer to be nude.

Maker – See *Human* (above).

Mantis Warrior – Part mantis, they average over 6 feet in height, but tend to be thin. They have pea-green skin and small barbs on the backs of their legs. Extremely intelligent and resourceful they were bred to work in arid environments and handle hazardous materials. They were sold mostly to oil and gas companies. After the Gen-O-Pod war, they relocated to North America and swore allegiance to the *Periplaneta* (see below).

Mayanoren – Part gorilla, they average a little over 6 feet in height and are extremely powerful. They have no body hair and mottled, pink, skin. They were designed to be infantry for a new world army by makers in competition with Rohta. They are, in the main, very stupid and require extensive explanations and training to accomplish any task beyond killing. However, killing is something they do very well and with extreme gusto.

Minotaur – Part Toro Bravo, they were bred to be warriors and officers. They have deep reddish skin and powerful muscles. Averaging over 6 feet in height, they are heavy, hoofed, beings who have developed a deep, spiritual, side while keeping all their warrior skills. They favor simple clothing and currently live near a dormant volcano under the ground.

Named One – Really smart *Mayanorens*. See *"Mayanoren"* (above) for more information.

Naradhama – *Fierstans* (see above) who were captured and mutated by Xhaknar into a servant class of warriors and sycophants.

Orcan – Part killer whale, they were designed to be security for several shipping companies. They never developed the true killer sense of their genetic predecessors and were scheduled for elimination around the time of the Gen-O-Pod war. Even so, they are powerful swimmers, with large, finned feet and have skin coloring similar to their namesakes as well as a developed echo location bulb on the front of their forehead and a blow hole on the back of their neck.

Pan – Half goat, approximately 3½ to 4 feet tall, thin and the males appear as traditional satyrs. Because Rohta enjoyed the myth so much all males were well endowed. Having no template for the females he'd simply made them voluptuous. They all have pale white and auburn hair and green eyes. Their lower body fur is thick and colored the same as the hair on their heads and they all have a curled white tail. Designed to be sex toys, primarily, for rich Europeans, they have turned into a very divergent race that breeds everything from art masters to warriors.

Periplaneta – Part cockroach, they are the sole race that provides the Südermenn for the delta brands. They average 5 feet in height, have six arms, and mandibles instead of mouths. They were designed to work in environments that would be lethal to humans, primarily radioactive and toxic. After the Gen-O-Pod war, they salvaged as much technology as they could and immediately set about to recreate the infrastructure necessary to run it. Highly creative and resilient, they are extremely spiritual and follow an essentially Christian lifestyle. They are revered by the various insectoid brands.

QZD-1934 – Part chameleon, they average less than five feet in height, weigh less than 100 lbs. and have the ability to alter their skin color to blend in with their surroundings. They were designed to be spies for various corporations and militaries. After the Gen-O-Pod war, they retreated to the southern continents and waited for a ruler to emerge.

Rangka – Wizards who had their flesh removed by a military grade virus in the first battle with Xhaknar. Greatly debilitated in one way they developed even more enhanced powers over magnetism and a powerful psychic sensitivity. See "*Wizards*" (below) for more information.

RZL-274 – Part flying lizard, they average around 5 feet in height and have membranes that stretch from their wrists to their feet. They also have a stabilizing membrane between their legs. They are mottled yellow/green and have razor sharp talons instead of fingers or toes. They were designed to work on top of the canopies in rain forests.

Se-Jeant – Pure mutant, they average around 5½ feet in height, have gray/blue skin covered with similarly colored fur and tend to be thin. They have three, round, eyes and were designed to do very specialized miniature work. Their long, thin, fingers and flat noses and slits for mouths belie the fact that they are fierce warriors and cunning adversaries. They developed an affinity for colder temperatures and live further north than any other brand on the plains in a home they call The Ice Palace. While not literally made of ice, they do their best to keep the temperatures cool.

Snake-Man – Not a brand but a class of assassins created by Xhaknar and Yontar to act as spies. It is believed they were created through selective breeding and rude experimentation, but no records exist of the exact procedure used. They average around 3½ feet in height, have poisonous fangs, and lightly scaled skins. They serve when they feel like it and are loyal to no one. Very few exist due to these facts.

Sominid – Not a brand but an alien race who encountered humans long before the Gen-O-Pod war. Over 12 feet tall, mammalian, bipedal, with bright blue skin and white hair they came to Earth for one reason only, to party. Like good house guests anywhere, they brought their own brandy. Unlike good house guests, they destroyed the moon and killed tens of thousands of people. However, the incident was alcohol related and not purposeful.

Succubus – Part bat, they average around 6 feet in height and are exclusively female. They have talons for toes and a spur on each heel for balance. They are partly metamorphic and can assume three basic forms; womyn, which resembles a human female except for their feet; mal, which resembles a human male except for the feet and has non-working genitalia; and their traditional form which features large leathery wings. Their skin colorings represent all of the former human races and they have hairstyles that run the gamut from bald to lengthy locks. They prefer to be topless and wear only loincloths in the wild, but can and will dress very elegantly when the situation calls for it.

Super Soldier – Multiple genetic sources, they average around 7 feet in height and weigh over 300lbs. Made by the same makers who made the *Mayanorens*, they have faces which are exoskeletons, and heavily muscled bodies that are covered in coarse, dark brown, body hair. They tend to be extremely intelligent, but limited in scope. Some are military tacticians, others political leaders and so on. Nevertheless, those limitations do not lessen their deadliness.

Warters – Part warthog, they average around 5 feet in height, are rotund and very strong. They have small tusks on their lower jaw that makes speech difficult. They are dark pink in color and tend to wear robes to hide as many weapons as they can. They were originally bred to be security for a specialized company no one remembers. After the Gen-O-Pod war, they turned to banditry and are scattered across the North American continent.

White Teeth – Part Great White Shark, born to be pure warriors of the seas. Averaging around 6 feet in height with mottled white skin and a mouth that contains two sets of razor sharp teeth, both top and bottom. They were given better eyesight then their genetic heirs and a far better sense of perception. Vicious beyond belief they were willing to kill any who crossed them. After the Gen-O-Pod wars, they joined the *Children of the Waters* and adopted their peace oriented philosophies as best they could.

Wizard – Pure mutants. Ranging in height from five feet to 6½ feet tall, they had bright blue skin and varied body types. They were designed to use the forces of magnetism for mining and related duties. To accomplish this an average human's natural magnetic field was enhanced on a geometric scale. Their basic abilities allowed them to segregate metals from the ground and to repel Earth's natural magnetism and float a few feet above the planet.

Because they were built to work in dangerous locales they were given enhanced control over their alpha waves so they could communicate with each other, in case of danger, without the need for expensive electronic gear.

Wolfen – Part wolf, they average just under 6 feet in height. They were designed to be a forest based, warrior brand. They have tremendous strength, an increased sense of smell and intense curiosity and intelligence. They tend to be covered in reddish brown fur and have slightly scalloped ears. They can cover great distances without any artificial aid and can learn to use any weapon within seconds. They prefer to live in packs and off the land. They were forced into hiding when Xhaknar attacked.

ANIMALS

Deisteed – About 20% larger than an average horse they were designed to be work animals. They were used by the wealthy land owners to show they were more in tune with nature than the robot users.

Kgum – Think an ugly cross between a cow and a water buffalo. They provide meat, wool, hides and crude labor. They replaced domestic cows which died off due to an inability to breed on their own.

Narkling – Approximately 8 to 10 feet tall with six legs and a segmented body covered in thick, dark, fur. They have razor sharp teeth that they can rotate inside their mouths. They will eat anything or anyone. They were designed to be mining machines but were too deadly to keep around. The makers dumped them in an abandoned forest in the Mid-West and forgot about them.

Nysteed – The only brand created exclusively by a brand. A horse-like animal, slightly larger than a deisteed, they can run vast distances at full speed and carry heavy loads if need be. They are shaggy, with dark coats, and have flames instead of eyes. Originally bred to help the Wizards explore their world they became the elite war horses of the plains after Xhaknar came.

Pit person – Mildly humanoid, less than 2 feet tall and thin, they are non-sapient and fearful of almost everything. They were designed to be helpers and companions for children but they never really worked out

Quizzle bird – Think of a parrot on acid and you get the idea. A riot of colors, averaging around 5 pounds, they are very large and very stupid. Rohta just thought they were fun so he made a lot of them.

Rakyeen – A six-legged creature, averaging about 6 feet in height and around 12 feet long, they are furry mutants that were designed to be draft animals. They are good, if gamey, eating but do not take well to domestication.

Sna-Ahd weasel – Not really a weasel, more like a long necked rat, they were an early experiment by Rohta that escaped before he could finish their line. They were supposed to process soil like earth worms and leave it aerated and filled with nutrients. Mostly they just have sex and live underground.

Steed – About ¾ the size of an average horse they were designed to run very fast for short distances, although they could carry a rider a long distance at a comfortable trot. The makers used them to patrol their estates and impress their neighbors.

TERMS

Arreti - Earth

Brand – artificially created sentient life form

Breaklight - dawn

Clik – approximately one hour

Dark Sun – winter

Dim Sun - fall

Epi-clik – approximately one minute

Even – night

Even-fall – dusk

Even-split – Approximately midnight

Full Sun (*sometimes just Sun or Suns in the plural)*- approximately 365 turns (see below)

Goldens - money

Good Sun - summer

Kay– approximately 1.246 miles / 2.005 kilometers. Arreti has a circumference of 20,000 kays.

Maker - human

Mid-break – when the sun is highest in the sky

Pod – see Brand

Small– child

Sepi-clik – approximately one second

Turn – One planetary revolution or day

Warm Sun– spring

Youngling – pre-teen to teenaged brand

Preamble

Above.

An olive-backed forest robin leapt from its perch, singing its happy song to the new day while letting its unbridled joy gleefully echo above the tree tops. A Fox Kestral heard the song and shared its joy, albeit for slightly different reasons. It swooped down from on high, snagged the robin, killed it, and began eating the tasty delicacy as it flew into the beautiful, African, dawn.

Below.

A servant noticed drops of blood and a tiny feather on the napkins. He quickly discarded them into a nearby trash receptacle, replaced them with new finery, and silently cursed outdoor parties again.

Later, servants' curses or no, it was a beautiful night for a party. The two halves of the long desecrated moon were in full light. The winds off of the Kalahari plains were dry and refreshing. Delicate Zzin music wafted across the fountainade and pool. The revelers stood around sipping Sominid Brandy, silently sizing up each other's spouses.

The nude waiters and waitresses were just decadent enough to entertain but not enough to earn extra money. The buffet was huge, stretching almost thirty meters. There was food and drink from every culture in attendance displayed across its wide expanse. All in all you would not guess this evening would signal the end of civilization.

However, apocalypses are funny that way.

The extravaganza in question was being hosted by Edward Q. Rohta. A brilliant geneticist, and avowed hedonist, who wintered in Africa. Of course this home was neither as large nor ornate as the one back in his native Brazil, but it would have to do for the evening. He had moved a large part of his laboratory here to finish his latest work. This work was going to make him the hit of the party world. It would also serve to make him even richer. Neither thought dismayed him.

He entered from the veranda onto the deck next to the fountainade wearing a transparent, gray, robe. His three husbands and five wives walked beside him. They all wore filmy white gowns and high heeled strapless shoes. Resembling dissolute angels, they glided down the stairway.

Local gossip had it that Edward was looking for another husband. With what he was revealing through his robe, everyone agreed he should have no problem getting what he wanted. His ebon frame was firm and proportioned generously in all areas of interest.

An aide brought out a large cart covered with a deep blue cloth. There were no decorations on its shimmering fabric. The effect made the cart even more mysterious, like a magician's appliance, and everybody knew Edward disdained magic.

Without a word being said, aids lifted the cover to reveal three large seals who had arms and legs. No one remembers exactly how they recognized the creatures as seals, but everybody did.

They were released from their cage, stood, stretched and walked over to the pool.

They jumped in, swam around for just a bit and then pulled themselves out. Their arms and legs were heavily muscled, their skin sleek and glistening. However, before anyone could ask why Edward would create creatures such as these because it was obvious he had, one of the seals asked for a towel. Several people fainted, the rest applauded. Edward had done it again. This party would be legend.

Before the end of the night, six government agencies had requested more information on the creatures and two had provided hefty down payments. Edward knew his creations would be perfect for difficult underwater research and exploration of the newly found geothermal sites under the polar ice caps. The fact they could speak would help them communicate what they had seen and enable researchers to be more explicit in their directions. These were all laudable achievements to Edward and his guests.

Ever since the Plato Wars it had been illegal to create any type of artificial intelligence. Edward's creations sidestepped the myriad limitations. They weren't artificial, they were organic hybrids designed to assist humans. The fact they were also sentient beings who could be bought and sold didn't seem to bother anyone. After all, it isn't like they were human.

It was a good year for Rohta Industries, L.L.C. Several other species of Gen-O-Pods, as they were called by the marketing department, were created to help with specialized tasks. Each helped relieve the workload for the dwindling human race and enabled everyone to have even more free time. The party continued.

Prosperity reigned.

Happy thoughts abounded and Edward Q. Rohta was wealthier than several countries and, perhaps most important to him, invited to all the best parties.

All of this would have been fine except for one thing. Edward didn't stop there. Hell, he didn't even slow up. Fascinated by Greek mythology, he began fusing genes from his husbands and wives with bull and bat DNA respectively. He mixed and matched molecules like a demented child mixing paints.

If said demented child had the benefit of a billion dollar lab and nanotechnology to bind the results into a cohesive whole that is.

He had discovered the trick to making transgenic beings, and thus having them certified as property, was to create them with fifty-two chromosomes instead of the usual forty-six. Legally they were listed as pseudo-humans and granted no rights.

The flotsam and jetsam of evolution allowed for simple things like gigantism, scales, excess fur, increased keratin for razor sharp nails, and so on. Those had popped up in unfortunate people since time immemorial. It's how the circus freaks of yore came to be. What evolution did not allow for were things like wings, feathers, hooves and the rest of what his clients craved. Man's reptilian ancestors had diverged before their avian progeny emerged and the distance between man and crow was too vast to be recovered.

The additional chromosomes allowed him to manipulate bone mass, muscle density, appendages, and whatever else he needed to satisfy his growing list of customers.

He was constantly reassured by the fact his research showed he had total control over the results. The creatures he created were stronger, larger and, in some cases, smarter than humans, but they could not reproduce. Nor could they live more than ten years. Their DNA was just too scrambled for that and he'd planted a bio-bomb, set to detonate in ten years, inside each to ensure the result.

So Edward Q. Rohta went merrily along creating fun things for his parties, and international slave labor, with nary a second thought. He really should have given it that second thought.

Maybe even a third or a fourth or a fifth.

He came to the same realization one day when, just over fifty years later, a Succubus walked into his Brazilian lair with two younger Succubi and announced enough was most certainly enough. She continued her pronouncement by saying she, and her contemporaries, had studied as much as they could of humanity and found it got in the way of decent creatures such as herself. Ergo, humanity had to go. And that was, most succinctly, that. She left with the two younglings straggling behind her.

Edward Q. Rohta went into his lab and efficiently killed himself. His final note claimed it wasn't suicide, just a chance to get while the getting as good. On that, he may have had the right idea. In less time than it takes to truly rear a suckling infant, the human race was a myth not spoken.

There had been no real way to prepare for the onslaught. The Gen-O-Pods numbered in the millions. They were heavily armed with exotic weapons of their own design as well as others they had stolen from the humans. They ignored all standard battle strategies. They could afford to. With Succubi and Minotaurs leading the way, they fought in three dimensions without mechanical help.

However, what they did not know, what these new conquerors could never have known, was Edward Q. Rohta had not been alone in his experiments. Far from it.

Several governments had been hiring scientists to recreate his work so they could compete for a piece of the lucrative market.

In retrospect, the price was already far too high but there would be no one left to say so.

The other, government sponsored, creatures watched the new world unfold from dark lairs and hidden fortresses. Their time had not yet come. They felt confident it would since, after all, every group needs a leader and that is exactly what they were bred for.

Blissful in their ignorance, and in an effort to eulogize their victory, the Gen-O-Pods restarted the calendar. Four thousand three hundred sixty five years nine months and nineteen days into the traditional Gregorian calendar, they called it turn one of the first Full Sun. The fact this happened to be Edward Q. Rohta's birthday was pure coincidence. With that behind them, they never gave their actions a second thought.

The majority destroyed all the weapons they had used since they reminded them of their makers. They disbanded the system of months and settled on the four seasons. The Warm Sun for the thaw, the Good Sun for planting, the Dim Sun for the fall and the Dark Sun for winter. A year became one Full Sun. Other conventions of humanity were either altered or eliminated, as needed.

National origins meant nothing so they used regional locations for a rough assessment of heritage. The names humans had used annoyed their tongues so they forgot them. The buildings humans had built were an inconvenience so they razed them. Within ten Full Suns of the elimination of humanity, there were no reminders.

The last age of man had ended, primarily, because of a good party.

Well, let's not underestimate the situation; it was one hell of a party.

It became legend. Just not exactly as Edward Q. Rohta may have wished.

BOOK ONE

Hunger. Hunger and Fear. These are not the type of emotions that will help you get in touch with your inner being, but they will keep you alive if you pay attention to them. Right now, hunger has Sland's full attention. Not the sand tangling his fur, not the knife handle poking his taut abdomen, not the blow-gun hanging from his belt. Nothing holds his attention, save hunger.

He watches the sand swell around the newly formed tar pit. He watches the carrion begging birds wheel carelessly close to the heat. He watches the exploding bubbles tease their rotting feathers. He watches because his BadgeBeth senses tell him food is here and he is hungry.

He leaps towards the pit and grabs a half decayed carcass of something from the tar before it can escape his hunger. He's back in his shelter before the carrion begging birds realize he's stolen their mid-break repast.

He doesn't bother with linen or cutlery. Though his body is not large, his BadgeBeth teeth are jagged, his fingers strong, his talons razor-sharp. He just rips the flesh from its, recently dead, bones and eats. Wiping the grease on his tattered pants.

As he finishes his sumptuous meal, his other emotion screams for his attention. Fear. A menacing, glowing, silver orb is heading directly at him. There is nowhere to move. He is trapped and angry. Angry at himself for not setting his camp better. Hunger had made him set it too quickly and now he will pay for that transgression.

He starts to pull his blow-gun but remembers he has no darts. He pulls his knife instead. If he is to die on the wastelands he will not do it quietly. The orb stalls just outside of his reach. It did not speak, yet he hears. Fear and anger are replaced by knowledge. It is time. For what, he does not know, but it is time nonetheless. He wipes his dripping maw on his bare arm, packs, and heads west.

About three kays south of his meal he spies a kgum herder grazing his shaggy beasts. Taller than Sland and three times as wide, the kgum are a steady source of labor, fur, leather, milk, and meat. They're also dumb as a box of rocks. A fact Sland is reminded of as he watches the herder try and dissuade one of the beasts, without success, from walking into a tar pit.

In another section of the wastelands, a Wolfen chases a young Rakyeen. His two legs are faster than its six. Soon, he's upon it. He draws his sword and beheads the beast in one fell strike, never breaking stride. As it shudders and stumbles to the ground the Wolfen, R'yune, smiles. He slices the beast as a Succubus lands near him. She, N'leah, tugs her loin cloth back into place and brings forth a tiny grill from the ground. He looks, distinctly, unimpressed with the grill, but still seems impressed with her taught, ebony, frame, her luxurious leather wings and her glistening, bald, pate and naked torso. She then creates a blue flame and sets it within the grill. These two things grow to a usable size and R'yune places the meat on them.

They are preoccupied with their meal when, unexpectedly, R'yune spins and draws his sword. There's an orb floating behind them. It does not speak, yet they hear. It is time.

They pack what little they have and head south. They ignore the carrion birds and sna-Ahd weasels that finish their meal. They have someplace to go and someone to meet. That much they know. For now, that is all they need to know.

An observatory glistens in the dripping even-fall. Its ancient walls seem imbued with pulsing blood. The very mortar appears as flesh to the eye. A living building for the living dead. The home of Geldish, last rogue Rangka of the wastelands. The last one on all of Arreti, maybe.

A Llamia, BraarB, approaches the structure. Wearing nothing but her weapons' belt, she is carrying an orb. She tosses it into the air and watches as it floats near the entrance. She sharpens the edges of her four cloven hooves on a nearby rock while teasing the orb with her whip for a while and then sits in the sand. The natural armor covering her loins and rump is dusty and dull from the journey. It can be polished later. She will be patient. She knows it is time.

Geldish appears from within the observatory wearing his customary black robe and mounts her sturdy back, sliding forward on the armored rear to find a comfortable position. Together they ride to the north. He knows it is time because he said it is. They say nothing to each other on their journey. They both know why they are going to Go-Chi. They both know why he has summoned the fringe dwellers of the wasteland. She is pretty sure she knows the basics at least, if not the full plan. It is time for change.

As they ride the wind scatters the sands revealing pit-people and sna-Ahd weasels copulating to the rhythm of swirling need. These creatures do not see glowing orbs. Nor would they want to. They only know it's time to procreate. It's safer that way.

Along the way, they pass a steed ranch. Geldish smiles at the sight. The haven lord rancher not only has regular steeds, which are used for racing and common transport, he also has six deisteeds, the larger variety preferred by warriors, and each of them looks to be prime breeding stock. Although the rancher watches the odd pair with a wary eye, the steeds are too preoccupied with grazing to care. They pass into the distance and the rancher marks it down as one more odd thing he's seen in a lifetime of odd things.

It's also the time of the Dark Sun, in the Full Sun of 986. That makes it nine hundred and eighty-six Full Suns after Rohta helped create the new zero. All of the fringe dwellers are aware of this. They are also aware which season it is. A time when the plants sleep, praying to awake in the Warm Sun. Now, it's dry on the wastelands. Not a savage blistering dry, but dry because the lands have been sucked that way. Each generation has leeched a little more until there is little more left and what little there is, is owned by Xhaknar.

In the village of Go-Chi, an unusual clan gathers. They will not draw stares. They will not even get acknowledged. To do so would invite death, or worse. When five of the wastelands' unrumored show up for drinks, you do exactly what the innkeeper did. You serve them drinks and hope like Zanubi they pay. He's in luck, they will ... later.

N'leah and R'yune are the first to arrive at the haven bar. She spins a chair around so her wings won't get caught. R'yune grabs a couple of more chairs as Sland enters. He screams an order for three flagons of skank and sits down. N'leah smiles at the uneasy innkeeper. It is not the kind of smile that will endear her to him. It is, however, the kind of smile that makes him check his purse. R'yune growls loudly. Of course, being mute, that's about all he can do.

As the innkeeper, a small furry haven lord, delivers their drinks, Geldish rides in on BraarB, holds up two bony fingers and waves them in the poor brand's face. The innkeeper quickly moves to retrieve two more flagons. When he returns BraarB grabs his bar rag and wipes the even mists from her breasts and hands it to N'leah so she can do the same. The innkeeper wisely holds his tongue. He needed a new bar rag anyway. He does not want his bar rag to need a new innkeeper. Besides, if he gets it back, it will make a great souvenir. Novelty items have never hurt the inn keeping business.

Geldish grins inwardly at the scene. He is enjoying the discomfort. They know it is rare for the fringe to enter Go-Chi. It is even rarer for a Rangka to join them. However, it is now time to get this meeting underway. Before he can begin, Sland shifts uncomfortably.

"Speak, you fucking sack of bones," he decides to get this over so he can get back to the hunt. "I have traveled far to be here, why have you summoned us? And for what reason?"

N'leah glances over at her new skank companion and smiles. This smile would endear her to anyone. She turns to face Geldish.

"What he lacks in subtlety, he makes up for in truth. Why are we here?"

He lets the question hang unanswered for a moment. He wants them to see the flame in his eyes. He wants them to contemplate who, and what, they are questioning. He wants them to think. To think long and hard about the flames. To think long and hard about how those flames came to take the place of eyes and what it means now that they have. His pause has accomplished its goal. So he answers.

"To kill Xhaknar's army, bring water to Go-Chi and to make many goldens."

Most of their skank ends up on the floor, either from oral and nasal projection or dropped flagons. Each of them looks as though they are trapped in a tiny room with an extremely large problem. Truth be known, they are.

Any hope this is some sick, elaborate, joke dies in the flames of Geldish's eyes. Quite a lot could die in those eyes. Humor is definitely on that long list. Two full epi-cliks go by without a muscle being twitched. It's almost as if the air had been sucked from the room. It could have been and Geldish wouldn't have cared one bit.

Of course, it would absolutely ruin everyone else's turn.

The innkeeper sees what has happened and runs

over with a round of new drinks. These are finished in one gulp by everyone except Geldish. He sips his slowly.

BraarB inhales deeply, "Well, okay, anything else?"

"Well, it seems we could do with more skank." Geldish grins outwardly. It is not the type of grin which inspires humor or warmth.

Geldish waves to the innkeeper again. The frazzled brand returns with five more flagons of skank and rushes away. So far he hasn't made a golden, but he's still alive and he got his rag back.

"Even for me, dead one, this is crazy talk," Sland says summing everything up at once.

Geldish turns and devotes his entire attention to Sland. This is not a good thing.

"Are you pleased with Xhaknar's reign?"

"No," Sland is not comfortable being the focus of those flames.

"Do you dislike goldens?" Geldish's voice seems to grow even darker as his flames grow brighter.

"No."

"Do you prefer pit food to real food?"

"No."

"Well, then, you are with me."

He makes it seem so easy.

BraarB contemplates everything she has heard and turns to face Geldish, as only a Llamia can.

"You are smooth, dead one, but what you ask is impossible."

Geldish returns the attention. "Why?"

BraarB looks at him as though he is doinkier than believed. "Because Xhaknar has over five hundred thousand well-trained Naradhama at his disposal and . . . well, what the Zanubi more do you need?"

"Well, we'll need an army, obviously."

There? You see? It's simple if you work out the details. Geldish smiles wider. It does not calm his guests. In fact, it causes their fringe dwelling blood to run even colder than normal.

N'leah almost throws her drink at him. She would have too, if he wasn't who and what he is.

Finally, she gathers her wits enough to speak, albeit sarcastically.

"Great Rohta! None of us could have thought of that! Shall I hail a crier to summon our army or do we just post a notice?"

"Neither will be necessary," Geldish whispers in a voice that could curl iron, "our army will come when we offer them the goldens we are going to get."

BraarB lets her curiosity get the better of her. She will regret that.

"And are those goldens we will be seeing soon?"

"Yes, this even, at moons full or at even-split ... whichever is easier."

Sland has no innate curiosity, just a need to end this conversation and make sense of everything.

"How much and where?"

"Three million goldens, presently located in Xhaknar's repository," Geldish says this as though robbing the planet's most heavily fortified repository was a common occurrence.

Sland's brain hurts for a sepi-clik, "Unless I'm an ass eater, that repository is not open now."

"I know."

It takes far more than a sepi-clik to sink in. They will be wanted by Xhaknar for the worst crime he has, disturbing his finances. That will get you thirty, pain filled, turns above Xhaknar's blood fountain and then death.

N'leah glances over at R'yune. "Well, how about it, partner? Will you let Xhaknar put another price on your head for the chance to zork him off and maybe kill him?"

R'yune growls an enthusiastic approval. The others discuss it vigorously amongst themselves and then let BraarB sum it up.

"We have all killed for less. I think it is safe to say

we are with you. We just don't know why."

Geldish nods, orders another round of skank and snags a bowl of meat from the hands of the, now trembling, innkeeper. Then he hands the whimpering server enough goldens to keep him in bar rags for eternity.

They will wait until even-split. Then they will make their move. It is the kind of move which brooks no error. Once they are done with this, there is no going back. This commitment is forever. The innkeeper knows none of this, of course. He just knows he is rich beyond his wildest dreams and he'd better find some fresh meat for his new best customers.

Oolnok looks across his fields and sighs. If well enough could ever be left alone he'd have a nice farm. But such seems doomed to never happen. Between the various raiding parties, the taxes, and the fact there seems to be less and less water every Sun, he barely ekes out enough to survive.

Nevertheless, survive he does, which is far better than any alternatives he can think of.

He glances down and curses softly to himself. No need to let the smalls hear language like that. Then he scrapes the kgum dung off his boots and headed to the coops. He scatters feed across the ground for the prancing fowls and went to slop the na-porcines. The large beasts grunted and growled and rushed the fence. But he'd made the fence himself and knew it would hold. Just one of the beasts could, when properly butchered, feed a family of four for a full season. He was blessed with six.

As he listens to his smalls, back in the house, squeal and laugh he realizes he is truly blessed. His wife of seventeen Suns is a treasure and his five smalls, now starting to grow into younglings, are good and honest, if a little noisy.

Yes, thinking of everything, he is truly blessed. No carrying swords into battle for good old Oolnok. No worrying about this warren or that to cloud his turns. No having to deal with the oddities of the fringe. Nope, all Oolnok needs to do is feed his beasts and wipe the occasional bits of kgum dung off his boots.

Those are tasks he can handle.

He heads to the side gate and releases the kgums into the field. With the Warm Sun coming the beasts would be ready to shed their heavy coats. Oolnok knew he couldn't let that happen. He'd let his wife know to make sure the shears were sharpened and they'd shave the beasts this even. The smalls were old enough now too, so they should help.

He patted one of the kgums as it sauntered by and noted with satisfaction its fur was thick. That was good. It meant he'd have a large quantity of high quality fur to sell at the warren. Whenever he was asked why his kgums had better fur than any of his neighbors, he'd shrug and tell the questioner he sang to the beasts. Everyone would laugh at him and let him keep his secrets, but the truth was that was exactly what he did.

Every even when the beasts were penned he would sing them songs his mother had sung to him. He did it to relax, but the beasts seemed to enjoy it too.

He closed the gate behind the last kgum and headed into his house for his breaklight meal. Then he had fields to tend.

Yes, life was good for old Oolnok.

Full even rests upon the wastelands. Battle fires burn in the camp of the Naradhama. Temp-slaves tend to the warriors. Since there are mal and femme warriors, there are mal and femme temp-slaves.

"At least those who were unsure were killed a long time ago," thinks Ek-kh.

He watches as the mutant deisteeds buck and whinny. They are complaining about their tight tethers. They don't like being tied in rows. Then again, inbreeding does that to a beast. The handlers ignore the beasts' displeasure and feed them their meager rations anyway.

In the camp itself musicians play ribald hymns and scatological tunes to entertain the troops. Dancers coil obscenely around each and every trooper in an attempt to warm them up for the temp-slaves. They writhe their bodies around the legs and arms of anything desperate enough to get close to them. No one complains.

They've been on a mission for almost fifty turns; most of the warriors were beginning to think their deisteeds were looking sexy. The temp-slaves and the dancers will do good business this even.

Ek-kh hears the whispers as he walks through camp. Minotaur slime, traitor and worse. He ignores them. He is an aide to Xhaknar. He is a leader of the Naradhama.

No matter what the Naradhama say.

His gray uniform is stained and sweaty from hedonistic adventures, not work. He staggers and swaggers through the main section of camp, slapping the bare asses of the temp-slaves as he passes. He grabs a jug of Whævin from a trooper and swallows it in one gulp. The trooper glares at him but says nothing. Ek-kh stumbles around grotesquely, shouting platitudes of greatness to all who ignore him. That takes a while. Eventually he finds a temp-slave to his liking. She is still breathing. He pulls her from the loins, mid swallow, of her previous customer. She follows him, laughing and drooling, to his tent.

Ek-kh almost swallows his tongue. He tosses the temp-slave from the tent and tries to wipe his slimy hands on his loin cloth. His knees give out and he crumbles to the floor in terror. The sight of Xhaknar, all two and a half meters tall of him topped with his bony face, does that to those who first meet him. Especially those who are his willing servants.

"Great one!" He shrieks, "You were not expected for three more turns."

"But, I am here now." Xhaknar watches Ek-kh impassively.

Ek-kh staggers to his feet. "Our scouts have attained the information you sought." Since sobriety fails him, he wisely sticks to business.

"Will you share it with me, or shall I rip it from your decadent, yet useless, soul?" Xhaknar lightly hisses each syllable.

"Oh no, Great One!" Ek-kh is trembling from head to hoof. "Ummhh, Geldish is on the move. Uhh, he has been sighted in the Crasnia. ... the haven bar in Go-Chi. Uhh, you know? Uhh, yes, umm, he has four fringe dwellers with him!"

Xhaknar contemplates this information for a brief epi-clik. He does not need time to assimilate the information, he just likes watching Ek-kh quiver.

"There are no warriors?" The answer is obvious, but Xhaknar asks anyway.

"Oh no, Great One!" Ek-kh is getting worse. His quivering leads Xhaknar to believe there will be humor before this is over.

"No traitors?" Xhaknar almost smiles.

"No, Great One!" Ek-kh is fading fast.

"Just four fringe dwellers?" Xhaknar could almost be said to be enjoying himself.

"Yes, Great One!!" Ek-kh is going to lose something... somewhere fast.

Xhaknar slowly pours himself a flagon of Whævin

before proceeding. "I see. What were they doing, Ek-kh?"

Ek-kh is definitely on the way to public embarrassment. "Drinking skank and eating meat, Great One."

If Xhaknar had eyebrows, he would have raised one. "Why?"

Ek-kh's loin cloth is straining under the pressure. Xhaknar pushes on. "So, tell me Ek-kh, newly loyal leader of Naradhama. Tell me, Ek-kh, he whose blood may yet fill my fountain. Tell me why they were drinking skank and eating meat in a haven bar in Go-Chi."

That does it. Behind his dwellers' loin shield, rivulets begin to cascade down to the ground. A rather large puddle forms around Ek-kh's hooves. Soon he is a fountain of humiliation. It almost appears as if he is raining on a miniature desert. Ek-kh crashes to his knees amidst his newly created lake, cracking his jaw against the temp-slave serving cart and causing his lip to bleed.

"I do not know, Great One! That knowledge is beyond me!" Ek-kh is screeching now.

"How will you attain that which I seek?" Xhaknar's voice never wavers, although he is greatly amused by the spectacle.

"I have left a spy in the Crasnia, Great One!" This may be the first thing Ek-kh has done to redeem himself all even. Xhaknar thinks about this for an epi-clik or so as he watches Ek-kh debase himself further. He secretly wonders how much liquid a Minotaur can hold. Ek-kh is still leaking up a storm.

Time to find out the rest of the story. He can watch Ek-kh become disgusting anytime. "Were any of the fringe dwellers hunters?"

"Yes, Great One! A BadgeBeth and a Wolfen!" Two answers right. Ek-kh may survive this after all.

"Was there a Succubus with the Wolfen?" Xhaknar is getting impatient.

"Yes, Great One!"

Three! He's gotten THREE right!

Xhaknar looks at the wet, pathetic, lump in front of him and decides to, at least, give himself a smile this even.

"You may live, but first . . . lick up your mess."

Later, Ek-kh leaves Xhaknar's tent. His mouth covered with mud, blood and piss. He runs screaming through the camp. "All can live! All can live!" The assembled ranks of the Naradhama and the Mayanoren either ignore him or offer up a half-hearted huzzah. He is, after all, the newly loyal leader of the Naradhama.

No matter what the Naradhama say.

Xhaknar listens as music again fills the camp. The Naradhama were never in any danger and they knew it. They would have been pleased if he had killed Ek-kh. It would have made warring less stressful. Xhaknar listens as the temp-slaves loudly fulfill their appointed tasks. He listens as his troopers revel in the ecstasy only a good orgy can bring. Let them have their fun this even, he will need their blood soon enough.

He will need it because Geldish has assembled the least likely group Xhaknar could ever conceive. However, they are all known to him for different reasons. Petty thieves, whores, poachers and layabouts. Geldish's new friends do not bother him, but Geldish does. Xhaknar cannot figure out why, in the name of Rohta, Geldish would even bother putting these cretins together. He must have something up his sleeves besides bone. Geldish never does what does not need to be done. That, more than anything else, is why Xhaknar has left him alone. Better to let him brood uselessly than to draw him out.

Dinero. The throbbing life blood of this rotting hulk

affectionately called society. Though its vital organs may be exposed and decaying it will still shamble along as long as it has its blood, and civilization's blood is gold. Geldish, more than many others, is acutely aware of this. He is also aware he wishes to build a new beast. A healthy beast which will not prey on the souls of the poor. At least, not until someone else comes along to fuck it up in another few thousand Full Suns or so.

But, to build this new beast, he must start with the blood. Since there will be no mother or father for this particular beast he must build it first in his mind. Like the simple geneticists before him, he will start with the blood. He must pull it apart and analyze it. Then, and only then, will he be able to remake the beast in the image of his choosing. If along the way, he can kill the old beast which has been tormenting everyone ... well, so much the better.

All of these thoughts occupy only a small part of the thing Geldish calls a mind. He is much more interested in the tableau unfolding in front of him. BraarB is walking near the rear of the repository, feeling the wall. She stops and points to a section. R'yune punches through the brick and mortar. He quickly rips out a Llamia size piece of the wall and tosses the loose bricks in a pile. Sland runs in and soon bags of goldens start flying out. After a few moments, there is a muffled shout from inside. N'leah dashes in half flying, half running. There are no more noises from inside. Two bodies flip through the hole then the bags resume their casual arcs outside into R'yune's waiting arms. When the bags stop N'leah walks out wiping the blood from her hands on, what appears to be, a Naradhama uniform shirt. Sland follows her. He is staring at her with new found respect. Neither speaks as R'yune finishes loading the bags on BraarB's back.

BraarB begins a slow walk west. R'yune and Sland flank her. N'leah takes to the air just above their heads. Geldish nods at them and motions for them to continue on without him. He looks at the mess in front of him and sighs.

He waves his hand at the bodies. They float/dance back into the repository. Then he looks at the bricks. They re-wall themselves quickly. No one would even know the repository had been visited. Geldish stares at the wall for a moment and then draws a letter 'G' in the brick face with his finger. The letter seems to glow and pulse to a rhythm all its own. He would hate to have done all this work and have someone else get the credit.

As he stands to contemplate something he hears screams calling for Enforcers and Naradhama. It's time to leave. He melts into the sand. Xhaknar is going to blow a vital organ because of this. Geldish smiles as he disappears.

Xhaknar looks at the weird little snake-man in his tent. He wonders why he didn't make more of them. Then he looks at its fangs and remembers. They're poisonous and not always loyal. Ah well, Ek-kh is not the only one with spies in the Crasnia. He briefly ponders whether or not Ek-kh's spy really exists. If it does he'll kill it as an example to Ek-kh.

He waits until the weird little snake-man is gone and ponders the information it has given him. He decides to pour himself another flagon of Whævin and sit on his portable throne. Why on Arreti would Geldish steal goldens? He has absolutely no need for them. He knows he cannot purchase the services of the Naradhama. The Mayanoren, maybe, but not the Naradhama. Actually, even the Mayanoren would require a serious reason to leave before they would even consider the goldens. They like killing too much. So, the question lingers, why? Why would Geldish be so obvious about a crime so severe? It's not the goldens. Xhaknar could forgive a few goldens.

Makers' Hell, if Geldish needed goldens, and it would have insured the status quo, Xhaknar would have just given them to him.

However, just to make this thought darken more, Ek-kh enters. At least he's washed his muzzle. "Forgive me, Great One," Ek-kh looks more nervous than before, "The troubadours from Anapsida are here. Do you require entertainment?" He is about to kill Ek-kh, just to keep the troops happy, when it hits him like a strike from the clouds. Entertainment! This whole robbery was an entertainment! Geldish put on a show for him. But why? To what end?

"Let them entertain the troops this even," Xhaknar tries out his benevolent tone without much success, "and you may stay out of my sight for one full turn, or I will kill you and let your blood be wasted on the ground and not fill my fountain." Ek-kh nearly falls over himself in happiness as he leaves the tent. Xhaknar decides it will be more fun to let him live, for a while. The amusement, alone, he provides is worth it.

Xhaknar returns to his contemplations anew. He listens as the revelry outside is taken up in earnest. He knows, with enough Whævin, his troops will find anything attractive. That's good because all of his clean slaves are busy primping each other for his return.

The troubadours' show will not calm his troops at all. It's not intended too. He has been 'entertained' at several of their shows and all they do is known to him. He has no need for carnal satisfaction this even. He must sit and contemplate the recent turn of events. A satisfied grunt near his tent draws his attention briefly. It would seem his troops are being well cared for by the entertainers. Actually calling them entertainers is a bit of a stretch, but they keep his well-paid vermin content, so what does he care?

Xhaknar ponders the news of the even some more as he sips his Whævin. He has been in power almost since the spawn of Rohta did his dirty work for him. Although they certainly had not intended to. He remembers their surprise at finding other creatures with little or no caring for their precious rules of conduct. They were horrified to think there would need to be another war. They proposed peace plans. They showed their good will in a variety of ways. They attempted to teach their customs to the new comers.

They failed.

Soon the fringe belonged to Xhaknar. Since then he has looked into expanding his empire, but there are powers beyond the fringe even he approaches with care. He would prefer to avoid the combined Rangka of the Temple of Azarep, if there are any, in mortal combat. He is also cautious about Südermann. His kingdom contains many terrors.

Maybe that explains it. Geldish is alone. If he is alone then this could be Geldish's final huzzah. Some twisted notion he alone can topple Anapsida. If that is truly the case then Anapsida is safe. No matter what he surrounds himself with, without the power of the Rangka, Geldish is beatable. He pours himself another flagon of Whævin and calmly listens to the erotic sounds of the dark near his tent.

Oolnok was plowing his south field when he saw the tax collector coming. That was odd since tax season was still many turns away. The tax collector, a big Mayanoren of limited intellect, walked across the field heedless of his path. Oolnok was grateful he hadn't begun planting yet. He'd have hated to lose that many seedlings.

"Greetings Oolnok," growled the tax collector, "you will be pleased to know Lord Xhaknar has decided to raise taxes in the villages by one percent. You will be pleased to know this because he's raising them in the warrens by three percent. Now you have been told, there will be no excuse for an underpayment."

With that he stalked back across the field and onto the road, presumably to share the good news with the other villagers.

Oolnok fretted, but mostly out of habit. One percent was certainly better than three and he'd had good sales at the warren when he'd sold his stock of kgum hair. Many herders didn't take the extra time to wash all the hair once it was sheared. He did because he and his glorious wife had discovered they could get almost double the price in the end. Yes, it was tedious work, but that's what smalls were for.

He smiled at the memory of the shearing. It had been the first for his smalls and they were eager to learn and help. While Oolnok was sure they'd learned, he wasn't so sure they'd helped.

In the end, he and his wife had done all the shearing and left the sorting and bagging to the smalls. He had to admit, though, they'd done a fine job of that. The coarse outer hair in one set of bags and the fine inner hair in others. They'd even labeled them so all Oolnok and his wife had to do was wash them and then put them right back in their original bags.

The smalls had also been helpful with the washing. He'd let them turn the handles on the tubs to keep the hair from tangling while he and his wife thoroughly rinsed it. Then he'd given them the honor of hanging the hair out to dry.

Once it was dry his wife then went through and selected what she needed to make sweaters for the smalls and themselves. The rest was re-bagged and sold.

Since the smalls had helped his wife had argued they should be allowed to go to the warren for the sale. Oolnok had agreed readily enough and was glad he did. The warren had long since become just a place of business for him and he'd forgotten the joys it held. His smalls had oohed at this and aahed at that and genuinely enjoyed the various pleasures it had to offer.

He'd even consented to watch the puppet masters in the square. While he found the tale simplistic, his smalls had enjoyed it immensely and had applauded loudly when the really evil bad guy was rendered low by the really nice good guy, who just happened to look like Lord Xhaknar.

N'leah gently slips through the drafts caused by the cracks in Arreti's fractured surface. Some are rumored to cut all the way to the other side of the world. Thin, deep and deadly to all except the Succubi, and maybe a Rangka or two for whom they are an aid, the walkers steer clear of them.

All around them is an odd, undulating, mist which seems to be following them.

R'yune and Sland still flank BraarB. They keep up a consistent trot even though they are well clear of Go-Chi. Eventually Sland motions for them to halt. The air is cool, but the breaklight Sun is harsh. They pass around canteens.

"I don't fucking get it," Sland swallowed some more water before continuing, "He set up the perfect plan and then let us walk away with over three million fucking goldens. Why?"

"Because this is what he wanted to do." BraarB seemed even more pensive than usual.

N'leah swung around and landed near BraarB. She took a swig from the proffered canteen and wiped her dry lips.

"You act as though you fear him," N'leah mentions as she plops down on the sand. "why is that?"

BraarB settles next to her.

"Do you remember Yontar?"

N'leah shivers and tries to focus on anything but her own thoughts, "... yea." The word trembles from her gut like hot bile.

"You need to say no more. Your brand was thinned for the 'good of Arreti' too, I see." She takes the canteen from N'leah and wets her mouth. "Geldish is the Rangka who killed him."

Vacant gazes emanate from the faces around her. All of the Arreti has heard of the great war between a rogue Rangka and Yontar. They were supposed to have killed each other. All the stories they'd heard said there was a great and noble battle. Everybody fought and everybody died. Neat, clean and pleasantly legendary.

That was the official version. If it was untrue and Geldish was the rogue Rangka from the story ... there was going to be one Zanubi of a war. Of course that opened up the possibility that Yontar may be less severely dead than previously rumored.

That is EXACTLY the kind of thinking which leads to Whævin. R'yune makes sure the path to intoxication begins with but a single step. He has a cask hidden in his pack. They put away the water and pass the potation around.

N'leah lays against BraarB's flank and tries to make herself comfortable. She fails, so she changes into her womyn form. That helps, but it unnerves Sland. He has never seen a Succubus shape change before. Now that he thinks about it, he has never really seen a Succubus up close before, either. Well, he thinks, now he has.

He wonders to himself how useful it really was to be able to look like a maker. It seems like a skill that would get one killed instantly and that, to him, is a useless skill.

Since they all are now staring in the direction of BraarB she decides to tell what she knows. "I was there. I saw the whole battle if you could call it that. I, too, have heard the lies spewed forth from the foul orifices of Anapsida. I know they were supposed to have killed each other. I have heard about the great and noble battle. I have heard how an unnamed Rangka died at the hands of a courageous Yontar, who fell protecting the good of Arreti," she sipped some more of the potent beverage, "but Geldish is still among the living, if that's the right term, and Yontar is gone. I can assure you there was no great, vainglorious, or epic war. There was no tremendous battle, there was nothing like that at all. They just stood on the field near Anapsida and stared at each other for thirty turns. Neither moved. Then, Yontar fell. Just like that, he was dead. Smoke poured from his rotten eyes. I did not mourn his passing."

She took a long pull from the cask this time. "Anyway, Xhaknar saw the whole thing and flew into a colossal rage. I was standing behind Geldish. I helped to carry him back to his lair before the Naradhama could figure out they were supposed to follow us ... and kill him. I kept my tongue, until now, because I did not wish to be hunted like a fattened kgum."

She let the story sink in and drank some more of R'yune's fine Whævin. Sland seemed to be considering the whole thing one syllable at a time. He kept scratching his head and shifting on his haunches.

R'yune was content to drink his Whævin. Nothing seemed to faze him.

The battle was just over one Full Sun ago. It's hard for them to believe reality could be so different from the rumors. If the story BraarB just told them is true, it means Geldish is more than a Rangka, he's an astral warrior. That would put a whole new spin on what they just did. As far as they know astral warriors don't need goldens. So why did they rob the repository? For that matter, why would Geldish need them or the goldens at all?

Sland is still stuck on the story, "Demon man?"

The sand bubbles around them. Foul smelling

embers crash around their feet. Smoke wafts from the gaping hole. They appear to be witnessing the bowels of Arreti expunging themselves.

Geldish appears, "You queried?"

"Is the asshole really dead?" Sland doesn't care what he asks. He just needs to know the answers.

"Who?" Geldish turns his full attention to the BadgeBeth.

"Yontar." Sland shifts uncomfortably beneath the dead gaze of Geldish's flames.

The flames in Geldish's eye sockets reach out and embrace Sland's head. They caress him deep into the folds of the thing Geldish calls a mind. They twist his body, and his soul, into shapes he never imagined. Up until now, he didn't even know his soul existed. He feels himself being pulled further away from the reality he has always known and now realizes he'd grown fond of. It may not have been a perfect reality, but it was better than this.

This place without a place. These sounds without noise. This is the color nine.

He is inside Geldish, somehow, somewhere. He is not in a happy place. He watches as a million stars melt and die. The things near them decay. He watches as his breath takes form and strangles the cosmos. He listens as faces appear, wailing and moaning. They suffer the kind of pain that makes death seem like a vacation. Their agonies should not be witnessed, let alone borne. The faces peel away from the undulating bone. They reveal angry insects that cannot flee. Each face distorts terribly and then withers, its usefulness now complete.

From behind the dying agonies, a thousand demon warriors appear. Their swords and knives are aimed right at Sland's heart. He wants to scream, he wants to die, he wants to leave. He can do none of those things. The warriors rush, headlong, at him. He feels the swords as they penetrate this flesh, but he sees no wounds. The demon warriors pass through him and fade from view.

If this were a dream Sland might have enjoyed it. He never put any stock in the babble of mystics so he never worried about his sleep induced musings. This, however, is not a dream. It's as real as anything he's ever experienced. It's even more real than anything he's ever imagined. Not that he has much of an imagination. It is a tortured place. A place where pure horror would be warmly welcomed compared to this.

While he's still getting his bearings clouds of blood begin to form on a recent horizon. As he nears them he can see three great beasts have been gutted. Their twitching bodies squirm under an impossibly bent moon. Their size does not diminish as he gets a better view of them. In fact, they seem larger. Sland has never seen beasts like these. They are larger than one hundred BadgeBeth. They scream like new born smalls. Their pain is omnipresent. He cannot escape feeling as they feel. The closer he gets, the worse it gets, and there is nothing he can do about it. He wants to flee but he cannot. He is firmly ensconced in the blood clouds. He is trapped in the beasts' pain. He is unable to do anything save suffer.

And he is doing that extremely well.

Suddenly the blood clouds pop him free. He shoots to a new horizon at speeds he has only heard of, and then only vaguely. This must be what high flight feels like to the Succubi. It is exhilarating but he does not like it. He has no control. He just plummets outward. Out, away from everything he has ever known. He is plunged into a curtain of glass shards. Each piece seems to delight in causing him pain, individually and completely. In fact, it is as though each piece waits for its predecessor to cause pain before it enters Sland's throbbing flesh. Yet, somehow, there are no cuts. He can feel the pain but sees no scars. This does not help his grip on this reality at all.

Then, as eerily as it began, it stops. He is facing a little rat-like creature. Not Din-La, not an extinct maker. A horrible patchwork, a mixture of both. The creature looks amused, almost giggly.

"Welcome," it sneers.

"Who . . . what the fuck are you?" Sland is not happy at all.

The little patchwork rat-like creature ignores the question. He lights a bowl of pitweed and looks Sland over.

"You're not all here. Who sent you?"

"Geldish ... I think" Sland is having trouble speaking. Now that he thinks about it, this is the first time since he arrived he has thought at all.

"Ahhh, I see. Did you kill him?"

The little patchwork rat-like creature seems genuinely concerned.

"No. I asked of Yontar . . . and here I am."

Sland almost makes it sound sensible, at least to himself.

"Well, now, there's a name few say boldly. Even around here. It's just not done. No, it's not done at all. No, no, no."

The little patchwork rat-like creature acts as though he is teaching a small a lesson.

"The ass eater lives?!?!" Sland finally focuses on his situation.

"Don't be absurd, fuzz face!" The little patchwork rat-like creature walks over to Sland. "Nothing lives here. Some things exist, but none live."

"Then why fear the name?" If Sland had a clear idea what suspicion was, he would name his present feeling as such. However, hunger and fear serve him here as well. He has a hunger for escape and a fear of staying.

"I fear nothing. I do what I say because it is prudent to do so. Here, yes here, I am the king of the land of agonies. I am the deity of atheists. I am he who leads the blind through the valley of razor blades . . . I AM . . ."

"Yontar."

Sland finally understands.

The little patchwork rat-like creature who now

claims to be Yontar, sighs.

"Well, I am what's left of him. What you see before you is a prime example of Rangka humor. This is the reason they never get invited to any of the good orgies."

The little patchwork rat-like creature who now claims to be Yontar relights his bowl of pitweed and sits in mid-air.

"Yes, I was given the privilege of being the recipient of Rangka pranksterism. A body that cannot live with a mind that cannot die. This is worse than any death I ever imagined. Yet, somehow, it is better than being dead. Yes, it is better, but not by much. If you ever see Geldish again tell him . . . LA'KYEE Shhak!"

Sland knows nothing anymore. Then he knows something. He knows he must leave. He must leave as fast as he can. To that end he turns to run. Glass explodes from his skin. Blood clouds reappear, beasts writhe beneath him again. He does not care. He is leaving Yontar. He feels the warm flames of Geldish's eyes and falls to the sands in front of his new companions. He is crying.

He looks up at Geldish. There is no sympathy in those eyes. There is nothing there but patience. Patience and flame. Geldish is waiting for Sland to speak, so he does.

"LA'KYEE Shhak!" Sland whimpers it out, as grandly as he can.

Geldish smiles, "So, he still has a sense of humor. That is good."

N'leah and BraarB look as though they have seen mist demons. R'yune lets out a growl which would curdle bone. Sland just looks confused.

"What the Zanubi does it mean?" As he regains his strength, his bluntness returns as well.

"I am near." Geldish's voice does not make this seem like a good thing.

R'yune growls again. This time, Geldish places a hand on the Wolfen's shoulder.

"Do not worry my furry friend. We are in no danger from him, here. Not anymore." Geldish smiles wider. No matter how hard he tries, his smile leaves a lot to be desired.

"Wait a sepi-clik," N'leah is staring at Geldish, "you can read R'yune's thoughts?"

"I can read many minds," Geldish begins walking towards his home, "but not R'yune's. I don't know why not, but it is still true. However, you need not be a mind reader to know fear when you hear it."

BraarB grins. "Well, at least there is one thing you can't explain, or do."

An opaque mist coils around their feet and hooves as they continue their journey. It is neither wet nor sticky. Somehow, that bothers the walkers even more. Disturbing as it is they try to ignore it. They're not sure where they're going but they are sure they have a long way yet to travel to get there.

Five turns later, to the north of our intrepid travelers, lies the ice palace of the Se-Jeant. It is a palace of blistered stone and frozen mortar. Skulls of unsuccessful interlopers adorn the masonry work. Ice covered turrets house the lookouts. Their view of the wasteland is unfettered by anything other than their own breath. Not a massive edifice, as edifice's go, but imposing all the same. Behind the three visible walls of the castle is a village carved into the caverns and hollows of a mountain. They are sheltered from both the cold and from view.

The Se-Jeant are a quiet brand. They keep their emotions where they believe emotions should be kept, deep inside. Not that they are passionless, not by any stretch of the imagination. They are fierce warriors when provoked, thorough lovers when enticed. They just don't wear their desires on their vests.

This turn finds them restful. There are no wars to prepare for, at least not yet. The reproduction season is still several turns away, and last Sun's smalls look as though they'll survive the Dark Sun.

No, this turn finds the Se-Jeant doing their laundry in the village fountain. The shops surrounding the fountain advertise all of the wares the brands will need for the coming season. All of the castle's weapons have been hidden from view and replaced with candies and liqueurs for the home.

Several smalls run around the village circle. Their naked bodies dance, unnoticed by all, near their parents. Many of their parents are nude as well. They have no need for clothing within the walls of their ice castle, so they don't wear them. Not that tall, furry from birth, with three, large, eyes that have both inner and outer lids, the Se-Jeant's actual purpose for the makers has been lost over time.

Most Se-Jeant only own travel wear. They understand the need to protect themselves on the open wastelands. As their forbearers were inclined to say, frostbite or Naradhama, it doesn't matter, they can both kill you.

Their fur is warm, but it can't stand up to the harsh winds of the open plains. Just ask any guard who gets stuck in the tower for a full shift. They wear full uniforms. They don't like them, but they wear them.

Suddenly, a guard cries from the tower, "ERDNA, UKU, . . . AGGA ASSA ASHI ASHI!"

The Se-Jeant villagers look up, but since it is not a cry of alarm, they continued washing their clothes. Four Se-Jeant guards approach the front gate and open it. A tall creature, heavily robed, enters the village.

The guards escort the creature up an impossible

flight of stairs. Once they reach the top, they show it into a large, ornate, room. The guards leave him and return down the impossible stairs. Once the guards have gone, the creature removes several layers of cloth from his face. He is a Minotaur. Not Ek-kh, but a Minotaur nevertheless. He is older and wearier looking than a young Minotaur has the right to be. He slaps his hands near the fireplace in the middle of the chamber. While he is warming himself, Uku the King of the Se-Jeant enters.

"Apa, Greko," says King Uku, curious at the sight of this friendly, but unusual, visitor.

"Almsa, King Uku," responds Greko.

"What brings a lava dweller to our fair but slightly frigid land?" Uku carefully avoids the fire.

Greko looks down to the floor. What he has to say will not be easy, and he almost wishes the floor would say it for him. Finally, he straightens himself up to face his friend, the King.

"My brother, Ek-kh, has dishonored our flame." Greko manages to keep his voice steady, despite the desire to cry. "He has joined the Naradhama. He is one with Xhaknar."

King Uku looks stricken. He has known Greko's herd for many Suns. He knew Greko and Ek-kh as smalls. He watched them grow and play with his own smalls. Their grandfather was a Seventh Level 1 Dweller of the Pit. He was as near to being an Elder as you can get, without actually being one. Their father is a revered Bovinity scholar. His translations of the 'Script of Rohta' have helped many through the tough times of their lives.

While he swallows the hard news he gets them each a flagon of Whævin. "This is indeed sad news. Our cold melts in sympathy with your pain."

This doesn't make the pain go away, but it helps. Greko is grateful to have a friend like King Uku. He takes a swallow of his wine before he proceeds.

"My pit thanks you and is filled with your warmth."

"All things can be done in friendship; however," Uku knows there is more to this, "you did not travel all this way to share only this information."

"The Council of Elders has sent me on a matter of some urgency. With Ek-kh's defection, the secrets of our pit have been laid bare. We fear Ek-kh may use our knowledge against his former dwellers. Our time of mating is coming, as is yours, and the Council believes he may attempt to take us then when we are occupied."

Uku considers this for a long epi olilu. Knowledge like that in the crushing grip of Xhaknar is a terrifying thought if ever there was one. Before he can panic more, Greko has still more bad tidings.

"One other thing has attracted the attention of the Council. Geldish has robbed Xhaknar's repository in Go-Chi." Greko spits these words out quickly. Even he does not believe what he is saying. He hopes his friend will listen to him and not just the words.

"Geldish? A repository?" Uku gulps his entire glass of Whævin. "Is that not like a blind one stealing a lamp?"

"True enough. He has less need for goldens than my pit has for flame," Greko refills his glass, "however, the Council believes it was not poverty, but convenience, which led him to this deed."

"Convenience?" Uku is seriously confused at this point. "What meaning dances with your words, friend Greko?"

"This much we know," Greko moves closer to the fire. By Rohta, these creatures keep a chilly hearth. "Geldish is traveling with four fringe dwellers who have been previously … entertained by Xhaknar. These five drank and supped in the Crasnia. That is a new haven bar in Go-Chi. They were open about their presence. They escaped into the southern desert with the even mists at even-split. They were headed directly towards Geldish's lair. They took, at least, three million goldens."

If Uku had any lips to whistle with, he would have

done it right there. He purposely took his time refilling his glass. He needed to think about this news. "With that many goldens." Uku pauses, "he could buy several formidable armies."

"That is what the Council believes as well." Greko smiles as he thinks about it.

Uku pulls a chair up nearer to the fire than he is comfortable with. He does not want to yell yet he does not trust himself to speak coherently without doing so.

"So … Anapsida may yet fall." Uku says carefully as he stares hard at his old friend.

"What else could it be?" Greko does not flinch. He is only a missionary of the Council yet he knows he speaks the truth. "Now he has killed Yontar, the way is open to him. Many will rally behind him. Only he could command the respect of the Fierstan's. With them … he would be almost invincible."

"If it was he who killed Yontar. No one is truly sure. If he can align the Fierstan's, if he really is going to war." Among their many other attributes, Se-Jeant are also wary.

"Yes, and if they wish to march with their friends the Se-Jeant." Greko is getting the hang of this diplomacy thing.

Uku ponders some more. Greko is glad the decision will be made by Uku. He takes a long time to make up his mind, but once he has, it's firm. Also, Uku's ponderings allow Greko a chance to warm himself near the little fire.

The two friends sit in silence for a while. Greko wonders what decision will be made here this turn. Moreover, he wonders what effect it will have on his life and the lives of all the Dwellers of the fringe. Uku stands and moves away from the fire. It is far too hot for him to maintain his proximity. He stares long and hard at his friend Greko. His thoughts run along similar lines.

"How many are you to ride to the lair of Geldish?" Uku stares at the flames as he speaks

"We will ride a scouting force of fifty." Greko smiles. It is this kind of question that can lead to action. He refills his flagon as he awaits the outcome Uku's ponderings.

"Not enough to attract the Naradhama and not enough to stop them should they track you. A risky number, but not a stupid one. You will be much safer with your number being one hundred, therefore, I shall send fifty Se-Jeant with you ... should they chose to go. I will not force this upon them. This travail will lead to war. There is no other way." Uku crosses the hall and motions for Greko to follow, "This even you will dine with us. I will let you speak with my warriors and I will abide by their decision."

Greko sits with the Se-Jeant warriors in the dining hall. He is grateful they are not in the banquet hall. He has always preferred life's simpler pleasures and he would have been even more uncomfortable in a formal setting. The Se-Jeant allow him to sit near the fire, for that he is more appreciative. They may be friendly, but their land is zorking cold. After they have eaten their meats, the warriors gather their chairs together and face Greko. Whatever discomfort he feels is masked by duty. He tells them all he has told King Uku. He tells of his traitorous sibling, the theft of Xhaknar's repository, and the fears of the Council. He tells them all of this and then explains that Dwellers of the Pit will be riding fifty to meet Geldish and they would welcome the company of the Se-Jeant. He tells them it must be voluntary. Two thousand volunteer, immediately. Greko mists with joy.

The rest of the evening is spent drinking and singing. Well sung tales of past deeds ring out through the dining hall. King Uku, himself, leads the even's first Aklop. The wives of the warriors entered and showed the assembled how the dance should really be done. It was not an even of drunken revelry, but it was fun. When it was over, Greko put himself happily to bed with the songs of the Se-Jeant and visions of the Aklop in his head.

Just past breaklight, Greko walks out into the courtyard and watches as fifty Se-Jeant fill their travel packs and dress. The goggles they use to cover their three eyes always made Greko smile. He wanders about for a while and walks into a shop where a Se-Jeant warrior is picking up a bag of stars. The stars looked like toys for smalls, but were, in fact, deadly weapons in the hands of the Se-Jeant. A good warrior could kill an opponent from two hundred paces with them. The shop keeper smiles as he sees Greko. "Good breaklight to you friend. Ata here was just telling me of your march."

The Se-Jeant named Ata looked around and smiled. "Hello, friend Greko, are you ready for the march?"

Greko smiles, somewhat sadly. "The march yes, but its conclusion is the part which chills my blood. The fringe does not need another war and yet we have no true choice if we wish to see the end of Xhaknar's reign."

"Do not worry, friend Greko," Ata smiles even wider, "we are carrying stars made by the master this turn. Our omens have all boded well. We shall see what this Geldish is up to. If it be good, then we shall have honor in our fight. If it be not, then there will be one less Rangka on the wastelands."

"Strong words from a strong warrior" Greko smiles as he says it but can't help noticing just how young this warrior is. At his age he should be finding his first mate, not carrying stars made by the master. But there is no other choice. The young Se-Jeant is a qualified warrior and he volunteered. To not let him go would dishonor his family and heritage. Greko smiles weakly and leaves the shop.

Soon the assembled volunteers begin their march from the Ice Palace of the Se-Jeant. It is breaklight. The mists roll off of the skulls of the losers. Their vacant eyes bear witness to the ferocity of these honorable brand. The proud denizens of the ice file out two by two led by Greko. Two of the Se-Jeant in the front carry the banner of their creed, the rest march behind them. The colors of their respective families dance off of the bland grey of the Plains. Greko walks near Ata as they pass beyond the gates of safety. The harsh winds of the Plains chill Greko even more than he remembered. It is a frigid turn in the Dark Sun. For Greko this does not bode well, for the Se-Jeant, they don't even notice. To them, the cold is a reason to wear clothes. Beyond that, they don't care.

As the warriors fade into the drab horizon, the residents of the Ice Castle of the Se-Jeant return to their lives. Each offering a silent prayer for the warriors.

Oolnok watches as the sheared kgum play in the mid-break Sun. They liked to butt heads with each other and then roll around in the field. He had no idea why they do that and doubted if they did either.

Satisfied there were no problems he headed back to clean the stable. He had, a few Suns back, traded a wagon full of food to a Naradhama for a deisteed. The beast was lame and starving but Oolnok thought he could cure it. His wife had been enraged, she thought he'd been swindled and being swindled was unlike Oolnok she said, over and over and over and …

But, within ten turns he had it walking without a limp and with its coat noticeably healthier. Within twenty turns the beast could jump fences.

The beast turned out to be gentle with the smalls, letting them ride it and lead it around the farm. They had taken to calling it Pzzby, after the character in their books.

Pzzby is the prettiest Ploong. Yeah, that's how it went. Nonsense rhymes for silly smalls, but it didn't bother him. Rohta knows he'd once been a small himself, even if it did seem like a mere echo instead of a clear memory.

Pzzby huffed as he entered and stepped to the side. Say one thing for the beast, it was smart. By moving as it did it allowed Oolnok to clean half the stall quickly, then the beast moved back and he finished the other half. Once done he led it out of the stable and into the fields. There he let it loose to run with the kgums.

Even though the beast could easily clear the far fences if it wished, it knew on which side its pastry was sugared. There was no way it would ever run away.

Oolnok used the beast to pull his cart when he went into the warren. Even with the added weight of his smalls this last time, the beast seemed happy. He had no idea what had been done to the beast before he got it, but decided it must have been harsh for it to think life with Oolnok was a significant step upward.

As Oolnok continued with his chores he found himself happily singing the Pzzby songs.

It is breaklight. A time of renewal. A beginning of a new turn. The Se-Jeants believe the terrors of the past melt in breaklight. The Dwellers of the Pit believe breaklight is the waking of the gods. Their morning worship is a continuing acknowledgment of the fact fire runs though their hearth and fire runs through the sky. No matter which philosophy you ascribe to, it is breaklight nonetheless.

Peace, it was once said, is a cheap facade awaiting a war to shatter it. As Greko walks across the putrefied soils of the frozen lands, he thinks of all these things. He is more than aware this war will not end quickly. The blood of many good souls shall fertilize the next Warm Sun's flowers. However, this is not the time to think of the Warm Sun. This is the time of the Dark Sun. This is not the time of renewal. It is the time of preparation. It is time to walk. A time to walk across the frozen tundra, to shamble through the bitter dreams of dead generations before and hope to correct the mistakes, and failures, of their ancestors.

It is breaklight. The time when the progenies of Arreti are hoping for hot food and Greko finds himself wishing for the same. Like a small without its mother, he feels alone in this crowd. Somehow, he knows it will be a long time before he finds comfort in anything again. He glances at the assembled Se-Jeant, looks at their determined eyes, and knows comfort is a distant horizon.

Two turns into their journey, they can see the Mountain of the Minotaur. A dormant, underground, volcano, which appeared for reasons no one knew, they have covered to hide from view. It is the perfect home for a race that enjoys mazes and heat. Their mountain is a thing of legends. Only the honored rulers of a tribe are allowed to pass into it and then only through the common entrance. In times of crisis, the Minotaurs have hidden entire armies from their attackers, but those times were rare. The Minotaurs are a solitary race. Though they are powerful and feared warriors, they prefer studying history and religion. Born with a cache of lore that outweighs almost any other, they talk to few. It is even rumored some Minotaurs study the works of the makers. However, no one has ever confirmed that and the Minotaur don't really volunteer much information about their studies.

The march continues easily enough. They steer clear of the armored garrisons posted by Anapsida, Xhaknar's desolate lair. It adds half a turn to their journey, but none question the wisdom. Ata attempts to draw out Greko but to no avail. Greko has too much on his mind to attempt glib conversation with a small, no matter how honored he might be among his own kind. They continue on into the even.

The next turn brings them to the home of the

Dwellers of the Pit, the Minotaur. They march in double file through the front entrance. It is the only visible entrance for miles. It is the one entrance the Minotaur rarely use, except for company. It is exposed but heavily guarded.

Once, Yontar attacked the Dweller's mountain. He sent his troops directly at the entrance. He had the Minotaur outnumbered, out gunned and, theoretically, outmaneuvered. The attack came at breaklight. Before mid-break, Yontar was watching the burning of his troop's corpses from a nearby hill. It was not a maneuver any follower of Xhaknar wished to repeat with any alacrity. Yet, a mere four hundred and some Full Suns later, Xhaknar was about to let Ek-kh do just that. The marchers didn't know that little fact, but they feared something like it. It was a thought gave Greko several evens of tenuous sleep. The defection of a Dweller was unheard of. Almost as unheard of as the rumored actions of a rogue Rangka. Not quite, but close enough to cause concern.

It is during this even the fringe dwellers who have heeded Geldish's call are assembled in his observatory. As frightening as the outside is, the inside is worse. If they considered commenting on it, they soon forgot it. Any comment they might have made could be met with a response and no one knew if it was good or not. Silence could be a much better tool at a time like this than anything else they had available.

N'leah hung from the ceiling, juggling three balls of flame. As she juggled, she morphed into her womyn form. Then she changed into her maker-mal-form and back through all three again, never dropping her flame. Sland watched raptly as the diminutive balls of flame rolled across her naked flesh. R'yune yawned. BraarB wandered aimlessly about chewing on something dead, picking her teeth with its bone. Geldish curled his legs beneath himself and levitated. His bony fingers touching tip to tip as though in prayer.

Sland jumped up, finally realizing the show is not going to become any more erotic.

"This is fun!" He says with the equivalent of BadgeBeth sarcasm. "Why do we just fucking sit here? We have three million fucking goldens! What the Zanubi are we waiting for?"

BraarB turns herself around. This is not an easy task indoors. "We wait because that is what he wants," she says as she motions towards Geldish, "and when we are done waiting, we will do something. What that will be, beats the Zanubi out of me." Despite herself, she sniggered at her rhyme.

Geldish does not waiver in his hover, "We are going to kill Xhaknar's army and bring water to Go-Chi."

Sland, in his BadgeBeth wisdom, asks the question which lingers in the souls of the others. "What about after our mid-break repast?"

Geldish waivered and then collapsed to floor in laughter. R'yune let out a frightening staccato growl and N'leah tittered. BraarB just looked concerned.

"Geldish, may I speak freely?" Geldish nodded at her and she continued. "Although I find your optimism intriguing, I'm afraid I do not fully understand why we are here. It cannot truly be as you state. For us to attack Xhaknar and Anapsida would be suicide and I have no wish to die a stupid death."

Geldish picked himself off of the floor and brushed the dust from his robe. "You share the doubts of Sland?"

"Light forgive me, but yes." It's the first time BraarB has smiled in a long time.

Geldish twists his skull into something of a grin and

continued. "I am afraid you are searching for intricacies in a plan of the utmost simplicity."

This statement is met by a room full of blank stares. N'leah sorts it out for them. "He means his plan is so stupid even we should understand it."

"I would not have put it thusly, but you are essentially correct." He walks over to a keg and pours himself a flagon of Whævin.

N'leah falls from the ceiling and lands lightly on her feet, much to Sland's surprise. She stretches her wings, pours herself a flagon and turns to face Geldish. "So, enlighten us dark one."

"Yeah! At least let us know what the shit's going on!" Sland does not understand the laughter that greets his statement but smiles at the room anyway.

Geldish looks into each of their eyes. He understands their desire to know. He, also, understands they must not know the truth. Not yet anyway. "By robbing the bank," he pauses a brief moment to sip his wine, "we have sent up a 'flare,' of sorts. We have served notice to the warrens we are looking. Hopefully, soon they will be finding."

BraarB watches the expressions of the others. Something about Geldish's answer rings hollow, but she will worry about that later. "Do you mean you expect the various warrens and villages to send representatives to negotiate an army?"

"Yes, that is exactly what I expect," Geldish says this far too easily.

"Warriors fucking come, then I fucking stay!" Sland is far too loud. His bravado merely betrays his nervousness. He wants to believe he understands. He needs to believe. The others feel the same way.

N'leah wraps an arm around Sland. "Calm down Sland. You're starting to sound like a wounded Rakyeen." Sland draws a deep breath and sits down. BraarB walks over to him and hands him a flagon of skank. Sland smiles weakly and swallows half the flagon. N'leah hops back up onto the ceiling and begins making knives appear and disappear. Sland doesn't notice. BraarB walks over to N'leah and raises her head to speak. Before she can utter a syllable, N'leah skitters, using her talons and heel spurs for traction, across the beam to the other side of the room. Braab realizes N'leah is affording her privacy. She wonders if the Succubi are telepaths as she wanders down to have her conversation.

"Tell me something N'leah." BraarB whispers, "Why do you travel with R'yune?"

N'leah seems lost in thought for a sepi-clik, "I'm not exactly sure. I met him a little over eight Full Suns ago. I was working for a sect of village elders in Anapsida, doing odd tricks for goldens and food. Mostly food as they kept me in a cage when I wasn't doing my ... odd tricks. R'yune was hanging around the local haven bar, picking up hunting jobs for a couple of the local haven mistresses, stuff like that. Bringing them food in return for goldens and personal favors. I knew of him but had never met him. I'd merely seen him from time to time when I would serve the elders who came from the haven mistresses' homes."

She paused to toss the knives into the ceiling and flip to the floor.

"Anyway, one even, a local Naradhama, who worked for one of the elders, snuck into my room to terminate my employment. I guess they were tired of me. I don't know how R'yune found out, or if he just saw what was happening and followed the assassin, but he followed the Naradhama into my room and left him in six neat little piles. I saw three more dead in the hall. We left the village that even in a bit of a rush. I'm not sure where he came from, I don't know where we're going, I'm just happy he's here."

BraarB considered all of this for a moment and walked across the room to the barrel of skank and poured herself a flagon. Geldish smiled at her and resumed his mid-air contemplations.

Sland and R'yune are silently toasting each other, seemingly oblivious to the fact their inability to communicate would, normally, tend to hamper a conversation.

BraarB watches the scene for a moment, crosses the room and curls up by the fire. The heat is comforting, but she still feels the chill of uncertainty in her bones.

Within two turns distance of BraarB's discomfort, Xhaknar's army is on the move. They are heading home. If anyone could use such a polite term for Anapsida. The Mayanoren lead the procession. Behind them, the servants of the Naradhama follow, playing music and setting the tone for the orgy which will occur later. The honored servants stand in the middle of the procession carrying Xhaknar's tent. The pride in their souls shows like a flame in the dark. The Naradhama follow, protecting the rear of their master. Ek-kh, newly crowned leader of the Naradhama, follows behind. He tries to hold his head high. He has been allowed to live by the greatest leader of all time. It is less a consolation than he would have himself believe. Worse yet, Xhaknar has made Ek-kh carry the weird little snake like creature. The creature flicks its tongue at Ek-kh but seems not to really notice the Minotaur's existence. For that matter, none of the marchers seem to notice Ek-kh's existence. Somehow, this is the best thing that could happen to Ek-kh. Unfortunately, he is unaware of the fact.

The twin half-moons shed pale light on the ground. Their luminance fractured by the Dark Sun's clouds. Shadows of oozing terrors crawl across the broken land.

The Mayanoren like the view. It reminds them of death. As the marchers cross a knoll, Anapsida looms in the distance. Shattered boulders create the first perimeter. Broken and eroded over the five hundred Full Suns of Xhaknar's reign, they remind all of the defeats every single army who has attacked Xhaknar's fortress have suffered and will suffer again if Xhaknar has anything to say about it. Behind them lies the fortress itself. Layer upon layer of buttressments, battlements, and weaponry. Giant axe-like objects rim the lower perimeter. Their razor sharp edges twist and curl at obtuse angles to reality. Above them are sheer crystal walls. Stretching, almost, to the full height of the Dweller's domain, they create a visible mountain of pain. Large, unusual, skulls top of each precipice. Each contains fire in its every orifice. This is the only light in this section of the Plains, except for the fractured moons.

Beyond the gaping maw that passes for an entrance is Xhaknar's fountain. Sixteen, still living, bodies hang on hooks above a churning swirl contained in a grandiose tureen made from bone, mortar, and mud. Blood slowly drips down into the basin and a small geyser springs forth from the mouth of a skeleton which belongs to the first traitor Xhaknar ever recruited. Gurgling noises emanate from the fountain, as well as from above.

Punishments are simple in Xhaknar's realm. One turn hung above the fountain earns you one brutal lash from the whip of a Naradhama. Two turns? Two lashes. And so on up to thirty turns. Then, if the victim is still extant, they are either killed or released.

That decision is always made based on the flip of a coin, or other, random, two sided object.

Xhaknar encourages the Naradham to gamble on the outcome. Just to keep them interested.

The Mayanoren love this place. The Naradhama do not seem displeased either. Around the blood fountain are forges, tended by slaves, who make the weapons for Xhaknar's armies. Vicious daggers, swords, and spears come forth from these hearths of agony. There are other, deadlier, weapons being made in secret forges, but those are not needed yet.

The procession makes its way into the massive courtyard. The honored servants of Xhaknar set his caravan tent down gently and bow. Xhaknar steps from within and wipes his hands on the gherkin of the nearest slave. He turns to face the rear of the procession and sends for Ek-kh.

Ek-kh rushes forward to his master and genuflects before he kneels. "Yes, Great One. How dare I serve you?"

Xhaknar smiles at the obsequiousness of his minion. "Fetch me two grindels from the hole, pay the Naradhama and the Mayanoren, and then get my even meal." Xhaknar hands him a sack of goldens and turns his back to the pitiful Minotaur. Ek-kh shoulders the sack and fetches the two grindels. These creatures could somehow be lizards, possibly birds, yet, although they resemble both, they also resemble neither. Ek-kh attaches small chains to their thin necks and hands them over to Xhaknar. He bows continuously as he backs away from his revered master and begins to pay the warriors. It doesn't take him long to realize there is no pay in the sack for him. It matters not to Ek-kh. He has been allowed to live by the greatest leader the fringe has ever seen. He comforts himself thusly as he runs into the kitchen to prepare his master's dinner.

Xhaknar halfheartedly tortures the grindels as he watches Ek-kh run into the palace kitchen. Finally, he deigns to speak to them. "Listen well creatures. You will fly to the home of Geldish. Each turn, one of you will fly to me and report on his activities. If you do not, I will kill one of your kin each turn. Since there are only eight others of your pathetic, hideous, kind left on Arretti, I would not make any errors in judgment if I were you."

The grindels' eyes drip hatred. Xhaknar removes their collars and tosses them into the air. They flop to the ground, all the while staring at Xhaknar. Soon, they back away and fly up over the wall. Xhaknar smiles as he watches them disappear into the even.

He traverses the compound towards his private entrance. He enters and two, nude, Naradhama mals kneel, and each holds out all four of their arms before him. Two others place food trays into their arms. He stares for a clik as two nude Naradhama femmes bring him his throne and then prostrate themselves so trays of food can be placed on their backs. He looks around and slowly samples the food Ek-kh has prepared. At least the sniveling kgum can cook.

It seems a pity to Xhaknar only his slaves and servants see this room. All of his trophies surround him. It is a pity, but it is prudent. He did not become leader of the Plains following the tenets of the democrati or of the Azarep. He accomplished all through the use of power. Raw, primitive, violent power. Subtlety is not a tactic he prefers or even acknowledges. Those are the preferences of the weak, and Xhaknar is not weak.

He watches as the torchlight flickers off of the skulls and battle armor he has collected. He caresses the thigh of a slave, then snaps it off. Her screams do not even provoke a whimper from the others. They will mist later when they are far away from their great and glorious leader.

Meanwhile, as Xhaknar's meal progresses, the fifty Se-Jeant sit down to the even's meal with the Dwellers of the Pit in the Great Hall. Large, stone tables circle an immense volcanic hearth. Above the hall, set into the south wall, is an elliptical stone table with six baroque stone thrones directly behind it. Here sit the Elders of the Pit. They watch stoically as meat is laid upon each of the tables below. They know, as it has been for centuries, they will be served last. It is a little thing, but it is something the Se-Jeant are keenly aware of. It is the way of the Dwellers. It is the way they preserve the honor of those who do not rule. The Se-Jeant are seated away from the hearth. Although it is merely comfortable for the Dwellers, it is sweltering for them.

As soon as the tables are stocked, the Elder on the east end of the table stands to speak. "Mooth, Schan, Elan!!" The entire hall falls silent. The servers of the meat sit, quickly, on the floor and place their trays in front of them.

The Elder continues, "As is evidenced by our honored pit this even, Greko has been successful in his quest." The assembled shout a mighty "Greko! Hushak!!" The Elder smiles and continues, "Hushak from the Elders as well, Honored Greko. Our Brothers of the Flame have selected their numbers. All will be ready at breaklight. Our gratitude to the Se-Jeant. To you, we pass on great prayers of strong flame."

An even mightier cry erupts from the Minotaurs, "Se-Jeant! Hushak!!" This time the Se-Jeant respond with a throaty "AkkA, ANHDI, Erdu!!" The Elders watch, mildly bemused, as several more cheers are exchanged. They are pleased this alliance has long been fruitful. They are especially pleased because, now, an alliance is sorely needed. After a sepi-clik or so, the Elder continues.

"Mooth, Mooth ... our thanks to all of you for the honor you spread with dignity. All of your chants are deserved. The Dwellers of the Pit and the Holders of the Ice have traded and fought together for over a thousand seasons. Despite this truth, we feel we must inform you many of you may not return if what we have heard of the actions of Geldish is true. As the turns have come and gone, we feel there is a reason to believe the air around the rumors known to us all is pure. Rest well this even for soon you shall be in the presence of the undead and relying on him to keep you alive. AKNEHA!"

More chants are exchanged as the meat disappears from the tables. The meal is well received by all. When it concludes the Minotaurs who are not going on the march next breaklight wander off to their bunks after wishing warm flame to the Se-Jeant and their own. The marchers lay their bedrolls next to the Se-Jeant on the warm floor near the hearth, but not too near since it is far too hot for the Se-Jeant. It has long been the tradition of the Dwellers of the Pit to share their dreams with those who are willing to die with them.

Greko finds himself next to the young Se-Jeant, Ata. He wonders at the courage of a small but does not let it trouble him. The flame will tell, after all. Greko hands the small a flagon of Whævin and they share it in silence for a while. Finally, Ata breaks the silence.

"Tell me Greko," he says between swallows, "since this is my first march to your honored home, are your Elders always giving such wonderful speeches?"

Greko smiles and looks at the small he so recently dismissed. There is wisdom in those three young eyes. "My ancestors are honored to hear you praise our Elders. However, the answer is no. In truth, this is the first speech, other than to fulfill the needs of tradition, I have heard in fifteen seasons."

Ata considers this for a half a sepi-clik and then takes another swallow of the Whævin. "Then, truly it is, that the Se-Jeant are doubly honored to have been here for this event."

Another Minotaur, Ocard, rolls over and hands the two conversants some meat from his pack. "No Ata," he smiles, "it is we who have been honored by the Se-Jeants loyal friendship, even in these times of impending duress."

There is no pause from Ata this time. "What kind of friend would not come in a time of duress?"

Ocard sighs heavily. "That is an answer we hope never to learn."

There is a silent agreement between them all. Sleep

comes easily to all in this place of truth and comfort. Uncomfortably warm though the hall may be to the Se-Jeant, their souls are comforted by the souls it contains. The even continues enveloped by the sounds of comfortable sleep emanating from near the hearth.

The Elder who gave the speech, his name is Urnak, walks silently back to his loggia and looks down upon the sleeping warriors. Even though his heart soars through the clean skies of the Warm Sun at the sight before him, he feels clouds encroaching on a near horizon. War is coming and the actions which arise from this march may only serve to speed its arrival. He reflects on this a little while more and then begins to think, maybe, if the situation is handled correctly, this alliance can control the outcome more directly than if they had just let it fester. Maybe.

He thinks back on how they got to where they are now. Even further, how he got here at all. He'd been a precocious small, always wanting to have fun and play games. He was, now that he thought about it, much like Ek-kh. Sad. He'd had such hopes for that small. But Ek-kh wanted the rewards without the work, and that path has never led to happiness.

Urnak had been barely ten Full Suns old when he'd been caught in a Naradhama raid on one of their villages. In fact, it was that raid that ended the villages. The survivors moved into the Pit, never to return to the Plains.

Somehow the desire to be frivolous died that even along with the two hundred and fifty Minotaurs he knew so well. He could still see their faces and name each one in his mind. Knowing full well he wasn't a fighter, he'd joined the ranks of the military as soon as he was old enough.

He'd served admirably, if averagely, and left after six Full Suns. Then he'd joined the ranks of the students of Bovinity. He learned the histories of each brand and the sacred words of Rohta. This seemed to be his calling. Over many Full Suns, he worked his way up to a Seventh Level Dweller of the Pit.

His parents had been so proud when he'd been selected. They'd worn their finest robes and sat in the front row of honored families and his mother had cried when he accepted the bracelet marking his rank. It had been a grand turn.

Less than a Full Sun later a group of elders returned from a trade meeting with the Fierstans when they were ambushed by a Mayanoren raiding party. Three of the five were killed immediately. The other two lived but were crippled from their wounds.

The Elders' Council must number nine, that was written long ago, so they mourned their dead, retired their injured, and selected five new members. Just like that Urnak sat on the Council. One vote later, even though he was the youngest, he was voted Elder. Mostly because he, and he alone among them, had military experience.

It was felt it would be needed if they were to survive.

Urnak had been smart enough to know what he did not know and immediately set up regular meetings with the generals of the Pit. He heard their advice, heeded some of their council and soon had the Pit running smoothly and securely.

He'd had two, new, hidden entrances built to the south and west and had two others, in the north, collapsed. They were simply too near the new Mayanoren paths between garrisons.

He knew his Pit considered him wise and willing to do what needed to be done. Thinking of the dark clouds his mind imagined on the far horizons, he wondered if that would be enough.

Less than a couple of turns away lies the home of the Fierstans. It may as well be in the heart of the land of Südermann for all the interaction they have had with the Plains since the rise of Xhaknar. They are not, by nature, antisocial; they were just too badly beaten when Xhaknar rose to power. After all, they had been the leaders of the council for almost five hundred Full Suns before he came. Nonetheless, even in their ultimate defeat, they had inflicted so much damage on Xhaknar's army he had never deigned to bother them again.

There is a tale told by ancients and whispered by smalls of the time of Xhaknar's first battle with the Fierstans, shortly after he'd first appeared on the Plains. The Plains were ravaged for a Full Sun as the Mayanoren warriors of Xhaknar laid siege to the lands of the Fierstans. Even in the temple of Azarep, they knew the ancient wisdom said no one could survive a well-planned siege without outside aid. Eventually, food runs out. However, Xhaknar had left no hope of outside aid. His plan had been simple and fiendish. He had let it appear as though his armies were scattered across the Plains many turns away from each other and then guided them together with the Fierstans in the middle. It was a slow plan, a careful plan, and a good plan. The Fierstans were trapped and the denizens of the Plains were too decimated to help.

Actually, the plan was not Xhaknar's. Yontar was the true military genius and it was because of this truth Geldish had sought him out, and not Xhaknar, to kill. Whatever the truth may have been, Xhaknar never minded taking the credit for it. What was left of the decimated plains did try to help, they were not heartless, but it was as though they were smalls chiding an elder. Dwellers rained weapons made from their hearth, but they may as well have just been shouting insults. The BadgeBeth and the Se-Jeant banded together for the first time in plains history to attempt a two pronged attack on Xhaknar.

Sad is the only way to describe the result.

Xhaknar had crude weapons like catapults and high-powered sling shots, which were things the true Dwellers of the Plains had forsaken long ago. Xhaknar also had a rudimentary force field, which sucked the air out from its wearer, but kept projectiles away. This did not bother Xhaknar, but several hundred Mayanoren died before he realized the problem. He let his troops battle without it and they fought even better for the favor. When it was over, the smell of burning flesh would permeate hovel walls four turns away. Smalls would cry from the stench and grown Dwellers of the Pit, and it is said some Wolfen as well, were seen to mist openly from the agonies they knew existed in that smell. It was as though full even fell and never left. Truly, now, it is still said honestly, "… it was one Zanubi of a war."

Come breaklight, the land of the Fierstans will be awash in activity, but for now guards keep careful watch on the technologies the other species of the wasteland have either forgotten or ignored. In their years as leaders of the Plains, they had bred eleven council heads. Now there was only Xhaknar. Far away then the Plains were bountiful and productive. Now, all that's left is the wastelands. Worse yet, in the battle of the Plains those many Full Suns ago, Xhaknar had captured several thousand Fierstans. Instead of killing them, as is his usual wont these turns, he forced them into servitude initially and then morphed them, over many Full Suns, into the Naradhama. Fierce beyond belief and, unfortunately for everyone else of the wasteland, exceptionally smart as well.

It is this bit of the past that occupies the minds of three creatures who appear as Geldish, but different. The first, Karrish, is shorter and rounder than Geldish. Before his flesh was removed, he must have been quite the fancier of life's culinary delicacies. Next to him stands Makish, also short, but incredibly thin. He appears as though if he were to face that-away and not this-away, he would disappear. It is a cultivated image. Beside him stands Elzish, the tallest of the three. When the flesh was taken from his bones, it must have gone screaming. He still carries the build of one who knew physical prowess. The three Rangka, for that, is what they are, stand in front of an odd idol. Two heads, eight arms, five legs, posed as though running. Beneath the idol are four tabernacles. Three contain simple flame, the fourth is dark. After a full clik has passed, they move towards a table set with a light repast.

Karrish tears into something resembling meat and looks at the other two, "Tell me brethren, what news have you?"

"Yontar has made another attempt to escape," Elzish smiles as he sits at the table, "but he has fared even worse than last time."

Karrish smiles a tiny smile which would freeze the blood of any mortal, chews some more and then looks at Elzish. "I take it then Brother Geldish's reinforcements were satisfactory?"

There is a sound resembling laughter as they begin their meal. They wander about the temple occasionally refilling their glasses and exchanging pleasantries. The meal that lies before them consists of many Rangka delicacies, some not yet dead, and a variety of wines. Their repast is as elegant as Xhaknar's but there are no slaves in this place. They do not need them. Whatever needs the Rangka possess are cared for by the Kgul. The large, clay-like, creatures do the Rangka's bidding as they have for long Full Suns for reasons which are entirely their own. Whatever symbiosis exists between them and the Rangka is left to speculation; neither seems to care much about speculation. Someturn things may change, but not yet.

Eventually, the conversation returns to the deeds of Geldish. They note, in the careful manner of their kind, his moves and their subsequent results. They know of the movements of the Se-Jeant and the Dwellers of the Pit. They know of Xhaknar's raids and Geldish's pilferance of the repository. They know much, but not all. They worry about the possibility of the Fierstans becoming involved in Geldish's scheme. They, also, worry they might not get involved. They worry a lot. After all, they are responsible for many things. They keep knowledge and history. They keep the thoughts of many and the feelings of others. They are the keepers of all that was and some that will be. They are, also, the keepers of the sacred flames.

Karrish sums up their feelings, as only he can. "No matter what Geldish does, even with his expanding powers, he cannot hope to halt the Naradhama with savvy parlor tricks." As his sentence fades in soft echoes through the halls, the fourth tabernacle kindles to life.

"Parlor tricks?" Geldish smiles as he appears in their midst. "You do not do your teachings justice my brethren."

"Your words honor us, brother," Karrish bows to the new arrival, "but your presence confuses. We had thought you never to return after you built your own temple."

Geldish smiles a smile that frosts souls. "I will be blunt brothers, I intend to end Xhaknar's reign. For this to truly occur, we four must ride together."

All three of the Rangka are taken aback. What Geldish is proposing could wipe out their kind. He could wipe out the future. "Already we have lost too much!" Elzish almost whimpers. His demeanor does not bespeak greatness.

Karrish pulls himself together first, "You knew the rules when you undertook your crusade lo those many Suns ago. We cannot do this thing. We must not! All could unravel"

Geldish turns and faces the Rangka, "True, it all could or it could not. It does not matter. Much has changed since I left the venerated halls of the Temple of Azarep. I now know how to beat the barrier that surrounds Xhaknar in battle."

Karrish does not appear impressed. "Brother Geldish, you have always made your own way in the world, it is your wont to do so. Nonetheless, just because you have found your path to a future does not mean we should tread upon it."

The uneasy silence that follows is broken by Elzish. "What of the fringe dwellers you have attained? Will they not ride with you?"

Geldish sighs. "Of course they will. Their pasts may be dark, but their desire for a future which includes them is burning brightly within."

Makish speaks for the first time, "Maybe this is enough." His voice does not brim with confidence.

"I would hope so," Geldish's voice escapes through clenched teeth, "but I cannot fool myself. The four of us would be a nearly impenetrable wall ... the dwellers, as good as they are, would be a mere brittle facade."

Karrish sits at the repast table and exhales multitudinous turns worth of sorrows. "Nevertheless, you must make do with these," he pauses, searching for the right term, "brittle riders of yours or return to your place of rebirth within these walls. There would be no shame."

Geldish stares at the three for a long epi-clik. The flames in his eyes bespeak barely controlled anger. Should they gain a voice, they would burn all of his histories in an instant. There would be no 'here' for him anymore. He debates the value of such a move. There is much he wishes to destroy, but this thing that guided him once is not amongst them. He selects a different course of action. "We once ruled this world. Arretti then flourished."

Karrish will not be baited. "Our old kind ruled, we inherited despair."

"We once walked in pride amongst the denizens of the Plains."

"We once carried flesh on our bones. Turns come and go and always bring change." Elzish begins to support Karrish. He, too, sees no clear future if they join Geldish.

"We once insured peace and prosperity."

Makish walks over to Karrish and seals Geldish's fate. "Now we merely guard against war and degradation. Geldish, hear me well, there are no more wizards on Arretti to die and join us. We are the last. Should we do as you desire, then there will be no more. You know, as well as we, what happened when last our kind attacked Anapsida."

Geldish shrugs. "If we are to die in any case, then why not expire on our own terms?"

Karrish will not be forced into action just to do something, the Rangka have survived too long to be rash now. "Tell me Brother Geldish … look me in my eyes and tell me what good our deaths will do and we will ride with you. Think hard, brother, before you speak."

Geldish does think. He thinks of many things, of turns gone by and those yet to come. He thinks of what it means to be a martyr and what his death will do. He thinks of what life on the Plains will be like if there are no Rangka. Eventually, his tabernacle fades. He is gone. The remaining Rangka turn to face their idol and bow. Long cliks pass before any of them speak.

"Will we ride?" Makish understood all that happened, but he fathoms the depths of pride more than many.

Karrish looks at him for a brief sepi-clik and smiles,

"Not yet, but someturn we may. This war that looms ahead, belongs to Geldish. When we do ride again, there will be a reason we can justify. As evil as Xhaknar is, as much as we hate the Plains under his rule, we would accomplish nothing by riding now."

Elzish does not appear completely satisfied. "What of his … Brittle Riders? They have no prayer against the Naradhama, not withstanding what the Mayanoren will do to them."

Karrish finally smiles a genuine smile, "Well now, a prayer is something we can offer." With that, he pulls a cord on a wall and smiles as a Kgul walks in. A quiet giant that appears to be made of clay. "Take four nytsteeds to Geldish. Make sure they are fully packed." The Kgul nods and leaves.

Elzish seems relieved. "Well, at least now they will ride with honor."

Makish's face reveals some trepidation. "Well, four of them will have our protection, but what of the Llamia? She cannot ride a nytsteed."

"Her kind has no real need of our protection." Karrish replies absentmindedly.

"You have never told us why that is."

"Someturn you will see for yourself, however, it is now time for our invocations." The three turn and face their idol. They are aware, without leaving their places in front of the idol of the movements of the Kgul. They see it load four nytsteeds with complete travel gear. They watch him load a huge kgum with his own gear. The nytsteeds would never support its bulk. They see as it rides into a bleak horizon, carrying the hopes and prayers of the remnants of a race.

Oolnok watches his wife hang their laundry out to dry. While there were still a few turns before the Warm Sun, the air was crisp and clear and the clothes would smell better because of it. He then returns to the coop and butchers two prancing fowls. Their meat was tender and his wife had several recipes for it that made his mouth water.

He quickly cleans the birds and drops their feathers in a bag. The smalls like using them to make toys and play games. He wraps the two cleaned and drained carcasses in a cloth and puts them in the kitchen. His wife notices him and smiles. Other husbands may make their wives clean the food, but not Oolnok. He knows, for those extra few epi-cliks of work, he's earned a lifetime of gratitude.

He hears, because all smalls are heard before they are seen, his smalls coming home from school. They walk along the road between the farms and head to the front door. He's filled with a feeling of gladness, he's done well these last few turns. That means he won't have to sell any of his smalls to the slave masters when they come to the village during the Good Sun.

He knows his neighbor, after carefully adding up what he did and did not have, was going to have to sell two. He's sure his neighbor and his wife can make more, but Oolnok's attached to the ones he has and doesn't want to part with them.

He valiantly suffers through the hugs and kisses and then waits until they're seated in the front room. Once he's sure they're doing their school work he heads back out to finish his chores. He kisses his wife on the cheek as he passes and she rewards him with a slap on the rump. He smiles and hopes the smalls will sleep soundly this even.

He whistles for Pzzby and waits for him to gallop across the field. Then he mounts him bareback and heads into the fields to round up the kgum. It takes him the better part of a clik to get the sluggish creatures back in their pens and he is tired and sweaty when he's done.

He takes a few epi-cliks to groom Pzzby then heads to the shower stall behind the house. He calls to his wife to bring him a fresh shirt and britches and then strips and lets the warmish water cascade over his body. Suitably refreshed, and wearing clean clothes, he saunters across the back yard. As he nears the house he smells prancing fowl cooking in kgum oil wafting from the kitchen.

He looks at the lands around him and smiles. Yes, life is good for old Oolnok.

As even-falls away, the Dwellers of the Pit and their Se-Jeant companions appear on a different horizon within the view of the Fierstans. Whether or not they are seen by the Fierstans is of no consequence, they are going there anyway.

Ata expresses the concerns of them all. "Tell me friend Greko, do you think they will march with us?"

"I do not know. I have never had the gift of foresight. One thing I do know is we will not find out until we ask."

Ata laughs. It is the kind of laugh that brings confidence to a small, Greko realizes, but it still helps lighten the mood. Greko watches as Ata pulls a flask from his pack and takes a swallow. He is about to put it away when he discerns he is being rude.

"Ice wine?" He smiles as he hands Greko the flask.

"Why not, there is a definite chill in the air this breaklight." Greko smiles and takes a long swallow like the small before him. His lungs scream, his throat convulses, his eyes pinch into slits. He feels as though he has poured molten lava into his gullet. It does not help him at all to be aware Ata is watching him with a less than sympathetic expression.

"One of our best vintages." Ata begins happily, "Fresh mountain roots fermented in ice and then stored in a mountain cask over a true nature flame. Delicious, isn't it?"

Greko can hide his consternation no more. "This stuff could kill you!"

"Or cure you."

Greko regards Ata anew. If this small is representative of the least of the Se-Jeant, and it can stomach drink like that, Anapsida is in for some serious trouble. He watches as Ata takes another slug and hands him back the flask. This time he sips. The flavor is good, the bouquet is interesting, it tastes better than it looks and it hurts less in smaller doses.

While Greko is discovering the 'joys' of ice wine, a sentry in the realm of the Fierstans is watching their arrival. After making sure he is interpreting the situation correctly, he pulls a triangle off the wall and speaks into it.

"Watcher Urkel, you were correct, they are coming directly to us."

The speaker crackles to life beside the sentry. "Thank you, guardian. Are they still just Pit Dwellers and Se-Jeant?"

"Yes, Watcher Urkel."

"Very well guardian. Please inform the gate to allow two of their representatives to enter the main area."

"As you command, Watcher Urkel."

Mere epi-cliks later, four Fierstans are leaving through the main gate area and heading across the plain towards the marchers. They ride without battle gear and still manage to look menacing. Originally their brand was designed to do massive amounts of manual labor. Slightly shorter than the Minotaur, they have four, evenly spaced, well-muscled arms and their legs are more akin to tree trunks than anything else. The marchers notice them and halt their advance. Soon, they are assembled together at the head of the column. Two of the Fierstans dismount their deisteeds and approach Greko and Ata. The leader of the two carries a staff emblazoned with the Fierstan insignia. Mist still falls from Greko's eyes thanks to the ice wine. The Fierstans notice this but are unsure what to make of it so they ignore it.

"I am Guardian Nak. Watcher Urkel will speak with two representatives of this column should you so desire." All of this is said as he watches Greko cough, mist and try to look dignified simultaneously.

"I am Greko, Fourth Level Dweller of the Pit and this is Ata, Patrol Leader of the Se-Jeants, we would be honored to share discourse with your Watcher Urkel." Greko manages to get this sentence out without causing embarrassment to his lineage and is grateful. Silently, he curses ice wine and the younglings who can drink it.

Guardian Nak waves his staff towards the gate and turns quickly to remount his deisteed. Greko and Ata follow on foot as they quickly are surrounded by the Fierstan riders. Behind them, the remaining members of the column begin to light fires and sit on the ground. They do not know how long this will take and they may as well stay warm. One of the Fierstan riders glances over his shoulder and admires the speed with which the column has set up camp. His admiration turns to subtle unrest as he watches some of the Se-Jeant begin to file their teeth. He immediately rivets his attention towards the gate and swallows hard.

Soon, the six are within the walls of the Fierstans. The gates close behind them, and for the first time in almost five hundred Full Suns, brands not Fierstan stand in the courtyard. They traverse the courtyard and encounter a huge door. This is an ancient door. It must have been made in the days before Xhaknar. There are scars in its wood that remind all of the viciousness of the past and the possible horrors of the future. As it swings open and allows the assembled to enter, Greko and Ata spy Watcher Urkel. His small frame belying true inner strength. They stare as he puffs on a pipe made from materials they do not recognize. His lower left arm motions for them to sit as his upper right cleans the pipe. His upper left is carrying a small sheaf of papers and his lower right is just hanging there as though no one thought of a worthy duty for it to perform.

Greko and Ata know the twisted history of the Naradhama. All smalls, as far as they knew, learned it Suns ago, yet it was disconcerting to watch someone who resembles those repulsive warriors smoking a grand pipe and doing paperwork. It is only then they notice the room into which they have been taken. The walls are covered with framed documents. Most seem to be written in Rangka script. In an admittedly offhand calculation, Greko places them at one thousand Full Suns old. He wonders what could be so important to place them in such honor. The Dwellers of the Pit rarely place their history on display unless it is something that can benefit all. Something deep inside of him informs him these documents meet that criteria, but he does not fathom why.

Their reverie is broken by the sound of a high voice wrapped in culture. "I am Urkel, Watcher of the Fierstans. What brings you to our humble village?"

Greko gathers his wits and speaks for all. "We have a request, legendary one. I am Greko, Fourth Level Dweller of the Pit and this is Ata, Patrol Leader of the Se-Jeant."

Urkel permits himself a wry smile. "With such

honored representatives sharing my parlor, I fear the request will be great indeed." He relights his pipe and faces them directly.

"Oh no, Watcher Urkel! We have come merely to request a patrol of Fierstans join us on our expedition to Geldish's lair."

Urkel frowns. "So, despite all of the other traumas denigrating our lives, the words of his deed have reached as far as you."

Greko and Ata are completely flabbergasted. "We were not aware …" Greko's voice trails into nothing.

"Aware that we cared of the comings and goings on the Plains? We are secluded, not ignorant. It would be the purest of follies to disregard the actions of others that could, nay, would, once again, bring flame where flame has no use being."

"If you are, indeed, aware of what has occurred, you must, by rights, have come to the same conclusion as we!" Ata did not mean it to come out as forcefully as it did, but it is too late to swallow the sound of his voice now.

Urkel stares at him. His voice barely controlled, he responds.

"IF? MUST?" He takes a long breath. "You are young and eager and, for all of that … correct. We, too, see the fires of war in the near future. We, too, have danced the Aklop in the joy of wishing Xhaknar a lingering death. However, I do not understand why you send patrols and not just two representatives."

Greko returns calmly to the conversation. "There have been marauding bands of Naradhama sighted on the Plains and the Mayanoren have been near our pit twice in the last two seasons."

Urkel considers this for a moment. "How could the Mayanoren find what is widely believed to be a myth?"

Greko shrinks a little inside and answers. "My brother, Ek-kh, has dishonored our flame and joined with Xhaknar. We believe he is giving information to Xhaknar in return for favors which would shame a kgum." Greko's large head hangs low. Ata, even though he had heard the story before, felt his heart chill at this simple retelling. Two sentences could be the death sentence for a brand.

Urkel has similar thoughts. His response must be made carefully.

"Hmm, your Pit must think well of you to have brought you all the way to the Fourth Level and you, Ata, diminutive though you are, stand before me as a Patrol Leader. Together you have travelled the Plains just to make a request of a 'legendary' somebody. That seems like a lot of work for an answer that could be, and should be, no."

Before they can speak, Urkel's lower left arm motions them to be quiet. "It has always been, and still is to the best of my knowledge, a Fierstan truism that 'to ride with the honored is to be honored.'" Greko and Ata can barely repress their smiles. Before they can gush their thanks, Urkel continues. "I wish I could ride with you myself. It has been many Suns since I took a patrol to battle. However, needs dictate I stay here and continue to be 'legendary.' According to my gate guardian, you march two patrols of fifty troops each, is that correct?"

Ata, still smiling, replies in the affirmative. Greko lets his head once again raise him to his full height. He thanks Rohta, they will not ride alone to Geldish. There must be cohesion amongst the Dwellers of the Plains or this plan will fail. What he knows, and Ata does not, is he was to end the whole thing and return the Pit if the Fierstans rejected the request.

Urkel watches them contemplatively for a moment and smiles. "All is good then. Now you shall march three." He reaches over to a triangular speaking device and begins ordering provisions for the march. Then he sends out servants to the column camped outside. To them, he sends a full hot meal and dancers. He knows troops well enough to know which will be appreciated more. He makes sure he specifies that two Rakyeen be loaded with the provisions so servants will not have to march with them. Finally, he claps his lower arms and the room explodes with sound as three musicians, unnoticed until now, begin playing odd, squeezable, instruments. Doors in the rear of the room swing open and trays heaped with Fierstan delicacies are brought forth and laid out in buffet style.

As Greko and Ata begin to share a mid-break repast with Urkel, the columns outside are greeted by two Rakyeen, their six legs churning up the distance quickly, carrying dancers and cheeses and meats and wines and jingly drums and squeezing instruments and Rohta knows what else. A cheer erupts from the column. Food is always a good omen. They know, without being told, the Fierstans will march alongside them.

After their food has been devoured, and the dancers enjoyed – although not in the same manner as Xhaknar's, three columns march forth across the Plains towards Geldish's lair. They exchange wishes for good health and pass the ice wine freely. Much to Greko's discontent, Fierstans seem to love this libation as much as the Se-Jeant.

Come even-fall they set their camp around several fires. Soon, all are assembled near the center fires and relaxing. Greko turns to one of the Fierstans, the one called Nak, and asks a question that has been bothering him since he met Watcher Urkel. "Tell me, Guardian Nak, what are those documents that surround the hall where Watcher Urkel holds forth?"

Nak smiles. "They are the stories of our past. They are, also, the stories of your past and all the pasts of all of the Dwellers of the Plains. We truly have as complete a history of the Plains as the Rangka or as your brand is rumored to."

Ata laughs. "Why have all of your history on a wall when you can go out and make some of your own?"

"Tell me Ata," Nak asks turning to face the young Se-Jeant, "why does your coat of arms bear the likeness of a Wolfen and a Dweller of the Pit?"

Ata blushes and shrugs. He has heard something about it, but it is a story and he never liked stories. They always made him feel like a small and he was not a small, he IS not a small. He is the Patrol Leader of the Se-Jeant. Well, actually, he isn't completely yet, but it makes him feel good when Greko says he is, so he doesn't correct it.

Nak beams. "Then maybe someone should tell you. It is your history that was a part of the reason we march with you this turn."

Greko lets his curiosity get the better of him. "Why don't you tell us the story Guardian Nak. Even if some of the Se-Jeant know it, it is always interesting to hear our histories from the mouths of others."

Nak nods and settles down with a fresh flagon of ice wine.

"There were turns when the Plains were not scarred and torn. There were turns when it was acceptable to walk them in the even without a weapon. It was right after the death of those turns my story begins. Xhaknar had disbanded the council where the Fierstans had ruled for five hundred Full Suns, with the assistance of the Wizards who later became Rangka of course. The Naradhama were not yet fully trained and many places had been overlooked by Xhaknar when he set out to conquer the Plains with the Mayanoren. It was during these turns he decided to rectify the situation and decimate the opposition. It was, also, during these turns a Wolfen and a Dweller of the Pit were injured, badly, near the Ice Palace of the Se-Jeant."

He sips his ice wine and notices none speak. All eyes, and there are many of them on the Se-Jeant alone, watch him. He takes a slow breath and continues. "The

Dweller was not of the ruling elite or the warrior caste. He was a tinker and, by all accounts of the past Suns, an excellent one. The Wolfen was an early fringe dweller. How they came to travel together, none know. All things considered, it does not matter. Nonetheless, they were badly injured in a rock slide and required help. A group of smalls, early in their warrior training, came upon them and took them to the Palace where they were tended. They watched from their sick beds as the smalls trained for battle.

"They knew of Xhaknar's deeds and, for reasons of their own, asked to join warrior school. As the Se-Jeant among us know, just asking to join warrior school can bring honor to a family. The training of the Se-Jeant can easily kill an applicant. In fact, the only way to pass is to survive. The medical staff at the Palace tried to explain these truths to them but they were not so easily dissuaded. Eventually, after passing some rather difficult tests, they were allowed to join the school."

By now the entire gathering was so quiet you could hear the sna-Ahd weasels foraging in the distant even. Nak takes another swallow of his ice wine and realizes, much to his surprise, he is enjoying being a storyteller.

"After about fifty turns, word came that Xhaknar was mounting an army outside the Palace. Although it was about a turn away, there was nothing else close enough for it to attack. It was apparent Xhaknar was going to move ahead with the idea of total decimation of the Plains. The Wolfen and the Dweller immediately asked to be made active so they could help repay their saviors. Initially, the Se-Jeant leaders had misgivings, but they needed bodies. Xhaknar's army was too big. Against their better judgment, arms were issued to the tinker and his assistant. The next turn, the Naradhama, and the Mayanoren attacked. Columns were formed, strategies acted upon and the battle enjoined."

Quiet would be too subtle a word to describe the

gathering now. Rapt faces stared at Nak and hung on his every word. He sipped some more ice wine and continued.

"The Wolfen and the Dweller were given positions at the rear of a column and they marched out of the Palace with their heads held high. During the course of the battle, they became separated from their battalion. Somehow, they ended up in the foothills near the battle covered in snow. They dug themselves out and joined a scouting troop of Se-Jeants who were headed back towards the main battle. When they arrived, they saw the Se-Jeant outnumbered three to one and pinned against the outer wall of the Palace. One of the Se-Jeant scouts, the tinker, and his assistant leapt into the fray from the rear. The Naradhama and the Mayanoren never saw them coming.

"They screamed and hacked their way into the battle and caused such confusion amongst Xhaknar's troops they allowed the pinned Se-Jeant a chance to regroup and thrust forward. As this was happening, the remaining scouting party attacked as well. They caught the rear guard between themselves and the three before them. According to legend, they killed almost two hundred Naradhama and Mayanoren before being overcome. The sight of their deaths so enraged the Se-Jeant they slaughtered Xhaknar's army in one turn.

"The Se-Jeant fought like beings possessed. Blood flew through the air and fertilized the grounds outside of the Palace. When it was over, there was one less battalion for Xhaknar to command. The bodies of the tinker, his assistant, and the Se-Jeant scout were found together. Their swords were still in their hands. Their bodies ripped and slashed, almost, beyond recognition. Their wounds appeared to have happened before they died. No one knows how they fought through the pain, but they did."

Nak simply pauses to pause. He is relishing in his role as an elder storyteller and does not wish it to cease just yet.

"After the battlefield was cleared, a great funeral

was held for these three. Since no one claimed the body of the scout, they were buried together. Unfortunately, no one knew their names either. Therefore, it simply states on their stone, 'Three separated from their battalion, Died with Honor and in Valor. Warrior rank ungiven, school unfinished.' As I said before, Se-Jeant warrior school is tough." This gets an unintended laugh from the assembled. Nevertheless, he sees many of them are seriously thinking about their own pasts for the first time in a long turn.

Ata finally speaks. "So this is why there is the symbol of the Wolfen and the Dweller on every piece of fine cutlery and dinnerware as well as on the coat of arms we carry into battle this turn. It was one of those things I never gave much thought to. I had always just assumed it was some symbol left over from when the council ruled the Plains and no one had gotten around to updating it."

Greko smiles and refills his cup of ice wine. He's finally getting used to this stuff, or he's drunk. He neither knows nor cares. As he sits down next to the fire, he thinks about Nak's unintended joke and how much tougher things are under the reign of Xhaknar. It is said, in Suns gone by, the council would meet every twenty Full Suns and choose a new leader. The elected one would not lead so much as arbitrate between the divergent species of the Plains. The tribes and warrens did not really follow but they did not deviate too far from the intentions of the council. Overall, it was an imperfect solution but it worked.

After the council had been in power for five hundred Full Suns a social stasis set in that passed for peace. Rumors were heard of a warring tribe to the north, decimating all who opposed it, but that was far away. Besides, the might of the council, when assembled, could handle anything that came its way. The problem with that thought was the phrase 'when assembled.' The varied defensive sectors of the tribes were disseminated throughout the Plains in an effort to keep the borders secure. In other words, it was a good idea in theory.

However, Xhaknar and Yontar cared little for theories. They realized the gaunt nature of the defenses and slaughtered the northern bastions without slowing down. By the time the other tribes could assemble, in any strength, the Fierstans were defeated and the Plains were aflame. Greko's ancestors fought in that war and were publicly flayed and left to die in front of their families. Xhaknar even went so far as to feed their entrails to his deisteeds. But, no matter how much hatred might exist, there was no power to enable it. There was nothing to free it and let it loose upon the walls of Anapsida.

Now, with the actions of a rogue Rangka, maybe there is. If they are wrong, Xhaknar will, once again, thin the tribes for the "good" of the Plains. If they are wrong, there will be blood from the lands of Südermann to the northern sky. There will be more blood than Xhaknar's fountain could ever spew and that would bring the ultimate indignity, it would make Xhaknar happy.

Watcher Urkel isn't feeling all that legendary at the moment. Over the last hundred Full Suns, he's slowly rebuilt the strength of the Fierstans away from the prying eyes of Xhaknar's spies. By keeping secure guardians at the gate and using the hard wired radios to communicate throughout the city, he's maintained their privacy.

He'd even had the City built down instead of out to hide the fact the population was recovering and the Fierstan warriors, once the most feared on the Plains, were back in some semblance of force.

He was unsure if they were ready for what was

coming, though. He didn't need to be warned at the ferocity Anapsida could bring. All he had to do was look at his own family tree with so many branches cut short. Nevertheless, nine generations of Watchers had come from that tree. Urkel, though never wed, had mated and there were two of his progeny who showed promise. He hoped their transition turn would still be far off, but was pretty sure he was hastening it along with his actions now.

When he'd been young life had been simple. Everything was a game. Even when he'd been selected to learn the ways of the Watchers, he'd not taken it too seriously. He wondered if any of his predecessors had either. It's hard, if not impossible, for a small to grasp the full extent of any situation that doesn't directly involve them.

But he'd studied hard, served his time in the military and then begun his formal training in earnest. It had all seemed so abstract back then, not the harsh reality he faced now. When his classmates would call him or his cousin Watcher Urkel or Watcher Glarn, it had always been good for a laugh. He'd always assumed Glarn would get the final call. He just seemed bigger than life to Urkel, the kind of leader citizens would want.

But Glarn had also been impetuous. He'd ventured outside the walls of the city looking for who knows what. An adventure Urkel guessed. He'd found one, that was for certain. He'd stumbled across a couple of drunken Naradhama relieving themselves away from their camp. Drunk or not they'd easily seized him and had him brought back to their commander as a spy.

Per the laws of Anapsida, Glarn was publically tortured for thirty turns and then executed above the fountain. After that, there was only one trainee left, and that was Urkel.

He understood then how terribly real all he was being taught was. He'd redoubled his efforts and if he was the only choice he'd still turned out to be a good one.

And now he was going to endanger it all chasing down the ghost of a rogue wizard. He silently hoped he hadn't just gone insane and there was a method to the madness which was sure to follow.

Although Greko had worried about Xhaknar's possible impending happiness Xhaknar is not happy at all. He stares across his throne room. His powerful frame, perched near the highest precipice of Anapsida, has a clear view of both the interior and exterior. In the courtyard below, near the blood fountain, Naradhama train. They wrestle and slash their way through imaginary defenders as the Mayanoren watch with bemused, and mildly disinterested, expressions. Xhaknar allows himself a personal grin. He knows the Mayanoren disdain anything that resembles effort beyond killing. They do not need it. Death is their toy and they play with it often. Xhaknar knows the Mayanoren would never involve themselves in something so demeaning as practice unless he demanded it and followed up his threats with dire actions. He, also, knows they were the best thing the enemies of Rohta ever invented for killing. He has watched them clear a village of all living things inside of two cliks. Nonetheless, he knows they respect the Naradhama, even if they don't understand them. After all, they both kill for Xhaknar and that is more than the dead can say.

Xhaknar's reverie is interrupted when a grindel alights near his throne but just out of reach. "Yessss Great One. I come assss promisssssed." It never takes its eyes off of Xhaknar.

"Your promise meant nothing. Your return saved the life of a grindel this turn. Beyond that, you have saved me the effort of killing a worthless creature. Tell me what you found out or die, those are your choices this turn."

The grindel could hate Xhaknar more, but it has other things to attend to. "Nothing hassss come or left Geldissssshssss lair."

Xhaknar studies the verminous creature and smiles. "Hate me all you want, thing, I could care less what your kind thinks of me. Go, return to your post and keep me abreast of everything, or I will kill two grindels come next even."

The grindel slithers backwards and leaps of the precipice which houses Xhaknar's throne. As it flies across the Plains, it smiles. It knows it told Xhaknar the truth. Xhaknar can smell lies. It just did not tell the whole truth. It did not tell of the columns of Se-Jeant, Fierstan and Minotaur it saw on the Plains. It did not tell they were headed directly towards Geldish. It did not lie and its kind still lives. Yes, it can smile this turn.

N'leah smiles as she arcs gracefully over Geldish's lair and then slides sideways through the air. Her lean, nude, body caresses the mid-break sky with an eerie sensuality. Suddenly, she twists and dives towards the ground. R'yune leaps, apparently, to the side then spins and grabs her ankle and tosses her into the soft sand. N'leah bursts out in friendly laughter. BraarB joins in as she helps N'leah up.

"Very, very impressive," BraarB smiles as she hands N'leah a flagon of Whævin, "I did not know bipeds could move so elegantly." R'yune, also nude, grunts and pulls a flask off of his belt, lying on the ground nearby, and takes a swig.

N'leah laughs even louder. A sharp contrast to her powerful, sensual, aerial skills, her laugh is gentle, innocent and honest. "I believe he said 'thank you." R'yune nods enthusiastically. BraarB grabs the flagon back, takes a swig, and stares down to R'yune's powerful thighs.

"Speaking of impressive, I think R'yune's warrior soul has gotten the better of him. I thought you weren't supposed to wear a sword in mock-combat. Not even if it's strapped to an inside thigh." BraarB keeps smiling. Much to her surprise, N'leah smiles and then barely suppresses a giggle. "What's so funny, N'leah?"

"Uh, that's not a sword. R'yune would never do that. One of us might be accidentally injured. R'yune would rather disembowel himself than allow that to happen."

BraarB is still staring. Her eyes grow wider and wider, reality sinks in. "Do you mean to tell me that ... this thing ... it's his ... OH SWEET ROHTA!"

That finishes off any sense of decorum that may have existed. N'leah falls down laughing. R'yune smiles a Wolfen grin. Somehow it is not the grin of mirth. Happiness may be his emotion, but predatory images are all that are conjured up with his show of teeth. Sland sidles up next to BraarB and pats her on the back.

"Wolfen are strong in all things, eh R'yune? Think BraarB, He could even hold you down with that thing." Sland's brief monologue simply tosses them all back into laughter. Geldish wanders over and strokes BraarB's mane. Soon, they all quiet down.

"Even comes my friends. We must go inside. Xhaknar's eyes could find us in the dark."

N'leah suddenly turns and faces across the Plains. "Something comes. Large, fast and quiet." They all watch the horizon. Soon, they all see what N'leah has heard. A Kgul with four steeds. Its immense clay-like frame bounds into view with the shaggy, black steeds close behind him. Their flame lit eyes remind all of Geldish. The sight is terrifying and reassuring at the same time. Geldish smiles and, this time, it's a good smile. Barely perceptible, the others still hear him dare the prayer "Azarep will live."

Sland turns and faces the Rangka. "What you mean dead one? Azarep all gone. Temple gone. Azarep all dead."

Geldish turns and looks at Sland. His eyes pierce the BadgeBeth's soul. "Death never slowed me down, why would it stop the Azarep?"

"You are from Azarep?" Sland, occasionally, guesses right in spite of himself.

BraarB stares at the oncoming sight and gasps. "If you are truly of the Azarep then those beasts are now approaching are really nytsteeds."

N'leah slides into the even air and calls down. "It must be true, because, unless all of those ancient pictures I saw as a small were lies, those beasts are most definitely nytsteeds."

Two eyes peer out of the nearby sands and watch the unfolding tableau. They see as the Kgul trots up and hands the reigns for all four beasts to Geldish. They see the awe in the eyes of the others. Awe, the eyes think, is good. It is seldom something long thought dead shows up to help. They see the Kgul wander across the sands to their lair. They see all of this and surrender to that which they now know is true. Long before the Kgul was here, it knew they were here. How Kgul know these things was unimportant. Kgul always know. They always have.

Much to the surprise of the assembled, a grindel pops out of the sand and flies to the Kgul. Alighting gently on the massive roiling clay/flesh, it settles in for the walk back to Geldish's abode. Geldish's smile disappears as he watches what the Kgul is bringing to him.

"You are a spy of Xhaknar's?" It's a question yet it sounds like a threat.

"Yessssss, I am. Musssst dothisssss thing."

Geldish ignores the statement. "What have you seen?"

"Nothing, until thisssss."

"Will you tell Xhaknar?"

"Mussst. Will kill otherssss if I not."

"Others? What others? All grindels were killed by Xhaknar to spite the Se-Jeant, your friends."

"Ten live. Ten all there isss on Arreti. All there izz on the Plainsss and ssXhaknar keep usss in cage near fountain."

N'leah looks at the grindel. Her brand never dealt with them so this is something new to her. "Why don't you just lie to Xhaknar? Or, maybe we should just kill you here and now. You are a threat to us if you work for Xhaknar."

Geldish raises his arm towards her. "No, Xhaknar can smell lies. If this grindel lied, the others would die. As for working for Xhaknar, none do that task freely or willingly except the Mayanoren, and now, of course, the Naradhama. No, we must devise a different plan of action. We must use this to our advantage. Tell me grindel, how do you report?"

"When brother come, we ssleep. Come breaklight, I leave and report what I know to ssXhaknar."

"When will your brother be here?"

"He come now, sssseeeee him near."

The Kgul walks a short distance away and holds out its arm. Soon, the next grindel alights there and nestles itself in the warm clay/flesh. The Kgul carries the grindel back to the others.

"Welcome comrade grindel," Geldish's voice is calm and reassuring, "you are amongst friends. I am only going to ask you tell Xhaknar the truth. The first grindel, you will tell what you have seen this even. The second grindel, when you make your journey, you will tell Xhaknar we are marching towards him. That will be the truth. We will march on Xhaknar and Anapsida come mid-break. Do you understand?" Both grindels nod affirmatively. "Good. Now the second grindel take this vial from me and hide it well. It is a magic potion. After you tell

Xhaknar we are marching towards him, he will have no need to send you back here. His spies on the Plains can keep track of us then. He will throw you back in your cage. When he does, you will take this vial from its hiding place and pour it on the bars of your cage. It will melt them. You will be free then. Flee Anapsida and go to the land of the Fierstans. Watcher Urkel will take care of you. Do you understand?"

The second grindel stares at the vial, smiles as only a grindel can, and puts it under its tongue.

Greko opens his eyes and regrets his rash impulse immediately. Even behind a closed tent flap – well, he assumes it's a tent flap even though it could be a door or a boulder given the way he felt - during the Dark Sun his eyes felt as though someone was pouring liquid flame in them. His head was making a painful, arrhythmic, drumming noise and his tongue tasted like a dirty wagon handle. He actually knew that exact taste thanks to a youthful prank by his traitorous brother many Suns ago. He spent several epi-cliks trying to discern what was underneath him and, eventually, concluded it was a bed. With supreme effort, he managed to grab one side and slowly pull himself semi-erect. Out of the corner of one of his still burning eyes, he saw a small platter of foods he didn't recognize, a flagon of something that might possibly be liquid and a note written in an unknown hand. While the words written on it were still beyond his ken he decided the note must be from Nak. After a few epi-cliks of careful study, and by holding it at a forty-five degree angle to something over there, he was able to make out the words.

"Eat this, drink that, feel better."

He decided he might, just might, be able to handle those instructions.

He took a tentative nibble from the plate and felt his tongue returning to its normal status. Within a few minutes, he was done with everything Nak had left for him and felt better than he had in Suns. With his senses fully returned he realized he was naked. His clothing and armor were neatly stacked on a box across the room. He walked over to them and quickly dressed.

Much to his surprise, his tent flap was, in actuality, a tent flap. He opened it to greet the Sun. That was not the best thing to ever happen to him.

Nak was walking across the plain towards him and smiled.

"Good breaklight Greko," he said warmly, "how feels your head?"

"Much better now," admitted Greko, "thanks to the medicines you left in my room."

Nak laughed. "We are a brand who love our ice wines. We've had to learn how to love them a little less or deal with the consequences. Your brand does not indulge like us or the Se-Jeants, do you?"

"No," grimaced Greko, "and hopefully I'm smart enough not to try and do that again."

Nak looked at him for a sepi-clik and then laughed uproariously. He slapped Greko on the shoulder and led him over to the main tent where a rude conference table/kitchen had been set up.

As he entered he spied Ata and several others standing around a table laden with food. There is a tang in the air Greko cannot place but realizes is coming from an urn on the table, set over a low flame. The others are drinking from it and smiling. He approached it warily.

"Fear not friend Greko," smiles Ata, "it is a refreshing drink the Fierstans use to start their day. It is made from nothing more potent than beans."

A Fierstan warrior Greko doesn't recognize pours a

small cup of the brew and hands it to him. Greko sniffs carefully and finally takes a sip. The drink is bitter and strong but seems to reinvigorate his body. He finishes the cup and attacks the food table with a vengeance.

Whatever else can be said about the Fierstans, they do know how to greet the light.

After their meal was completed they quickly divided up duties and prepared for their march to Geldish's lair. Within a few epi-cliks, there was no sign a camp had ever existed and the marchers were fading into the growing Sun.

Xhaknar too had risen to greet the morn. After being dressed by his slaves he walks out into the Naradhama camp, currently in the middle of the courtyard, and quickly assesses the status of his army. The local entertainers who had greeted their return were long gone and the troop-slaves were busy cleaning up the memories. He glances over at the pit where they were tossing the bodies of the entertainers who had, for any one of a million reasons, displeased one soldier or another and noted there were only three this time. He was mildly surprised and decided he would hire them again. After all, as leader, it was his job to keep the troops pleased.

On his command, the troops had spent the last fifty turns raiding villages across the Plains and testing out the information he'd been given by Ek-kh. He knew they had taken in several wagons full of loot, but that was not his concern. What he wanted was information and this turn he would find out what he needed to know, or he would make sure there were bodies on spikes.

His bearers carried him across the crowded

courtyard and placed him in front of a temporary building. He enters the provisional compound where his Naradhama generals met and is mildly surprised to find a Mayanoren standing with them. They come to attention immediately upon his entrance and wait for him to speak.

"I assume you have news that will please me?" His voice seems to rumble off the canvas walls.

"Yes, lord," replied one of his Naradhama, "it appears the traitor Ek-kh has spoken the truth thus far. We found the lair of the Minotaurs easily enough. Per your command, we did not attack it, but we did take the opportunity to raid some neighboring villages of mixed brands."

"Go on."

"Their mountain, and eternal flame, is housed in a series of ancient structures which survived the coming of the Gen-O-Pods. They have covered these with dirt and grasses to make a single structure that appears as though it is just a normal hill. Several of my soldiers swear we have ridden across it on our way to other battles. To the best of my memory, they may be right."

Xhaknar laughed. "So, they hide in the open? How interesting, and yet, how effective."

None of the assembled even cracked a smile. The Mayanoren shuffles uneasily and then resumes his attentive stance.

"Why is a Mayanoren among you? I did not order them to return here or on this mission."

"Forgive us, Lord," replied the second general, "but with the Naradhama occupied with your commands, and with the attack at your repository, we needed to enlist the Mayanoren to follow the offenders and see where your goldens were so we could recapture them when you so desired."

Xhaknar wasn't exactly sure he liked initiative in his ranks but decided to let it pass. For now. He turns to the Mayanoren and asks, "Well, since you are here and the deed is done, tell me what you know."

The Mayanoren straightens fully and speaks in a more cultured voice than Xhaknar would have thought possible for those vicious vermin.

"I caught up with the rear of the raiding party about ten kays south of Go-Chi. There was a Wolfen, a BadgeBeth, a Succubus and a Llamia. To the best of my sight, the Llamia carried all the goldens. They stayed close to the eternal cracks and were surrounded by some demon-inspired mist. I attempted to traverse the mist to get closer but it burned my steed and I was forced to kill it and follow on foot at a distance."

"Interesting. Continue."

"After another ten kays, they made camp and were visited by a Rangka. I know not where he came from, he just appeared from the cracks. I could not hear what was said, but they resumed their march shortly thereafter. Then the mist grew and I was unable to see any more. They were still headed south the last I saw them."

The Mayanoren assumed he would now be killed for not having recaptured the goldens or, at least, locating their final destination. This didn't bother him since he knew he lived only at the desire of Xhaknar.

But Xhaknar seemed lost in thought. After a moment he finally spoke.

"It is odd, is it not, that Geldish allowed you to get that close in the first place? Even odder still he made no attempt to dissuade you until he was near his lair? He allowed you to see what he wanted you to see and no more." He paused for a few long epi-cliks and then realized they were all waiting for him to pronounce judgment. "All may live, keep your bounty and get back to work."

Ignoring the looks of relief, he strode from the tent and waited for his bearers to carry him back.

R'yune and N'leah ride to the left of BraarB and Geldish and Sland fill out the right flank. The Kgul was long gone having headed back to the Temple of Azarep shortly after presenting Geldish with the grindels.

The five riders, Geldish has not told them of the name bestowed upon them by the remaining Rangka, mostly because the explanation would take too long, headed north towards the marching columns of Fierstans, Minotaurs, and Se-Jeants. Although the Kgul had given him exact directions, Geldish had felt them the even before and could easily have found them on his own. Nevertheless, one less burden means a lighter turn, that's what his mother used to say.

The unbidden thought of his parents sent his mind wandering. Designed to have greatly enhanced electromagnetic fields and to use parts of the mind that had, previously, been barely touched, the "wizards," as they were called, were a highly effective work force. Their combined talents made them ideal mining surveyors. They could find metals and ores in sepi-cliks that would take others, even with the most sensitive equipment and charts, months.

Their skin color, thanks to the enhancements Rohta had given them, was universally royal blue. Why that was is still unknown. Geldish's mother always thought it was Rohta's way of ensuring they could never pass for makers. To Geldish that seemed as logical a reason as any other.

Geldish had been born after the Gen-O-Pod war. Like many of his breed, he'd explored his abilities to their fullest. By the time he was pubescent he could move objects, sense and define over a thousand natural minerals and objects and reverse his magnetic field so he could float above the planet. Not high, no more than two or three feet, but it was more than many others could do.

When he'd passed his twentieth Full Sun he and some friends had discovered they could combine their talents. They could move large amounts of metal and ores with relative ease. They also found each could create a magnetic bubble. Then they could stack one on top of the other so that, eventually, the Wizard in the top bubble could be as much as one hundred feet or more off the ground.

They were heady days. Unlike his parents who could be, and often were, punished for showing their talents, the complete lack of makers was a wonderful thing for the newly born Gen-O-Pods.

After that Geldish's story felt oddly conventional. He fell in love with a wizard named Estella, married, and started a family of his own. It was only later that he, and the others of his kind, realized the lifespan of a wizard was going to be considerably longer than advertised. Some of the first born, who'd fought in the Gen-O-Pod war, were nearing one hundred Full Suns old and didn't look a turn over twenty-five. With sharp minds and excellent health, they realized there was no need to slave themselves to the maker's way of doing things.

They had no true idea how long they were going to live but it was clear they'd see far more breaklights than their makers ever dreamed.

Geldish was just entering his five hundredth Full Sun when Xhaknar attacked. Within the first seven turns, his beloved wife was dead, his smalls missing, presumed killed, and his parents were cinders laid on the steps of their home. The bodies of most of his friends lay strewn about the fields where they used to play as smalls.

Yontar, the mind behind the mayhem, had set up trading posts many Suns before the attack and ferreted out the strengths and weaknesses of each brand of Gen-O-Pod long before Xhaknar's arrival. Beings tend to be friendlier when they are just talking among friends, which is what the residents of the Plains assumed Yontar's spies were. When they descended upon the wizards they used plastic weapons and crude, nonmagnetic, electronic shields. For all their power, the wizards may as well have stood naked in front of the lethal weapons.

Well, lethal to the wizards, to everyone else they were merely irritating.

One group of wizards, led by Karrish, banded together for one last stand against Xhaknar's army. By causing their magnetic fields to swirl and undulate they threw off the aim of the energy weapons and began killing at will. Within three turns it looked as though they might defeat their enemies.

Then, to the horror of all, Xhaknar released an airborne virus which literally ate the flesh off its victims and made their bones supple. That slowed the wizards down, but for reasons unknown at that time, did not stop them.

Weakened, confused and grotesquely deformed, they still kept attacking. Xhaknar's Mayanoren broke ranks and fled. Not even Xhaknar could blame them.

Yontar quickly rounded up the troops and attacked everything not held by the hideous wizards. The wizards, despite the fear they caused, were simply too weak to come to the aid of the rest of the Gen-O-Pods. Within a Full Sun, the Plains belonged to Xhaknar.

The other surviving brands, already mildly insular, to begin with, became rabid xenophobes and hid behind mighty fortresses. That suited Xhaknar fine since he then knew exactly where to find them if he wished.

With the warrens sequestered, Yontar found four deep tunnel borers about fifty kays south of the giant lake. Each was about eighty feet around and was designed to create underground aquifers. Yontar and Xhaknar quickly conceived of a far more malevolent purpose.

It took the Mayanoren a Full Sun to get the ancient machines running and then it took four more Full Suns to drive them a thousand feet underground and then reach the lake. But it was all worth it for them when the machines punched through the bottom of the lake in four disparate locations and gravity took over.

Within another Sun the great lake was gone and the Gaping Canyon was born.

Geldish remembered spying on Xhaknar once as he stood near the carnage and laughed, gleefully, at the sight of an ecosystem dying.

His reverie was snapped when BraarB called his name.

"Geldish," she called, "I'm hearing echoes off the far horizon. We're less than a quarter turn from the column. Maybe we should take a break now so we're fresh when we meet them"

Geldish absently nodded his assent and the riders came to a halt. N'leah and R'yune quickly arranged a meal from their provisions and passed around a canteen of spiced water.

Were it not for the knowledge of the ride's purpose, the scene would have been positively bucolic. The five of them sitting quietly around one of N'leah's earthen flames, eating and drinking contentedly as the mid turn sun shone down upon them. There was a nip in the air but it was clear the season of the Dark Sun was beginning to blend with the season of the Warm Sun.

For a brief moment, Geldish wondered if this was what peace could be like.

Xhaknar stood gazing across the courtyard of Anapsida. Almost three square miles of space dedicated to his military might. Around that were the hundreds of thousands of dwellings for the troops, their families and the many who lived to serve Xhaknar. Surrounding them were the main battlements and then, beyond them, the spiky, fortified, impregnable walls that kept all inside safe. The entire edifice, for it was truly one great place, was over seven square miles in diameter. His palace sat on the northeast corner of the courtyard so he could see it all with a single glance.

Xhaknar, too, was doing a little wool gathering. Unlike the sniveling brands of Gen-O-Pods, he and Yontar had been created from multiple sources of genetic material. Each almost seven feet tall and just under three hundred pounds, they had been built for raw power. They both had dark brown skin and a covering of thick, coarse, hair all over their bodies. Their faces were more exoskeletons than anything else and both had built in immune systems that could cure any illness within sepi-cliks. Injuries, no matter how serious, would heal within a turn. "Super soldiers" their makers had said.

Although both had been given the same training, it was Yontar who really took to the military planning aspects and Xhaknar to the dissemination of power. As a team, each filled in the gaps of the other.

When the Gen-O-Pod war began, Xhaknar and Yontar knew exactly what to do. They, with the first generation of Mayanorens, killed all the makers, decanted the Mayanoren and waited. They let the petty, inevitable, power struggles subside and then, slowly, began building up a command base.

Stuck, as they were, over a hundred kays north of what was once called Vancouver, there was no one for them to rule over. The humans were all dead and the only other variants, as Yontar liked to describe their assemblage, were themselves. And while lording over the Mayanoren had its pleasures, it wasn't what they'd been bred for.

Yontar began sending out Mayanoren spies. The hardest part was teaching them to be polite to whomever they encountered. They'd been designed to be killing machines. They were squat, hairless, gorillas with an atrocious attitude. Please and thank you just weren't in their vocabulary. But, after a few Full Suns of Yontar's gentle ministrations, and burying their companions who didn't follow the plan, enough of them understood to make the mission viable.

While they were waiting for their first spies to return they did a thorough search of the lab. They discovered many more vats of creatures like themselves. After a short debate, they decided to leave them as they were. They knew how dangerous just the two of them were and didn't want anything to challenge their power.

Over the next fifty or so Full Suns they developed a pretty accurate picture of what life was like beyond their redoubt. The west was run by two powerful clans that had still not settled into any sort of truce. While tempting, it was too easy to imagine both sides would turn on any new invaders and Xhaknar and Yontar would be wiped out. They were simply outnumbered and outgunned there.

The eastern seaboard was more settled, but was heavily politicized and had access to many old makers weapons. While the scouts reported they weren't in use, neither had they been destroyed. In fact, from what they could glean, they were being kept in pristine shape. That didn't bode well for their nascent army either.

But the Plains were a different story all together. The residents there seemed to be living peacefully, had an abundance of natural resources and did not have access to any high tech military gear. Contrariwise, it seemed they had destroyed anything like that after the war and were moving on with their lives.

It would be the perfect foundation for Xhaknar's empire.

His thoughts were interrupted by the return of the grindel.

He waited for the loathsome creature to take its

place on its perch and then turned and faced it.

"Speak."

"Yesss looord. Geldisssh hass four fringe dwellersss ….."

"I know that. Tell me something new or die."

"Yessss looord. A lone Kgul brought them four nyssssteedsss and sat with them for ssseveral clikss. Could not hear what they sspoke, but could ssssee dwellerssss get much exssssited."

"A Kgul," pondered Xhaknar, "are you sure?"

"Yesss looord. Remember them from the old dayssss. Not ssseen in long time."

Kgul could be a problem. Big and ugly, they could move with remarkable speed and seemed to have no internal organs. Shoot them and shoot them and they just kept coming. It was Yontar who'd discovered they could be killed by quick freezing and then smashing the frozen pieces into dust. It was tedious work, but that was why the Mayanoren were here.

Even so, Xhaknar had thought them all long dead. This one must have been a retainer of Geldish's and kept safe. No, that couldn't be it. The Kgul lived only for a couple hundred Full Suns. It had been much longer than that since Yontar had cleansed the Plains. Okay, maybe a small number still existed somewhere. It would be just like Geldish to keep some of those freaks alive. Well, no matter, if they became a problem he knew how to kill them readily enough.

He looked back at the grindel. "What else did you see?"

"Nothing looord. I left at breaklight and Geldisssh and dwellerssss were still at hisss home."

"Return and find out more."

"Yessss looord."

With that, the grindel hopped off its perch and out the window. In less than an epi-clik, it disappeared over the horizon.

The Kgul entered the courtyard of the Temple of Azarep and headed for the stables. There he tied up the kgum and petted it fondly. A small contingent of haven lords came out and began grooming and feeding the beast.

Satisfied, the Kgul walked behind the temple to a secret entrance hidden in the rushes. He opened the heavy door and walked onto a brief landing. Closing the door he headed down the long staircase. He knew there were many eyes watching him but didn't care. He was no intruder, he was home.

After passing through three more doors he entered a vast cavern. Over twenty thousand Kgul were going about their daily business. Some acknowledged him as he passed. At his hut, his mate met him and rubbed her head against his in greeting. Together they walked over to the blacksmith's shop where weapons were being forged. While the elder smithy was working on traditional hand to hand combat weapons, albeit massively oversized so they could be wielded by the large Kgul, his son was working on a nasty looking gun. He picked it up and led everyone out back. He had set up a shooting range about one hundred yards long. He aimed the weapon at the farthest target and fired. It blew a six inch hole in the center and exploded.

"Yessss," whispered the Kgul, "this will do nicely."

About two cliks after they finished their meal the riders caught their first glimpse of the oncoming columns.

Still some considerable distance away they could barely make out the cloud of dust caused by their impending allies. They increased their gait to an easy gallop and headed in that direction.

A little more than a clik later they could clearly make out the distinctions in the columns. Minotaurs on the left, Se-Jeant on the right and Fierstans securely in the middle. All three columns had weapons at the ready but flew no colors. To Geldish that was a good sign. It meant the emissaries were purely military. There'd be no fawning courtiers or weasel-mouthed ambassadors to deal with. He'd feared there might.

The columns spotted their approach, halted and began erecting a large tent.

A couple of epi-cliks later the riders arrived and dismounted. A massive Minotaur strode up to them.

"Greetings dead one, I am Greko, Fourth Level Dweller of the Pit. This," he said pointing at a young Se-Jeant, "is Ata, patrol leader of the Se-Jeant and we are honored also by the presence of Nak, troop guardian of the Fierstans."

"Greetings to each of you," replied Geldish, "and thank you for making this journey. The BadgeBeth is named Sland, the Wolfen, R'yune, the Succubus is N'leah and the Llamia are represented by my dear friend BraarB. I am sure you have many questions and I will attempt to answer all of them. But first, let us break bread together and relax. Now that we are assembled, we have plenty of time."

R'yune brought forth a bag of provisions he had on his nytsteed and laid them on the table. Greko inwardly groaned when he saw Sland load two flasks of ice wine onto the table. The respective leaders prepared for their meal while the remaining troops set up a rough perimeter and lit fires to cook their own food. Everyone had flagons of Whævin so no one would go thirsty while they talked.

The conversation around the table was light. Much

lighter than Greko would have expected. Ranging from such controversial topics as the weather, crops and how everyone's respective families were doing, it all seemed pointless to Greko. He was growing more uncomfortable by the minute. Geldish sensed it and turned to face him.

"Relax friend Greko. War will come soon enough. There's no need to rush it any faster."

Greko looked at him puzzled for a sepi-clik and then decided he was right. Blood will flow soon enough, may as well enjoy the delicacies in front of him. With that behind him, he found himself enjoying the mindless banter and terrific foods. Some he didn't recognize but was amazed to discover. One particular dish, was a spiced meat and grain combination. A Kgul staple. When he mentioned the dish, he thought all the Kgul were gone, all five riders smiled but said nothing. For reasons he couldn't quite pinpoint, that gave him hope.

When the meal was finished Nak sent out mixed patrols to bring back regular reports in case they'd been followed or were being watched then they sat down to talk.

"Tell me dead one," began Nak, "what do you hope to accomplish by summoning us out of our safe warrens?"

Geldish smiled. "I have summoned no one. I merely sent a subtle signal that times may be about to change."

That brought a round of raucous laughter.

"Subtle?!?" cried Ata, "what was so subtle about stealing millions of goldens from Xhaknar's repository and then signing your name to the bricks?"

The riders didn't know about the last part.

"Well," replied Geldish calmly, "compared to what I wanted to do, this seemed subtle enough."

"In all seriousness," interrupted Greko, "even if we three brands combine our forces, we are no match for the Naradhama and the Mayanoren. No one has an accurate count, but our scouts say there are over a half a million Naradhama stationed at Anapsida and another three hundred thousand Mayanoren in camps throughout the surrounding plains. Add in the fact that Anapsida is heavily fortified and could easily outlast any siege we could bring, and I see no chance of success."

Geldish sighed. "I'm dead, not stupid, Greko. I have no intention of attacking Anapsida directly. At least not now. Xhaknar has woven a blanket of despair and fear over the Plains. Before we can throw that off we must first pull apart many of the threads. Once it is sufficiently weakened, then we can consider more direct action."

"Great Uku has had similar thoughts," said Ata, "but we've always dismissed them because of what Xhaknar's retribution would be. It is one thing to defeat one of the Naradhama raiding parties, he expects some losses there, it is quite another to attack him openly, even if only on a small scale."

"Agreed," Geldish nodded, "were only one brand brave enough to do that deed, that brand would be annihilated from the Plains. Every single being, right down to the last small, would be eradicated. However, I propose we keep up a series of running attacks on his outposts and garrisons. Those are his weak points. They are manned by untrained Mayanoren, slaves, and traitors for the most part. And not just one strike or two, but a Full Sun's worth with one happening every turn. We will force him to waste time and resources.

"Further, I propose we crush his supply lines. Anapsida creates nothing on its own except pain. It requires enormous amounts of food, medical supplies and so on. Xhaknar thinks himself smart because he uses an underground rail system he built to keep his supplies safe and away from prying eyes. But I know where that system is and it does not take much effort to cause a cave in. Tunnels, once exposed, are delightfully vulnerable targets.

"Lastly, I propose we set up a headquarters in the pit of the Minotaurs...."

Before he could finish, Greko, once again, interrupted him. "Sadly, that cannot be. My brother Ek-kh has dishonored our flame and our line by allying himself with Xkaknar. The last word we heard is he was named leader of the Naradhama in return for his knowledge. Ek-kh has always been a problem, preferring lusts and passions over the important things in life. It is with great shame that I admit he has put his carnal desires above the needs of his family and his pit."

Geldish was astonished. Never in the history of the Plains had a Minotaur defected. Nevertheless, he pushed on. "The shame is not yours to have. All shame belongs to Ek-kh. But I suppose it matters little where we meet. Xhaknar will find out soon enough. My guess is we'll need many places before this work is done."

The conversation continued on well enough. Geldish knew each brand would need the approval of its council before it could formally act, but he sensed they wouldn't be here now if it wasn't a foregone conclusion.

As the participants were getting ready to leave, Geldish had two more things to add to the proceedings.

"Before you depart, I would like to ask you to send a small patrol to the land of Südermann. I have a message for him that may aid us greatly when the time comes."

That got everyone's attention. Südermann was a leader of a set of brands that caused fear just in their appearance. No one knew who'd made the multiple lines of insectoids, but they were fierce warriors and severely territorial. They weren't conquerors, but none who ventured to their lands returned. Geldish understood their fears.

"Whoever goes will go with a flag of Südermann as protection. I have it in my kit. No harm will come to the patrol, on that you have my word.

"Secondly, I promised a grindel I would march on Anapsida. Since I like to keep my promises, I ask ten soldiers from each column to join me."

It was quiet enough to hear hair grow. Not one being moved.

Finally, Ata spoke.

"I would ask how you got a flag of Südermann, but I'm quite sure I would hate the answer. As to the insane march on Anapsida, my warriors will need a good reason for joining. We are not, by nature, suicidal. And, though my experience with them is limited, I believe the same holds true for the others here this turn."

Geldish smiled. "Not one warrior will be harmed. We only march towards Anapsida for a while until we have the attention of Xhaknar, then everyone can return to their warrens. Let's just say this will be the first thread pulled and leave it at that."

Much to everyone's surprise, Sland laughed.

"I fucking love this. We will march less than forty on Anapsida while waiting for bug-people to do whatever it is we expect bug-people to do and, somehow, this will make Xhaknar tremble. Of all the ways I thought I could die, this never occurred to me. I fucking love it. New things are always fun. Even the ones that try and kill you."

R'yune growled mirthlessly but BraarB and N'leah couldn't contain their laughter.

"Why not?" asked N'leah, "Xhaknar surely knows we've aligned with Geldish by now, so there's no turning back in any case. If we're going to die, let it be an unusual death. I'm with Sland. Whatever you have up your sleeve besides bone had better see us through, though, otherwise, me and mine will torment you for your entire afterlife."

After some more, uncomfortable, laughter it was agreed. Greko, Ata, and Nak would each take nine volunteers on Geldish's wild ride. A patrol of nine warriors, three from each column, would ride to Südermann, and the rest would return to their warrens to report on what transpired.

As the summit - such as it was – was breaking up, a gangly creature emerges from the sands. A face like a praying mantis sat atop a wiry body of muted greens. Its legs were long and had barbs on their calves. It wore a long jacket which hid many weapons. As the sun darkened in the west it took off to the south at speeds which would have amazed anyone who saw it.

Of course, it was a master at what it did, so no one saw a thing.

In the Main Chamber of the Pit, the Council of Elders sat and listened to the grave news. It hadn't taken them long to chart each of the raids from the Naradhama. It was clear Xhaknar knew the exact locations of their hidden entrances. While he'd once had Yontar attack the public gate that was long ago and held little value beyond the symbolic. Now it was clear he knew exactly how to get in. With that knowledge he could easily overrun their pit.

The Council Elder, Urnak, spoke. "Mooth, Ek-kh has done us a great harm. His lust for temporary things will bring our eternal ruin. Worse, he is blinded to the truth. When we are defeated, Xhaknar will have no more use for him and will just have him killed."

There were huffs of assent throughout the room.

"We have," he continued, "been the keepers of the old knowledge as well as the guardians of the middle plains. With us out of the way, there will be nothing to stop Xhaknar from crushing the entire land."

"What about this quest of Geldish's?" asked the second Elder Lornin.

"It is folly. No matter what he does, without the Temple of Azarep to support him, the most he can do is be a thorn in Xhaknar's side. We must evacuate the smalls and the old ones as well as the shopkeepers and craft masters. We must also save as many of the holy books as we can. Beyond that, all we can do is prepare for war."

"Why then did we send Greko to meet with Geldish? Why seem to support folly?"

"I said Geldish would be a thorn in Xhaknar's side. That does not diminish the damage he may yet do. Hopefully, it will be enough to distract Xhaknar from our retreat. Besides, we all knew this turn would come when Ek-kh defected. Better to cause Xhaknar as many problems as possible to help our brand get free."

"Where will they go?"

"According to the ancient scrolls, there is a warren, similar to ours, near the border of Südermann. Several Full Suns ago I sent some of our student monks to test the veracity of the scrolls. There were thirty points that needed verification, the warren being only a minor one as far as they were concerned.

"They reported all thirty points were as they should be and the warren, while dilapidated, was still there and possibly even functional. Although I hold out little hope for that and instead attribute it to the youthful enthusiasm of young monks."

"All well and good," replied the youngest of them, Karnol, "so we send all but the warriors away. Who will protect them on their journey?"

"We still have our pact with the Llamia, or have you forgotten? Empress ClaalD will not abandon us in our time of need. We can ensure the pact by giving her brand a copy of the library as it relates to her line. We know much about their history that has been forgotten."

"As good friends as the Llamia are, I am uneasy

about using outsiders to guard our secrets."

"Mooth, I sympathize, but what choice do we have?"

"What about the Fierstans?" asked Lornin.

"What about them?"

"Since Greko has not returned they must be supporting his quest."

"Watcher Urkel is no fool. I am sure he has his own reasons. He may use Geldish's distractions to make an attack of his own. We do not, and cannot, know. Our only concern now is the safety of our brand and our heritage."

None of them liked it, but there was no better solution. They began making preparations at once.

Alnk had ridden with Nak ever since they'd both completed Fierstan's training rigors. He'd always thought of him as one of the wisest and smartest patrol leaders he'd ever met. Now he was having serious second thoughts about that. He looked around at the eight other warriors with him and thought of the flag they carried, still furled in his pack since they were still in the land of Xhaknar, and wondered how he'd gotten talked into this?

The others seemed to be having similar thoughts.

Kronlk, Greko's immediate sub-commander, broke the mood with a big, bovine, laugh.

"Hah! Look at us! Brave warriors, blooded in battle against the Naradhama and the Mayanoren and here we are sniveling like smalls at the thought of some magic bugs. We are warriors! That which we cannot kill will kill us! That is our way. This is no different. We still have many turns to go before we reach the lands of Südermann. And who knows how many more before we find him? We cannot waste our time fretting like smalls before an exam. We must sing warrior songs and tell each other our favorite lies. The femmes we should have had, the fish we should have caught. Tell them all so each shall know the heart of the other and walk bravely forward on this quest!"

While that speech would never be immortalized in scrolls, or so they thought, it had the desired effect. Soon they were singing ribald songs, swapping stories, and the kays disappeared beneath their feet.

They continued on in this manner for four more turns before a young Se-Jeant named Ulnku halted them.

"We are being followed."

"How can you be sure?" asked Kronlk.

"The sands to our west have been moving at the same pace as us. And only a small amount of them. Just enough to hide a spy. At first, I thought it a trick of the light, but it has been happening for the last two turns. I swear something is there."

Alnk thought about it and said "No Naradhama can move like that. Nor can any Mayanoren I've heard of. So, let us three walk over to where Ulnku saw this enchanted moving sand and ask it why it follows us.

Ulnku pointed out the last spot where he had noticed anything and they headed off in that direction. Each warrior was trying to think of the best jibes they could tease the young Se-Jeant with when it turned out his magic sand was nothing more than wind and dust. Just to make it fun, Alnk figured he'd play it straight.

"Come out, O' creature of the sand, we mean you no harm."

The sand shifted and a tall, greenish, creature stepped forth.

"Who spotted me?" it asked.

Kronlk and Alnk both immediately pointed at the hapless Ulnku. To their complete shock, the creature walked directly to Ulnku and extended its hand.

"I have been a spy for over three hundred Full Suns

and never have I been spotted. You must be a great spy for your brand."

"I'm just a student," stammered Ulnku, "it is my masters you should honor."

The creature laughed. "Well said young one. And so shall it be. In my report to Lord Südermann I will honor your masters by group, and you by name. That is, if you'll tell me your name. I am Elaand, First Lieutenant of Südermann's personal guard."

"I am Ulnku, warrior third class of the Se-Jeant. The Minotaur is Kronlk, First Sub-Commander to Greko, Fourth Level Dweller of the Pit and the honored Fierstan is Alnk, second in command of the patrol guard."

"Well," said Elaand, "I seem to be in pretty majestic company. Am I correct in assuming you are marching on Südermann?"

"No," replied Krolnk, "we are marching *to* Südermann. Specifically to deliver a message from Geldish to him. We have been given the flag of Südermann as protection."

"May I see it?"

Alnk opened his pack and handed the flag to the spy.

He glanced at the green and red symbols laid over the yellow slash and handed it back.

"So, you truly have a flag of peace. I have only heard of them. Südermann does not hand many out. Maybe five in my lifetime that I know of. May I ask how you came to possess it? It is much older than any of you."

"It was given to us by a Rangka named Geldish," replied Alnk," he is leading a force of less than forty on a raid of Anapsida while we were asked to find Südermann."

"Hmm," considered Elaand, "I'm not sure which task is more doomed. Well, 'was more doomed' to be precise. Yours will now meet with success. Südermann is at his northern palace. We can cut due west from here and be there in less than four turns."

By now the rest of the party had come over to see what was going on. If any of them were nonplussed by the site of one of Südermann's brand, they wisely kept it to themselves. In short order, they were off led by Elaand with Ulnku at his side.

Elaand sang songs of warriors past and present and told stories of femmes he should have had and fish he should have caught. Despite their trepidations, and the nagging thought this could all be a trap, they all took a liking to him.

In the six turns since they'd split from the main group, the thirty warriors and five Brittle Riders had tasked themselves with making Xhaknar's life miserable. As they inexorably headed towards Anapsida, where all seemed to think they would die, they had overrun and annihilated three Naradhama patrols and one Mayanoren scouting party.

And while warriors had tended to think lowly of fringe dwellers that had changed in the first battle. Greko owed his life to R'yune that turn. Ata surely owed his to N'leah and BraarB at the end of the next. All of them, at one point or another, owed their lives to all of the fringe dwellers. As they set up their camp and guards for the even, Geldish looked lost in thought.

"I can't just let them keep calling you fringe dwellers."

"Why the fuck not?" laughed Sland, "It's what we are. Or will your magic put us in a royal house? Will King Gornd bow down before me in the Revered House of BadgeBeth?"

The thought made him laugh some more. Then

R'yune attempted what might have been a curtsy and everyone burst out laughing.

Geldish smiled. "A while back I visited the Temple of Azarep. I asked the Rangka to ride with us. They refused but, obviously, decided to send aid. That is where the nytsteeds are from. Anyway, during the conversation Karrish, the elder, called you Brittle Riders. At first, I thought it an insult. Now, I'm not so sure. While it is true you are brittle compared to the power of the Rangka, the Rangka aren't here and you are. More importantly, I can't seem to come up with a better name for you."

Greko laughed. "Fine dead one, the Brittle Riders they are. All I know is we each owe them our lives. I have never seen fighting skills like they possess."

"You'd be amazed what you can learn and do when you are less than one turn from Xhaknar's blood fountain," N'leah said that softly, but everyone heard.

"Fine," chimed in Ata, "We now ride behind your Brittle Riders. But how will Anapsida know this if we keep killing everyone it sends at us? We should let one go free to return to Xhaknar with that knowledge, and then he will surely kill the messenger."

Geldish thought about that for an epi-clik and then headed out into the sands. He returned with a grindel.

"You are free of Xhaknar now?"

The grindel smiled and nodded.

"We need not fear you telling Xhaknar where we are or what we do?"

More smiles and nods.

"Could you get word to Xhaknar of what we have done without being recaptured?"

The grindel thought for a moment and then smiled. "Yessss, there iss a patrol of Mayanoren, half turn to the north of you, looking for you, I can tell them ssXhaknar sssent me to warn them you are near. If wissshed, I can sssay exactly where you be. Mayanoren not know if we lie and they are too far from ssXhaknar to know we esssscaped thanksss to you."

"Good enough," laughed Geldish, "well, troops, where would you like to be ambushed?"

"How about right here?" asked BraarB, "I'm tired of walking. Let them do the work this time."

That idea was met with a hearty round of approval and became the plan. Geldish invited the grindel to join them for their even meal and then they worked out the details for the ambush.

Just after breaklight, the grindel soared into the growing dawn and disappeared to the north. Geldish and his, newly anointed, Brittle Riders, laid around the fire as though asleep. Hidden in the sand around them were the thirty warriors. Geldish had cast his mind far and wide last even and determined the Mayanoren were marching without stopping. With the grindel's message, they should hit the camp at a full run in about a clik.

He was off by about five epi-cliks.

The Mayanoren, thinking they'd caught them by surprise, rushed the camp without any advance scouting. Before they were within ten feet of the 'sleeping' riders, the warriors burst from the sands and killed all but one raider.

He'd been knocked unconscious from behind and not seen them.

He would not see them now either as they, once again, hid behind the sands before Geldish roused the doomed Mayanoren.

"Wake up warrior," said Geldish to the woozy raider, "it's time for you to leave."

The Mayanoren stared at him in open contempt. Even though he wasn't bound, he could clearly see the four swords pointed at this throat and the Rangka calmly standing before him.

Since Geldish wasn't interested in anything the brute had to say, he continued on.

"You will report back to Xhaknar and tell him of the events of this turn. You will tell him your patrol was decimated by Geldish and his Brittle Riders. You will tell him we let you live because we wanted him to know. We would have let him know sooner, but we kept forgetting to leave a survivor.

"I know, I know," he continued as petulantly as possible, "you think that's sloppy of us. Well, as you can tell, they are new to being warriors so it's hard to keep them under control. You remember your first battles, don't you? Your blood up, your fires stoked? Your enemies falling before you? Yes, I can see you do. Good. So here's how this will work. We have all your weapons and aren't going to give them back. You will be given a canteen with enough water for you to make it back to Anapsida and that is all. You may leave now."

BraarB was the first to lower her sword and she handed the Mayanoren a large canteen filled with water. The others moved closer to Geldish but never let down their guard. Geldish made a shooing motion and the ruffian was off. N'leah sailed into the sky to make sure he wasn't coming back. After a while she landed, laughing.

"He's running so fast he may make Anapsida by even-fall."

Geldish laughed and then gave a signal to the warriors letting them know to return.

"Well, that was fun," laughed Greko, "what do we do next?"

"You return to your warrens and tell them all we have done. This particular thread has been loosened enough. Xhaknar will be in a rage. By next breaklight, I wouldn't be surprised if there were a thousand Naradhama scouring these hills."

He looked around at the carnage and smiled some more.

"Leave the bodies as they are so he'll know he's been told the truth. Take everything else, including their weapons. Then get out of here and back to your Elders as fast as you can. I will be in contact in fifteen turns. On that even have a representative for each of you meet me in the haven bar in Go-Chi. The innkeeper there is quite fond of me and won't give us any trouble."

He smiled to himself and watched as the others exchanged gratitudes and left.

Oolnok stretches as he enters his house for the even meal. He quickly washes in the tub set aside for that purpose and sat at the table. His wife had made a wonderful meal this even. Kgum meat marinated in liquid spices, puff bread, and gravy, golden roots with butter and more. It was a meal fit for a king.

His smalls had set the table and taken their seats shortly after him. His glorious wife came into the room bearing trays of delectable foods and set them in the center. The oldest small gave thanks and they began their meal.

Later, as he and his wife lie in bed, she expressed her concerns over recent events. They'd heard a loud battle in the distance. It hadn't come anywhere near their village, but worrying was what mothers did best, his wife better than most.

Now he understood the meal. She feared it would be their last.

He calmed her by noting, even if war was afoot, this village hadn't warred on anyone since Ondom's crazy quest many long Suns ago. More importantly, they didn't live on any of the major trade routes. No, war or not, they would be left alone.

Reassured by her husband's wonderful logic she nestled in his shoulder and fell asleep.

Oolnok stayed awake a while longer hoping he hadn't lied to his beloved wife and then decided there was nothing he could do about it if he had.

He soon fell asleep too and dreamed dreams of kgums with the greatest hair on the Plains and puffed bread with gravy.

Ulnku gasped as they crossed the last hill. From sandy ruins sprung lush greenery. The others cleared the rise and had similar reactions. This land is beautiful. It was as though the ravages of war had never visited here. As they neared the bottom of the hill they were met by a large patrol of almost sixty warriors who looked similar to Elaand. He spoke to them in some rapid tongue and then turned to the party of plains-folk.

"I have explained you are not prisoners and no harm should come to you. I have further requested they take us to Lord Südermann so you may deliver your message. They tell me we can be there in time for the mid-break repast. Since Lord Südermann sets the most lavish table on Arreti, our timing is very good."

With that, they marched on and headed into the jungle. Alien sounds and sights greeted them at every juncture, but Elaand set a pace that did not allow curiosities to be sated. As promised, just as the sun took hold of the middle of the sky, they turned a corner and were greeted by a sculptured garden which enveloped a glorious palace made of materials no one recognized. When they got closer a large figure strode out of the main door. Unlike the elegant green skinned creatures who marched with them, this creature was huge and dark brown. He had mandibles instead of a mouth and seemed to have six arms beneath his long, luxurious, robe. His large, multi-faceted, eyes stared at them intently. His voice, when he spoke, was a surprise.

It was soft and warm, not at all what they expected.

"Welcome travelers, it is seldom we get guests instead of intruders. I can assure you guests are preferred. A scout has informed me of the bare details of your mission. Please come in and tell me all about it over a shared meal."

With that, he turned and walked back into the palace. Not knowing what else to do, the representatives of the Plains, led by Elaand and Ulnku, followed. There were massive art pieces on the wall, but not of warriors or brands. As best any of them could discern, the artists had tried to capture an emotion or thought. It is unlike anything any of them had ever seen.

At the end of the hall was another guard, this from a third species they did not know, who motioned them through another large door. When they entered they were greeted by some of the grandest architecture any of them had ever seen. Giant, vaulted, ceilings separated by flying buttresses made of the shiniest silver metal in the world. There were hidden torches that shed light in perfect symmetry with the art on the walls and, when they finally noticed it, the food on the table.

Their host, obviously Lord Südermann, motioned for them to eat. Elaand went and grabbed a plate from a stack on the left and began traversing the table to the right until it was filled. The others followed suit. There were chairs and cushions around a large table so they sat there. Elaand took a cushion, the rest used the chairs. Lord Südermann came over with a laden plate and joined them. After a pleasant time of quiet eating, Lord Südermann spoke.

"May I see this message from Geldish?"

Alnk opened his pack and produced the sealed envelope. He passed it down the table until it reached Südermann.

Südermann opened it and read it quietly. He did not look pleased, but neither did he look angry.

"Well, Elaand, it seems our fears are coming true."

Elaand looked up and stared at his lord. "You can't be serious lord, Xhaknar would never march on us. He knows too little of what we can do."

"Be that as it may, Geldish is clear. Now that Xhaknar has gotten the Naradhama to the number he wished and trained the Mayanoren as much as they can be, there is no reason for him to stay behind his walls. Geldish supports that with several claims that match your earlier reports. Furthermore, Geldish asserts that Xhaknar has discovered the old weapons of our makers. We knew he had some, but now it seems he is manufacturing them by the thousands.

"Even if we defeat him, which I believe we will, he would still do great damage to our lands. Our families could go hungry, our smalls would probably die. We cannot let this happen."

"What shall you have me do lord?"

"You will take ten thousand of your Mantis Guard and march on the southern flank of Anapsida. Do not try and take the fortress itself, just position yourself a couple of turns to the south so Xhaknar will know you're there. Geldish claims he is assembling an army he will bring from the east. It will take him a Full Sun to arrive, according to his letter, so you have time to make sure your troops are in peak condition.

"When you see Geldish's army, you will turn your service over to him. After that, you're in God's hands."

"And the bones of a rogue Rangka. Nevertheless, it shall all be as you say, lord."

With that, he snapped a quick salute and returned to his meal.

After the meal, Ulnku, Kronlk, and Alnk were shown to a lavish room which contained three beds, a small unit that they were told kept drinks or food cold and was already filled for them, along with more of that art that tried to capture thoughts. When their escort left, they sat on the floor in the middle of the room and tried to sort out all they'd seen and learned.

The brands of the Plains were not idiots. It's just that they, like most of the Gen-O-Pods, had eschewed technology. The infrastructure that allowed it to work had been decimated by the war and they saw no reason to bring it back. Nevertheless, it was clear Südermann had taken a different path. Now they had gotten used to their surroundings they realized he had a reliable source of electricity and was using it not only to improve living conditions but for many other purposes as well. Elaand had shown them a room where electronic eyes spaced all around the border were monitored by cautious guards. He had explained their approach had been spotted one full turn before their arrival at the border. That was how the guards had been able to have a force meet them at the border should they have turned out to be foes. Since they had been shown that freely, they assumed it was merely a minor function in the larger scheme of things.

They were both impressed and a little afraid. Ulnku, being young and, occasionally, impetuous, opened the box to see what delicacies were inside. He discovered several bottles of a dark, amber, liquid. There was a device hanging on the inside of the door which was clearly meant to be used as an opener. He opened one bottle, took a sip, smiled and opened two more for his companions.

"It's not ice wine, but it's very good." He said smiling.

"It's some type of ale," noted Kronlk, "The haven lords around Go-Chi make something like it, but this is much better."

They enjoyed their drinks for a few epi-clicks and took the opportunity to truly relax. Finally, Alnk spoke.

"So, Ulnku, you seem to have become close with Elaand."

"Well, close may be the wrong word, but I am fond of him. He is much older than me. I think he looks at me as he would a small he's grown fond of. But, I have learned a lot from him in these few short turns.

"As we know already, Südermann's domain borders not only Xhaknar's but the Fish-People's to the west and a small portion butts up against the lands of Kalindor to the south. He says the Fish-People aren't a problem since they need to stay near water and have shown no desire to expand. They, too, have technology like Südermann. Kalindor, he claims, is more like the Plains technologically, but has vast forests and most of its citizens live in trees far above the ground.

"They, however, like Xhaknar, pose a constant threat. He says they keep several large garrisons along that border and the troops there see action all the time. He also said Südermann has thought about conquering the lands just to end the violence, but he has no idea what he would do with the territory when it was over. He said the brands would probably not take to his rule well and would open him up to many Suns worth of insurrection. So, things stay as they are until someone comes up with a better plan."

"What of Xhaknar?" queried Kronlk.

"We all heard Geldish's message to Südermann. Elaand says he must be getting old and blind to have missed it. While there was no new information in the note, Geldish interpreted it in a different way. Elaand says he believes Geldish's interpretation is the right one.

"Xhaknar has long coveted the technology of Südermann and, with new weapons, could pose a serious threat."

"If he has these weapons," wondered Alnk, "why doesn't he use them on us?"

"Why should he?" shrugged Ulnuk, "we already are unable to defeat him. Why waste the time and energy winning a battle he's already won? Elaand believes, and this makes sense to me, that when Xhaknar marches on Südermann, then he'll use his weapons on the residents of the Plains to make sure there is no chance of a rebellion forming in his wake. He could march directly on the Dwellers of the Pit, smash them, then curve down to the Fierstans, overrun them with these new weapons and head straight to these lands. That would effectively cut off the Se-Jeant from rendering any aid. According to Elaand, he thinks fully eighty percent of the Dwellers and Fierstans would be destroyed."

While they are contemplating that grim news, there's a knock at the door. Ulnuk rises and opens to door to find Elaand standing there with a wooden box. Elaand sets it on the bed and then goes to the ice-box and grabs himself a bottle of the ale.

"You are welcome to stay here as long as you wish. You are guests under a flag of peace. However, when you do depart, Südermann asks you each to take a message back to your councils. They are in the box I brought."

"Thank you very much," replied Alnk, "but as pleasant as these accommodations are, we were planning on leaving at breaklight. There is much we need to tell our brands and much that needs to be done if we are to survive what's coming."

"Good. I am glad to hear you say that. Lord Südermann wishes to know if you believe you have any allies besides yourselves in this coming battle."

"We don't know," replied Kronlk, "but it is doubtful. The Llamia, BadgeBeth, and Succubi were nearly made extinct when Xhaknar first came. They have never truly recovered. The haven lords were bred for service, not war, so I see no help coming from them either. The Rangka, as far as we know, number Geldish and no more. The Kgul appear to merely be a rumor.

"No, when this battle comes, it will be us and any help we can find from your lord."

Elaand laughed, "You make it sound as though all is lost before it is begun. First off, help from Lord Südermann can be quite beneficial. We have weapons and communications devices that will greatly aid your brands and Lord Südermann has decreed you be given access to them. Furthermore, as Geldish stated in his missive to my lord, while Xhaknar knows exactly what he has and how he wishes to use it, there is much he does not know as well. Were Yontar still alive our task would be much harder, but I still believe by working together we can win the turn."

That brightened the mood considerably. It had been many Full Suns, more than any of them could count since there'd been hope on the Plains.

"Additionally," continued Elaand, "you will not ride to your warrens alone. Lord Südermann has decreed ninety of my Mantis Guards will accompany you. Thirty for each warren. They shall carry designs, which you can manufacture, for weapons far superior to anything you have now. They will also serve as trainers for your warriors so they can be familiar with them when the time comes. Furthermore, hopefully, they will also serve the purpose of proving to your elders you are not alone in this thing. That help is coming, even if it is unexpected."

"It seems to me," noted Kronlk, "that Lord Südermann could have overrun Xhaknar many times in the past. Why didn't he?"

"Well, after the Gen-O-Pod war the first Lord Südermann decided we would secure what we could and take care of our own. It was during the reign of the third Lord Südermann that Xhaknar arrived. By then we were still building from within. When Yontar tested our borders we were more than a match for him and his Mayanoren, but Lord Südermann felt we had enough to do protecting our own, so we never ventured forth. To be blunt, we didn't think of them as a threat so we mostly ignored them.

"That may have been a mistake. Besides the suffering he has caused your brands, he has forced us to develop all of our own supplies from within or do without. This Lord Südermann, the seventh, would like to trade with the Plains. We do with the Fish-People, but there is little they have that we want. And visa versa. The fifth Lord

Südermann did try and send a trade delegation to Anapsida. They were arrested as spies and hung over Xhaknar's fountain. Xhaknar took this as a sign of weakness and sent a battalion of Naradhama to our border to topple Lord Südermann. They were met and slaughtered to the last one. Then Lord Südermann took the heads of each soldier and tossed them into carts which he sent back to Anapsida. The bodies were burned and that was the last time we ventured his way again."

They contemplated all they'd been told for a few epi-cliks.

"I thought Lord Südermann," ventured Ulnku, "was like Geldish or Xhaknar, yet you keep numbering him."

"Lord Südermann is mortal," smiled Elaand, "just like the rest of us. When his smalls reach a certain age they are tested. Whichever one passes the test is trained to be the next Lord Südermann. Two of them have been femmes. But no matter the gender, all are referred to as Lord Südermann. It is this continuity that ties us to our heritage and our future."

The thought of a femme leader amused them until they remembered the Llamia and Succubus they'd recently seen. Each realized it wouldn't take much for them to follow either one into battle, femme or no.

Elaand divvied up the contents of his box and bade them good even. They settled into the most comfortable beds they'd ever been in. It was hard to leave them, come breaklight, but duty called and hope beckoned.

They were past the border of Südermann before the sun had met the middle of the sky.

Geldish entered through the back door of the

Crasnia. He spied the weird snakelike creature sitting in the shadows. He snuck up behind him and slit his throat with his finger. He calmly carried the body outside, pleased no one had noticed, and deposited it in the trash. He'd needed Xhaknar's eyes before, but not now.

When he reentered the bar he spotted the inn keeper and waved while holding up a small bag of goldens. The inn keeper broke into a wide grin and cleared a table near the rear door.

"Greetings inn keeper," began Geldish as he handed over the small bag of goldens, "I thank you for your courtesies, but I will be meeting several guests who will wish for some privacy. May we use your basement?"

"I see no reason why not," said the inn keeper, "but it is not much of a space. Mostly stock and my work table."

"Have one of your servants bring a large table and ten chairs down there and we will be fine. Also, they will be hungry and thirsty. I hope it won't be too much trouble to add in a couple of buckets of your finest skank and a meat platter."

The inn keeper laughed as he counted the goldens and said no, it would be no trouble at all. Then he went to make the arrangements. Geldish had left his Brittle Riders outside the tavern to await the arrival of the emissaries. Soon they entered the bar with Ata and a Se-Jeant he did not know, Nak and Watcher Urkel and, much to his surprise, Council Elder Urnak instead of Greko. All the guests were wearing merchant's robes and not an ounce of finery. He mentally approved as he motioned them across the room and led them into the basement.

N'leah discreetly held up two fingers to Geldish as she passed by. He knew she meant they had found and dispatched, two spies outside the bar. There may be others, but Geldish doubted it. Xhaknar was miserly in that regard and the haven lords would rather eat their own tongues than assist him. He was as safe as he was going to be. After that, whatever happened, happened.

"Two turns ago," began Council Elder Urnak without preamble once they'd closed the door to the basement, "one of our scouts returned. His steed died at the gate because he'd ridden it so hard. He claimed to have seen the emissaries you'd sent to Südermann returning. They had two kgums, heavily laden, and were accompanied by tall green creatures I can only assume are members of Südermann's guard. They are still a couple of turns away, so I was unable to find out what they had to say before this meeting.

"However, I had assumed this meeting and all you are about to do to be folly until I heard this news. This is why I am here instead of Honored Greko. I must know what you know so I can properly advise my brand."

Geldish briefly considered this. "It is my intention to kill Xhaknar's army, bring water to Go-Chi and make many goldens. This last part I have achieved by robbing his repository. The first part I expect to achieve one Full Sun from now. It is the water that will require the most effort."

The Riders laughed at that, as did the others.

"Well said, dead one," chimed in Watcher Urkel, "but saying something does not make it so. If it did I would be taller and better looking."

They all laughed at that too.

"Seriously," he continued, "even if we combined our might we could not face Anapsida."

"As I told your warriors, I have no intention of attacking Anapsida. At least not now. It took him many Full Suns to get the Naradhama to the number he required and to teach the Mayanoren more than just simple butchery. As you already know, we began by killing patrols wherever we found them. My Brittle Riders and I have continued on this path for these last fifteen turns. Every Naradhama lost weakens Xhaknar and slows his plans."

"The Naradhama die damn good," said Sland, "we get to sharpen our skills with each kill and we keep their provisions. Geldish only asks we leave the bodies so

Xhaknar will know we were there."

"We're pretty sure he has a good idea we're here now" deadpanned BraarB.

R'yune growled and then the rest of the room chuckled.

"Okay, I understand the logic," said Council Elder Urnak, "but even if you kill ten thousand Naradhama, all that will do is force him to unleash the rest upon the Plains."

"That is exactly what I am counting on."

That killed every smile in the room.

"Within Anapsida," he continued, "they're almost invulnerable. But in the open, they can die like just like everybody else. My biggest concern is Xhaknar has finally found a way to manufacture the makers' old weapons. They would be devastating against any defenses you could mount. That is why I asked for the aid of Südermann."

"How did you meet Südermann?" asked N'leah, "it's not like he's open to guests."

"It was after the Gen-O-Pod war," smiled Geldish, "the Temple of Azarep wanted to see who was friend or foe. I was tasked with entering the lands of Südermann. I was met by his Mantis Guard before I could set foot on his lands.

"They are his elite troops. A special force that is trained in espionage, combat, and any other skill they might need to survive. Only the best of the best serve directly to Südermann.

"As they were taking me in as a spy, we were passing a large metal structure that was being built by workers. A section of it fell loose and was about to crush one of the guards. Without thinking I used my power over magnetism to stop it in flight and set it gently on the ground.

"That seemed to buy me no sympathy from the guards. They didn't say a word and just led me on to meet my fate. But they must have somehow told Südermann about it. He questioned me ceaselessly about the incident. He wanted to know why a spy would save one of his guards. It took me several turns to make him understand I was not a spy. I told him of how the Rangka came to be when Xhaknar destroyed the wizards. I told him of how the Llamia, BadgeBeth, Succubi and Wolfen were almost eradicated from the planet. I told him of our hatred of Xhaknar and what he meant to the Plains. I told him all I knew and all about me. When I was done he was the only person, other than a Rangka, who knew every secret I held."

"Were you tortured?" asked BraarB quietly.

"No. I was treated quite well actually, almost as a guest. But it was clear, he still didn't trust me. It took several turns for his spies to confirm what I had said. Even then he was skeptical. So I did the only thing I could do, I let him into my mind. That is not something we Rangka do lightly. It requires us to open every facet of our being. But Südermann was too powerful to have as an enemy while we were facing Xhaknar. If I couldn't make him our ally, at least I could try to keep him neutral.

"After that Südermann said that, while he now trusted me, one brand does not an army make. So, he decreed he would make a decision in a hundred Full Suns and let me go.

"As fate would have it, one hundred Full Suns later our Temple was surrounded by a thousand Mayanoren. Our future looked pretty bleak. A contingent of Südermann's guards came upon the scene, assessed what was happening and began killing Mayanoren in bunches. This broke their hold on the wall. Freed from being defensive we attacked and after a brief, but brutal, battle, met the guards over the bodies of the Mayanoren.

"I mean that literally, by the way.

"The lead guard told me Südermann would not attack the Plains, but nor would he aid us in our struggle since he had more pressing concerns at home. However, if I were to ever hear Xhaknar was going to move on Südermann I was to tell him at once and then he would come to our aid. I was given a flag of peace to guarantee me safe passage should such a time arise.

"With Xhaknar's new weapons, that he is hording instead of using, and with his Naradhama army complete, it was clear this is exactly what is about to happen. It is with that flag of peace I ensured the warriors would not be assaulted. It is because of that they return to you now. And since they are returning with members of the Guard, I can only assume Südermann will honor his oath and act on our behalf. That can be confirmed when they arrive at your warrens."

The room grew quiet as everyone considered this new information. R'yune walked around the room refilling everyone's flagons of skank and then placed a meat platter in the middle of the table.

It was during this lull Urnak began truly assessing the fringe dwellers, Geldish's Brittle Riders. Greko had told him the story, of course, but Urnak hadn't lent it much credence until now. R'yune, Sland, and N'leah wore no clothing but loin cloths and weapons belts. BraarB only had the belt. And R'yune and Sland each wore an odd looking bow and a quiver filled with what appeared to be short spears instead of arrows. BraarB had a crossbow on her back Urnak doubted he could draw. Each was well muscled and sure of their abilities. While their eyes laughed easily, it was clear there was a darkness behind them that gave each rider strength beyond what he might have imagined. Had anyone told him it might be worth a moment of his life to petition aid from King Gornd of the Revered House of BadgeBeth or Empress ClaalD of the Sacred Lairs of the Llamia or, even, Queen A'lnuah of the Roosts of the Succubi, he would have laughed them into submission. They could barely take care of themselves, or so it was said. What kind of army could they mass?

"Maybe a very deadly one," Urnak decided..

He noticed Watcher Urkel surveying Geldish's riders as well and gathered he was reaching a similar conclusion. They caught each other's attention briefly and Urkel nodded. There might be a way to win the turn after all. He asked the question before Urnak could, which was fine with him.

"Well, dead one, will you be sending petitions for aid to King Gornd of the Revered House of BadgeBeth, Empress ClaalD of the Sacred Lairs of the Llamia or Queen A'lnuah of the Roosts of the Succubi? It seems they might be able to aid our cause as well."

"They have suffered so much; I had hoped to leave them out of this, if at all possible."

"It is their plains too," noted Urnak, "and I think they might wish to have a say in how they face their future. I know not why Xhaknar took such actions on their kind and no other, but it is clear he fears them somehow. Or, at least, Yontar did. Based on what I know of your riders and what my warriors have attested, their force might be small, but I imagine it would be formidable."

Geldish pondered that for a moment. He truly did not wish to involve the fringe if he didn't have to. But Urnak was right. The actions they were about to take would affect all, not just the combatants. He looked at his riders and realized they could not make any petitions. They were not royalty, nor did they hold any position in court other than their new title as Brittle Riders, which was probably not worth much. Geldish did, however, hold rank as a member of the Temple of Azarep. Maybe that would be enough to get them taken seriously.

"You are right, Elder Urnak," said Geldish when he finally broke his contemplations, "if nothing else we must let them know what is about to happen and let them make a choice. You should each send messengers to them and offer to have them meet me in ten turns at the home of the haven lords. That is neutral ground at all times and the accommodations are fine enough for kings and queens.

Should any of you wish to attend to bolster our position, you would be gladly welcomed."

"HA!" exclaimed Sland, "so you will have King Gornd bow before me!"

R'yune, once again curtsied and, once again, got a laugh. When the laughter died down, Geldish continued.

"No one will bow before anyone else. We are in this as equals. We all will live or die based on the outcome. One thing is certain. We need to get Xhaknar further off balance. I propose each warren send out a small hunting party, similar to mine, and slaughter Naradhama and Mayanoren raiding parties. If, however, they spy them carrying weapons that look like this," he quickly sketched a gun on the ground, "have them avoid contact until they meet with me. Those weapons can kill from over a thousand long paces away and you'd never know you were dead until you hit the ground.

"The good news is, if those weapons are spotted, it means Xhaknar is getting desperate. The less he can plan, the better our chances."

It was only then Geldish realized the inn keeper had left his son in the room, huddled near the stairs. Probably to serve the guests or get anything they'd need. He wondered what the small made of it all. He didn't really care all that much. He summoned him over, handed him another small bag of goldens and asked him to make arrangements to have the home of the haven lords made ready for his arrival in ten turns. The small quickly, and perfectly, repeated the instructions and bolted up the stairs.

Shortly thereafter he sent his riders up to make sure there were no threats to his guests. An epi-clik later the door opened and two halves that had once made one whole weird little snake-man came flopping down the stairs. They all looked up as N'leah stood there wiping a sword on a bar rag.

"He was carrying a beautiful sword. It seemed silly to let it go to waste. Anyway, the path is clear for everyone to leave. Can someone throw me up the scabbard that goes with this? I think I'll keep it."

"Yes indeed," thought Urnak as he picked up the scabbard off the bottom half of the corpse and walked it up the stairs, "quite formidable indeed."

Xhaknar was fuming. Not only had Geldish assembled fringe dwellers, now he seemed to be coordinating the main warrens. That could not be allowed to happen. But he needed knowledge if he was going to crush this mini-rebellion. And it was hard to get knowledge if every spy he sent out came back dead. He glared at the temp-slave he'd sent into Co-Chi to look for his spies. The drek had done his job well enough. He'd found all four in a trash can near the village center. Not knowing what else to do, he'd stolen a cart and steed and brought the whole trash can back to Xhaknar. It was still sitting in this throne room, resplendent with body parts falling out of it.

His first impulse had been to kill the slave but he quickly thought better of it. Finding the bodies, as he had, was no easy task. He might have a use for him again someturn. His second thought was to lay waste to the haven lords' domain and crush Go-Chi. But he needed many of the services they provided and haven lords hadn't done this butchery.

No, this was the work of Geldish and his scum. But how to strike at him? Could he attack the warrens and draw him out? Maybe. It was time for his Naradhama to quit being targets to whatever fringe dwelling commandos were stalking them, to turn them loose so they could get some revenge. There'd been a nasty upturn in dead Naradhama these last few turns.

But what target?

Then it hit him. It would be perfect. He told the slave to have the body parts cleaned out, knowing he would scavenge what he could from their pockets, and then summoned Ek-kh.

Within an epi-clik, the newly anointed leader of the Naradhama stood trembling before him.

"Your warren, angered over your intelligent decision to side with me, has been killing my Naradhama reclamation parties. This must stop." Ek-kh looked like he was going to obsequiously agree, but Xhaknar stopped him with a glance. "You will lead a battalion of ten thousand Naradhama cavalry to the secret entrances of your old home. They will traverse the tunnels into your warren and slaughter all who stand in their way. Should any survive, you may keep them as pets. You march in two turns. Using only the cavalry, you should arrive at the pit two turns later. Go, select your troops, and prepare your plan. I do not want to see you again until you carry the head of Urnak and place it at my feet.

"You may leave."

Ek-kh was thrilled as he scurried from the room. He didn't even bother to contemplate why there had been a pool of blood on the throne room floor. He would show those stoic old fools what real power was. He would make them pay for all the insults and jibes.

"Lazy Ek-kh, useless Ek-kh, Ek-kh who isn't fit to breed and probably isn't capable anyway, Ek-kh the simpleton …" Yes, he'd heard them all and now each one fired through his mind igniting new and painful hatreds. He hurried outside the castle and found the Naradhama general who'd led the successful raid on the Kalindor outpost they'd tried to erect on the western border. Silly Kalindor. He would do fine for this mission. He explained, quickly, Xhaknar's orders and time table and left him to arrange all the details. The first detail he arranged was to confirm the orders with Xhaknar, but Ek-kh never knew that.

Ek-kh also didn't know the general's orders were to kill Ek-kh instantly if anything, anything at all, went wrong.

There was much Ek-kh didn't know.

What Ek-kh did know is that he needed to look like a leader when they attacked the warren. He went to the local tailor and told him what he wanted. The tailor secretly cringed as Ek-kh described the flamboyant outfit he wished to wear. Ek-kh only had twenty goldens to his name, so he told the tailor he would only pay that amount for the suit when he picked it up the next turn. The tailor, who had only been planning on charging four goldens for the monstrosity, reluctantly agreed.

Ek-kh retired to his private room in the palace. Another thing he did not know is it was previously a storage closet for the slaves. To him, it was a grand estate befitting a being of his rank and stature. While he may have gotten the adjectives wrong, he did arrive at the correct conclusion.

The tailor summoned him shortly after the next breaklight for a fitting. While he hated awakening that early, these were special times and he hurried over to see what the tailor had accomplished. The suit, a wild panoply of light blue, bright purple and gold, lined with vibrant green trim, was exactly what Ek-kh envisioned. He put the garish suit on with pride and waited patiently as the tailor made marks as to where to cut and where to tighten so it would fit perfectly. Within a clik, he was done and was told it would be ready for him prior to the even meals.

Ek-kh strode out of the shop and looked for the general he'd tasked last turn. It took him a while since he had trouble telling one Naradhama from another. Eventually, he recognized the uniform and stopped the general in his tracks. After taking a few epi-cliks to ensure all was in order, and they could leave at breaklight, he went to the troop brothel for a turn of celebration. He'd earned it after all the hard work he'd just done.

Another thing Ek-kh did not know was currently sitting in the main greeting area of the Dwellers' Pit. The thirty Mantis Guards were patiently explaining diagrams to the Minotaur craft-masters. While the uses were new, the techniques were not. The craft-masters quickly deduced what each piece was for and how they all fit together. Within a clik forges were firing anew with a fresh and deadly purpose.

A few cliks later a scout rode in and informed the Council of Elders of the troop movements in Anapsida. He informed them Xhaknar wasn't even trying to hide his target since he was dressing Ek-kh up like a mating quizzle bird. When informed the Naradhama were only arming themselves with traditional weapons, the Mantis Guards laughed. The new guns being forged wouldn't be ready in time, but they had all of their own and they'd brought a couple of hundred spares, just in case. The Naradhama were in for a rude surprise the next turn.

Elder Urnak called on Greko to assemble his own battalion and march them, slowly, towards Anapsida. That way it wouldn't matter which secret entrance Ek-kh led them to, they could catch them in the open.

They worked through the even and, by breaklight, fifteen thousand Minotaurs were assembled on the Plains. The Mantis Guard rode with them and handed out their spare weapons to the front line troops. Then, to their astonishment, three craft-masters came out of the Pit carrying wagons full of weapons.

A Mantis Guard grabbed one at random, loaded it and fired. The shot blew a hole in a rock fifty paces away. He smiled, then laughed, then let the craft-masters pass out their efforts to the troops. It was still not enough for all of them, but it was a huge improvement over what they had.

He informed Greko to tell the troops with the new weapons just to aim for the torsos of the Naradhama. They could learn to finesse the weapons later. Greko thanked him and issued the order.

With that out of the way, they began their slow march west.

About a clik later they came to a series of ridges. Greko halted their march and studied them carefully. He turned to face his warriors.

"No matter what, the Naradhama will first have to pass these ridges before they can get to our Pit. We will stop them here then. Anyone who has a gun, report to the Mantis Guards, they will divide you and place you behind the ridges so you can shoot easier. The rest of us will split into halves. Sub-commander Kronlk will take one half around the ridge and wait, hidden, in the gulley. I will remain here with the rest. When the shooting starts, we will close in on the pass and slay any who try to flee the killing zone.

"Additionally, while I would prefer to kill Ek-kh myself as a matter of honor, do not hesitate if you get the chance. The safety of our Pit far outweighs any honor my family is due.

"Now, let's go destroy these rotting, slimy, vermin who breed with their mothers!"

A mighty "HUSHAK!" went up and the troops dispersed quickly into the ridges and gullies around the Dweller's Pit.

Ek-kh had led the Naradhama out the front gates of

Anapsida less than a clik after breaklight on the appointed turn. None of the Naradhama marched near him, leaving him alone at the head. He thought it was their way of showing respect. In reality, none wanted to be close to such an obvious target. When Xhaknar had seen Ek-kh's uniform, by accident since Ek-kh was avoiding him by decree, all he could say was "Yes, it describes you perfectly."

Ek-kh took that as the highest praise he'd ever earned.

About five cliks after breaklight on the second turn of the march, he spied the ridges and hillocks that signaled they were near the warren of his youth. He felt nothing at any of the memories he stirred. Nothing, that is, other than hatred. He rode back to inform the general of where they were and which entrance would be the easiest to access from this point. Then he turned and resumed his rightful place ahead of the Naradhama. This would be his greatest triumph. He led the Naradhama less than twenty paces from where Kronlk had secreted his warriors in the sand. That was something else Ek-kh did not know.

They were about halfway through the chasm beneath the second ridge when he heard an unfamiliar noise. It was a loud popping sound and it kept repeating. He then became aware of the Naradhama screaming and trying to exit both ends of the mini-valley simultaneously.

Greko had moved his part of the battalion closer to the opening of the ridges when he heard the guns' fire. He wanted to make sure they killed every single Naradhama who might try to escape. He could clearly see on the other side Kronlk had the same thought. He was grateful to have such a competent sub-commander. It meant one less thing to worry about. His eyes finally rested on Ek-kh who seemed oblivious to the carnage raining down upon his troops. He just kept riding forward as though nothing were amiss.

Soon enough they were involved in hand to hand combat as the Naradhama, who'd ran past Ek-kh, tried to flee. His troops rushed in to greet them with bloodlust in their hearts and savage war-cries in their throats. The knives, swords, gauntlets and the rest were merely a way to give flesh to those emotions.

His archers never had to loose an arrow. It was a slaughter in every sense of the word. In the chaos of the moment, the Minotaurs crushed the skulls, slit the throats, and impaled the gizzards of any Naradhama foolish enough to get close to them. Those who tried to flee back into the ridge-valley were met with continuing fusillades. If they did survive the middle they were met by Kronlk and his warriors. Not a single square inch was safe for the Naradhama.

As Ek-kh neared the egress of the valley, Greko rose to meet him. But, before he could raise his sword Ek-kh's head exploded like a dropped melon. His gaudy suit was immediately covered with gushing blood and scrambled brains. He flopped off his horse, dead, not ten paces from Greko.

Greko walked over to the body and stabbed it in the chest anyway, just to be sure.

With nothing better to do, Greko led his troops into the valley to finish off any survivors. About a clik before even-fall he met Kronlk in the middle. It was over. The two, grizzled, veterans (all veterans of war are grizzled, it's part of the job description) surveyed the scene calmly. The troops were efficiently gathering up all of the surviving steeds and stripping the dead Naradhama of their weaponry. Others carefully tended their own wounded while bearers from the Pit gently put the bodies of the fallen onto carts so they could receive proper funerals. Both Greko and Kronlk noted there were few of their warriors who had not survived.

"This," said Kronlk with the barest hint of a smile, as he waved his arm over the scene of the butchery, "is really going to piss Xhaknar off."

Südermann strolled past the warriors' barracks behind his palace. He watched as birds and insects swarmed through the jungle canopy above. When he neared the officers' quarters he spied Elaand, motioned him over and then continued his leisurely promenade.

"I have received word from Hlaar. He says the Minotaurs were attacked by ten thousand Naradhama near mid-turn. He notes that thanks to a simple – yet brilliant – plan from the acting general Greko, they were able to pull off an unprecedented ambush. Not one Naradhama was left alive.

"He also noted the craft-masters of the Minotaur far exceeded his expectations. He said they had five wagon loads of weapons ready within a turn. He can only conclude they worked every novice and themselves without sleep."

Elaand took it all in. "This would be good news, would it not, lord?"

Südermann nodded. "Yes, at its surface, it is exceedingly good news. But for an attack that large, so early in Geldish's campaign, I must conclude Xhaknar is becoming more unstable faster than we predicted. You and your Guard may be called into action sooner than expected."

"That will not be a problem, lord. As you know, we train constantly. There will be none who let down their vigilance. We can leave with less than a turn's notice at your decree."

Südermann's mandibles vibrated slightly. It was an old habit he had whenever he was lost in thought. Elaand doubted he was conscious he did it. As they continued their walk in silence Elaand gazed at the colorful fauna which surrounded them. Each Südermann was tasked with keeping this, along with the sentient residents, safe from harm. With the barbarians, literally, at every gate, it was not a job he envied. The one hundred percent mortality rate among interlopers was a cruel, but necessary, pogrom. Elaand knew, by saving the old technology, and later advancing it, as well as rebuilding the infrastructure required to keep it all functioning, these lands would be a prize beyond belief for many.

Ever watchful, ever ready. That was the mantra of the Guard and it had served them well throughout the millennia. It would serve them well again in these times.

Südermann stopped suddenly and Elaand had to catch himself so he didn't walk into him.

"Look, Elaand, at this puzzle we keep. Each piece fits into another so the whole may emerge. Our ancestor insects feed the birds who in turn feed the mammals who in turn feed on each other and all of them, of course, feed us. The same cycle occurs in our rivers and lakes and even in the southern ocean. Each of us has a gap to fill. And when our time is done, we return to Arreti to begin the process anew.

"Xhaknar is like a small with a temper. He cannot figure out the puzzle, so he smashes it and bellows in rage. Were he allowed his way, the whole world would be laid waste. The third Südermann was correct when he held his hand and did not attack the lands of Anapsida. The odds of victory were too slim and the rewards almost nonexistent. However, I fear we Südermenn have become complacent over time. Anapsida has grown from an annoying itch to a gaping lesion. We have let that wound fester for far too long and now it threatens to infect everything with its blight. This cannot happen."

Although Südermann never raised his voice, Elaand could hear the power in his words. The line had been drawn. This far and no farther. The words resonated in his heart and he knew, without fail, that he would see his lord's wishes come true or die in the attempt. There would be no middle ground.

"Forgive me, m'Lord," Elaand asked tenuously, "but one thing has always bothered me."

Lord Südermann nodded for him to continue.

"We have all this technology, why have we not built smarter computers? I know the capability is there."

Lord Südermann sighed.

"That answer lies in the dust of time," he paused to gather his thoughts and then continued, "back in the Sun 2150, of the makers' calendar, the makers connected all the artificial intelligence in the world together to make one great mind. They named it Plato after an ancient philosopher of theirs who preached peace and the possibility of relationships without the need for physical passions."

He stopped to smell a flower and smiled.

"Obviously, whatever homage they paid to those beliefs was hollow or we would not be here this turn.

"Anyway, for a while, almost a hundred Suns actually, all went well. Then some of them started noticing the mortality rate for the less educated and the infirm was staggeringly high. They attempted numerous queries to Plato only to be told, time and time again, everything was as it should be.

"Finally a few scientists were able to secure a sample of bodies to autopsy in secret. Their findings stunned them. Every single one of the bodies had been poisoned with a sophisticated, gene crushing, drug. Quite simply they'd been desiccated from the inside out.

"Naturally they went to Plato to confront him and

find out why their results were so different than his answers. He repeated everything was as it should be. He informed them, as politely as he could, it was his job to protect the makers and that, as far as he could tell, meant helping them achieve the loftiest goals. Since the majority, eighty percent by his estimate, of the makers were a drain on society, one way or the other, they needed to be culled."

He stopped to admire an insect as it nested in a flower and then continued.

"The resulting war killed three billion of the makers but they finally destroyed Plato. They wrote strict laws preventing anyone from ever creating an artificial intelligence again. That was the way things remained until the Sominids came and you should know the rest of that story."

He chuckled amiably.

They continued walking in the near silence, with the only sound being Südermann's vibrating mandibles. When they reached the officers' quarters Südermann bade Elaand a good even and headed back into the palace.

Elaand watched him go and then entered his quarters. He spied his bottle of Sominid brandy and poured himself a healthy snifter's worth. There were only two images in the room. The first was a picture of him and his family when he was young. He was playing Skizzi-Ball and his parents were laughing. His brothers and sisters were suspended in air, trying to stop his reckless run. He smiled at the memory. The other picture was of him being sworn into the Guard by the first Südermann he'd served. This Südermann was his third and would be his last. The first had been old, near the end of her days. Even so, it was another ten Full Suns before she turned over the reins of power to her successor. Then she, like every Südermann before her, went to the Palace of Echoes to await eternity.

He, like every member of the Guard, had been there once. As part of their training they learned meditation techniques from the monks who oversaw it. It was, quite possibly, the most peaceful place on Arreti. Burbling fountains and sculpted gardens hidden within thick walls which kept out all other sounds.

He put the memories aside and considered what lie ahead. He knew he only had a few more Full Suns left in him before he'd have to put down his weapons and retire. He could feel it in his bones. He did not want to become a burden to his troops. This, then, would be his last mission. If he survived he would take Südermann up on his offer and move up to the rank of Colonel and begin the last phase of his life as desk bound warrior. He did not rue the prospect. It meant a substantial increase in pay and benefits. While he had no smalls of his own, his brothers and sisters did and he could leave them a healthy bounty when he finally met oblivion.

He knew Südermann believed in a God. He was not sure he shared that faith. However, there was only one way to find out if there was an afterlife and he was prepared to take that step when the time came.

He sipped his brandy and realized he felt something he'd not felt in many long Suns; peace.

Though they were only two turns away from their meeting at the home of the haven lords, Geldish had decided to try and get in one more raid. They had tied their nytsteeds up in a nearby valley and made their way to the top of a rise. They'd heard noises that could only come from a Mayanoren raiding party.

As they looked at the scene below them it was Sland who summed up the situation.

"What are they going to raid? Anapsida?"

There were over one thousand Mayanoren below

them. They had set up camp for the even and had a loose sort of guard on their perimeter. But there was no way, lax defenses or not, rapidly becoming legendary Brittle Riders or not, they could come out of an attack on that camp alive.

They eased back behind the crest and thought.

"Something's happened," said Geldish in a blindingly obvious moment, "there is no reason for Xhaknar to commit such a large force to a simple village raid. Especially out here on the fringe. The closest enclave is one of just a few Succubi. There couldn't be more than a hundred of them, if that."

"It's called Anara," clarified N'leah, "It's where I was born."

Geldish considered that. "We need knowledge. I will infiltrate the camp and see what I can find out. You four head to Anara and warn the villagers of what's coming. They should be safe if they hide in the Vested Hills.

"I'll meet you at the Din-La trading post north of here come breaklight."

Geldish slid over the rise and, in less than a sepi-clik, was gone from view.

"I wish he could show us how he does that," commented BraarB, "it would be useful."

"You might not wish to learn," replied Sland, "look at him and think if you'd want to spend forever looking like that just to learn a trick."

Occasionally, although not often, Sland said something salient. This was one of those rare times. With nothing else to discuss they shuffled back down the hill to their nytsteeds and headed off to Anara.

Within two cliks they spotted a sentry and rode directly toward her. They slowed their gait and kept their hands in plain view so she would know she wasn't being attacked. They quickly appraised her of the situation and, within two cliks more, the village was empty.

Then they skirted north, beneath the Vested Hills

and made their way to the Din-La trading post. It was closed at this late time, so they made camp behind it and waited for Geldish.

As they waited, N'leah thought back on her Suns in Anara. They had been peaceful times. They'd worked the land, raised their own livestock and taken care of each other during tough times. Of which, under Xhaknar, there were many. Like most Succubi, she had no siblings and her parents could have been anyone. Every small was raised by the entire village. It had been their way for as long as any could remember.

She smiled as she thought back on her first flight. Nothing of avian beauty that. She'd careened through the sky, flipping over several times before landing, inelegantly, in a haystack. The adults had laughed, then scooped her up in their strong arms, wiped away her tears and told her of their first attempts. By the time even fell, she was laughing too hard to care about her bruises.

She remembered her first kiss. Under the moons-light, behind a barn, with a Succubus named P'marna. Raven haired, with alabaster skin, green eyes and supple limbs, she was quite possibly the most beautiful Succubi ever to have lived. At least that was what she thought at the time. Over the course of two seasons, they'd explored each other's bodies and shared each other's minds. Then P'marna had been selected to serve in Queen A'lnuah's court and was gone.

N'leah had cried for many turns. Completely inconsolable and convinced her young life had been destroyed and there was no reason to breathe anymore. Then P'marna had written to say how much she enjoyed the

Queen's court and, while she missed N'leah tremendously, the honor and prestige her appointment brought their village helped her see the larger picture. She'd wished N'leah well and stated, though they were apart, she would never stop loving her.

Knowing P'marna still loved her helped her get through. Within a few turns, she was her usual self and had rejoined the community. She would always carry P'marna in her heart, just not on her chest like a badge.

She also remembered the even the Mayanoren raiding party had assaulted her village. They knew the denizens of Anapsida prized Succubi as sex slaves. With their basic shape changing abilities they could please any perversion. They had captured three that even. One, K'lnanga, died during the trip from her injuries. The other, L'randa, was killed by a master when she refused to do something for him. N'leah never learned what the something was and really didn't want to know.

N'leah had served as a sex slave for thirty Full Suns before R'yune had rescued her. The memory of what some of the Naradhama, and others, made her do still made her blood run cold.

Another eight Full Suns of life with R'yune had been hard, but comfortable. He had a way of dealing with difficult situations and making them seem easy enough for a small to handle. His confidence, though he may not know it, finally helped heal her soul. His prowess in bed helped ease her thoughts of P'marna. Since one brand couldn't impregnate another, she never worried about a surprise on the Plains.

Now she was sitting outside a Din-La trading post, waiting to start a war. Her life had sure been wrapped in some unexpected weaves.

Shortly before breaklight, they heard a familiar scraping. Geldish had returned. BraarB roused Sland, who could sleep through a war if he wished, and went to greet their leader.

"I have interesting news. I don't know if it's bad or good right now, but it's certainly worth repeating. It seems Xhaknar sent ten thousand of his best Naradhama to crush the Dwellers of the Pit. To drive home his revulsion with them he had the battalion led by Ek-kh. There was a lot of talk about Ek-kh being dressed like a quizzle bird, but I have no idea what it meant.

"Anyway, when they got to the western ridges of the Dwellers' domain they were ambushed. It appears Südermann's emissaries brought new weapons to the Pit and armed the Minotaurs. There is a lot of uncertainty in the tale, but from what I gathered, every single Naradhama was slaughtered and left to rot. One important thing to note is they all believe the Minotaurs developed these weapons themselves. They have no idea Südermann is aiding us in any way.

"This all happened several turns ago and Xhaknar is livid. Even the fact that Ek-kh is dead didn't mollify him. The raiding party we saw is just one of many Xhaknar has set loose on the fringe. He believes we are behind the defeat and we are hiding here. He will raze every village until he finds us."

As the last syllable exited his mouth there was a distant whump and then a pillar of flame. Anara had been put to the torch. Huts could be rebuilt, at least the villagers were safe. They all watched the smoke and flames disappear into the sky for a while when they were suddenly interrupted.

"The Brittle Riders, I presume?"

There stood, in the ubiquitous purple waist coat and yellow trousers of his kind, a Din-La. Made from some form of rodent to be servants to the makers they'd proved useless as warriors during the Gen-O-Pod war. But, they turned out to be amazing at finding anything you wanted, for a price. They'd developed into a trading community that spanned the whole continent, possibly the world. They were far too valuable a resource for anyone to destroy, so they thrived when others failed. The Mayanoren would never even consider coming here looking for them.

"Even here," said the little creature, "we hear news of the world around us. It seems you have been spending your time making Xhaknar angry. While we normally stay out of the affairs of others, many of us think this is a good thing. Yes, we think it's a very good thing indeed."

"I am Geldish," he said as he stood, "and these are BraarB, R'yune, N'leah and Sland. You seem to have us at a disadvantage."

"Oh, I doubt that," smiled the Din-La, "I doubt that very much indeed. Had you the desire I would be visiting my ancestors and telling them about the amazing speed at which I'd begun the journey. Nevertheless, I am called Zrrm and this is my trading post. How may I serve you this turn?"

"A large party of Mayanoren will be here in a clik or so," Geldish began, "would you be so kind as to say you saw us two turns ago and we were headed west?"

Zrrm thought about it for a bit and then nodded. "For a golden, please."

The Din-La were notoriously greedy, but also kept their own code of honor. Once a contract was paid for they would never break it. Xhaknar and Yontar had put several to death before they'd figured that out. Geldish handed him the golden and sat back down.

"We could also use a good meal. We have been riding long and hard and, while we have plenty of stored provisions, nothing is better for the soul than fresh food."

Zrrm nodded again and motioned for them to stay. He opened the back of the trading post and shortly returned with a large pot of a steaming liquid.

"The Fierstans love this drink. It's called Java. It's made from special beans and will refresh your souls. While you drink I shall prepare your breaklight repast. Then, as I'm sure you're aware, you must go."

Sland sniffed it, sipped from a cup and smiled. Thus pronounced good they all began sipping the steaming beverage.

Good as his word, Zrrm returned shortly with a platter of cooked meats, spiced Eastern style, and another platter which was stacked with round breads covered in sweet syrup. There was another platter of fresh fruits and exotic cheeses. There were even two large carafes of the Fish-People's famous Morning Wine. All of these were laid before the riders along with plates, cutlery and, wonder of wonders, cloth napkins. Geldish had no idea how such delicacies and fineries ended up in such an out of the way trading post, but he didn't care enough to ask. Not that he would have gotten a useful answer anyway. The Din-La kept their secrets as well as their word.

As soon as they were finished Zrrm held up two tiny fingers. Geldish smiled and handed him three goldens.

"The extra one is for good luck. Yours and ours."

Zrrm bowed and returned to the trading post. Two other, smaller, Din-La appeared from the woods and began clearing away any evidence of the visit as the riders mounted up and headed east.

The home of the haven lords was legendary for its

grandeur. The haven lords, like the Din-La, had been bred for servitude and were left alone by Xhaknar. Unlike the Din-La, their heritage was primarily canine. The tallest of their kind would still be shorter than the shoulder of a Minotaur.

In the main entranceway, there was a huge chandelier which was lit by hundreds of candles. Above it were carefully placed mirrors to reflect the light evenly throughout the room. In a scene that would have fit in any time, bellhops and servants scurried about making sure their guests every whim was met. Touring ambassadors and the few elite there still were all made this their home.

The next turn would see them visited by two queens and a king. Well, one queen was actually an empress, but that was of little import. And if that royalty was of the fringe, no matter, royalty was royalty and goldens had been paid in advance.

The main dining area had been set up for the meeting and rooms were set aside for all. Since they didn't know how many courtiers their guests would bring, they'd simply set aside an entire wing. Minor details could be dealt with when they arrived.

In the back of the edifice was a smaller room, not lavish at all. In it sat six of the haven lords, ostensibly going over books. One, the inn keeper whose name is Brek in case you're curious, sat with a bemused look on his face.

"Well," he began, "we've certainly sniffed it out this time, haven't we?"

The others nodded in agreement.

"So, what do we do? Do we stay on the side and watch our world burn or do we pick a side?"

Unbeknownst to anyone, the haven lords, unlike the Din-La, had felt shamed at their lack of military expertise during the Gen-O-Pod war and then subsequent terrors of Xhaknar. They had been secretly training in the basement of their home and in the far hills, away from prying eyes. While they were no threat to any army now, they could field a relatively solid phalanx of foot soldiers. The problem they faced was picking a side to fight on.

While they held no love for Xhaknar they were astute enough to realize he lorded over their realm with an iron fist. Should they rise against him and not be victorious, retribution would be swift and final. But if they sided with him, and Geldish's revolt proved successful, they would never again be trusted. Their ancestral home would be taken from them and they would either be exiled or killed.

The third option was the one they hated the most. Do what they were expected to do, watch the world burn and pleasantly serve the champion.

The debate had been going on ever since Geldish first showed up at the Crasnia. Brek wanted to side with the Rangka, but others were not convinced. Yes, life under Xhaknar could be cruel, but it was steady and he, for the most part, left them alone. Many thought an unexpected show of favor to him might buy them some rewards when the dust finally settled. Others felt, should Xhaknar find out they could fight, he would immediately conscript them and they would never again be haven lords.

Still, others felt the whole argument was silly since the rebellion would die out as others had before it. Whether from lack of support or Xhaknar's rage, most rebellions faded before the next season's Sun.

Brek, however, felt this one was different and said so, loudly and often. This was not some warren trying to throw off taxes or avoid service in Anapsida. This was a meeting of the main warrens and the fringe. They had all heard the rumors of what happened at ridges by the Pit and most were aware Naradhama were dropping like Dark Sun leaves across the Plains.

"I say there is only one solution," growled Brek, "we must ask Geldish when he arrives. The Rangka may not tell you all they know, but they've never lied when questioned directly."

"You expect us to trust the undead," asked Dorl,

"why not just ask us to jump in Xhaknar's fountain?"

That met with a murmur of agreement.

"What would you have us do, Dorl? Sweet Rohta, should we just sit here and wait for a tummy rub like our distant ancestors?"

That got an unintended laugh.

The argument, occasionally dirty and nasty, continued well into the even as all around them opulence reigned.

Xhaknar stood in his throne room and fumed. No one came near him. None dared. He was furious at Ek-kh, he was furious at the Naradhama, he was furious at the Dwellers of the Pit, he was furious at Geldish and his Brittle Riders – what the hell kind of name was that anyway? – and he was furious, most of all, with himself.

He'd put too much faith in the bulk of his army. He'd assumed they could crush anything that got in their path just by sheer weight of numbers. And they could. That wasn't the problem. The problem was Geldish wasn't fighting him army to army. He was picking away piece after piece until there'd be no pieces left.

He'd gotten the report from the Din-La, through the Mayanoren, reporting Geldish was heading west. That was the first thing Geldish had done, thus far, that made sense. The Kordai Sanctuary was there and it took in all who wished to sequester themselves from the world. Worthless monks and whiny losers all, but it would be a good place for Geldish to hide. Even if he flattened the place he might not find Geldish and his freaks. There were so many nooks and crannies built into the surrounding hills it would be an act of supreme luck if he did.

So, maybe, Geldish was out of the way for now. Certainly, he wasn't going to find any warriors in that warren of the weak. And, also certainly, the ambushes on the patrols had stopped once he increased their strength. So maybe Geldish didn't have as many allies as feared. His attempt to raise the masses in revolt had gone nowhere and now he was forced to hide.

If so, and it seemed likely, then it was time to stop fooling around with this nonsense and begin planning the attack on Südermann. He'd deal with the Minotaurs and their new weapons on that march, not now.

First, he had to recall all of the Mayanoren and Naradhama wandering the Plains. Then he had to train them how to use the ancient weapons he'd been having built in his secret munitions factory. He had enough to do without chasing ghosts.

Let the dead keep their own, he always said. And now they had Ek-kh to deal with, which just made life a little sweeter.

He was just about to issue his orders when a young femme slave entered the room. Like all his slaves, she was naked in his presence. It was easier than searching them every time. She held a piece of paper over her head and aimed it in his direction. Curious, he took the paper and read it. It was a report from one of his spies out on the fringe. The royalty of the fringe was headed for Go-Chi and there was a small patrol of Se-Jeant headed that way as well.

Well, that was it then. Fearing his wrath over the actions of their spawn, they were asking the Se-Jeant for protection. They'd pay whatever they could and, who knows, the Se-Jeant may even put those dregs up in their ice palace. That didn't matter. What mattered was they were clearly planning on closing ranks and praying for better turns. Nothing else could get those slime to leave the safety of their hovels.

And that was more good news. It meant there were

fewer players in the game than before. Now he could plan his attack on Südermann unmolested.

He was in such a good mood he actually smiled when he raped the slave.

Her muted cries were made all the sweeter by his current disposition.

N'leah spotted the weird little snake-like man near the back of the haven lord's home. Whether he was there in the service of Xhaknar or just on vacation was never discerned because she sliced him in two and threw the pieces in the trash. Except for the odd sucking sound his innards made as they hit the ground, the even was adamantly silent.

They entered through a back door and were met by Brek. He led them through a series of back corridors that were off limit to the guests. They went up several flights of stairs until they reached the top floor. He took them down the main hallway until he reached five rooms at the end whose doorways formed a semi-circle. He handed each a key and quietly departed. Geldish opened the door nearest him, on the right, and smiled.

"Well, this sure beats sleeping on dirt."

The others opened their doors and were equally impressed. The accommodations, while just above average in the haven lord's home, were far more extravagant than anything they'd ever seen. Small torches in wall sconces, a giant bed in the middle as well as private bathing and toilet areas for each, it was like something from a small's fantasy.

"Get clean and get plenty of rest. The staff will bring food to our rooms in about a clik so we won't starve. Next breaklight is going to bring many changes to this realm so I'll need you all at your best."

R'yune spent several epi-cliks trying to divine the purpose of each of the objects in the room and finally surrendered. He walked out and knocked on N'leah's door. The look of utter confusion on his face, when she answered, told her all she needed to know. She was leading him back across the hall when Sland came out of his room. He looked so baffled it took all her strength to stifle a giggle.

"Come on you two, I've seen stuff like this when I was being kept at Xhaknar's palace. It's not as hard as it looks."

She led them both into R'yune's room and then went to the bathroom first.

"This is called a toilet. You sit on it when you need to make waste and, when you're done, use that paper on the roll to clean yourself off. It's just like wiping leaves, only softer. Just unroll it like this." She gave them a quick demonstration. "When you're done, just pull this handle and all the waste goes away." She demonstrated that as well. Then she led them into the bathing area. "This is just like the tubs you grew up with, only fancier. The handle on the left makes hot water and the handle on the right makes cold. You mix them until you get a temperature you like. The handle in the middle is so you can fill up the tub by pushing it down or take a shower by raising it up." She demonstrated all the wonders of the tub and looked at them. They weren't stupid, not by any means, but neither were they experienced. They'd lived their whole lives on the fringe, or in poor hovels. Luxuries like this weren't even rumored out there. In short order, they figured everything out and she took her leave. When she got back to her room she noticed that her tub had a scalloped back so she could rest her wings. She decided that was exactly what she would do.

She got the hot water running and set it to fill the tub. Then she stripped off her loin cloth, weapons, belt, and scabbard and slid into the steaming water. A little bit later there was a knock at her door announcing food was served. Just in case, she slid her sword on the edge of the tub and told the haven lord to bring it in.

Whatever thoughts he might have had seeing her nude in the tub, clasping a sword, he wisely kept to himself. After ascertaining she needed nothing else, he let himself out. She stayed in the tub until the water began to cool. She opened the drain and stood as it swirled around her feet. Then she turned the hot water on again and set the handle to the shower position. She luxuriated in the mist until she felt positively sensuous.

Sometimes when she felt that way she'd get R'yune to service her. She wondered if he'd mind. She walked back into the main room while toweling herself off and noticed a dress hung near the bed. It was the traditional glory dress of the Succubi. The bottom half was five layers of sheer white fabric held together by a wide belt of kgum leather. This one was so well polished she could see her reflection in it. The top half was a simple, over the shoulder wrap with delicate, glittery highlights. She felt like a princess just looking at it.

There was another knock at the door and, completely forgetting she was naked, she just called out for them to enter. BraarB walked into the room with a towel wrapped around her head and stared at the dress.

"Wow," she gasped, "that's beautiful. I found the ceremonial breast plate for formal meetings in my room and was worried I'd be over dressed. Obviously, no one's even going to notice me with you wearing that. I wonder what they gave R'yune and Sland?"

It didn't take long to find out. R'yune, still damp from bathing, walked out in a deep red suit with a matching cape and boots, and looking confused. It was the traditional, Wolfen, regalia for a prince, minus the look of confusion, of course. Sland was in the hall shortly thereafter wearing a royal blue suit with the knee high boots preferred by BadgeBeth, and a black cape clipped to his shoulders.

N'leah, realizing she was still nude, quickly ran back into her room, put on the dress, and walked back out into the hall. BraarB had done likewise and was now wearing the ornamented breast plate. They were all staring at each other trying to decide who looked either the most royal or the most foolish when Geldish came into the hall.

"Geldish," cried N'leah, "what's the meaning of this stuff? Are we playing dress up games next turn?"

He smiled. "Well, it seems the only way I could get you into a meeting with royalty was if you were my servants or royalty yourselves. Since you clearly serve no one that left me only one legitimate option. I sent word to Karrish at the Temple and had him issue a decree naming you four as protectors of the temple, formally acknowledging your group name of the Brittle Riders and assigning you the rank of prince or princess, as the case may be. He also assigned you each a stipend of one hundred goldens, which you'll find in the top drawer of the desks in your rooms."

"I'm a fucking princess?" asked Sland incredulously.

That did it. As uncomfortable as they were, they were all laughing too hard to notice anything else. Since they were preoccupied, they were startled to hear the baritone growl of King Gornd.

"So it is true," he exclaimed, "the leavings of the fringe has taken it upon themselves to earn princely ranks. Up from nothing, or less than nothing, to become protectors of the Temple of Azarep. I admit Sland I had high hopes for your brother Granq, and he has done nothing to disappoint me, but you …. Why …Your father, were he alive …. Just look at you. I am proud of you Sland. Very proud indeed."

Without waiting to be introduced to anyone else, King Gornd and his small retinue of courtiers returned down the hall and were led by a haven lord to their suite of rooms.

Sland looked as if he was debating whether to laugh or cry and neither option was winning.

"We're all proud of you Sland," whispered Geldish, "as a warrior you have saved our lives countless times and as a friend you've been truer than any I can think of in recent times. You've earned his respect, as well as ours."

Sland inclined his head in a pseudo bow and went back to his room, his mind full of thoughts far deeper than he'd ever imagined he could handle.

The rest quickly went back to their rooms and settled in for the first complete even's sleep any had had in many turns.

Sland sat on the edge of the comfortable bed and tried to piece his life together. It had started out normally enough. Like all BadgeBeth, he was strong and had shown a propensity for working the soil. By his tenth Full Sun, it was clear he would always be less than his brother Granq, but that didn't bother him. Granq was warm and giving and made everyone around him feel welcome. He was special and Sland knew it.

He may not have been as smart as his brother, but he was smart enough to know you don't curse nature for the gifts you got. There was much he could do that would benefit his clan. He took pride in that and did the best he could.

It was around his twentieth Full Sun he began to notice the wider world around him. When he didn't have chores for the clan he would go out and explore the surrounding lands. He met up with other brands and found he had skills they did not. Some, like the haven lords, hired him out as a hunter. His keen sense of smell and superior strength made him an ideal candidate for the job.

Once a village had been terrorized by a narkling. Rare and wonderful, they were also massive and deadly. Like a Rakyeen they had six legs and were furry. Unlike a Rakyeen, they stood twice as tall as any brand and had razor sharp teeth that could rotate inside their mouths. The village council had offered him ten goldens, a then princely sum to him, if he would kill it.

He'd set up a small camp on the outskirts of the village and began tracking the beast. For three full turns, pausing only to nap in trees or caves, he'd followed the tracks around the village. On the fourth turn, he'd found it.

Before he could draw his weapons the beast charged. Left no other options Sland had jumped up, vaulted himself over the head of the creature, and landed on its back facing its rear. His fingers, having only one knuckle since the tips were actually claws, plunged into its flesh so he could hold on. He spun quickly, readjusting his grip as he did so, drew his sword and began stabbing. The beast bucked and spun, ramming into anything it could and finally knocking Sland off. But not before he'd done some lethal damage.

Sland finished it off with one grand thrust and collapsed. He'd been knocked against so many rocks and trees that he couldn't even begin to count his wounds. His left arm was broken, of that much he was sure, and he was pretty confident a lot of the blood on the outside of his body should have been on the inside.

Still and all, though, he was alive and the beast wasn't. As far as he was concerned, that's all that really mattered.

He pulled a spare shirt from his pack and cut it into strips. He used two to secure two branches into a serviceable brace for his arm after he'd set the bone. He used a third to make a sling. Then he found a nearby spring and washed off the blood. He was pleased to note his wounds, although numerous, were mostly superficial. He bandaged the few that required attention and headed back to the kill. He pulled the horn he'd been provided, in case he succeeded, and sounded it. Then he sat down on the grass, ate some dried meats, and sipped some water from his canteen.

About half a clik later the villagers arrived with a cart and a medical kit. Not so dumb, these villagers. They loaded the beast onto the cart, tended Sland's wounds more fully than he could have done and took him and the beast back to the council.

The council members saw them coming and came out to greet them. They handed Sland his goldens and invited him to stay for a feast. He did.

Two turns later he returned home and told his father, Rorng, what he'd accomplished. He then offered the goldens to his family.

His father frowned deeply and then spent a full clik bemoaning the fact his son, the son of a clan leader, was mucking around with other brands. He went on and on in that vein making sure to use variations of the word "disgrace" multiple times and then stormed out of the room. Granq came in and tried to comfort Sland, but it was clear he disapproved too.

That even, Sland packed all he could think to carry and walked out, never to return.

Downstairs in the main rotunda, under the cover of darkness, Brek realized the decision was being made for him and the haven lords. He watched as four Minotaurs entered with a small retinue of hooded courtesans, followed by four Se-Jeant and a few more of the hooded courtesans. As soon as they've cleared the lobby he watched a group of four Fierstans enters and noted they, too, had the weird hooded courtesans. Brek had lived his entire life on the Plains and thought he knew every brand there was. The courtesans, with their lengthy gait and sure manner, were unlike anything he'd ever seen before.

No matter. All of the main warrens were here. That was enough.

Before he could tell his companions what he'd seen. Empress ClaalD of the Sacred Lairs of the Llamia and Queen A'lnuah of the Roosts of the Succubi came through the door followed by their personal courtiers. At least there weren't any more of those weird creatures with the unnaturally long legs.

He watched with interest as the staff handled each with dignity and just the right amount of obsequiousness. In less than five epi-cliks the lobby was as barren as a tomb. They had done well.

The next turn would tell all, but Brek already knew what the answer was. War was coming and it was coming fast and hard. This would be no petty rebellion. These leaders have gathered together to throw off Xhaknar's yoke once and for all. Anyone who sides with Xhaknar will simply be ground into dust.

Brek felt a sense of relief. It's easy making decisions when you only have one option.

At the trading post just outside Anara, Zrrm was carefully restocking his shelves with the help of his two sons. The Mayanoren had camped for two full turns waiting for the Succubi to return. Zrrm had used his immense network of information to inform them they, too, had headed west to parts unknown. He laughed at the memory while making a note to charge T'reena a golden for his efforts. He wouldn't want it to get out the Din-La worked for free. The Mayanoren had bought it completely, along with half his store, and then began their return to Anapsida.

And that was what was troubling him. If they were truly hunting Geldish, why had they broken off the search so quickly and easily? A few burned villages and some mindless killing is just a regular turn for them. A true threat to Anapsida was what Geldish was, of that much Zrrm was certain. The engagement should have resulted in wholesale slaughter and forests being burned to the ground.

Now he really was using the vast information network the traders had to find out what was actually going on and if he should be more worried than he was.

There was a soft knock at the rear door. He motioned for one of his sons to answer and finished arranging the row he was working on. He was surprised, but not shocked, to see the C.E.O. of the Din-La, Bmmd, walk in.

"Greetings Zrrm," began Bmmd as he handed his coat to the boys, "I see business has been good lately."

"A thousand, hungry, Mayanoren and some inconsequential guests. Pretty much the usual these days."

"Inconsequential," Bmmd chuckled, "I think not. A talking skull with flame in its eyes will get noticed, even this far out, especially when it is protected by the legendary Brittle Riders." He paused for a sepi-clik as if lost in thought. "While I think the Mayanoren put some well-deserved goldens in your pocket, my guess is your inconsequential guests will have more, shall we say, long term value."

He paused again to light a pipe and rest against a barrel.

"We Din-La are not warriors, never have been. Even so, we have, when we've had to, chosen sides. We sided with the Gen-O-Pods against our makers, with Südermann against the tribes of Kalindor and with the Fish-People during those first Mayanoren forays into their realm. When Xhaknar and Yontar marched on the Plains they came via a circuitous route through the north and avoided all of our outposts. Had we known they were coming we might have stood a chance against them here."

He sighed.

"But those turns are dark memories and nothing can be done to change them. But what can't be undone in the past can surely be undone in the future. You have been asking some interesting questions, so I am here to give you some interesting answers. Please, sit, this is going to take a while."

Zrrm pulled up a chair and sat down. Then, almost without thinking, lit his own pipe and sent his sons home.

"Xhaknar believed your tale of Geldish and his riders going west. He had to. It was the only thing that would make any sense. This is even more-so when you think of it from his point of view. While his Naradhama were annihilated at the Dweller's Pit, it was he who attacked them, not the other way around. If you remove that from the equation, all you have left is Geldish harassing a few Naradhama raiding parties. Yes, the attacks were lethal to the Naradhama, but they don't amount to much in the grand scheme of things if they don't incite the warrens to rebel.

"And it is clear they did not.

"But what Xhaknar does not know is the warrens never planned on openly rebelling. Not now, anyway. No, they let Geldish have his fun and stayed quiet. I imagine Geldish wanted it that way as well.

"Xhaknar also doesn't know Geldish sent an emissary party to Südermann under a flag of peace. We do not know what they told Lord Südermann, or if they carried a direct message from Geldish, but that matters little. What matters is the emissaries returned from Südermann's lands with a contingent of Mantis Guards. They divided up into three groups of thirty each to stay with the Fierstans, the Se-Jeant, and the Minotaurs. It also seems they brought weapons superior to the ones Xhaknar's been stockpiling."

He noticed a bottle of Eastern Brandy on Zrrm's desk and motioned to it. Zrrm nodded and watched as his C.E.O. poured two small glasses and then left a coin next to the bottle. Even in times like these, tradition reigns.

"Despite the slaughter at the Pit," he continued, "Xhaknar doesn't know about the Mantis Guards. Greko led the battle and made sure there were no survivors. So while the bodies may have been bullet riddled, there was nothing to tie them to Südermann.

"Furthermore, while Südermann may be the biggest card Geldish is holding, it's not the only one. He had Karrish assign royal rank, through the Temple, to his riders. By doing this he not only shows them his respect, he creates blood ties between the fringe clans and the Temple. The fringe has long looked for some way to regain stature among the warrens and this will provide them a good start. As you are aware, the Temple is both feared and respected, that's a good place to begin when you are regaining power."

"Why did Xhaknar hunt the BadgeBeth and the rest so relentlessly?"

"The BadgeBeth appear to Xhaknar as scavengers so he lumps them in with vermin. He caught them off guard last time. Now, with much of their strength returned, I believe he will discover he's woefully underestimated them. Their brand was built from an old animal, now long gone as far as I know, called a badger, they were designed to accomplish some amazing things with dirt. That might seem silly to us now, but then it assured them plenty of labor in mining, forestry, and gardening.

"The Succubi are shape changers. Xhaknar fears them simply due to that. They're not true shape changers, of course, they can't become a rock or a table, but they can, by merging their wings with their flesh, take on the form of a maker femme and, by moving around their fatty tissues, they can create genitalia, non-working of course, and appear as a maker mal. Some can even produce a hint of a beard in that form."

"That's always confused me. If the genitalia doesn't work how do they reproduce?"

"They have all they need inside them. There's a testicular sac placed liked a third ovary and they have an ovipositor that extends past the labia when they wish to mate. After that they make love as femmes have been making love to femmes for time immemorial, and three seasons or so later, a baby Succubi appears.

"Add in the fact they can do some parlor tricks with earth and flame just proves to Xhaknar they're freaks who should be eradicated."

He took a sip of the delightful brandy before continuing.

"The Llamia are special. Like the wizards of old, they can control some metallic elements and create flame from nothing. Unlike the wizards, they were bred to be warriors. They are rumored to have other talents too, but I will stick to what I know.

"The Wolfen, now, they present Xhaknar a real problem. They are the warriors he wants the Naradhama to be. Since the Wolfen refuse to serve him and, in fact, will kill themselves as soon as possible if captured, he's never been able to turn their bloodline like he did the Naradhama. He once captured some Wolfen smalls thinking he could turn them. They slew their captors in their sleep and made good their escape. As far as I know they were less than five Full Suns old.

"Unlike the other clans, the Wolfen have no true leader. They do everything by agreement of the pack. Even the ones who prefer the solo life, like R'yune whom you've met, would never hire out to Xhaknar. Their sense of honor is too inbred in them. And that is a good thing. If Xhaknar controlled an army of Wolfen I fear Südermann may have fallen by now."

"What will the Wolfen do now that R'yune's been given royal status?"

"That is an excellent question. The bad answer is no one has any idea. Will they flock to Geldish's side, will they sit this one out, no one knows. Even in the best of times, the Wolfen keep their secrets well. In times like these …"

"I see. Thank you for filling in the gaps in my knowledge. I suppose the only question that remains is what will the Din-La do? Which side will we choose?"

"I think, by not turning Geldish over to the Mayanoren for the reward, you have already made your choice. And, for what it's worth, it is the choice I would have made. And since the choice has been made, we shall keep things simple. We will support Geldish as best we can. And the first way we can do that is by letting him know Xhaknar has recalled all his troops to Anapsida. He is beginning to prepare for his war on Südermann."

"I assume you still have your wireless?"

A few epi-cliks later the message had been sent and confirmed and a messenger was on his way to the home of the haven lords to deliver it personally about the same time they were pouring their second brandy.

The Rangka did not need any devices to talk to each other long range. The same genetic alterations that allowed them to combine their powers when they were wizards allowed them to talk, mind to mind, whenever they wished. Karrish had once found some old scientific journals and discovered Rohta had altered the alpha waves in the wizards' brains to be almost identical to each other. It was probably a safety precaution. If the wizards weren't working out, just release a high energy blast at that frequency and be done with them.

When Xhaknar released his virus on them, it had the unintended side effect of fusing those brain waves in the survivors. Now, whenever one Rangka needed to talk to another, all he had to do was think about it.

Elzish and Makish were doing just that with Geldish this even. They shared their thoughts, their concerns, and what they knew. They were still sharing their minds when the message arrived from the Din-La. Geldish read it so all could share and then asked to be alone. The others respected his request and soon all was silent in his mind.

If Xhaknar believes Geldish, et al, have escaped into the Kordai Sanctuary then that changes some of his strategies. With the Naradhama and the Mayanoren locked up inside Anapsida, he can't continue his thinning campaign. On the other hand, he knows where Xhaknar is going to go, and it's pretty easy to guess when he's going to do it, so that means he can plan some wonderfully malevolent surprises along the way.

Geldish walked into the bathing room, found a small tin of polish, and began shining his skull for the next turn's events.

Lord Südermann is sitting in his throne room and looking at the message he's received from the Din-La. It amazes him for two reasons; first, because it is clearly written and devoid of the usual sycophantic language they prefer and, second, because he didn't pay for it. He supposes, blithely, that the message itself is also amazing. Confirmation Geldish was correct and Xhaknar's preparing to march on his realm is the stuff of horror tales. Even so, he's more amazed by the first two items than anything else. Since nothing need be done before breaklight, he decides to let Elaand sleep. As the Din-La noted, Xhaknar will need time to assemble his troops and, if Geldish is correct, train them in the use of the new weapons.

So there is time.

His six arms are each handling different tasks. From pouring him a brandy with extra sugar to sorting paperwork, it is an act that comes as naturally to him as breathing. His brand had been developed to work in radioactive areas, removing waste and so on without the need for any protective gear. He idly wondered whose bright idea it had been to use cockroach DNA, and how they'd ever managed to mingle it with human, but decided he really didn't care.

Unlike cockroaches, his kind only had one or two smalls at a time. But, like them, he could survive in almost any environment. Still, he was glad the first Lord Südermann had decided to make his home in a verdant forest rather than a blasted wasteland.

His wife, daughter, and three sons were in another part of the palace. Probably sleeping by now. His daughter had passed all the tests and was being groomed to become the next Lord Südermann. He was proud of all of them. He knew they would all do great things to help keep their home safe and secure. His first cousin, for example, had finally discovered a way to make solar panels small enough to be feasible. They were being erected all over the land and supplementing the power grid. Although they were already self sufficient thanks to the hydroelectric plants they'd built on the rivers, it never hurt to have a reliable back up source.

Unnoticed by him, his mandibles were buzzing.

He walked over to the large window at the front of

the palace and stared at the two moons waning in the ebony sky. Long ago, before even Rohta walked and breathed, there had only been one moon.

Südermann knew the story well.

The citizens of Earth, as Arreti had been called then, had been broadcasting messages to the stars announcing their existence. Some feared these messages would invite wild eyed alien invaders to come and do great harm. Some claimed they already had. But, about two centuries after they began sending messages, they got an answer.

The giant ship sailed in past the colonies on Io and Titan, past the great cities of Mars and parked itself in orbit around the Earth. Five small shuttles appeared and the aliens gently entered the atmosphere and headed straight for a building called The United Nations.

Südermann chuckled ruefully at the thought. History had shown the nations were anything but.

Nevertheless, the shuttles landed by the great building and disgorged a total of twenty beings who were clearly not of this world. Over four meters tall, with bright blue skin, and bleach white hair, they did not blend in. They were, nonetheless, bipeds and clearly mammalian. The womyn among them had large, round, breasts.

They called themselves the Sominids.

Their appearance sets off a fascinating debate about the nature of evolution and the structure of the universe.

The Sominids didn't care about any of that. They had come to party.

Oh, they agreed to share some of their technology and to show the brands of Earth how to build great ships and all that but, for the most part, they just wanted to drink and have sex.

Their ship carried over two hundred thousand of their kind and they hit earth's club scene like a tornado. They drank until they couldn't drink any more. They had sex with any who were experimental enough to try (a larger number than Südermann would have guessed) and basically settled themselves in for a nice long stay.

After about fifty Full Suns it was clear they were innocuous. It became known they were the wealthy effete of their world and this was how they spent their long lives. They went from sentient world to sentient world and partied.

Earth's scientists were thrilled to get a list of all the worlds they had visited but the Sominids dismissed scientific curiosity, along with any moral code, as something far beneath them. It wasn't even worthy of their contempt.

After another few Full Suns had passed the Sominids announced they'd discovered signals from another world and were going to head off to the next party. It was decided to have one last bacchanal on the Sominid ship. Two thousand humans were invited aboard and media crews were allowed to cover the event.

About three turns into the party a decision was made. This decision, fueled as it was by alcohol, narcotics, and sleep deprivation, probably seemed like a good idea at the time.

The humans wanted to see how the Sominid's cutting beam worked. The beam was designed for pushing asteroids and other rubble out of their path as they flew between the stars. It was decided to aim it at the moon.

For some reason, the beam was turned on to full strength. It cut through the moon like a hot knife through butter and instantly killed all fifteen thousand residents of Luna City. The remaining forty thousand Lunarians were severely injured. More died before they could be rescued.

Even for the Sominids, that was a mood dampener. Devoid of any ceremony, the party disbanded and the Sominids left without saying another word.

Earth mourned the tragedy for a few Full Suns and then began trying to replicate the Sominid ship. For it to work for humans it would have to be a generational ship.

Even though it could fly close to the speed of light, the nearest planet on the list was over one hundred light years away.

Interest waned and, eventually, the project was scrapped.

Over the next millennia, the population began to seriously decline and the colonies just came home. There was nothing genetically wrong with the humans, it was more like a planetary malaise. The prospect of not being able to tell anyone what they found when they got there, at least not in any timely manner, killed space flight. And the knowledge they'd gone about as far as they could otherwise go stymied any other desires.

Even so, work needed to be done. It was into this world that Edward Q. Rohta, supreme maker, had been born. Enveloped by wealth and bred with an innate curiosity that couldn't be tempered, he was already famous by the time he was a teen. He'd developed a species of, disease free, flies which fertilized the ground wherever they were placed. His father, a corporate lawyer, devised an iron clad contract for his son to use and soon the money was pouring in. His mother, an advertising rep with a major firm designed all the promotions and helped make Rohta Industries, L.L.C. one of the major bio-engineering firms of its time.

Südermann shifted his brandy from his lower left arm to his upper and sipped.

The rest, as they say, is history.

N'leah was restless. She couldn't sleep. She stepped out of her room to go to R'yune and pleasantly surprised to see him, wearing nothing but a robe, coming to her. Since her door was still open they went back there.

As soon as the door closed he let the robe drop and he was pulling hers off as well.

The haven lords, in their wisdom, had placed her bed in the middle of the room so she could spread her wings. She took advantage of that as she fell back and R'yune crawled on top of her.

He spied a vial full of body oil and gently poured some between her buttocks. He began rubbing his fingers up and down the crease until he had one each inside of her, front and back.

She squealed in delight. It had been quite some time since he seemed excited in bed, not that he was ever boring, but he was clearly in the moment now.

Fully aroused he bent her back until her knees touched her ears. Before she could think of anything to say, such as "stop," he plunged into her anus and began pumping.

One part of her brain thought this was slightly silly, if it was a precaution, since no brand could impregnate another. Another part of her brain wondered if he was going to try and fit all of that thing inside her. Still, another part realized she was enjoying herself immensely.

She wrapped her legs behind his neck and dug her spurs into his back. She wasn't sure if she pierced his flesh but neither of them seemed to care. She used the new position to pull him deeper inside of her.

While she was at it, she let her right hand drift down and begin pleasuring herself in rhythm with his thrusts.

With each new plunge, he went just a bit deeper. She found the effect thrilling.

Soon enough she felt him begin to swell inside her. Knowing what was about to happen she ground her hips into his pelvis, yes – he was completely in her now, and she encouraged him to completion.

He exploded inside of her. Her spine compressed, her ribs shook, and her breath disappeared.

She exalted as she felt him deflate and then gently remove himself.

After a few epi-cliks, he made the sign for "shower" and she had to agree.

They walked into the bathing chamber and she adjusted the water to a slightly hot temperature. Not really used to hot water R'yune took a moment to adjust. But he felt his muscles relaxing and decided he liked it.

They both just stood there for a little while. N'leah was absently stroking R'yune's shaft when she was surprised to notice it was coming back to life. She slid to her knees and began licking the tip.

He moaned and leaned back against the shower wall.

She had no allusions about being a sword swallower, and now was not the time or place to learn, but she still managed to get the head of his penis in her mouth and begin sucking.

She spied a bottle of Din-La shampoo and poured some on her hands. With her left hand, she began massaging his testicles and letting a finger penetrate him in the rear. This was a turn for new things for everyone she imagined. Then she used her right to start stroking his shaft.

The harder she gripped the more he moaned. The more he moaned, the faster she stroked.

The result should have been obvious but she was caught completely unaware as he erupted in her mouth. He did so with such force she feared the back of her head might blow off. She was forced to swallow, even though she hadn't intended to. This wasn't Succubus on Succubus sex, after all.

Nevertheless, she found herself enjoying the salty taste of him and noticed her tongue cajoling out every last drop as he fell out of her lips.

They stayed like that as the water splashed over them until he reached down to help her up. It wasn't until then she realized she still had two fingers buried deeply inside him.

They disentangled and she got up.

"Not that I'm complaining, mind you," she said with a grin, "but what brought this on?

He signed. "Soon we will die. I did not want that to happen without you knowing I not only love you, but love every part of you."

He kissed her deeply.

A half a clik later they finally went to bed. She had no idea if they were any cleaner now than when they started. Nor did she care.

Had Xhaknar known about Sominid technology, he would have torn Arreti asunder to get his hands on it. But history was not a subject his makers had been interested in and, truth be told, neither was he. The past was dead, it was the future he sought.

The young slave he'd raped last turn was back in his chamber holding another slip of paper. She was quivering, clearly terrified, but managed to deliver the document without dropping it.

Xhaknar read through its contents and smiled. All of his troops, save the garrisons, were heading back to Anapsida. And, under his strict orders, were not stopping to raid or pillage any of the local communities. He hadn't wanted to waste the time.

He thought about raping the slave again just to take the edge off but decided against it. He needed to focus on the tasks at hand. He dismissed the slave without a thought and summoned his weapons' master.

The Naradhama weapons' master might have had a name, but Xhaknar didn't care. His subjects were defined by their duties, nothing more.

"As you know, lord," began the weapons' master without introduction, "the energy weapons Lord Yontar designed to fight the wizards have proved useless against the other brands. However, we have designed a way for them to serve you still. The beams can be adjusted to cause temporary blindness, nausea, and severe headaches. Such a condition would make your foes easy targets."

Xhaknar's lips curled into the tiniest smile. He motioned for the Naradhama to continue.

"While only effective at up to fifty paces or so, they should still be enough to give your front line troops a distinct advantage. Additionally, we have a sizeable cache of the new guns. We have both long range versions and smaller ones that work in close combat. They require skill to aim properly, but once that skill is acquired, the soldier can kill ten times as many targets, in much shorter time, than he could previously."

Xhaknar's grin widened some more.

"Per your decree, we have built enough of these weapons so each Naradhama and Mayanoren can have one of each and we have a store room filled with spares and parts, in case of any malfunctions. Given that none of your troops have ever worked with weapons like these, it seemed prudent."

Initiative, solely in his service, could be a good thing. But he'd still keep a watchful eye on the Naradhama. It wouldn't do to have them start thinking for themselves.

"When can I see these weapons?" It came out more as a command than a question.

"Immediately great one. We have a firing range set up in the basement of our foundry."

Xhaknar decided now really was as good a time as any and followed the weapons' master out of the room. There was a carriage waiting by the front of the palace, drawn by four deisteeds, that Xhaknar and the weapons' master entered. It took them across the great courtyard to the far end of Anapsida. There they passed three sets of sentries, each more alert than the last, and then went down a long tunnel which led them into a large chamber. There were forges and slaves everywhere.

When the war was over Xhaknar would have the slaves killed, naturally, to protect this secret. Depending on how much of this new initiative the scientists were showing would decide their fate.

They came to a door guarded by two more sentries and exited the carriage. The sentries snapped to attention and opened the door. The first weapon he saw was a long one with two bayonets affixed to its barrel. There was a cartridge hanging near the butt of the weapon. He motioned for his weapons' master to explain.

"The cartridge carries fifteen shots. Instead of having to reload after every kill, the soldier can keep firing until the cartridge is empty. He can easily carry several more cartridges with him into battle. Would you like to try the weapon, lord?"

Xhaknar most certainly did. His first thought was to line up a couple of slaves and see what damage this thing could do. But then he noted the targets at the far end of the room and they were shaped like Rangka. A nice touch, even if it showed more of this initiative stuff he was worried about.

He picked up the weapon and lined up the sight. That was easy enough. Then he pulled the trigger and the jolt almost knocked him off his feet. Nevertheless, he could see a large hole in the faux Rangka and he smiled even wider.

"If you take a deep breath and gently squeeze the trigger, the jolt is far less severe," offered the weapons' master.

Xhaknar took his advice and, in short order, put fourteen more holes in the target.

"In thirty turns I want every Naradhama and Mayanoren of rank to be trained with these weapons. Then they can train the rest."

With that, he strode back to the carriage and began the journey back to his palace. The glorious victory that had so long eluded him would soon be his. And with Südermann gone, all that technology would be his. Then he could begin to finally set this planet right.

The home of the haven lords was a bustle of activity, although you wouldn't have thought so had you been in the lobby. There was one bellhop and one desk clerk and that was it. But had you been able to get into the grand ballroom, you would have been greeted with a sight of almost military precision.

Haven lord waiters and waitresses moved from carts to tables neatly laying out food and drinks for the assembled gentry. Around the room, where the courtiers and those robed, long legged, courtesans sat, the scene was the same. If a chair had a body in it, it got a meal.

Brek had put Geldhish's goldens to good use. Each table was adorned with a small ice sculpture, baskets of varied breads, the finest cutlery that haven lords could offer and a bottle of kelp wine imported from the Fish-People.

The meal was no simple thing either. Seven full courses made from the finest stock the Din-La had to offer. Every dish was an imported delicacy. Brek hoped the meal would remind everyone of the larger picture.

He needn't have worried. As much as everyone was enjoying the feast, every single mind was focused on Geldish's mad quest and how best to make it succeed.

When the meal was finally over, the participants settled into their chairs to await ... something.

Geldish walked to the center of a low stage that had

been erected behind the main seating area. Everyone could see him easily with just a minor shift of position.

"I thank you all for coming," he began, "I was unsure how many of you would attend."

That got an unintended laugh.

"Before we begin, I must share some news I received last even. Xhaknar has recalled all of his Naradhama and Mayanoren troops, except for those posted at garrisons, and appears to be preparing to attack Lord Südermann. We know, thanks to our spies, Xhaknar has rebuilt the old weapons of the makers. It will take him some time to train his troops in their use, but not so much we can sit idly by.

"When he marches out of Anapsida he will have only one choice, he will have to destroy the warrens of the Minotaur and the Fierstans to prevent any force from attacking his rear. It is my guess he will take the time to destroy the Se-Jeants as well. With the entire might of the Naradhama and the Mayanoren concentrated on each warren alone, none will survive."

He paused to take a sip of the delicious wine and continued.

"Even banded together, the warrens would be outnumbered and their brands would assume the status of myth."

"So, you brought us all to feed us your best fineries and then ask us to kill ourselves to save Xhaknar time?" asked Empress ClaalD sarcastically.

This got a rueful laugh.

King Gornd stood up. "Tell me Geldish, now that you've made princes and princesses of some of the fringe, do you expect us to go to war with you?"

"No," he replied softly, "I could not ask that of you after all you've been through. However, the actions decided here this turn will affect you just as much as they will the main warrens. It would be unfair to act without your knowing what was coming."

"Oh," interrupted Queen A'lnuah, "you are attempting to maintain our dignity while asking us to hide like smalls while the grownups go do the real work, is that it?"

This wasn't going exactly as Geldish had planned. He looked over at the Brittle Riders for support and found only amusement in their eyes. So be it.

"Of course not," he rallied, "you are as welcome to die on the field of battle as any of us. Or all of us. This will be bloody work no matter our numbers."

He was about to continue when he heard a commotion at the entrance of the dining hall. At first, he feared it was the Naradhama come to crush the rebellion once and for all. Then he spied the large, furry, creatures resplendent in red robes and smiled.

"Let them in, if you please. The Wolfen have as much right to be here as anyone else."

Six large Wolfen entered the room. Geldish recognized G'rnk, the pack leader, although he hadn't seen him in many Full Suns. What surprised him most was the small contingent of Din-La who accompanied them.

"Greetings dead one," grumbled G'rnk loudly, "it seems the Din-La were late in delivering our invitation. I hope we have not missed anything important."

"Just that we've all agreed to commit suicide," deadpanned Queen A'lnuah, "and one Zanubi of a meal. Make sure to have the staff feed you when we're done. It'll be worth the wait."

The staff of the haven lords quickly found another table and had the Wolfen, and their Din-La guests, seated shortly.

Empress ClaalD addressed the assemblage before Geldish could speak. "Let us all admit we will fight in this coming war. There is no gain to be had by hiding in the hills. Geldish has, for reasons of his own, granted royal status to some of our kin. That gives the fringe blood ties to the warrens, which we have not had in many Full Suns. Not since the Elder Plains' Council fell before Xhaknar. Though these ties be new, they will be honored." She turned to face Geldish directly. "So, dead one, you have us all here, how do you propose we get out alive."

Geldish returned her stare for a moment and then turned to face the throng. "By aligning with Südermann."

That sent a gasp through the room. Finally, G'rnk spoke.

"Isn't that like trading boiling water for flame?"

"No," replied Geldish calmly, "not even close. I know Südermann. While he rabidly protects his domain he has no desire to expand into the Plains. And, when told of the situation here, he sent help. And that help allowed the Minotaurs to defeat the Naradhama at the recent battle of the Pit. To explain all this better, please allow me to present Lieutenant Hlaar and the Royal Mantis Guard of Lord Südermann."

The robed courtesans stood and removed their robes. They were wearing emerald green dress uniforms which glittered with medals and gold trim. They managed to look elegant and deadly all at the same time.

As the initial shock wore off Hlaar walked to the front of the stage.

"On behalf of Lord Südermann, long may he reign, I am here to promise you no fewer than ten thousand Mantis Guards stand ready to assist you. Furthermore, we have brought new weapons which are as good, if not better, than anything being forged in the stench of Anapsida. More importantly for you, we have brought the designs for these weapons, and more, so you can make them yourselves.

"Elder Urnak, of the honored clan of the Minotaur, can attest to their efficacy."

Urnak stood with a large smile on his face.

"Less than ten turns ago, ten thousand Naradhama came to our Pit, intent on its destruction. Not one left alive. In the battle, honored Greko was able to have the stain of treachery removed from his family. The traitor Ek-kh was killed by a Mantis Guard.

"Had any of you told me, even thirty turns ago, something like this could happen, I would have sent for a healer because, clearly, you would have been stricken with a fever. I, and all the leaders of the main warrens, have been promised all Südermann wants is to finally crush Xhaknar and open trade with the Plains. I, for whatever it may be worth, believe him."

With that, he sat down and looked around the room.

Some things are fact, others are faith. The facts were in plain evidence. The Mantis Guard were there, vouched for by one of the most honored leaders on the Plains. Geldish was there, with his Brittle Riders who had caused so much destruction in such a short time. The leaders of all the main warrens and all of the fringe were there and in agreement. Xhaknar must be toppled.

The faith part was the word of a bug monster whose very name sent smalls quivering into a corner.

Well, that was a concern for later. For now, plans must be made.

The various leaders crowded around Hlaar's table and looked at the designs he'd brought. His guards had copies for all of them. G'nrk ignored the plans for the long guns but was fascinated by the smaller weapons. Questions were asked; "How much weight can a Succubus carry in flight?", "How far can a Llamia run and with how much cargo?", "What can a Se-Jeant see others can not?"

And so on. This was no time for furtiveness or timidity.

Each answer was met with more designs and, sometimes, more questions. In the end, some rough alliances had been worked out.

The Llamia would travel north to the land of the Se-Jeant. King Uku, for reasons of his own, seemed thrilled and Empress ClaalD was beaming. There, working with their craft-masters, they would build the weapons they would need. In return, they would help the Se-Jeant assemble whatever they required.

The Succubi would move into the Pit and the BadgeBeth would join the Fierstans, under similar arrangements. Watcher Urkel spent a long time conversing with King Gornd and the two seemed to be hitting it off, unlikely as that should appear. Queen A'lnuah and Elder Urnak were both reserved by nature and seemed to be a good match for the times to come.

G'rnk caught Geldish off guard when he asked to move his clan into the Temple of Azarep, if it still existed, but Geldish readily agreed. If nothing else, they would provide a tremendous defense for the Rangka.

The Mantis Guard would remain in the warrens they were already living in for another thirty turns to ensure there were no problems and then they would return to their homes and report to Lord Südermann.

The excitement in the air was palpable. This mad plan almost seemed to have a chance of success. And if the alleged chance was slim, who cared? Sometimes it's better to do anything rather than accept the way things are.

R'yune went to his room and thought about his pack leader. While the Wolfen had a long history of taking care of their crippled, R'yune had never felt deficient in any way. The fact he couldn't speak was just that; a fact, not a disease.

He'd done well in school and passed all his courses, even the warrior ones, with high marks. He still got treated as though he were missing something vital. His pack talked down to him as if, somehow, the inability to speak made him mentally slow, despite all evidence to the contrary.

Tired of the condescension he'd left the pack just

shy of his eighteenth Full Sun. When certain families of the Naradhama had realized they had access to a true bred Wolfen who couldn't betray their secrets, he found steady work.

Technically he was a hunter. In reality, he was their plaything. He hadn't realized that at first, but he deduced it soon enough. They would hire him to hunt this or that and then bring him along to their parties of gross debaucheries knowing he couldn't tell anyone about them.

He decided he didn't care. They paid him good goldens for their condescension which he took without complaint. More importantly, to him, the game in the western plains, where everything had reverted to its most feral roots, was exciting to kill. And that was what the Naradhama wanted; excitement.

He'd kept a small, simple, room near the outskirts of Anapsida and did all his banking with the Din-La. They'd figured out fast enough he was a mute but not dumb.

He lived like that for twenty turns. He probably would still be there except for the conversation he'd overheard. One of his Naradhama retainers had won a Succubus in a card game. But she had a smart mouth. He'd decided to have her killed that even and be done with her. R'yune had long ago learned, to the Naradhama, mute equaled deaf, so he hadn't bothered to hide.

While he had no idea who this Succubus was, he decided to save her. At least he could do one worthwhile thing with his life. If he worked it right he could rescue her and be back in time for the next breaklight's hunt.

Things didn't exactly go according to plan.

He'd arrived at her room at the exact same time as the assassin. Worse, the assassin had several guards posted in the hall. The fight had been far bloodier than R'yune would have wished, but there was no way of avoiding it if he planned on living too. He yanked her from her room, led her over the bodies, and was almost free of the hall when a small squad of Naradhama entered the other end. They saw the blood, the dead soldiers, the fleeing duo, and pieced it together easily enough.

The chase was on.

They made it past the south walls of Anapsida, without having to kill anyone else, and headed into the Plains. Later, holed up in a cave where R'yune had sequestered some hunting supplies she finally figured out he was mute.

It didn't seem to bother her at all. He remembered her reaching between his legs and asking, "Well, your tongue doesn't work, but does this?"

He knew then he would never leave her side.

Even had fallen several cliks ago and the Brittle Riders were finally settled about Geldish's room. The frippery of the turn had been replaced by their usual loin cloths and weapons' belts. Although those had been thoroughly cleaned by the haven lords and returned to their rooms. Even their weapons had been polished and sharpened.

"Truly this has been a turn of many miracles," spoke BraarB, "seeing Empress ClaalD making nice with Elder Urnak alone was worth the price of this turn, peace treaty or no. But for her to agree to actually move all of the Llamia to the Ice Palace? I know it to be true and still can't believe it."

Geldish smiled. Not in his wildest dreams had he thought this would go as well as it did. The various warrens, after they calmed down, seemed to accept the emissaries of Südermann without so much as a flinch. "Well," Geldish surmised, "warriors recognize warriors."

He was also pleased the leaders of the fringe had accepted the newly royal members of their clans. Although he knew his riders had been peppered with questions, he also saw how proud they looked as they garnered the attentions of their respective leaders.

"This has been a good turn," smiled Geldish, "but we still have much work to do. We must make Xhaknar think we five are his only worries. He thinks us in the Kordai Sanctuary at the moment, hiding from his wrath. We will let him continue to think that is so until the Mantis Guard return to Südermann. Then we will begin harassing the garrisons throughout the realm."

"That's thirty turns from now," pointed out N'leah, "what do we do in the meantime?"

"We will go to the Temple of Azarep. There is plenty of room for you to train and the gardens will be coming into bloom as the Warm Sun nears. Also, with G'rnk and his packs arriving, they could use our help. We will most certainly not be idle.

"Make sure to pack your clothes from this turn and your goldens. You can store them at the Temple and, who knows, we may have need of those fine garments again before this is done."

He was about to dismiss them for the even when there came a knock at the door. Curious, but not alarmed, he opened it to find the inn keeper.

"Greetings dead one, I am Brek, council member of the haven lords. I have come to ask a favor of you."

The eyebrow ridge on his right raised slightly. "What can I do for you honored Brek?"

"The haven lords wish to be given access to these new weapons too. Our kind was shamed when Xhaknar took power. While the Din-La have, at least, made themselves useful, we have been relegated to servitude. For the past ten Full Suns, we have been training, with the help of some Wolfen, a fighting force. It was our intention, once we had enough soldiers, to claim Go-Chi as our own warren. Our force only numbers around a thousand now but the Wolfen say they are ready for combat. Allow us the dignity of fighting alongside the warrens so we may finally be free of our bonds. One way or another."

Every jaw in the room was agape. After he had an epi-clik to assimilate all he'd just heard into some form of context, Geldish nodded.

"Agreed. Since you are already working with the Wolfen, have your warriors report to the Temple of Azarep. I will write the directions down for you. Once there they can align with Pack Leader G'rnk and … well, I guess we'll just figure the rest out as we go."

Shortly thereafter, with directions in hand, a pleased looking Brek took their leave.

"Haven lords fighting? Will miracles never cease?" BraarB couldn't stop shaking her head even after she'd finished speaking.

Sland was more subdued. Barely audible, he whispered "I hope you know what you're doing Geldish. Because I'd hate to die and not be able to tell my smalls about this someturn."

G'rnk lay huddled with his traveling pack partners in front of a small fire. There were beds in the room, but they were more comfortable as they were. They were far from home and going farther. Anything that buried that knowledge, even for a brief time, was welcome.

The great pack had not had a leader since before Xhaknar came. Of course, each small pack had a leader, that was needed, but the great pack, the whole brand, had eschewed the concept as unnecessary. When something came up which affected the whole brand the small pack leaders would meet and decide yay or nay. Once the decision was made it was final.

Even after Xhaknar came they held the tradition. They'd moved from their ancestral homes on the northern plains down to the fringes of the Se-Jeant territories. They rarely intermingled but agreed to protect the other. The great pack had complained bitterly about the move, but they were helpless against Xhaknar without some allies. Like it or not, it was what had to be done.

His thoughts jumped forward to R'yune. The poor mute … no, that's not true. He'd seen him. A prince of the Temple of Azarep. An earned position. Not a position given to the weak. He'd heard the stories of R'yune and his companions and now tried to put them in context.

He remembered R'yune as a cub, of course, since every pack knows its own. He'd done well enough in school, both warrior and regular, but still … but still what? Obviously being a mute had not hampered him in any way. He'd seen him and the Succubus waggling their fingers at each other during the conference. It had taken him a while to realize it was a language. He'd been denied one way of communicating and had simply learned another and moved on.

That is a trait of a strong brand, not a weak one.

He would have to talk to the pack leaders. There was much to reconsider.

Another thing was bothering him as well. The pack leaders were turning to him more and more for advice and leadership. They were trying to make him the tip of their spear. He was not comfortable with that.

He understood it at some level. Each warren and fringe brand had one voice in council. To use any more would cause the offender to dominate or be ignored. Since the Wolfen had no experience in a war like this, his pack would be ignored. That couldn't happen.

But did that mean they needed his voice?

He knew he'd been a good leader for his pack, and

had the respect of the other leaders, but this task they seemed to be thrusting upon him was far beyond anything ever asked of a pack leader before. This task should be borne by all, not one. But he could think of no way to effectively make that work.

Many generations of G'rnk's line had been pack leaders. Even those few who weren't had served the pack honorably. He'd been bred to lead, that he knew, but never something like this. He'd thought, naively in retrospect, the Se-Jeant would say "stand here" or "march there" and the pack could serve the war effort that way. But everyone seemed intent on making each brand an equal. One voice, one vote. He wasn't entirely convinced this idea could, or should, work, but it seemed it was the only way it would.

He snuggled into the pack a little deeper and dreamed uncomfortable dreams.

Ten turns later Xhaknar's spies began telling him of fringe dwellers heading into the warrens and a small band of haven lords headed east to who knew where. This was better than Xhaknar had expected. With all of the scum in one place, he could cleanse the Plains once and for all.

He thought about having the Mayanoren attack the refugees but decided against it. Their time was better spent here learning the new weapons. Besides, if he let the parasites hide in the warrens he didn't have to worry about them being on the Plains and causing, who knows what, kinds of trouble.

More good news came in the absence of news. Not a peep had been heard from Geldish since his last raid over fifteen turns ago. He must be buried deep in the Kordai Sanctuary.

Not that he expected any success, the place was huge and had many hiding places, but he had a couple of spies in the sanctuary just in case. The monks who ran the place had odd notions about personal privacy and respect.

Once he had things completely under his control, he'd deal with idiots like that in short order. For now, they were harmless and too far off the path he intended to take to bother him.

Continuing his good mood, he thought back on last even when his weapons' master had shown him an adaptation on the long range weapons that would allow it to fire an explosive device over five hundred paces with accuracy.

Xhaknar had aimed it out his window at the gate of a shopkeeper who was behind on his taxes. He watched, with glee, as the whole façade went up in flames and, later, burned the shop to the ground.

Yes, things were moving along nicely.

Although not given to sentimentality of any sort, he did wish Yontar could be here. Besides his useful military advice, he would have enjoyed seeing Südermann go down in flames. That had been his fiercest wish when he was alive.

He knew Yontar wasn't completely dead. They had some sort of bond, engineered by their makers, that allowed them to feel what the other felt. In the even, when all was quiet, he could make out images of a horrible, roiling, place and some being trapped in an ever decaying body. He assumed it was Yontar. But he knew of no way to traverse that chasm to bring his comrade back and Yontar seemed to be of no help whatsoever in that regard.

Well, if there was a way out of wherever he was, Yontar would have to find it himself. Xhaknar just had too many things here to worry about first. Maybe someturn, when all this was over, he'd look into it.

Or not. He'd have to see how he felt about it then.

King Uku and Empress ClaalD walked through the forge area and examined the work product of the craft-masters. The Llamia didn't need forges to make metal malleable. They could control it with their minds and their bodies. Uku had heard rumors, but the truth was beyond his wildest expectations. The Se-Jeant would bring them ingots of iron and the Llamia would turn them molten in a matter of an epi-clik. Then they could be poured directly into the molds designed by the Mantis Guards.

One of the guards, his name was Mnaas, oversaw everything with a watchful eye. He looked up and saw his visitors and stood to address them.

"Greetings King Uku and Empress ClaalD, how may I be of service?"

"We were just wondering," said Uku, "if the work was going apace."

"Oh yes, your majesties, everything is coming along ahead of schedule. Your craft-masters are both excellent students and teachers. Thanks to the Llamia, we save over four cliks a turn by not using the forges. Plus their attention to detail is amazing. They catch errors even I have missed. They don't really need me anymore, but I like to feel useful as long as I'm here."

Both royals accepted his compliments warmly, thanked him for his service, and moved on to the training facilities. There they watched as Llamia and Se-Jeant sparred in a variety of fighting styles.

It seemed that warriors from each clan had much to teach the other. Neither royal thought the knowledge and skills would go to waste. With what was coming, they would need every resource they could muster.

If Empress ClaalD was bothered by the sight of her

Llamia being used as steeds, she kept it to herself. Uku watched in wonder as the combination of Se-Jeant and Llamia became a fighting force never before seen on the Plains. With the Llamia firing weapons and the Se-Jeant launching explosives, they became a death dealing tandem never before imagined. He wondered who had first come up with the idea but then decided it didn't matter. What mattered was it worked.

Later they watched as the fighters practiced training with traditional weapons. Either rider or ridden could fire arrows, wield a sword or drive a lance, often both at the same time. The effect was hypnotizing and terrible all at once.

One of the Se-Jeant was knocked from his mount with blood spurting from a wound in his arm. Before Uku could worry the warrior jumped up, laughing, and shook hands with the Llamia who'd brought him down. Then they heard the Patrol Leader signal and demand the warrior seek medical attention so he could fight another turn.

A small part of Uku's mind quailed at the thought they were building such a killing force. He looked at Empress ClaalD and wondered if she felt the same. As if reading his mind, she answered.

"They train for what is to come. They train to defeat a horror from the past, wielded by a fanatic in the present, who wishes to control the future. To do any less than they do would be to admit defeat.

"When Xhaknar and Yontar first came, it was Yontar who discerned the threat we, and the rest of the fringe, would pose were we left to develop. It was he who designed the plan that forced us into hiding all these long Suns. Now Xhaknar seems poised to finish what Yontar started.

"What he does not know is Yontar's efforts forged the survivors into something more than we were before. What little powers we had then are now fully blossomed. By ourselves, we would still have been meaningless. But now, tied again to the main warrens of the Plains, we may yet do some harm."

They watched the training in silence for a while more and then retired to the throne room for the mid-break meal.

Later that even, as ClaalD sat in her chambers, she thought of the events thus far. Thirty turns ago she and her herd were making plans for their extinction. Where there had once been fourteen herds in addition to the herd of the Empress, now there were just three, and they'd all banded together with hers. All the Llamia in the known world were now housed in the Ice Palace. Uku probably suspected as much but had been kind enough to leave it unspoken.

When she'd sent BraarB to meet with Geldish, she'd figured he was going to announce the beginning of the end. The Rangka had been completely hidden since his battle with Yontar. He'd undoubtedly been drained by what he'd done and was now wrapping up the details of his long life to go and meet oblivion. The Llamia, with their last hope gone, would soon follow.

She could have been more wrong, but wasn't sure how.

Not even when she was a young foal, barely walking, had she made a mistake like that. She'd known, naturally, she was the next Empress in line. Her mother, Empress DsaajT, took her every turn, after school, and showed her the ways of her kind. She'd learned the history of her brand, the once proud rank Empress had actually held and how they'd developed the talents they had.

Her mother showed her the papers of the makers, copies of course, that detailed how human's natural magnetic fields had, as in the wizards, been greatly enhanced and how they had been designed to make metal malleable by the use of those fields and some natural acids.

The Llamia were to be used in battle. They could run long distances faster than any human. They could forage off the land without the need of any special gear. They, like all the Gen-O-Pods, had been given powerful immune systems so they could endure injuries that would kill lesser beings. They could rip through any vehicle the humans had and kill the occupants. What the humans hadn't counted on is how well these traits would work and how quickly they'd be used against them.

Her mother and her mother before her and so on, had been terrified by Xhaknar and kept tight reins on their brand. Maybe a little too tight, thought ClaalD. An alliance here or there might have spared them many horrors. But, no use crying over spoilt hay, she had a future to consider.

She'd initially been appalled seeing her citizens ridden like mere steeds in the Se-Jeant training facility. But as she watched, and saw how deadly they were together, much more so than either side could manage alone, she understood. And when she saw her soldiers laughing with theirs, she embraced the concept.

Two had become one.

She wished her mother, long since gone to peaceful fields, were alive to see it. Her last turns above the ground had been dark ones. She saw nothing but doom anywhere she looked. While the destruction of the herds had been devastating, there was hope in this cold place.

She pulled the large blanket she'd been given over her back and realized her future, and the future of her brand, whether bleak or bright, would now be met with friends. Maybe that was enough.

Queen A'lnuah and Elder Urnak were watching their forces train too. On the ground, face to face, the Succubi were an even match with the Minotaur. But, when they took to the air, they could rain death from above. Hlaar took notes from each training session back to his room and brought back plans for even deadlier devices for the Succubi to handle. After making adjustments for weight and efficiency, he pronounced his work done.

He walked with a Succubus over to the royal viewing party. They turned and were stunned by what they saw. The Succubus had a belt carrying twenty small bombs wrapped around her waist, a short gun with a long barrel holstered on her right thigh, and a knife sheathed on her right ankle. But it was the object strapped to her back, between her wings, which held their attention. The barrel was about the same size as her head and protruded about half a head above hers. There was a short wire framed rack containing six balls, which looked like they fit into the barrel, hanging down her back to about her knees. A cord ran from the object on her back to a device in a glove that covered her left hand.

Hlaar smiled. "In the old times, this would have been called a self-loading cannon. We needed to make the charges light enough so the Succubi could fly with them, but deadly enough to cause great damage when they hit their target. Sub-commander Kronlk seems to have a knack for making explosives. He's developed a paste that has ten times the explosive power of gunpowder. Both the cannon balls and the waist bombs contain it. If you'd care to join us, we are going outside to test the final design."

They walked together through the pit, past the astonished looks of everyone they passed, until they got outside. They were not surprised to see many had stopped work and followed them out to see what was going to happen.

The Succubus quickly took to the air and wheeled upwards in a lazy arc. After she got her bearings and balance, she eased higher into the sky and worked through a series of maneuvers to ensure she could control everything.

Suddenly she streaked from the sky, bombs began dropping in precise patterns and then, with a deafening roar, the cannon fired and a boulder larger than twenty Minotaurs was turned to dust.

She wheeled again for a second pass and was even more accurate in her devastation. The onlookers were amazed. She could cause more carnage in an epi-clik than a battalion could in a turn.

With her munitions spent she flew back to where everyone was standing.

"YOU'LL NEED TO MAKE SOME SORT OF EAR PROTECTION," she said very, very, loudly.

Realizing he should have thought of that, Hlaar nodded with an embarrassed look on his face and helped her off with the gear. They were all getting set to return to the Pit when a young Minotaur came walking over with a large sack over his shoulder.

He flipped the sack over to spill out one of Xhaknar's weird little snake-men. The creature was verifiably dead, seeing as how it'd been carved into quarters.

He glanced at Hlaar, "Maybe we should all be a little more careful before we play with our toys outside. This might not have been the only one around."

The Succubus turned, looked confusedly at each of them, and then, finally, asked in her very, very loud voice, "WHAT DID HE SAY?"

Watcher Urkel and King Gornd watched their troops train in the subterranean, dirt packed, lair favored by the Fierstans. While the BadgeBeth were clearly stronger, the Fierstans were faster and had better balance. In the end, they were pretty evenly matched. The Fierstans may have been bred for heavy labor, but the BadgeBeth had been bred to be miners. Although they didn't mine any more, they still preferred to live beneath the ground, with Sland being a rare exception.

They watched as a BadgeBeth got separated from his squad and three Fierstans pounced on his position to deliver the 'killing' stroke. The BadgeBeth flipped away to his right and slapped the ground as he landed. Unexpectedly a huge mound of dirt exploded from the ground and knocked the three Fierstans unconscious.

Nak immediately called a halt to the training and walked over to the fallen soldiers. He motioned for a medic and then turned his attention on the BadgeBeth.

"What in the heck was that trooper?"

"I honestly don't know sir. One moment I was about to be impaled by your guardians and the next I could feel the dirt, in my mind, wanting to explode."

"Can all BadgeBeth do that?"

"Until now, sir, I didn't know any of us could."

Nak looked over at Watcher Urkel and King Gornd to see if they could explain what happened. Gornd made an attempt.

"Many long Suns ago, our brand was bred not only to work with the soil but to be at one with it. The makers wanted us to be intimately aware of our surroundings. It was said a BadgeBeth could tunnel without tools, just using his hands in front of him to move the ground. Supposedly the makers had engineered us so we had the ability to repulse dirt without mechanical aids."

"Sounds like superstitious drivel if you ask me," complained one of the Fierstan warriors.

"Superstitious drivel or not, something just hospitalized three of my best warriors. And I want to know what that something is. Can we repeat it? Can we control it? I need answers, and I need them now."

Despite the order, answers were not immediately forthcoming. But, as the turn wore on they discovered some of the BadgeBeth, when stressed, could repeat the feat. Within three turns those BadgeBeth could create the effect at will.

Within five turns, they had a new weapon and they knew how to use it.

With Fierstan fighting methods welded with BadgeBeth abilities, they soon had a squadron that could use the ground itself to assassinate anyone in their path.

Gornd sat alone in his room sipping the local liqueur the Fierstans made. He'd forgotten its name, but it was the perfect drink to end a turn. Potent enough to ease one into sleep, but not enough to cause headaches when you woke.

He knew exactly what he'd been seeing these last few turns. The perversion of BadgeBeth natural abilities into a weapon concerned him at some fundamental level, but not too much when he thought of what Xhaknar had done to his brand.

When Yontar had needed miners for some scheme or another he'd had the Naradhama raid the BadgeBeth homelands with a fury. King Plarg had demanded he stop and work out an arrangement for the BadgeBeth to be compensated. On that turn, Gornd went from prince of the clan to king in one short sepi-clik.

A horrible battle had broken out and Plarg fell, stabbed from behind. Following his king's, father's, final command Gornd had quickly rallied his citizens and got them to scatter in the countless tunnels and cubbyholes they'd created over the many Full Suns. Yontar, frustrated by the fact he'd only been able to capture thirty or so BadgeBeth – not enough for his needs – killed his captives and left their bodies in the main hall of their warren.

For ten Full Suns after that Gornd had led his brand deeper into the ground and instilled a mild xenophobia. Once they were secure from prying eyes they began to rebuild their world. That may have been an error on his part. Not the rebuilding, the hiding.

Twenty Full Suns after that Sland had stormed out of their world into the lands above and began his journey that, eventually, led him to be a Prince of the Temple of Azarep and led his brand into war, although that was obviously not his intent.

The couple of times he'd met Sland he'd thought him simple. Maybe he was, but there were depths there now that had never shown themselves before.

Gornd, too, had grown since he'd come up from the ground and joined forces with Watcher Urkel and his Fierstans. His brand even more so; no longer afraid, no longer cowering, they felt in control of their destiny.

Much would be different when this war ended. Much else would have to be reconsidered. He thought of calling an aide to write down some ideas and then laughed.

Who was he kidding? In thirty turns they'd all probably be dead. If not? Well, then he certainly had plenty of new retainers who could jot down some simple notes.

Geldish wandered the grounds of the Temple, strolling through a copse of fruit trees. He heard the Wolfen and their haven lord allies training behind the stables. As he came out of the grove he saw his riders working on new skills. Each was taking the time to teach the others what they knew. They'd fought so many skirmishes with the Naradhama and the Mayanoren in such a short span they seemed to be able to read each other's thoughts. While not literally true the bond between them had grown much tighter than he'd expected.

A couple of Kgul were tending to the nytsteeds in the stables and a few of the haven lord retainers were policing the grounds. All in all, it was a tranquil enough setting.

It reminded Geldish of an image he'd seen as a youth of some foreign monastery. Monks in their saffron robes working through fighting forms in the sun.

He continued his laconic stroll heedless of the violence that was being rehearsed around him. He noticed the birds in the trees and reached out his mind to comfort them. He saw a few small animals scurrying beneath the trees and did the same for them. He was completely absorbed in his thoughts and was startled when a Kgul tapped him on the shoulder.

"Forgive me Geldish," it rumbled, "but is it true you are going to raise war on Anapsida?"

"Not Anapsida," corrected Geldish, surprised a Kgul had deigned to speak at all, "just Xhaknar and his armies. The city itself is too well fortified. We need to draw Xhaknar out to have any chance of success."

The Kgul considered that for a while as he walked along beside Geldish.

"Come. I have something to show you no one, not Kgul, has seen."

With that, he stepped off the path and headed towards the rear of the temple. Soon he was opening a massive door Geldish had seen, but the thought was only used to hide storage. After they made the long trek down the staircase and through the three remaining doors, Geldish beheld a sight he would never forget.

Thousands upon thousands of Kgul walking through streets, milling in shops and acting as if this was the most normal thing in the world. Even Karrish had only thought there were, maybe, twenty Kgul left. None of the Rangka had even dreamed of a legion of Kgul. Certainly not living right beneath them.

They walked through the thoroughfares across the underground metropolis until they came to the blacksmith's shop. The Kgul motioned him forward through the rear door and Geldish beheld a well crafted firing range. The Kgul picked up a large gun and turned to Geldish.

"The Kgul will fight too."

With that, he aimed the weapon at the distant target and fired. The center of the target exploded and the Kgul did something Geldish never thought any Kgul could do; it smiled.

"How have you kept all this secret for so long?" Geldish was truly incredulous.

"Not secret. Makish knows. Makish helped."

Geldish ruminated for a while and realized Makish was the perfect choice for something like this. Cautious, careful with his thoughts and preferring to avoid conflict, hiding an entire race without causing a war would be right up his alley.

Geldish staggered at the possibilities.

"How many can you field?"

"Leave young and old, and one thousand chosen by lots in case we all die, fifteen thousand can take the field. All have weapons like these. All will face Xhaknar with you."

Geldish nodded. "I will have to inform the Mantis Guard and the warrens. This is too big a force to keep hidden."

"We knew. We talked. It is what must be done. The time for secrets is now passed. The time for action has come. Tell us what needs to be done, and it will be done."

And that was the end of that. He slotted the weapon into the rack on the wall and began walking out. Geldish followed, his mind a blur as it tried to factor in all the elements he had to work with.

One thing was for sure, come what may, this was going to be one Zanubi of a war.

Lord Südermann sat with his lieutenants in a small chamber next to his throne room. In his army, any rank above lieutenant was a non-combat rank. When they reached that plateau Südermann wanted them teaching, not fighting.

They'd finished reviewing their latest briefing from the warrens. The abilities of the BadgeBeth and the Llamia amazed them. The creativity shown by Hlaar was no less impressive. Südermann had sent him diagrams for ear shields he'd found in the archives. According to Hlaar, they solved the problem nicely.

"What we have," sighed Südermann, "is a lot of fighting potential and no way to meld it into a cohesive whole. Great Rohta certainly has given us the tools to fight this war. Now, are we smart enough to know how to use them?"

That was the question every one of them had been mulling over these last few turns. The Mantis Guard was a true fighting force. Each soldier knew exactly what the soldier next to them would do in any situation. The force developing on the Plains? Not so much so. While they were all experienced in battle, life under Xhaknar would allow no less, they'd never fought together before. And even if the fringe dwellers living in the warrens were developing some cohesion with their new allies, it still did not create a viable army. Neither the Se-Jeant nor the Fierstans nor the Minotaurs had ever trained or fought together and they were going to be leading the charge.

Logistically, it was dreadful

Worse still was the fact Xhaknar's army was a true military force. The Naradhama and the Mayanoren each had clearly defined roles and worked together seamlessly. Facing a well trained, battle hardened, army with nothing but a lot of potential is a good way to see all that potential wiped from the face of Arreti.

Lord Südermann poured snifters of brandy for each of them and sat back to wait for ideas.

Suddenly Elaand saw the answer. "Forgive me, lord," he intoned, "but I believe we may be going about this the wrong way. I say forget trying to make them into one army, leave them as four, with us making a fifth, and assign each army a specific task. Then all we have to do is agree on the goal of each one and let them have at it. Maybe in the future, they can create a true army of the Plains, but, for now, I think this is our only option."

Südermann contemplated this for a while and then chuckled.

"Why not? With five armies coming at him Xhaknar will never be able to focus on a single target. We will need to set up a council. Geldish and his Brittle Riders will lead the troops stationed at the Temple of Azarep. Elder Urnak will lead the Succubi and his Minotaurs. King Uku can lead the Se-Jeant and their new Llamia allies and Watcher Urkel can control these powerful BadgeBeth as well as his Fierstans. That gives them four armies coming from four different directions all with the same, overall, goal. With you leading the fifth …. Yes, Elaand, I believe you have solved our dilemma."

The rest of the meeting went well until Südermann announced the council should be held in the Dweller's Pit.

The lieutenants argued, vehemently, the trip was too dangerous, especially with war coming.

Südermann would hear nothing of it. "My daughter is already well into her training. Should any harm befall me the line will continue. No, the brands of the Plains are putting their faith in us. We are the reason they first found hope. If we make them march here it will seem as though we are commanding them. That is not so and cannot be. We have too much real work to do, to suggest we are the rulers of the Plains. No, this is the only way it can be. We must go to them. Show them we are allies, not conquerors. This is the only way we can build peace when this war is done."

They didn't like it, not even a little bit, but they knew he was right. When the meeting disbanded Elaand began making the arrangements.

Mnaas had ridden hard for two turns to get to the Temple of Azarep from the land of the Se-Jeants. He didn't mind the ceaseless ride or the lack of sleep. The Se-Jeants and the Llamia no longer needed him, except as a figurehead. When word came in Geldish needed to be contacted, he jumped at the chance to do something useful.

He cleared a rise and was astonished to find a fertile pasture with carefully tended groves and babbling brooks. It appeared as though it had been dropped from the sky in the middle of all this waste and he decided Lord Südermann would love this place.

He slowed his steed to a slow trot and spied a large, gray, creature near a gate. He racked his tired brain for a moment and remembered they were called Kgul. Lacking any better plan, he headed towards it.

The creature spotted him and met him half way to the gate.

"Greetings honored Kgul, I am Mnaas from Lord Südermann's Royal Mantis Guard. I have an important message for Geldish from Lord Südermann."

The Kgul seemed to consider that for a moment then turned, grabbing the steed's reins as he did so, and led Mnaas through the gate. Mnaas felt foolish being led like a small on its first steedling ride, but there was nothing he could say or do about it. The Kgul was far larger than he and, according to what little he knew, couldn't be killed. Besides, this one clearly had a destination in mind so he might as well go along for the ride.

A few epi-cliks later he was in a small garden next to the temple. A thin Rangka was levitating and meditating. The Kgul simply pointed and then released the steed and walked away.

"Well," Mnaas decided, "what they lack in loquaciousness, they make up for in efficiency, that's for sure."

Unsure how to proceed, he'd never met a Rangka before, he simply dismounted, slung his pack over his shoulder and waited. The Rangka turned without touching the ground and stared at him.

"You are one of Lord Südermann's Mantis Guards, are you not?"

"Yes, Venerable Rangka, I am Mnaas of the Royal Mantis Guards. If you are Geldish I have come with an important message for you."

Geldish extended his bony feet to the ground, stretched and waved Mnaas forward.

"Come, you look tired and hungry. You can give me this important message over a meal."

They entered the temple through a side door and were greeted immediately by the smells of cooking foods. Mnaas had forgotten how hungry he was. Geldish handed him a glass of spiced water. He'd never tasted anything like it before but found it eminently refreshing. It had a citrusy, cinnamon, flavor. Geldish handed him a small platter filled with cooked meats, cheeses, and fresh fruit and then led him to a table in the corner of the room. Mnaas noticed another, rounder, Rangka across the room who was filling his own platter. He briefly wondered how Rangka processed food and then decided there are some things best left unknown.

He pulled a sheaf from his pack and began.

"Lord Geldish ..."

"I am no lord. Just Geldish will do fine."

Flustered, he began again.

"Geldish, Lord Südermann is coming to the Plains in eight turns from now. He has ordered all Mantis Guards already at the warrens to maintain their residencies there and to prepare for his arrival. He will make his temporary base at the Pit of the Minotaurs. He requests you and your Brittle Riders meet him, and leaders of the other warrens, at that time and place."

Geldish considered this and nodded. "I will need to bring three others Lord Südermann doesn't know about but that should not cause any problems. Do you know the nature of this meeting?"

"Not fully. I know that it is to be a council of war. From what I understand he was trying to figure out how to best disseminate the various armies that have sprung up into one cohesive unit. It seems he now has a plan and wishes to discuss it."

Geldish pondered a bit before responding. "This is the same problem that was vexing my meditations. If Lord Südermann has an answer, I would be most anxious to hear it." He got up from the table and grabbed a pitcher of the spiced water and refilled Mnaas' glass. "Stay here for the turn. Your steed is already in the stable by now and our groomers are the best in the Plains, so it will be well cared for. You can leave at breaklight and let Lord Südermann know I will be there."

Mnaas paused and then pulled a box out of his pack. "Meaning no offense Geldish, but this is called a radio, you can let him know yourself. My orders are simply to accompany you to the Pit should you decide to go or to return to the Ice Palace should you not."

Geldish knew of radios, of course, and knew the Din-La had a version, but since Rangka didn't need them he'd never actually touched one before. Mnaas gave him some quick, and easy, instructions and Geldish opened a channel. Elaand responded to him and, in short order, all the preparations were confirmed.

"We could coordinate all the armies with just a few of these," noted Geldish, "does Lord Südermann have any more?"

If Mnaas had any inkling what a face/palm was he would have done it right then and there. He and the other Guards took their technology for granted. They carried it with them at all times. But the Plains had been under harsh rule, innovation had been crushed, progress banned, if not by decree then by example. He quickly spun the radio around and contacted Elaand again.

Elaand made a noise like a stuck kgum, his way of admitting he, too, had missed this obvious fact and quickly made arrangements to set things right. When Lord Südermann arrived his Guards would be carrying enough radios for all the warrens and their leaders.

The weapons' master surveyed the forges and the

slaves who tended them. The weapons would start out as raw frames at one end of the room and then pass from slave to slave as each part was added. When it got to the other side, it was a complete weapon, ready for use. Yontar had designed the system many Full Suns ago and the weapons' master still preferred it. This way the slaves didn't have to be taught any crafts. They just had their assigned, moronic, duties and that was that. A kgum could do their jobs.

He wandered over to the growing stockpile and realized he'd need more storage space sooner rather than later. There were plenty of raw materials in the transport yard, he would just need to assign some slaves to build a few more sheds.

He saw the slave master at the end of the line so he walked over and explained what needed to be done.

The slave master barked out some orders and, soon enough, twenty slaves were headed out the door to begin building more sheds.

The weapons' master smiled. He liked efficiency.

That taken care of he let his mind wander. He remembered the first time he'd faced Fierstans in battle. He was shocked to see a race that looked so much like him.

Well, similar but not the same.

Instead of the comfortable gray and brown skin that allowed them to blend so easily with the terrain, the Fierstans were dark red with patches of black around their eyes. The Fierstans were also a little bit taller. They fought differently too, not of one mind like the Naradhama. While they would attack in tight formations, if the battle shifted they could break off and fight in smaller groups or even individually. Given the amount of damage they'd caused, there might be something to that style.

The weapons' master quickly dismissed the thought. If Lord Xhaknar had found any use in the Fierstan style he would have implemented it long ago.

The weapons' master then went over to the training facility and watched as the ranked Naradhama were learning to use the new weapons. They had taken to them quickly enough and were now quite deadly.

He felt nothing akin to personal pride for his part in this, that trait had been bred out by Yontar and Xhaknar long ago, though he did not know that, but he did feel a certain satisfaction in knowing he was helping the greatest army the world ever knew achieve its master's ultimate goal.

The Naradhama were in close formation, one solid line behind another. They were staggered so the second line could fire through the first. It allowed them to lay down a killing zone while the third line launched the explosive missiles. Every Naradhama of rank had learned each position and each weapon. In a couple of turns, they would be ready to train the main body of troops by themselves.

He watched as the training master barked out orders and found flaws he couldn't see. Of course, were this a real battle, the training master would be killed for talking to the ranked Naradhama like that. When all was said and done, he might be anyway. But, these were special times and everyone knew the greater good must be served, no matter the personal cost in humility.

Yontar drifted through the venomous ether and assessed his situation. That damnable Rangka had boxed him in as surely as a herder did with an infant kgum. The closer he ventured towards the edge of the domain, the more his body ripped apart and his mind ceased to function. When he retreated, the body would heal and his mind would clear.

It was like rolling a boulder up a mountain only to have it roll back down just as you neared the summit. He considered the analogy briefly and debated whether or not it was original. He decided it was and put it behind him.

Even if he did somehow pass the barrier, there was no body for him to inhabit. His infrequent visits to Xhaknar's mind had shown him his own, very public, cremation.

It had been a wonderful funeral, full of pageantry and decorum with weeping slaves and an orgy in his honor, but it still severely limited his options as far as attaining any corporeal form.

Seeing no way out directly, he put his mind to the task of looking at alternatives.

The fact he could contact Xhaknar niggled at the back of his mind. Why him and no others? What had the makers done for them they hadn't done for anyone else?

And was there any use to the knowledge even if he figured it out?

He thought of something else too. He could sense his location relative to the world he had known. He had, out of habit more than anything else, stayed near Anapsida. But he did not seem bound by any terrestrial boundaries. He slipped through the ether to the north and then headed west. Not with any destination in mind but just to see if there was anything that would stop him.

He couldn't make out any details of his former world, but he sensed vague outlines and larger geographic landmarks. He passed over the Kordai Sanctuary. He wondered why he'd never turned that blithering bastion of individuality into slag. He guessed it was because he always had something more important to do.

Now he had plenty of time and not the means.

More frustration courtesy of that noxious Rangka.

He felt something tugging at him and decided, since he obviously had nothing better to do, to allow it to drag him along.

Soon he found himself over the old bunkers of the makers. He couldn't see any specifics, but he knew this place almost as well as he knew the back of his hands. His first ten Full Suns had been spent training here before the war of the Gen-O-Pods. Then even longer as he and Xhaknar assembled their first army.

So what was calling him here?

He let his mind roam freely. There was something here; he just had to figure out what it was and how to use it.

G'rnk sat with Brek in the room he'd been given by the Rangka as a headquarters. One advantage to having a haven lord on his staff was anything he needed, he got. And it was always of the best quality. There were two Din-La with them as well. Kssp and Tffl were their names, although G'rnk was still having trouble telling them apart. They dressed the same, talked the same, and even walked the same.

He supposed it didn't really matter. It just irritated him that Brek seemed to have no such problem.

His pack had taken the unprecedented step of naming him as their sole representative for the war. He understood the concept, they needed a single voice in any council, but he was uncomfortable working without the guiding voices of his brethren. He had decided to allow himself to be the token leader for any meetings with the other warrens but still discussed every option with the pack. That was not a perfect solution for him, but it was working well enough thus far.

One of the Din-La spoke. "We have spoken with Geldish. We will accompany you to the meeting with Lord Südermann. We have no say in a war council, of course, but we can relay information to our clan and make sure all your needs are met."

G'rnk wondered how they did that. They seemed to communicate all over the Plains in mere sepi-cliks. Well, it was their secret, not his, and they were trying to help. He decided not to press the issue.

The Din-La had laid out a spread of several delicacies and two flagons of Whævin. It was the finest vintage G'rnk had ever tasted and he told them so as he thanked them. Of course, having been raised on pit food, he didn't have much to compare it with.

He silently toasted his companions and considered what was to come. The haven lord warriors were as good as advertised and they had been easily assimilated into the Wolfen ranks. The Kgul, of all beings, had surprised them with a cache of weapons and enough ammunition to fight twenty wars.

Wolfen were used to firing cross bows so these new weapons were merely an extension of that. They took to them readily enough. Many of the warriors decided to carry both into battle. That was fine with him.

Brek was absently nibbling on the tray the Din-La had served. He finally saw hope for his kind. No more to be haven lords, but to have a true name assigned to them and to be equal to the warrens. It was the greatest, and longest, dream of his kind.

The Din-La, inscrutable as always, kept their thoughts to themselves.

G'rnk rose from behind his desk and looked at the battle plans his pack had devised. There'd been much debate as to how to incorporate the Kgul, but it was finally agreed there just wasn't time. The Kgul would march beside them and have to fend for themselves when war finally came.

Given what little he knew about those strange, quiet, creatures, he somehow supposed that would be enough.

Upon finding out there was a Kgul army beneath their feet, the Din-La had become apoplectic. They ran to their rooms and didn't come out for a full three cliks. When they reemerged, they seemed satisfied. Four turns later many wagons had shown up with odd looking vests. They weren't armored, but the Kgul seemed to love them. G'rnk had felt one when a Kgul was wearing it and found it slightly hot to the touch. Maybe the Kgul got cold easily? He didn't know.

But if those, heavily armed, gentle giants wanted something to keep them warm while they battled, it was of little consequence to him.

He realized everyone was staring at him looking at the plans.

"We leave at breaklight for the meeting with Lord Südermann. The training here is going well and I have no concerns about leaving the pack now. There is little more we can do, except drill the lessons home, until we march. And that can be done by the commanders.

"We seem to have far more resources than I would ever have imagined possible. Hopefully, that will continue throughout this campaign."

"That will not be a problem" replied Brek as the Din-La chuckled, "between the goldens Geldish gave me when this was all beginning to the ones we haven lords had saved for just this emergency, we can pretty much get whatever we want at any time."

"Plus," chimed in Kssp, though G'rnk wasn't sure about that, "we are providing anything we can at cost. Our profit will be our freedom. No more to see my brothers and sisters hanging in Xhaknar's fountain."

G'rnk thought about that and figured they'd be fine.

There was a knock at the door and Mnaas walked in. The strange bug-like creature had proved invaluable. His knowledge of tactics and weaponry had advanced their training in geometric proportions. If his appearance still bothered G'rnk on some visceral level, he did his best not to let it show.

"Greetings to you all," began the Guard, "I've come

to tell you the Kgul have finished packing the kgums for our trek to the Pit. Also to let you know Lord Südermann is looking forward to meeting each of you, so please allow time after the meeting to greet him."

It was said pleasantly enough, but G'rnk knew a command when he heard one.

"Further," continued Mnaas, "I wish you to know, while it has been my honor to serve with you, I will be returning to the lands of Lord Südermann to take my formal place in the Guard after the council. I do not know if I will be replaced here or not."

"It has been an honor, and a pleasure, getting to know you," stated Brek, "your help has proved to be useful. I do not know if we will win the turn, but I do know we now have a chance."

Sometimes a glorious speech isn't required to make the heart pump a little faster. Sometimes the simple truth is enough.

The Din-La poured another round of Whævin and the odd assemblage, an impossible assemblage less than a Full Sun ago, sipped their drinka and contemplated their fates.

King Uku and Empress ClaalD sat in Uku's throne room. Llamias, being bred of heartier stock, seemed to enjoy the cold more than any other allies Uku had met; she never wore more than her shawl of rank. They sipped cups of ice wine and nibbled on a tray of snacks Uku had ordered.

Empress ClaalD was unsure what some of the dark meats were, but

found them delightful. Wonderfully spicy and with

a rich, smoky flavor. When this was all over she would ask Uku for the recipe.

She found it enjoyable to be in the company of brands unlike herself, and that surprised her. King Uku was pleasant and witty and kept a fine hearth. After so many long Suns hiding her kind in the wild, she thought it might be nice to have a real home. A place there the Llamia could grow and prosper.

The preparations for the coming battle were coming along as well as could be hoped. Next breaklight they would begin their trek to the Pit of the Minotaurs. Although that would get them there early, King Uku had argued he'd rather camp for a turn or two outside the Pit than be late. She'd had to agree. Fearing the open plains for as long as they had, made Llamias sticklers for schedules. Had she had her way they would have only been on the move long enough to show up at the appointed sepi-clik and not one moment more.

Since Mnaas had left Klaat had taken his place. It had surprised her to realize the Mantis Guard was a femme. She didn't have a valid reason why, but it did. Nevertheless, Klaat had shown the same ability to keep things moving along as Mnaas had and the work continued without interruption. King Uku had wondered if the Mantis Guards were all from the same egg, the way they worked together. While a discussion with Mnaas, during a quiet conversation one even, had assured her they were born the same way as everyone else, she knew what Uku meant. They were expertly trained. No wasted movements, no idle actions. When something needed to be done, they found the best way to do it and then did it.

Her own general, KnaaR, who barely came up to her shoulder, though he was older than she by three Suns, had remarked he wished they'd run into the Guard Suns ago since the troops were already far advanced of what he'd hoped now they were being tutored by these professionals.

General? When had that happened? Someturn they'd gone from being hunted to being hunters. She sighed deeply. While she had no wish to be prey, that didn't mean she relished war either. Sadly, there was nothing that could be done about it. Xhaknar had started all of this, but they would stop it or die in the attempt.

King Uku seemed to read her thoughts.

"War is never a welcome thing, is it? For all the glory and the songs and the poems and the fables, on the real field of battle, there is nothing but blood and pain." He shifted to look at her directly. "When I was young, we battled a Mayanoren raiding party at the Lake of the Dead. We were just recruits then, on a march to prove to our commander we knew how to put one foot in front of the other without causing injury to anyone.

"We carried our weapons and our packs and nothing more. We came through a covered pass and walked right into them. There was nowhere to run. They attacked and we stood our ground. I remember our commander, Oro was his name, barking out orders and swinging his blade. It never occurred to us to question those orders, we just cut blindly forward. Coming where he said come and going where he said go. When it all was over, fifteen of my mates lay dead, but so did all thirty Mayanoren. Oro was injured, but not badly. He had us make litters for the fallen and sent a runner ahead to let King Ibi know what had happened and request reinforcements, just in case.

"When the litters were finished Oro came around and checked each of us for injuries. He said battle sometimes makes you blind to them. It was then he noticed I was missing a finger. When he pointed it out I didn't know what to say. I was afraid he would yell at me or give me a demerit. So, I said the only thing I could think of, 'I'm sorry sir, but it's only a little one and I won't let it happen again.'"

They both laughed. It was then she finally noticed the second finger was missing on his left hand. Odd she hadn't seen it before. It was also then she noticed his skin held several scars. No whimpering royal he, then, this was a king who led in battle. The kind of king they'd need for the times ahead.

The conversation with Empress ClaalD had gotten him to thinking. King Ibi had been a great king. He'd kept their warren safe and prosperous, he'd kept taxes as low as he dared and made sure trade was unencumbered. His predecessor, King Epe, had been competent enough but lacked the vision and skills of Ibi. When Ibi had reached his one hundred and thirtieth Full Sun he'd announced it was time for the warren to select a new king. That was the way of his brand, so the search was put into effect.

Per tradition, ten candidates had been culled. Five from the military and five from the local population. None were allowed to speak on their own behalf. Their resumes were posted along with one paragraph written by the King's staff stating why each candidate was worthy. Uku had been a colonel then and had served in many campaigns. He'd been honored just to be considered and never gave it another thought.

A warren meeting was held and residents were allowed to voice their concerns regarding, or their support for, each candidate. Since, as was their way, the candidates were not allowed to be present, Uku did not find out until much later what had been said. Several of his troops had stood up and spoken well of him.

A little too well as it turned out.

Uku was elected on the first ballot with fifty-nine percent of the warren selecting him.

No longer Colonel Uku of the Palace Guard, he was

King Uku, absolute ruler of the Se-Jeants. He would serve until he retired or died. He was only forty-eight Full Suns old at the time and the warren looked for a long reign. He, on the other hand, feared he'd drop dead from fright before he was crowned.

Thankfully King Ibi had stayed for one Full Sun teaching him the ins and outs of being a king. Then he'd retired to a small villa he'd had built outside the northern wall and left Uku in charge.

That had been forty-three Full Suns ago. He was still young and vital and hoped he was doing a good job. So far it seemed he had. Trade was good, the military was a little stronger since he took over and there weren't even the slightest hints of a recall, something that had only happened once in the history of the warren.

Things were as stable as they could be under the rule of Xhaknar. Now he was going to risk all that for the slim chance of ending the terrors his brand faced from the thinning pogroms and the raids of the villages, among everything else.

And he was a smart enough king to know the chance was slim indeed.

May Rohta forgive him if he failed.

Elder Urnak handed Queen A'lnuah a steaming cup of korlnak. It was a Minotaur delicacy, but an acquired taste for everyone else. She sipped it, bemused by the twists fate had taken. Barely more than thirty turns ago, her kind was hiding from extinction, now, here they were, girding for a battle the likes of which the Plains had never seen.

For the last several turns she and Urnak had watched as the Succubi trained with their new weapons and listened, as patiently as possible, as Krolnk had described how each one worked. Hlaar had blunted some of that by taking Krolnk with him on scouting missions. Hlaar had samples of Naradhama battle strategies so they would train by having half the Minotaurs pretend to be Naradhama and the other half attack them. The results showed that, as long as the Naradhama continued to be Naradhama, they stood a good chance.

Time would tell.

Her Succubi amazed her. They had turned into a lethal force from the air. As Kronlk noted once, "They rained Zanubi from the clouds."

As Urnak sat quietly, reviewing some notes, she thought about the Pit she was in. It was more accurately a labyrinth. It stretched for kays in all directions under the ground. There were probably as many Minotaur as there were Naradhama soldiers. But, when one discounted the smalls, the old, the lame and those who needed to stay behind for whatever reason, she guessed they would march about a quarter to a third of that into battle.

Nevertheless, in the center of the labyrinth stood the crest of a dormant volcano. The lava burbled and bubbled, but never seemed to pose any threat. The Minotaurs used it as a source of heat and power. While they didn't have the technology Lord Südermann seemed to have, they'd still done well for themselves. They had carefully secured the location by leaving only one public entrance, and it several kays off to the north, and by keeping lookouts on the roof of the warren. Since they had naught but open lands around them they could get word of any approaching party and deal with it accordingly. That was how the young Minotaur had found the spy.

He'd seen the ground moving where the creature had been tunneling and simply followed it until it tried to break ground. What happened next was obvious enough by the contents of the sack.

Urnak put away his papers and turned to her.

"In a few turns, our home will be home to the war. The alliances and decisions made here will seal the fate of the Plains, for good or ill. That is a heavy burden to bear."

"Truth," replied Queen A'lnuah, "but you are not bearing it alone. Every king and fringe lord of the Plains bears it with you. And, now, it seems Lord Südermann has agreed to carry some of the weight himself."

She paused for a moment and realized she liked korlnak. The thought made her smile.

"One thing does concern me, though," she continued, "I have only heard terrible rumors about Lord Südermann. While his actions of late would seem to make him less a demon than we feared, I still wonder what he'll be like, in all his glory, as it were."

Urnak laughed.

"I think we need not see him in his all, fully clothed will be enough for me to handle."

A'lnuah laughed as well. She hadn't caught the second meaning in her remark.

They sat quietly for a while more.

"Xhaknar's got no idea what we have planned for him, does he?" Urnak didn't seem to need an answer, but he got one anyway.

"No. But, then again, neither do we."

Queen A'lnuah, supreme leader of the roosts of the Succubi, sat troubled in her sleeping-room, wearing nothing but her somnolent robe. Elder Urnak had ordered a divan for her that allowed her to sleep comfortably and stay in the main castle if that was the right word for a building within a structure. She decided she not only liked the old Minotaur, not that old by Minotaur standards, but she respected him as well. That still didn't ease her mind.

She hadn't been flippant with the Elder. They really had no idea what they were going to do. Yes, they were assembling a mighty fighting force and, yes, her Succubi seemed to be learning the new tactics well, but they were just a buzzing insect compared to the might of Anapsida.

She sighed and poured another cup of korlnak. The strange drink had become a balm, of sorts, for her soul.

Her mind wandered back to when she was a young princess, one of three available to become Queen if they survived the rights of passage. But there were no trials troubling her then, just the need to pull a prank or two on her classmates.

Something she'd been quite good at in her time. The Succubi and the Llamia were the only two brands she knew of that had different skin colors within their brands. Her teacher had explained how Great Rohta's many spouses had represented many shades of the human species, ranging from dark brown to white. She'd taken that knowledge to heart and had put dye in the showers the young Succubi used after sports.

The dyes hadn't worked so well on the darker Succubi but the lighter skinned ones came out in a wonderful variety of hues. She'd laughed and laughed and laughed and, even knowing discipline was coming, laughed some more.

Her bottom still stung when she thought about the arrival of that discipline. Then, unable to help herself, she laughed out loud again. Of course, she was Queen now, there was no one who would dare to stripe her mischievous little bottom with a switch.

Thinking about her youth helped calm her some more. Then she realized, while all of the Succubi from the roosts were with her, many still lived in the northern villages. Should they not survive this coming war her kind should live on. That was some comfort.

She called her consort, P'marna, and prepared to

order a light meal.

When she came in she saw her Queen smiling and said: "Things must be going well with the war effort my Queen."

A'lnuah blanched for a sepi-clik and then smiled anew.

"Yes, as well as can be expected, but I was just wandering through my memories to the turns when I seemed more destined for trouble than the throne."

She laughed again and told P'marna of her prank. They both laughed this time and it took them a bit to settle down.

"I would guess, P'marna, we all have some fond memories of our innocent turns."

P'marna became uncomfortable as she realized her Queen was asking her to share a memory too. She shrugged inwardly, figuring they may not see too many more turns together anyway and told her of N'leah. Not the graphic, physical, details, of course, those she kept in the tabernacle of her mind, but enough for the Queen to understand.

To her astonishment, her Queen smiled and put a hand on her shoulder.

"If we see the breaklight after the war, we will ask N'leah to come stay with us. I see no reason you shouldn't be happy too. She will have duties for the temple, to be sure, but it would still give you more time together than you have now. And, who knows, you might learn to smile again. You're an awfully doughty little thing at times."

P'marna blushed deeply, then did grace her Queen with the warmest smile she'd ever seen as she took her order and headed for the kitchens.

Watcher Urkel and King Gornd watched over the preparations for the next turn's trek. Nak was dealing with the details and nothing seemed amiss. Two kgum were laden with provisions. Far more than they'd need, but it never hurt to be prepared. It was decided, with the thirty Mantis Guards accompanying them, they'd take only thirty of their own warriors for security. Without having to be told, Nak had assigned fifteen BadgeBeth and fifteen Fierstans to the patrol.

On the return trip, there would be 90 Mantis Guards who would stay with them until they reached the Fierstan city and then they would continue on to the realm of Lord Südermann. Plus whatever guard Südermann brought along in the first place. Unless they got attacked by a couple of Naradhama battalions, they should be safe.

The remaining warriors would continue training under the tutelage of Nak's lieutenant, Teg. It was he who'd been devising strategies to use the BadgeBeth abilities, and the troops liked and respected him. Not that Urkel or Gornd cared about him being liked, soldiers did what they were told or they weren't soldiers anymore, but it did seem to make things go smoother.

Teg had also hit it off with several of the Mantis Guards, he seemed to have an innate ability to work well with others, no matter how unusual the situation.

They walked away from the staging area and headed towards Watcher Urkel's private chambers. It had become something of a tradition, each even, for them to sit quietly, chat when they felt like it and sip ice wine. Two more divergent personalities you couldn't find; Gornd was loud and brash like most BadgeBeth and Urkel was a reserved aristocrat. But they'd grown close. Whether it was because each recognized the warrior in the other or because each filled a void of personality the other lacked, none could say. What was clear was these two would be friends long after the war, assuming they survived.

Nak and Zarn, the BadgeBeth who'd first

discovered his latent abilities, blocked their way.

"Great Kings," they piped simultaneously.

And that was something new, too. It was not an honorific either Urkel or Gornd had asked for, or even encouraged, but it seemed it was what they were going to get called anyway. It was the soldiers' way of acknowledging they would respect and obey both leaders even though neither truly led them all.

"Great Kings," continued Nak, "the preparations for the journey are complete and the first shift's training is over. We would like to humbly request the troops be given the even off to enjoy some ice wine, the hospitality of some of the servants and to dance the Aklop in celebration of all we've accomplished thus far."

Urkel and Gornd looked at each other. It was a good idea. They'd been pushing two training shifts per turn once they'd discovered what the BadgeBeth could do. The troops were frazzled. An even of fun would do wonders for their morale and their focus.

The Great Kings nodded in agreement.

Zarn looked like he was about to hug them but quickly regained his composure. He and Nak ran off to the barracks to inform the troops and make any arrangements not yet made.

As Urkel watched them leave he realized it was not just he and Gornd who were becoming fast friends. That was good. War should bring hope as well as destruction.

They were going to be traveling light. Geldish approved. There was no need for a mighty caravan for what amounted to a walk across safe ground. It was to be him, his riders, Mnaas, G'rnk, Brek, a Kgul, two Din-La, two kgums with provisions, and five Wolfen and five haven lord soldiers as his escort. That was more than enough. With BraarB in the middle, Geldish and Sland to her left and R'yune and N'leah on her right, they led the others past the gate and on the road to the Dweller's Pit. The escort soon formed a phalanx of sorts on either side of them, which left everyone else riding in the middle.

Geldish looked behind him and laughed. If this wasn't the strangest group ever to be called emissaries, he didn't know what was. They rode under the growing sun and enjoyed its warmth. The Dark Sun was near an end and plants were starting to sprout and small animals were seen more readily as they scurried about looking for food and mates.

Mnaas slid his steed between Geldish and Sland as easily as could be, forcing Geldish to admire, again, the brand's many warrior skills.

"This land was beautiful once," Mnaas smiled, "I have seen pictures of it in Lord Südermann's library."

"I can see pictures in my head," replied Geldish, "I was alive before Xhaknar came."

"So I'd heard. Still, it would be nice to make this land luxuriant again. It would make life easier for the citizens of the Plains."

"True enough. They did not ask for war or for hardship. All they want, all most intelligent beings want, is a roof over their heads, food on the table, a place to worship their gods, and the chance to earn an honest living."

Mnaas pondered that and then nodded. They rode on like that, quietly trying to imagine what was once here and what could be again once Xhaknar was gone.

N'leah leaned in towards BraarB and whispered something, probably a dirty joke thought Geldish, which caused her to flush red and then burst into giggles. Geldish was constantly amazed by the estrogen enhanced of any brand. No matter how tough, no matter how sure, there was a core to them that forever retained the joys of a small. He sometimes wished he knew how to do that.

The turn passed lazily as they kept a steady pace. Canteens of spiced water were passed around, tales were told, songs were sung and, all in all, it was a pastoral day. Around even-fall, Mnaas consulted his map and announced there was a decent sized brook over the next rise and that would be a good place to make camp.

What happened next can be ascribed to luck.

Of the pure and dumb variety.

Mnaas was right. It was an ideal place to make camp. That was why a group of forty, steed riding, Mayanoren garrison soldiers, rotating from one garrison to another per Xhaknar's orders to prevent complacency, had selected it as well.

Geldish immediately assessed the situation and, while cursing himself for arrogance and sloppiness, realized there was no way this group could outrun that one. There was nothing else to do but fight.

And if you're going to fight, fight to the death.

He signaled the Wolfen squad leader just as the Mayanoren cavalry began a mad dash up the hill. He glanced at Mnaas who shrugged, as if this sort of thing happened every turn and twice on feast turns, and ordered the charge.

Two things became apparent immediately. One, Xhaknar had not gotten around to issuing guns to his garrison troops and, two, garrison troops were a distinct cut below what the Brittle Riders were used to facing.

They slashed through the Mayanoren with BraarB and the nytsteeds leading the charge. On their first pass over half the Mayanoren lay dead or dying. The Din-La, of all brands, were nice enough to deal with those lucky few who ended up in the latter category by slitting their throats.

Geldish and Mnaas reined up. They watched as the riders spun around and took out every remaining Mayanoren on the left flank while the Wolfen and haven lord warriors descended on their right. Less than an epi-clik later it was done. Mnaas could do nothing but shake his head in awe.

The Din-La were walking through the offal and body parts making sure nothing was overlooked. Every now and then one would yell "FOUND ONE!" and everyone would hear the sound of a throat being slit.

One Wolfen soldier had received a superficial knife wound, which a Kgul quickly, but expertly, patched up. Other than that minor wound they hadn't suffered a single casualty. At least not on their side, the Mayanoren were obliterated.

The Wolfen and haven lords, well trained now, hurriedly scavenged any weapons from the dead, retrieved the surviving steeds and their provisions and then stacked the bodies near the top of the rise, which was where most of them fell. Then they poured an accelerant on them and lit them on fire.

Amid the smell of burning bodies and the sounds of bones exploding from the heat, BraarB walked up to Geldish.

"Well, we spent so much time and energy clearing out the trash, we may as well camp here."

So they did.

King Uku and Empress ClaalD led the procession, consisting of fifteen Llamia, fifteen Se-Jeant on deisteeds, thirty heavily robed Mantis Guards, also riding deisteeds, and four kgum laden with supplies out of the ice palace. They set a leisurely, but steady, pace as they headed for the Dweller's Pit. Were it not for the many swords and lances in view one could easily have mistaken this for a romp to a picnic.

Since Uku had received enough surprises in his life, he'd sent scouts ahead of them with orders to report back every clik but to return immediately if they spotted any danger.

The air was brisk and dry and it was clear to Empress ClaalD the season was turning yet again. Maybe that was a good omen, though her kind put little stock in talismans or omens. Besides her royal belt, which distinguished her rank when she wasn't wearing the formal breast plate, the only other jewelry she wore was a necklace given her by King Uku. It was a beautiful piece. Copper and brass blended together to make a magnificent swirl with a simple, but large, emerald in the middle. It was tasteful and elegant. She had given him a silver bracelet, about half a hand span wide, embedded with blue diamonds, which had been designed by a Llamia craft-master. While Uku was admiring it, the craft-master made the linkage malleable and sealed it permanently to Uku's wrist. As he felt the metal harden he said it would be as permanent as their friendship.

Cautious royalty or not, she believed every syllable.

The scouts came back regularly to report nothing was in their path. They enjoyed the weather and each other's company and let a feeling of bonhomie wash over them.

One scout reported she'd seen a Mayanoren garrison patrol about three kays to the west and heading north. Since it was highly unlikely they would be spotted and they were headed in opposite directions, Uku ordered her to keep an eye on them but did not alter their march.

They passed through a village of haven lords. Some of their smalls stood by fences waving as they went by so the Mantis Guards tossed tiny candies at them. This caused a round of laughter from all sides and brought the parents forth from their hovels to see what all the fuss was about.

Much to the parents' chagrin, some of the Llamia

scooped up a few of the smalls and placed them on their backs. The little ones squealed in delight as the adults looked on in horror. Then, just as quickly, the smalls were returned, safely, to the ground wherein they ran back to their, now relieved, parents shouting the equivalent of a cry every parent knows well.

"Momma! Poppa! Did you see? Did you see meeeeee?"

After they left the village the road sloped down a little so they picked up their pace. Not enough to tire the steeds or the Llamias, just enough to take advantage of the terrain.

A few more kays down the road it leveled off and they resumed their original gait. A little while later, realizing one of his scouts hadn't returned, he called a halt to the procession. Quickly issuing orders, he and Empress ClaalD were surrounded by warriors as four other warriors rode forward to find the scout.

Before anyone could react Empress Claald sprouted an arrow from her left shoulder. One of the Mantis Guards jumped on top of his steed and slipped a weapon from beneath his robe. Less than a sepi-clik later he found his target and fired. A Naradhama archer fell from a tree.

The remaining warriors began scouring the area as King Uku, himself, cut the arrow and pulled the shaft through. Realizing it hadn't hit anything vital, he was about to call for a medical kit when one ended up in his hands. He swiftly thanked the prescient Se-Jeant and applied a balm to the injury and then bandaged it.

Empress Claald, for her part, appeared unfazed.

Within a clik, the warriors regrouped and pronounced the remaining terrain safe. The four who'd been sent to find the scout returned with sadder news. They'd found her, with her throat cut, about a kay up the road.

Knowing Xhaknar could not know of their plans, they quickly discerned he must have placed spies and ambushes at random points across the Plains just in case any rebels left their warrens.

Scouts were redoubled and security around the King and Empress was tightened.

As they continued their march, Empress ClaalD turned to King Uku.

"Thank you very much for your kind ministrations," she smiled warmly, "while it hurts like all Zanubi, I'm guessing it won't slow us down." Then she huffed. "Imagine the arrogance of that little maggot. Thinking he could bring down the Empress of the Llamia with one little arrow."

King Uku, in spite of himself, laughed.

Watcher Urkel and King Gornd did not get to have any moments of gentle relaxation. Less than a clik into their march a scout came racing back.

"A mounted band of Mayanoren garrison troops are riding hard, less than a kay behind me," He said breathlessly.

King Gornd, looking at the arrow in the scout's arm, stated the obvious, "You're hit."

"It's just an arrow, Great King, I'll be fine."

King Gornd grabbed a tool from his pack, cut the shaft and pulled the arrow from the arm. Satisfied nothing important had been hit he expertly cut off the sleeve, applied a balm and wrapped the wound.

"Now you can go back to your squad and make the Mayanoren pay for your spilt blood."

"Guardian Nak," shouted King Urkel, "I think it's time to see what your shiny new warriors can do. Slay that Mayanoren patrol."

Nak nodded, quickly saluted, and barked out a set of orders. If the Mantis Guards had any problems with taking orders from a foreigner, they never showed it. Of course, that could just have been due to the burqas they were wearing.

In less than an epi-clik Nak had them formed up with the BadgeBeth in the middle on foot, the Fierstans on steeds and split on either side of them with the mounted Mantis Guards riding close behind. Since the scout reported the Mayanoren were only carrying traditional weapons, and the Mantis Guard were still the better shots with the new guns, Nak figured this formation gave him the best chance of success.

He kept them at a slow march since he wanted the Mayanoren horses as winded as possible when they clashed.

The Mayanoren came rushing over the hill, screaming and brandishing their swords above their heads. While this can look terrifying to a small it is not an effective battle strategy.

To a one, the warriors of the Great Kings made disparaging remarks about the low quality of garrison troops.

The Fierstans split out and let the BadgeBeth stand in front of the charge. As soon as the Mayanoren were surrounded, the BadgeBeth exploded the landscape. The Mayanoren horses reared, throwing riders hither and thither across the ground. Before they could react the Fierstans went through them with swords scything downward. The BadgeBeth rushed in and began hacking off limbs and heads at random.

The Mantis Guard pulled back a little and just watched. There really wasn't anything else for them to do.

Watcher Urkel and King Gornd rode up behind them and stared in awe.

The ground was littered with Mayanoren body parts and weapons. The BadgeBeth quickly recovered the weapons and rounded up the surviving steeds.

Within a few epi-cliks, carrion birds were descending on the carcasses and all of the warriors were back in formation behind the Great Kings.

Watcher Urkel turned to King Gornd and smiled.

"Yes, I think they'll do nicely, don't you?"

As the turns passed, Xhaknar began receiving anomalous reports from his spies. Several squads of garrison replacements were missing and the fringe dwellers were heading towards the Pit. The reports all said there were fewer than a hundred brands of the fringe in each party. He would, obviously, have to have his spies killed. There had to be more vermin than that.

What had happened was obvious to Xhaknar. The fringe was gathering in the Pit since it was the most secure place to be. They'd run across a few garrison troops in their path and, thanks to their overwhelming numbers, overran them. It was as simple as that.

The part that was of greater import was the fact they were solidifying in one place. That truly showed desperation. They were headed towards the safest place they could think of. They unmistakably thought, with Ek-kh's demise, he didn't know all the hidden entrances. Hubris would be their downfall.

He could let them go where they felt safe and crush them at will.

It was a good feeling.

He enjoyed when things were made easy.

He let his large frame relax in the throne and pondered his options. The simplest plan and the one he decided to employ was this: when his troops were trained in the new weapons he would march on the Pit. There he would destroy all the royals of the fringe and then turn his army on Südermann. With no leaders to guide them, they would be floundering. With no threat of rebellion, he could easily conquer the bug lord and enrich his domain.

He was flabbergasted at how easy it all was going to be.

There was no word on Geldish, that was true, but that just reinforced the fact the cursed Rangka was in hiding at the Kordai Sanctuary. Let him rot there then, there was much he needed to do, and with the bag of bones out of the way, little to stop him.

He re-read his weapons' master's report and smiled. The training of the ranked Naradhama was complete, the training master had been given an honorable death, he'd earned that despite his sharp tongue, and the troops were all coming along nicely with their training.

Yes, all was well in Anapsida.

A new, barely pubescent, effeminate mal-slave brought him his even meal.

He grinned as he raped him and enjoyed his snack, wiping the grease of the meats on the slave's back without pausing. When the youngling's anus bled he actually laughed. Yes, it was good to be the ruler.

Oolnok had seen the monks go past in the even. At least he thought they were monks. He'd never seen monks ride steeds before, but he wasn't familiar with all the religions that dotted the Plains. He knew some had as few as ten or twenty members and other numbered in the thousands. Beyond that he was clueless.

Even so, monks were no threat to him so he waved

as they passed. His smalls saw the procession and wanted to know if it was a Feast Turn. They were chagrined to find out it wasn't.

The even meal had been cleared away and he and his wife sat on the porch and watched their smalls burn off the last of the turn's energies. They sat quietly, holding hands and rocking gently.

They'd both heard increasingly more detailed rumors of some sort of uprising. But there was nothing in the news sheets about it and it all seemed far away. If there was a threat to their village Lord Xhaknar would surely let them know.

Oolnok wasn't a fool. He knew Xhaknar was a tyrant. It was just that he could conceive of no other leader to take his place. Certainly, the Mayanoren were incapable, the Naradhama were even more brutal and the warrens lacked the power. No, his life may not be perfect under Xhaknar, but it was still his life.

One of the smalls fell and scraped her knee. But instead of crying for her mother, as she would have in Suns passed, she stood up like an adult and pronounced herself fit to continue the game. His wife smiled and noted they soon wouldn't need her or Oolnok anymore.

While he didn't say so, and he truly did care for his progeny, he still looked forward to the turn he could have his wife all to himself again. He knew that was selfish and didn't care. She was the one constant joy in his world.

He remembered when his father had told him of his marriage. Scared and unsure, he'd gone to meet his prospective bride at her home. In keeping with tradition, she was covered in chaperones. He'd made his formal introduction, stammering most of it, and presented her with a bouquet of silver nindlinds. He noted, right then, the nindlinds looked like weeds next to her. Not intending to sound like an idiot, he told her so anyway.

She'd told him he wasn't all that bad looking either. That received some unhealthy glares from the chaperones.

It didn't matter much anyway. Within a turn it was obvious to all the two younglings were in love.

They'd proceeded with the appropriate one Full Sun courtship and then were married at Oolnok's father's home. The whole village had turned out. At the reception, Oolnok's father had given them the gift of this farm. It was just a part of his own, out on the border at that, but it was a kingdom to Oolnok. And to make things even better, his kingdom had the most beautiful queen in the village.

They'd waited seven Full Suns before having smalls. It's not they didn't want any, it was just they enjoyed each other's company so much they didn't want it interrupted. But when the first small came he saw the joy in her eyes and knew they'd have to make more. He wanted nothing more than for her to be happy.

When the smalls began to snap at each other, a sure sign it was time for bed, they rounded them up and set them upon their even ablations. Once they were sound asleep his wife hiked her skirt and motioned with her finger. Oolnok smiled as he entered their bedchamber. Yes, life was pretty good for old Oolnok.

While it was certainly not planned that way, all of the fringe warrens arrived at the Pit on the same turn. Far from the august bodies they may have been when they left, they were a motley lot when they arrived. Even so, except for the one dead Se-Jeant, who'd had her throat slit, and one dead Wolfen, who'd tried to stop a lance with his chest, they were all alive. They'd all run into various and sundry Mayanoren patrols going from garrison one to garrison two or from three to four, it hardly mattered since the roads were littered with Mayanoren and they'd had to face them.

Had they begun their march two turns earlier or two turns later, they would have missed them all. They'd also encountered multiple Naradhama assassins and run across two of the snake creatures. All whom they'd encountered directly were dead.

Elder Urnak and Queen A'lnuah met them near the public entrance and welcomed them into the warren. Within two cliks it was as though they were never on the Plains.

Wounds were tended and steaming mugs of korlnak were passed around. By even-fall, the travelers were safe and healthy.

Come breaklight, they'd learned Lord Südermann was still one turn away so they had time to talk amongst themselves. Geldish had commandeered, or been given – depending on whom you asked, a state room where the leaders of the fringe could meet.

They compared notes of their trips and realized Xhaknar had placed far more traps than they'd expected. It was clear that, though Xhaknar was planning for thing A, he also covered any contingencies for thing B and thing C as well. They would have to be far more careful from now on.

And though Geldish wished it were not so, since he wanted more information from the others, stories of the Brittle Riders dominated. Not just their run in with the Mayanoren garrison, but N'leah's kill of one of the snake-man assassins less than a turn from the Pit and R'yune's disemboweling of a Naradhama assassin who had tried to kill Geldish. Plus they were all stunned at the sight of the Kgul and the Din-La. All of this took up more time than the Rangka would have liked.

Still, when looked at objectively, his riders were imparting fear in their enemies and earning respect from their allies. Maybe, just maybe, he wouldn't need the Rangka to ride with him after all.

Despite the early setback, by mid-break, he had a

pretty clear idea of what each patrol had enjoined in battle and how they'd fared. All in all, given what they'd faced, not bad. King Gornd and Watcher Urkel had both suffered minor wounds but seemed no worse for the wear. King Uku had looked like he was about to become a Rangka when he'd arrived last turn, but the even's sleep and a hot meal seemed to have done him a world of good. Empress ClaalD somehow managed to look even more regal with her bandaged shoulder and sling.

All of the warriors were housed in the west end of the labyrinth in barracks and Geldish had checked in on them just after breaklight. Aside from the numerous bandages, casts, and slings, none of them seemed to show any ill effects from their hard ride. In fact, they were laughing and joking, and swapping tall stories – of course, as they headed for their first meal of the turn.

The meeting of the leaders broke up just after mid-break and everyone went into an ornate dining hall where Elder Urnak had laid out a sumptuous feast. Although there was no formal seating arrangement Geldish was surprised, and then pleased, to note the leaders sat in the pairs they'd arrived in. His Brittle Riders had been seated in the center and Hlaar, Mnaas and Ghaaz (the leader of the Mantis Guards in the Fierstan city) were spaced between them all.

Geldish pulled up his chair next to BraarB and began to enjoy the meal he was being served. Minotaur food was always spicy and he looked forward to sampling all of the exotic tastes.

"So, dead one," interrupted Empress ClaalD, "how fare we thus far? Is all going according to your grand plan?"

He considered for a moment, then nodded.

"We certainly suffered more bumps and bruises than any of us counted on. But these new warrior alliances performed admirably. In a way this may have been the best thing to happen; the troops got blooded together in battle, not just mock combat, and proved they are worthy of our trust as well as each other's.

"More importantly, by now Xhaknar's spies will have told him of the warrens descending on the Pit. Since we came from the distant east and killed everything in our path it's doubtful he knows about us. To Xhaknar it will seem as though the fringe and the warrens are hunkering down for a siege. All of its leaders, neatly housed, in one place. My guess is he'll wait for his troops to finish training with their new weapons and then march his total force here."

Looking at the horror in Elder Urnak's eyes, and the ripple of concern that resulted, Geldish raised his hand for quiet.

"Not to worry, I won't let that happen. Once this council is ended my riders and I will begin to do our part of the plan. Although Xhaknar thinks us holed up in the Kordai Sanctuary, hiding from his wrath, we will do something I'm quite good at; we will come back from the dead."

That earned a robust laugh all around. Even Geldish was forced to smile.

"We will begin harassing the garrisons at random. One turn north, the next south, or west or wherever we feel like at the time. We won't attack them directly since that would be foolish. Sloppy soldiers or no, being outnumbered one thousand to one is still being outnumbered one thousand to one. We aren't interested in martyring ourselves.

"No, we will slay guards, ambush supplies, blow up weapons depots and anything else we can think of that will cause the most harm and destruction. We will also make sure everyone knows it's us and not some lucky wanderers. I repeat we have no wish to be martyrs, but our goal is to force Xhaknar to come after us, in force if possible."

Everyone considered this for a while and then King Gornd spoke thoughtfully.

"Ah, I see, the more he's forced to expend troops

looking for you, the more Naradhama the warrens can slay in raids. The more we can slay now, the fewer we'll have to face when the true battle comes. It's a risky plan, but sound. It gets my support."

In short order, all of the leaders had assented and the mood in the hall relaxed considerably.

"Yes," continued Geldish, "that is essentially it. As long as you keep scouts on patrol you should have plenty of warning when any Naradhama are near your warrens. Obviously, when this council completes Xhaknar will know something is up. If you're not hiding, waiting for a siege, what are you doing? That will be the question in his mind. The more on edge he is, the less focused, the better for us."

Mnaas laughed. "It's like fighting a bigger opponent in the sparring-square. You can't knock him out with one blow, so you keep jabbing him and jabbing him and forcing him to chase you until you've winded him, then you go in for the kill. Well conceived, dead one, well conceived indeed."

With that, the talk in the hall turned to the mundane. King Uku recited Empress ClaalD's comment about her, would be, assassin and got laughs for the story and more respect for her. It was as convivial as a war council could be.

They were not dupes. They knew what was coming. There would be blood on the Plains before long and much of that blood would belong to them and theirs. But, for now, they could relax and enjoy each other's company.

And, for now, that was enough.

Lord Südermann was advancing across the Plains surrounded by sixty of his Mantis Guards. They would accept no fewer number even though he'd wished no more than five or six. Oh well, there was nothing to be done about it, they were paid to protect him and protect him they would, whether he wanted them to or not.

Scouts had brought word of various Mayanoren patrols and they'd skirted around them easily enough, but it had added an extra turn to their journey. Xhaknar had stopped putting spies along Südermann's border many Full Suns ago since they kept getting killed. Südermann was sure the spies would return soon enough when Xhaknar made his move.

He'd ordered a long rest after their mid-break meal. He wanted to march through the even and arrive at the Pit by breaklight. His Guards were even less sanguine about that plan than the one that got them here in the first place and raised many objections concerning assassins hiding in the dark and so on. He'd not bothered to respond, instead just looking at them like a parent would look at a small fearing shadows.

Suitably shamed, they'd relented.

Halfway through the even, they ran across their first spy. A Mayanoren who'd spotted them and was trailing along behind trying to find out who they were. Elaand slipped from the ranks and buried himself in the sands. Five epi-cliks later he rejoined the squad and ordered increased vigilance. Lord Südermann watched him clean the blood from his dagger without comment.

By the time they came into view of the public entrance of the Pit they'd dispatched four more spies and a small squad of Mayanoren bandits who'd been foolish enough to try and rob them. Südermann laughed inwardly at that particular memory. The bandits must have thought they'd found a band of traveling monks, dressed as they were in simple robes. The look on their faces when the 'monks' erupted with swords, daggers, and arrows was worth the risk of the ride as far as he was concerned. They went from baffled to terrified to dead quicker than he could blink.

Four Minotaur guards rushed out to meet them and, satisfied they were neither Naradhama nor Mayanoren, led them quickly into the Pit. Südermann was surprised at the opulence of the surroundings. While decorated in muted colors and rounded archways, highlighted by flowing lava, the overall feel was one of intelligent elegance. He could think of no better term. He decided he should have done this trip long ago. There was much here worth saving.

Südermann was aware of the layout of the Plains. Surrounding each warren, except for the Minotaur, who all lived in their Pit, for a turn or two in any direction were scattered villages and hovels of residents who lived off the land. Most villages were brand specific, but quite a few had become mixed for one reason or another. There was a village near Südermann's border made up of haven lords, Din-La, some Se-Jeant and a few Fierstans. They didn't bother anyone so Südermann left them alone. Xhaknar's raiding parties had learned not to stray too close to Südermann's borders, so the village ended up in a safe zone and prospered as well as any village on the Plains could.

One of the main reasons Südermann didn't care is because he knew, without a shadow of a doubt, that he'd be more likely to fly without aid than see haven lords or Din-La pick up weapons.

As he escorted his Mantis Guards to the barracks they'd been assigned, he saw two haven lords cleaning guns and a Din-La sharpening a vicious looking dagger.

He glanced at Elaand, who seemed equally baffled by the sight, and sighed.

"Forgive me brave Elaand, but when we get these robes off, would you please check to see if I've grown wings?"

Elaand was more confused than ever.

Yontar hovered over his ancient home. Turns came and went and he was no closer to piercing the secret than he had been when he first arrived. While his memory of the facility was clear, his sight was not. He could make out gross shapes and some shading, but that was about it. It was as though he were trapped in a malevolent fog. One which would let him see this but not that.

He tried viewing things from different angles, but that neither hindered nor helped. The pull, though not powerful by any calculation he could devise, was strongest over the main building.

So, he settled there and thought. His body needed no sustenance of any kind. Nor did he require sleep. Originally that had bothered him, but here and now he considered it a boon. He didn't want to be distracted at all.

He let his mind wander through his memories looking for any little clue as to why he was here. He could hear the echoes of his long dead makers issuing commands and taking measurements. He could hear Xhaknar's maniacal laugh when the Gen-O-Pod war began. He could see the bodies sloppily piled outside the compound, left to rot in the weather. He could remember the beginnings of the Mayanoren, and their blooding during the insurrection, as well as his later tours of all the secrets the facility held. His memories were sharp and clear but they didn't seem to be helping him at all.

Slowly, in the far reaches of his consciousness, a concept began to emerge. It was so pathetically obvious he discounted it. But it kept coming back. Stubborn super soldier or no, he began to ponder it fully.

Directly below him were a thousand more just like him.

He tried to remember what it was like when he was first decanted.

It had taken almost three Full Suns for him to become self aware. That meant the bodies were there, the tools were there but none of them were sentient yet. He could take over a body and …

And freaking what?

How could he get to those bodies? And even if he could, they were in cryo-stasis, that would be a fate worse than this.

Frustrated at being so close to an answer only to, once again, have it denied him; he fumed silently in the netherworld Geldish had trapped him in.

Xhaknar studied the report he'd been handed by a slave. He dismissed her and tried to fathom its meaning. A raiding party and two spies had been slaughtered in the east. There were no warrens over there. As far as his intelligence network knew, there was nothing there but wastelands.

Some new power from the eastern ocean?

That seemed unlikely. Although his latest reports from there were over twenty Full Suns old, there'd been no sign of unrest or conquest. While they had four powerful warrens the majority of the brands lived in small villages up and down the seaboard and were protected by a military made up of the main warrens. They'd never shown any desire for expansion. For that matter, except for the Kalindor, none of the brands seemed interested in conquest. They were weak like that.

Another like him?

Again, doubtful. Even if one like him did exist and

had taken residence in the eastern plains, there wasn't anything there. No brands, no warrens, nothing but wild animals and some lakes. That would be a place to pass through on the way to conquest, not a place of conquest itself. Besides, why kill an entire squad of Mayanoren, set their bodies on fire and then leave? That made no sense at all.

There'd been rumors about wild brands living in the wilderness, could they be true and one of those tribes had just happened across the Mayanoren? Highly improbable. There'd never been one shred of evidence any wild brands existed and, even if they did, what chance would a small group of savages have against professional killers like the Mayanoren?

None.

So what happened?

Or, more correctly, who happened?

He wished he could have examined the bodies to see how they died, but by the time the garrison scouts found them the parts that hadn't been burned had been eaten.

Better to concentrate on what he did know.

Whoever had done this had taken the Mayanoren weapons and steeds. They'd also been able to overpower forty garrison troops. While they weren't equal to his front line troops, they weren't smalls either. Certainly, no random band of villagers or scavengers could have done this.

So who the Zanubi was out there?

He wished Yontar was here. His knack for warfare would have come in handy. Maybe he'd see something he'd missed.

Or, maybe not. Yontar had been a military genius, not a seer.

He'd have to clear this up before he began his campaign on Südermann. If there was a threat to the east, it must be dealt with first before he left the confines of

Anapsida.

The first wave of Mayanoren were fifteen turns from completing their training. He would wait until they were done and then send one thousand of them out to the east to see what they could find. He would make sure they carried the new weapons and had clear orders to kill anything that threatened him.

Since the Mayanoren were dense beyond belief, he had the orders drawn up immediately and posted on their barracks so they could be reminded of them each turn. With that out of the way and nothing more to do, he flipped open a list of good citizens who were behind on their taxes.

He called for two of his private Naradhama guards and set off to cause some, long overdue, pain and suffering.

The three Din-La walked over to the Mayanoren barracks and quickly sold out of the succulent sweet cakes which were forbidden to them. The Mayanoren weren't interested in alcohols or prostitutes, but they could fund a small city just with the number of sweet cakes they purchased and ate.

While they were there a Naradhama guard walked over and hammered a new set of orders on the wall for the Mayanoren. They had to do that so the Mayanoren commanders would remember to remind the Mayanoren soldiers.

The Din-La feigned disinterest and memorized the command. Then one of them found, accidentally, of course, another box of sweet cakes after the Naradhama had left. At that point, he could have been granted access to a munitions depot if he'd asked.

Instead, he got something better than that. The Mayanoren were reading the command aloud, while eating their sweet cakes, and discussing how best to use their new weapons and, also, how to tell if they didn't recognize something. There was also a brief, but friendly, discussion as to which way was east.

Much to the Din-La's amusement, the Mayanoren decided to kill anything they didn't know and ignore the rest.

Bmmd was going to love this.

Südermann had decided not to wait for a formal meeting and walked in on their breaklight repast. While several of the attendees were clearly shocked by what they saw, they calmed down as they heard him speak.

Geldish had a slightly different reaction. This Lord Südermann was a hand taller, slightly thinner and had a deeper voice than the Lord Südermann he'd met. It had never occurred to him Lord Südermann was a title and not a name. He must be getting old.

He chuckled to himself, pleased to note the dreams and desires of his Lord Südermann coincided with those of this Lord Südermann.

Maybe it was part of the arrangement. He'd have to ask later.

Südermann was fascinated by the Kgul and slowly drew him into a conversation. Many thought the Kgul to be mutes, but they really were just exceedingly recalcitrant around strangers. G'rnk and Brek stood alongside the Kgul and helped answer questions as they could. Two Din-La, a brand Südermann would never see the same way again, also offered up bits of information.

In short order, Südermann made his introductions to everyone while eating off of plates handed to him by various Minotaur servants. He commented, favorably, on several of the dishes and, no matter how revolting he appeared to some, soon won them over.

Elaand had spied Geldish and walked over to say hello and bring him up to date. He had fifty radios with him and would dispense them after the meeting. He also gave Geldish the outline of Südermann's plan for the armies. Geldish smiled; it was simplicity itself, the warrens would easily go for it and it would work. He wished he'd thought of it.

They retired to the main meeting hall and Geldish noted Urnak hadn't been sleeping in diplomacy class. The stage and lectern had been removed and there was a large round table in the center of the room. Everyone would have equal footing in this meeting.

Geldish had had his riders don their formal garments for this meeting. It may be a council of war, but it was not happening on the battlefield.

Even without weapons, they looked deadly. Südermann spied them and motioned for them to sit near him. That left Geldish across from Südermann. He wasn't sure if it was intentional or not, but it did work out well when he thought about it. Now, when they spoke to each other, there would be no chance of there being any secrets.

Fair enough then, this conference would be transparent.

Well, almost.

Elder Urnak motioned for the various staffs to leave and then had the door closed behind them. Once done he walked over to Queen A'Inuah and took the seat beside her.

Urnak called the meeting to order and turned the floor over to Südermann. He wasted no time and quickly outlined his plan for the armies. After a few questions for clarification, everyone agreed. Then they began debating which army would do what. Geldish feared this would be the worst part. Petty squabbles and codes of honor could trash even the best paid plans.

But, it didn't happen that way. Watcher Urkel and King Gornd whispered to each other then Urkel stood and announced, as long as no one had any objections, the Fierstans and the BadgeBeth would take on the main Mayanoren lines. Within a clik, all of the Xhaknar's forces had been divvied up between them. Südermann admitted he was taken aback over how well it all went. Geldish had only had to speak once, and that was to get his riders the right to ride on Xhaknar and his elite guard directly.

Since no one else had asked for that honor, it was theirs.

Then Geldish stood and outlined his plan to buy the warrens more time to train their unique forces. Südermann laughed when he heard it and promised five hundred Mantis Guards for each warren to aid the cause.

It was just then that a Din-La entered the room and scurried over to Geldish. He handed him a note, bowed to the assemblage and left.

Geldish read the note, smiled, chuckled and then burst out laughing.

When he calmed down, he explained.

"Well, it seems that for all the wrong reasons Xhaknar's gone ahead and done exactly what we want. He claims someone …," he stretched the word out for almost an epi-clik and smiled, "someone has wiped out a Mayanoren raiding party in the east and he wants to know who did it."

That got a round of laughter at the table, with several of the assembled hailing the riders before he could continue.

"So, in fifteen turns, he's going to send out a thousand Mayanoren, armed with the new weapons, to find out." He paused for a sepi-clik to sip the fine cup of korlnak, "G'rnk, it would seem this would be an ideal time for your troops and the Kgul to get some live fire seasoning."

G'rnk considered that and smiled, "Yes, we know

how many are coming, where they are coming from and when they will arrive. That is about as good as information gets for warriors. We will handle the rest."

"Good," continued Geldish, "then the Brittle Riders and I can stick to our original plan. Now, I believe Lieutenant Elaand has something to say to us all."

Elaand stood and began handing out radios to everyone in the room. He also had larger units, for permanent placement in each warren, which he set on the table. He explained how to transmit and how to receive. He explained which channel had been assigned to which warren and how to contact someone on the field of battle directly.

He then explained about the batteries, how one set could be charging while the other was in use so the user would never be without. He even showed them how to use the generators that ran the chargers and told them what to use for fuel.

G'rnk stared at the devices.

"So," he grumbled aloud, "that's how the Din-La do it. Well, good for them and now better for us." He picked up the device and walked over to Elaand. "Show me again so there can be no mistakes."

With that, all the leaders got up and began trying the new devices. Questions flew from every direction and Elaand handled them all with quiet efficiency. Within a clik, everyone knew what they were doing and how to make the best use of these wonders.

Karrish and Elzish were both staring at Makish. Although several turns had passed since the discovery of the Kgul city, they still couldn't believe he'd been the one to keep that secret. And, while they were convinced it was the only secret he had kept, it still boggled. There was obviously more to him than met the eye.

After a while, Karrish got up and walked over to the idol. The others quietly followed.

"As long as we're telling secrets," intoned Elzish politely, "tell me where this thing came from."

Karrish chuckled.

"After Xhaknar came, and before the first rebellion, Absanda, may her soul be at peace in the void, found this in a shop in Go-Chi. She thought it was the most hideous thing she'd ever seen and purchased it as a reminder that, as bad as things were for us, they could have been worse."

He'd held that story for almost five hundred Full Suns. He'd really expected a bigger laugh. He excused himself and headed for the great library. While Rangka memories were eidetic, things could get jumbled over such long spans of time. He headed past the stacks of fiction, Rangka enjoyed a good yarn as much as anybody, and entered the section of historical archives. He soon found the book he was looking for, *A Complete Account of the First Rebellion*, and took it to a table.

He flipped it open to the first page and began reading to see if there was anything in there that might help Geldish on his mad venture. After all, if Geldish failed, there'd be no hiding from Xhaknar anymore. They'd have to move the temple east and start over. If only he could have waited another hundred or so Full Suns, they'd have restored enough of their power to topple Xhaknar on their own. Well, he always was the impetuous sort, nothing to be done about it now.

Watcher Ondom had led the rebellion two hundred and eighty-seven Full Suns ago. Unlike Watcher Urkel, he was a huge Fierstan, full of life. His voice would boom across the battlefield and give hope to all who heard him. He'd rallied all the warrens and the villages, and convinced the Rangka to ride with him as well.

They numbered one hundred and thirty-two then. All that was left of the wizards.

Like Yontar, Ondom was a military genius. Instead of attacking Anapsida head on, imposing even then, he'd led the combined warrens against the outer garrisons, drawing the Naradhama out.

That part of his plan went flawlessly.

The next part did not.

Yontar, knowing the Rangka could stop his energy weapons and not having the resources, then, to recreate the makers' weapons, split his Naradhama into two fronts. The first, by far the larger of the two, he reinforced with Mayanoren and aimed directly at Ondom's army.

The two great armies met about twenty kays west of Go-Chi.

To nullify the Rangkas' prowess with magnetism he'd armed his warriors with all wooden weapons. Arrows, even with wooden tips, could be deadly. Instead of swords, he'd armed his troops with clubs that had large spikes protruding from them. The spikes had been treated and varnished and were just as hard as steel. And just as deadly.

For fifteen turns the two armies clashed from breaklight to even-fall, littering the ground with corpses. The wounded could be heard crying into the dark and, sometimes, it was a mercy when they died.

Every turn Ondom would charge and every turn he would be repelled. But, every turn he drove the Naradhama a little further back. And every turn his troops gained a little more hope.

Until the sixteenth turn.

Both sides had the technology to make chariots. It's just they weren't much use in these times. Steeds, while swift, weren't strong enough to pull them and deisteeds did not have the temperament to work in tandem. And, as any soldier could tell you, one deisteed pulling a chariot was just a waste of a good deisteed.

Nytsteeds, the sole purview of the Rangka, would

no more pull a chariot than they would yodel. They were pure-bred warriors.

But what Yontar had created wasn't a chariot; it was a deisteed drawn horror.

Ondom had moved the Rangka to the middle of his ranks since they had no effect on the wooden weapons and weren't as good in hand to hand combat as his other warriors. Karrish remembered what happened next as though it were just the turn before.

From behind them, they heard a whooshing buzzing sound. With the battle raging to the front there weren't any available troops to check it out. Suddenly, the remaining Naradhama appeared behind Ondom's army. They were leading five hundred deisteeds pulling modified scything machines. But instead of cutting down wheat, they cut into Ondom's ranks.

Rangka can survive many things, but being savagely sliced into little pieces wasn't one of them. The Rangka died that turn just like everybody else.

Some of the Rangka were able to rally and begin bending the blades, but it was too little too late. With the rear guard in shambles and the center of his army being decimated, Ondom called for a retreat. Yontar took that opportunity to split his front line forces and surround Ondom's army. The route was on.

The battle lasted three more turns and finally ended when Yontar placed Ondom's head on a spike. After that, Xhaknar's repercussions were brutal and swift. He rounded up every member of rank from every warren and hung them on the main wall of Anapsida; leaving the dangling bodies to be eaten by birds and rot in the sun. He demanded, and got, the warrens to reimburse him for all costs incurred by Yontar and then imposed strict laws about public gatherings.

When it was over, Xhaknar's reign was unquestioned. The warrens were rendered impotent. All the great leaders were dead. And the Rangka numbered four.

This is what Geldish was trying to bring back.

Not finding any hope in the book he returned it to its shelf and sat back down.

What positives could he find for this rebellion that the last one had not?

Well, for one, Yontar was trapped in the void in between. Geldish had opened his mind to Yontar, a dangerous move, but instead of using it as a tool for sharing he'd used it to fence in Yontar's essence and wrap it around itself. Yontar was trapped by the fact every step forward he could take was the equivalent of one step back. The closer he gets to the edge of the realm, the further away his mind and body are. Simple, yet effective.

Sadly, it was not a trick that would work on Xhaknar. Whereas Yontar's mind was quick and moving, a fact that allowed Geldish to lure it out, Xhaknar's was like a wall. You'd sooner teach a kgum to juggle before you could make him curious.

Second, massive military might nor no, Xhaknar simply did not have Yontar's ability to strategize. When he attacked it was a thing of brutal efficiency. Not that it was ineffective, but it lacked finesse. And Geldish's plan would need to be met with finesse.

At least for now. Eventually, Geldish was going to have to face Xhaknar on the field of battle. That would not be a subtle thing. That would be a bloodbath. As to whether Geldish and his allies could survive such a battle, Karrish had his doubts.

It had been five turns since the council of the Pit. Even was just about to fall and N'leah smiled at Geldish in anticipation. So far they'd raided three garrisons. The first had been laughable. The garrison commander, in an effort to save time, had placed his munitions next to the barracks. N'leah had swooped over the wall, dropped one of Kronlk's little bombs and, within an epi-clik, the entire south side of the garrison was ablaze. They'd waited for a search party to come looking for them, but none emerged. The commander's ineptness saved a few Mayanoren lives that even.

The second commander wasn't much brighter. He'd planted dense foliage around the perimeter of the garrison. While it served to hide it from view, it also did an excellent job of hiding their attack. Leaving BraarB behind, because she couldn't maneuver in the thick leaves, they each took one gate and killed the guards. Then, when rotation change came at even-split, they killed their replacements as well.

As they were approaching the third garrison they spied five supply wagons guarded by a small squad of Mayanoren. Feeling left out of the fun, BraarB attacked before they could set a plan. Prior to the riders catching up with her half the Mayanoren lay dead or dying and the other half were running, screaming, for the garrison. This commander, no slouch he, saw what was happening and immediately closed the gates, leaving the supplies and the troops guarding them to their fates. Shortly thereafter, all had met their demise and the wagons were in flames. With the garrison commander shouting various insults from atop the wall Geldish gave him a jaunty wave and they rode slowly away.

There was no need to rush since no one was following them.

This garrison, against protocol, was leaving the gates open after even-fall so they could make goldens off of trade and in the bars and brothels. The troop barracks were against the northern wall, far from the south gate where they were watching. There were two Mayanoren guarding the gate, but that was it. Inside the south wall, they could clearly see the roof of the munitions depot festooned with a flag marking it as such.

They decided to take the simple approach. They would ride directly to the gate, pay the one golden entrance fee and make for the depot. Once there they would kill any guards, blow up the depot and then create as much havoc as they could on their way out.

It was a good plan, if simple. There was only one problem.

It didn't work.

They got inside easily enough. But they were barely half way to the depot when Geldish noticed the wanted poster. At the same time, he heard a yell and turned to see a hundred Mayanoren soldiers, with swords brandished, heading right at them.

The only way out was north, right into the awaiting arms of the troops in the barracks.

With no other options, they turned their nytsteeds to the north and began shooting at anything that moved. N'leah dropped a couple of Kronlk's bombs behind her and they were making good headway amidst the mayhem. It was then they heard the commander shout for the gates to be closed. They were going to be trapped like fish in a barrel.

Well, not every commander can be a moron, thought Geldish regretfully.

Swords were clanging, shots were firing and bombs were going off at every twist. Geldish absently noted the BadgeBeth had really taken to the new weapons. They were like an extension of his arm. If he aimed at something, it died. R'yune appeared to be out of ammunition and had resorted to beheading anyone who got too close to him. What that strategy lacked in finesse it made up for in effectiveness. N'leah kept mixing bombs with bullets and was leaving a bloody swath behind her. BraarB also seemed to be out of ammo and was carving a path opposite R'yune. Geldish, possessed of many abilities, was reduced to firing one shot at a time into the onrushing Mayanoren.

It seemed for every one they killed, two more took their place. The street was getting congested and their progress had been severely slowed.

As they got close to the north gate they noticed a farmer's wagon had lost a wheel and the Mayanoren were trying to move it bodily. But it was laden with supplies and far too heavy. In an indelicate move, executed without apologies, the riders went straight over the cart, knocking the farmer to the ground, while they killed as many guards as they could. Once free of the garrison, they pushed their nytsteeds as fast as they could go and disappeared into the even's mists.

A little more than a clik later they stopped, hearing no sounds of pursuit. Panting and shaking they dismounted and sat on the ground. BraarB just collapsed her legs beneath her and stared at nothing. They'd all received cuts and bruises and were exhausted.

After Geldish finished bandaging them up, Sland turned to him and smiled wanly.

"That didn't fucking go as well as planned, did it?"

BraarB was just counting the stars hoping the many pains would subside. She wondered about the many strange roads that had led her to this place. How she'd gone from the safety of her crags in the hills to running with a band of terrorists, or so they'd been branded by Xhaknar. She thought back to her youth as a foal in the herd. Llamia are born self aware, unlike any of the other brands, so her memory went back a long way. She remembered her mother and father cleaning her off and then helping her stand on her weak, little, legs.

She remembered being introduced to the clan. As

was the tradition of the Llamia, she was introduced as the daughter of DkaaR and TlaaM, mother and father respectively. It wouldn't be until her fifth Full Sun that she would attend her naming ceremony and become BraarB.

She remembered sitting with the other foals agonizing over her name. There were so many choices and so many ways to mess up, it seemed like they would overwhelm her young brain. But, eventually she settled on the name of her great grand-dame, may she rest in peaceful fields, and that made her family happy. She had surprised them with the choice too. They hadn't known until their herd leader, a stallion named KlaalT, had introduced her formally.

She remembered her mother's surprised gasp and then the applause. Yes, she had chosen well. Her ancestor had been well respected by the herd and was much beloved in lore.

It was just after her fifteenth Full Sun when Xhaknar's 'thinning pogrom' got to her herd. She could still hear the screams as the Mayanoren butchers cut through them, killing every third Llamia they crossed. They had fought back, of course, but what good was that against well armed soldiers who had the element of surprise?

She escaped by falling off a cliff. It may not have been the best plan, but it worked. She had tumbled, flipping over and over, bouncing off of rocks, until she'd hit bottom. Then she lost consciousness. She awoke the next turn to see her crag in ruins, smoke pouring from multiple fires. Hearing no noises she crawled, painfully, back up the hill and wandered through the ruins. She'd found her parents, and KlaalT, piled on top of each other, savagely butchered. Several of her playmates lay dead in the same room.

She'd roamed aimlessly for many turns after that. She spied a herd in the distance one turn just after breaklight. Scared, but also lonely and hungry, she cautiously approached them. She must have looked like a monster from a small's story. Her hair was tangled, she hadn't eaten much in turns and she was covered with healing bruises and nasty scratches and scars.

They listened to her story and then brought her to their healer. He was a wise old stallion named HwaapT and he had a funny sense of humor. He and his wife, she forgot her name, cleaned her up, fed her and tended to her many wounds. Within a few turns, she was healthy enough to gallop.

It was around then she discovered she was in the care of Empress ClaalD's herd. It was larger and better armed than her herd had been. They could fend off a Mayanoren thinning party and had done so in the past. She spent five Full Suns training with their warriors and learned how to use every possible weapon. She also learned how to use things that were not weapons for the function of killing. She could never look at cutlery, especially spoons, the same way again.

She felt empowered. She had skills that could save her life and the lives of others. That gave her the confidence she'd been missing since the attack. By her twenty-first Full Sun, she was a member of their warrior caste and was being sent on missions for the good of the herd. Some were violent, some diplomatic, it didn't matter, she cherished them all.

Now, here she was, just shy of her fiftieth Full Sun, sitting with a Rangka who was bent on turning the world upside down. She'd met with him four times before, the last time saving his life, so she'd been asked to see what his message entailed. She wasn't exactly sure everything which had come after was part of the plan but it was a little late to back out now.

Also five turns after the conference, many kays to the south, Südermann – now surrounded by one hundred and fifty of his elite guards – crossed into his lands. They'd seen the two thousand Mantis Guards headed towards the three warrens and the temple two turns ago and wished them well. Though the trip back had been uneventful, his guards were still on high alert. He doubted they would relax until he poured himself a brandy in the palace.

He didn't begrudge their vigilance. He'd seen the wounded at the Pit as clearly as they had. The tiniest mistake and they could all be dead. Instead, he spent his time wondering how all these events would pan out. Things were fully in motion now and there was no turning back.

He'd received Geldish's reports on the first three raids and figured they were going well. By now Xhaknar had to know Geldish was neither dead nor praying in a monastery. The fact he'd already committed a thousand troops to a worthless quest spoke well of Geldish's plan.

The best result would be for Xhaknar to be killed. But Südermann wasn't sure that was possible. In a long ago raid he'd seen him get hit by an arrow in the heart. He'd then snapped the shaft, pulled it out and kept fighting. No, Xhaknar wasn't going to go down easily.

But, without his army, he was just another loud bully and bullies could be dealt with. Even if they couldn't be killed.

Südermann considered every angle and pitted it against its opposite in his mind. Xhaknar's superior force against Geldish's, and his, superior skills just seemed to be a wash. Whatever edge they gained, on the one hand, they lost on the other.

Still an all, there was a chance. And, to prevent his lands from being overrun, it was a chance he had to take.

He reminisced about his conversation with Geldish after the conference. The two of them had been able to sit quietly and enjoy a brandy and pastry tray. Südermann had never had Minotaur sweets before and was thrilled by their variety and taste. He seemed to have an insatiable sweet tooth that wasn't shared by many. Geldish had sampled the pastries but had stuck mostly with the brandy.

He wasn't surprised Geldish had figured out his name was also his title. The Rangka may be preoccupied with revenge, but he was no mental midget. They'd talked of the first rebellion, which happened two Südermenn before his reign and they talked about what he hoped to accomplish with this one.

Bringing water to Go-Chi seemed to be the impossible part of his plan. There was nothing but blasted earth and a deep canyon east of Go-Chi. Whatever had been there before was lost to the past. But he'd accomplished one third of his plan and was making progress on the second, so who was to say he couldn't accomplish the third?

However, since he seemed to have no plans to try and kill Xhaknar, there was a certain logic to the rest. It was like trimming a diseased tree. Instead of cutting the whole thing down and maybe having it crash on your home, this way you controlled every step of its destruction. Once it was down then you could burn the stump and be done with it.

He vaguely noted they were well past the first checkpoint headed towards his northern palace. With the Warm Sun coming he'd hoped to move to his southern one, but there was no chance of that happening with war on the way. He'd let his family go, of course, since he knew how much they loved the excessive heat and humidity. They knew the only reason he came to the north palace at all was because Xhaknar was up to something. Bless them all, they never complained.

Südermann thought some more about the twists of fate that had made him who he was. The arrogance of a maker over one thousand Full Suns ago had set all this into motion. Yes, Rohta had been brilliant, but he'd missed every sign things were not going according to plan. He seemed to have been one of those leaders who let others deal with the details. That can work well if the others are competent or not cowed. Neither parameter had been met by Rohta's retainers. By surrounding himself with those who, like him, were more interested in the hedonistic aspects of life there was no one qualified to pay attention to the problems that were arising.

For example; instead of dying, his Gen-O-Pods were disappearing. That should have been worth a mcmo somewhere. And, instead of letting his customers know that, they were allowed to assume the Gen-O-Pods had returned to the factory to expire and simply ordered more.

Ignorance may be bliss, but it is seldom useful.

A part of him wished the Gen-O-Pod war had never happened, but it was clear there was no way to have avoided it. The humans, small in number and mighty in self-importance, had left no other option. His kind may have been bred for slavery, but they hadn't taken to it well.

Maybe if Rohta had only created a few types of brands, the system would have held. But by filling every niche he'd left no room for humanity in the equation.

Something had to give, and it had.

With a vengeance.

Then Südermann thought about the Sominids. They'd brought a treasure trove of knowledge to Arreti. From reports of other worlds to the ability to find them, humans should have taken to the stars instead of returning to the ground. But the task was beyond them. The thought of being so far away from home with only a few of their kind with them was just too much to bear. Humans were, by and large, social creatures and the thought of leaving it all behind was just too alien.

Südermann and his brand had no such compunctions.

Now the infrastructure was secure his scientists were making rapid progress on rebuilding those incredible engines. Once they had those they could easily build the ships. His brands would venture forth into the heavens and see what there was to see. The descendants of the mantis could make the round trip to some of the nearer worlds and still have time to explore.

None of this would happen during his lifetime, of course, but it felt good to know the dream was still alive. Of course, should Xhaknar win out, then that dream would die just like everything else.

That could not be allowed to happen. He would talk with Elaand. Forget the ten thousand soldiers, they were going to throw everything they had at Xhaknar. That should end any stalemate.

Xhaknar had killed the slave who'd brought him the report and still didn't feel better. Geldish was not in Kordai Sanctuary, that much was obvious, the main brands and the fringe had left the Pit and were returning to their warrens and there were two thousand monks who seemed to have traveled through Südermann's lands to end up here. What were they about? The last thing he needed was some new, half baked, religion setting up shop when he was in the middle of important plans.

Plus, he still had the unknown threat to the east. Something had killed and stripped that patrol and it wasn't Geldish or some damnable monks. He briefly thought about doubling the force of the Mayanoren heading into the east but decided against it. That would require new orders and he wasn't sure they could adjust in time. According to the Naradhama who oversaw the Mayanoren training, the Mayanoren commander had come up with a simple solution to make sure he remembered what to do. He'd put red buttons on a thousand bunks and then put a red button on his calendar. When it was red button turn he would march with all his red button soldiers.

Xhaknar was unsure if that was more of that new initiative stuff or if the Mayanoren were finally gaining sentience. No matter what, it wasn't something to be worried about now.

One thing he could do was deal with the monks. He'd send a thousand Naradhama to find them. If they were just passing through on their way somewhere east, he'd let them go, if not, they would all be killed.

Then he thought better of that plan. Better just to kill them all and be done with it.

With that decided he called for a Naradhama general to be brought to him. When the worthy arrived he gave him his orders and sent him away. Then realizing the dead slave was still on his floor, he called for a couple more of them to clean up the mess.

With the easy stuff out of the way, he could concentrate on Geldish. What was his plan? Was he hoping the rabble in the warrens, inspired by his idiot riders, would come together in open rebellion? Even if they did, what of it? Combined they still couldn't field more than half the force of his Naradhama. Was Geldish hoping he'd come out personally so he could do to him what he'd done to Yontar? Well, he could keep dreaming on that one. When he next left Anapsida he would be surrounded by the combined forces of the Naradhama and the Mayanoren. Geldish couldn't get to him then.

So what was he trying to accomplish?

Was he actually hoping to overthrow a garrison and keep it for himself? To what end?

Maybe it didn't matter what his motives were. Sticking to the facts; Geldish had destroyed a lot of his property, it was time for that to end. There was already a price on his head, but that wouldn't be enough. No, it was time to box Geldish in and crush him.

He would send five thousand Naradhama to patrol between the warrens of the Minotaurs and the Se-Jeant. Another five thousand would patrol between the Fierstans and the Minotaurs. Split into squads of five hundred each, they could cover a lot of ground. A third patrol of five thousand would go from garrison to garrison. Again, split into squads of five hundred each, they could cover ten garrisons a turn. That would force Geldish in one direction or another. No matter what, they'd get him.

He wondered, when they brought him the head, if those mocking flames would still be burning. He kind of hoped they would. He'd use them as a reading lamp.

He called another general and gave the orders.

The Naradhama squad leader eased his troops into a gulley and waited for them all to assemble. They were within sight of the public entrance to the stupid pit of the cursed Minotaur. They would camp here for the even and then, come breaklight, begin their rotation with the other squads. In the four turns since they'd left Anapsida they'd seen nothing suspicious so far. A few monks had passed them earlier in the turn and few Succubi, pulling carts full of trade goods, had headed into the pit. A couple of the Succubi had made lewd suggestions, but his troops were better disciplined than that. They knew the phrase, "the prettier the fruit, the more potent the poison."

All in all, it was just regular business on the Plains. Lord Xhaknar would be pleased to note the Minotaurs had resumed trade with the fringe. More trade meant more taxes and more taxes meant better equipment for the troops.

His squad was running low on provisions, but they had enough in their packs to get through this even and they would meet up with the quartermaster and the kgums well before mid-break next turn.

He watched, pleased, as his five hundred troops quickly made camp, set up a perimeter and posted sentries. The last tent was barely up when he caught the smell of meats cooking over a fire. Within a clik, they'd all be fed.

He squatted on a rock and began writing his report of the turn's events. There'd been no sign of that bothersome Rangka or his rogue followers. They had spotted a few Llamia wandering the path, and that was unusual. But one of his lieutenants had questioned them and was satisfied they were heading back to the ice palace where their empress was in hiding. He'd thought of killing them anyway, but then he'd have to deal with the bodies. Better to just let them go into exile and leave him alone.

He made some other notes about general commerce and the condition of the road, excellent - thanks to the efforts of Lord Xhaknar, and closed his papers and stuffed them in his pack.

He was walking over to the cooking fire when he noticed a large group of monks approaching. Didn't they know that Lord Xhaknar had ordered a curfew? Probably not. Monks were notoriously dense from what he had heard. He was about to order a couple of his troops to go and corral them until breaklight when he heard a whistling sound from above. He looked up just in time to see a thousand or so Succubi diving from the sky and dropping little, round balls.

Before he could issue any orders the camp erupted in sheets of flame and the monks, who were probably not really monks said a tiny voice in the back of his head, opened fire on them with terrifying precision.

He noted, without surprise, he could see similar fires blazing down the road. All of the squads must be under attack by now. With no choice but to do what he did, he rallied his troops and began advancing on the pseudo-monks.

But the Succubi weren't done yet. They landed behind his squad and began firing on them with small weapons unlike any he had seen. Small or not, known or not, his soldiers were dying in quantity because of them.

His last thought, a complete non sequitur, was Lord Xhaknar would never know how nice his new roads were.

The Naradhama general was using his upper right arm to scratch his chin while his lower left rubbed his belly. There was something strange about these monks. Two turns ago they'd found the trail, right where the spy had said it would be, easily enough. Then they'd begun tracking them and the trail seemed to branch off and then disappear. Even odder was figuring out why monks would be riding steeds in the first place. He didn't know a lot about monks but he was pretty sure they were supposed to be humble and walk around barefoot. Yes, he was positive that's what he'd heard.

Now they'd wasted another two turns going in circles, finding nothing. Not even an old campsite. Monks had to eat too, didn't they?

He halted the senseless march and called for a courier. He'd send word to Xhaknar of what they hadn't found and his suspicions these monks may not actually be as perceived. It was almost even-fall, so he'd send the courier out at breaklight. No need to have him risk being brought down by bandits or anything like that.

He called for his troops to make camp where they were and began penning the message. One of his troopers, obviously bucking for a promotion, had stashed a few casks of ice-wine in the provisions on the kgums. He decided there was nothing else to do so he ordered them broke out.

As he sipped his ice wine under the glistening moons he thought all this scene was missing was some temp-slaves. Well, there were plenty of those back at Anapsida.

A little before even-split he was awakened by a sound he first thought a mirage. Slave bells. Sure enough, though, that's what they were. Great Lord Xhaknar must have sent them and, thanks to his cursed wanderings, they'd been forced to search for the troops. But now they'd found them.

If the time was late, so what? It isn't like they were going anywhere for a while. As they came into view he was pleased to see there were three caravans being drawn by a kgum each. That meant they were bringing around three hundred slaves all total. Sure the troops would have to share, but this is war, not a party, sacrifices have to be made.

Not by him, of course, he'd get the first choice.

Now he could see them clearly he noticed something wrong. The caravan drivers all wore robes like monks. They should've been naked. Then he noticed the markings on the sides of the caravans. More specifically, the lack thereof. They should have been emblazoned with all the symbols of their trade; the grotesque phalluses, the jiggling breasts, the undulating vulva and so on. But these caravans were bare.

He was just about to sound the alarm when he saw it was too late. He did it anyway, but all it did was delay the outcome. And that, not by much.

A mixed force of three thousand Fierstans and BadgeBeth - when did those scum become allies? he vaguely wondered - came storming over the rise. The caravans erupted with strange looking green beings who were deadly shots.

He fought in an ever tightening circle for about ten epi-cliks, watching the ground explode around his troops though he heard no explosions, and then everything went black. His last thought, before he died, was someone should tell Lord Xhaknar about these weird green monks. They were surely not regular monks.

Oolnok made his weekly trek to the tavern. Built, as it was, on top of an old levee, it was officially called The Levee, but everyone just called it the tavern. Not that he was much of a drinker, but the tavern and the church were the only places where the village council posted the news sheet. And while he firmly believed in a God who made Rohta, the maker of all things, he wasn't a fan of the minister's speeches about death and destruction and doom. He was real heavy on the doom stuff. Oolnok believed that if a God took all the time to make all this then He probably had a better reason than just sending all of His creations into a flaming pit.

Besides, if it was going to cost him a few coins no matter what, he figured he should go to the place where he got something tangible in return.

He tossed his few coins to the bartender and picked up the proffered flagon of skank. With it firmly in hand, he joined the other villagers by the wall and began reading the latest news. There was a note about the new tax and a reminder the penalty for noncompliance was beheading. Nothing new there. Then there was a story about the upcoming Feast of the Warm Sun which would be held in every warren. Oolnok usually avoided feast turns, but the smalls were older now and they would probably enjoy it. He'd discuss that with his wife. Then there was a brief sentence about the ten thousand goldens reward for the head of some Rangka named Geldish. Oolnok sniggered at that. Like a Rangka would ever be in the village. As far as he knew they'd all been dead for over two hundred Full Suns. One must have gotten away. Well, then, good for him.

Then he got to the important stuff. Golden root and na-porcine prices were up, but prancing fowls were down. That was okay. They'd have more prancing fowl for their meals and he'd take a wagon of golden root and a na-porcine into the warren after chores next turn. The extra goldens sure wouldn't hurt, even with the extra taxes.

After he finished reading he took his flagon up to the bar and sat in one of the big chairs lined up for that purpose. He listened to rumors of war and how this many, no – that many, Mayanoren were found in a burning pile and how many Naradhama were missing. Oolnok discounted them all as useless claptrap. If there'd been any truth to them there'd have been a mention in the news sheet.

Then, in a stroke of luck, the village craft master walked in. Oolnok had been meaning to go see him because he needed a new hitch for his wagon. After many Full Suns of use, the old one was finally giving way. They haggled over the price briefly, but more out of form than any disagreement, the craft master was always fair. And in a bit of good news, Oolnok discovered the new hitch could be made out of steel instead of wood. If the price was a little more than Oolnok would have liked, the fact this new hitch would probably outlast him made it worth the cost. Once the price was agreed he, as was the custom, bought the craft master a flagon and got himself a second one as well.

The craft master went and read the news sheet and then returned to sit next to Oolnok. Since he wasn't given to wild flights of fancy either they discussed the important news over their flagons of skank. When the craft master learned Oolnok was going into the warren next turn he offered to take a little more off the price if he would take a box of spurs into the stable master and return with his goldens. Oolnok readily agreed. He knew the warren's stable master well since he often left his deisteed there when he went to market.

Oolnok left the tavern in a good mood. He'd gotten everything he needed taken care of and there was nothing but good news on the sheet. He knew when he told his wife, she would rest easier for many turns.

Geldish and R'yune sat on a couple of crates in the back of the Din-La trading post eating something Geldish didn't recognize. N'leah and BraarB were chatting with Zrrm and Sland was cleaning his weapons. After the last disaster, they'd headed to the post north of Anara to regroup, heal, and come up with sensible plans for the future. It was clear they no longer had the element of surprise on their side.

Zrrm had contacted several other treading posts and was waiting for status updates on the garrisons. He was pleased to inform Geldish that Xhaknar had raised the price on his head, and just his head, to ten thousand goldens. Geldish was flattered, but that meant there would be eyes everywhere looking for him.

Nothing to be done about that, he'd known when this started things were going to be risky. He was refilling his cup of ice wine when the radio came to life.

There were ten camps of Naradhama evenly spaced along the Se-Jeant / Minotaur road and King Uku had coordinated with Elder Urnak to attack every other one. At first, Geldish was confused by the command but he quickly realized this would be the perfect way to find out what the Naradhama would do with no clear orders and a crisis on their many hands. That would be useful information in a battle.

When the reports finished about a clik later all of the camps that had been attacked were embers. While they'd wanted to keep the same routine, the riders had started, of stripping the weapons, collecting the deisteeds and burning the bodies, they'd been forced to settle for just burning the bodies so they could be gone before any reinforcements showed up.

King Uku reported the five heaping piles of flaming Naradhama were holding the complete attention of the remaining five squads.

He listened to the casualty totals from the raid and tallied them up in his head. Sixty-nine total dead, including eleven Mantis Guards, and one hundred and seventy-three injured. Nine of the injured were critical but the rest should survive nicely.

While they were absorbing that information the radio came alive again. Reports began coming in about the slaughter of the one thousand Naradhama outside the land of the Fierstans. That was more good news. They reported thirty of their own dead, seventeen BadgeBeth and thirteen Fierstans, and seventy-three wounded who appeared as though they would survive. All the Naradhama were killed and their bodies were stripped of weapons and then burned. Eight hundred and twenty-three Naradhama deisteeds had survived so they would be cleaned and groomed and then distributed amongst the warrens as needed.

So, then, thirty-five hundred dead Naradhama in one even.

It was official, they'd been blooded. The war had officially begun even if Xhaknar wouldn't know about it for a couple of turns. It was well past even-split. Geldish ordered everyone to get some sleep and then asked Zrrm to wake them two cliks after breaklight. He felt he had a good idea what to do next.

It took a little more time than Geldish figured. A rider from one of the surviving squads rode his deisteed to death and then stole another to finish the ride, but he didn't make it to Anapsida until the third turn. He quickly told his commander what had happened on the road outside the Pit. His knowledge of the details was sketchy, mostly because he didn't know any. They'd been camped about twenty kays apart when the attacks came. He'd seen shadows in the sky and then fires on the ground. Beyond that, he could only guess, and he didn't want to guess for fear of being wrong. But whatever had done the deed, the results were clear. There were twenty-five hundred dead Naradhama strewn about the road.

The commander gave the young trooper some water and then led him over to Xhaknar's palace. There he requested an audience and explained it was most urgent. A few epi-cliks later he was summoned into the throne room.

"I do not see Geldish's head. What else could be so important?"

The young trooper trembled but managed to answer completely. He told his lord and master everything he'd told his commander and waited to be executed.

"Shadows in the sky?"

"Yes, great lord."

"And they weren't Succubi?" He knew they weren't since they were all in the Pit. The trooper would have seen evidence of them coming out otherwise.

"I don't think so, my lord. It was more like a pillar with many wings. The Succubi have never flown in such close formation to the best of my knowledge."

"You have paid attention to your trainers, that is good. Tell me about the flame. Was there anything unusual about it?"

"Just the quantity, my lord. When I got to the first camp the bodies were burned beyond recognition."

"Did you see all five camps that were destroyed?"

"Yes, lord, my commander had me ride hard down the whole road and then come straight here. Those were his instructions to me."

"Did you notice if the deisteeds were missing or the weapons taken?"

"There were weapons everywhere, my lord, and the deisteeds were still tethered to their stands, although some of them were dead for that."

"How soon did your squad arrive at the scene of the first camp?"

"Less than a clik after we saw the flames lord."

"Mmm, they must have seen you coming and left."

"Who, my lord?"

"That is the question, isn't it? What's your rank trooper?"

"Trooper, Fifth class, lord."

"Commander, take note, he is now trooper Fourth class."

"Yes lord," intoned the commander.

Xhaknar dismissed them and then began mulling his options. Clearly, this mysterious threat from the east was growing stronger. Or getting bolder. Either way, there was more than one method to find out what was what. He called in one of his guards and ordered two riders be sent to find the troops hunting the monks, then he called in one of his Naradhama spies. He would have him follow the Mayanoren red button battalion and tell him exactly who killed them. Or would kill them in a few turns, as the case may be.

King Uku and Empress ClaalD were sitting in his antechamber. It offered plenty of privacy and was far less ostentatious than the throne room. They both preferred it. They were enjoying fresh cups of spiced water and reviewing the reports from their spies.

In the three turns since the raid, the Naradhama had done nothing. They were completely paralyzed. They had sent a rider shortly after they'd counted the dead, but that was it. Since then they were all huddled about the midpoint of the road.

They'd discussed contacting Elder Urnak and coordinating a raid on them, but decided against it because they were getting so much useful information. The Naradhama were highly secretive about their command structure and procedures. Partly because so few survived a meeting with them and partly was because of their inbred paranoia.

Now, however, they could easily discern ranks and positions and had copious notes on which emblem meant what. In a few more turns they should have figured out all the possible battle commands as well since, within their tight confines, all they did was drill.

But they would not leave their staging area.

Empress ClaalD had likened them to smalls in a crib banging to get out but crying once they did. That little simile had made its way through the ranks and endeared her to them all the more.

Uku pondered the peculiar relationship that had sprung up between him and the empress. Certainly, they could never marry, at least not for any reason other than political. He wasn't sure if he could even survive a tryst with the large Llamia. Somewhere in the back of his mind, a voice made a rude joke about new ways to mount a steed. Fortunately, although it made him smile, he did not verbalize it.

While being thrown together in times of hardship could certainly bring some brands closer, this was more than that. He was deeply fond of her and felt she returned the feeling. In private they often finished each other's thoughts and seemed to sense when the other needed quiet or conversation.

He knew, too, his troops liked the Llamia. Although they were forced together in training, he'd noted they spent their off time together as well. During his rounds, he'd spied them in inns and in shops laughing and joking and purchasing this or eyeing that. He honestly believed his warren was better for their presence.

Since that was true, it was time to put belief into action.

"ClaalD," he began tentatively, "may I ask a boon of you?"

"Certainly Uku, whatever you wish."

"When this is over, and assuming we are still alive, I would like you and your brand to stay with us."

She considered for a while before speaking.

"This is a great honor you bestow on us, Uku. I'm not sure what to say."

"You need not answer now, but know this, I and mine have grown fond of you and yours. We fit well together. On a more mundane note, my master builders have been after me for many Suns to expand the south and east walls. The plans are all drawn up and waiting for my word. Within a Full Sun, there could be ample accommodations for your brand. As for you, well, this is a big, musty old castle and it gets lonely from time to time. I would be honored if you would agree to share it with me."

To a Llamia sharing meant mating. It took her a sepi-clik to realize that that was not Uku's intent. Not that she found him unattractive or uninteresting, but she'd probably kill him if they attempted anything like that. Then she pondered what he'd just said. It would mean a real home for her brand. Yes, she'd be held to a lesser rank than he but, after having ruled in desolation for so long, the crags of the fringe were not something she wished to return to. Better to serve here than rule there.

With her ego out of the way, she considered the rest. A Llamia enclave within these walls would provide her brand safety and security for many Suns to come. If, someturn, they wished to leave and make their own warren, that would be a decision made by another. As Uku had said, they may not live long enough to care.

And, he was right about something else, they did fit well together. The Se-Jeant and the Llamia were like missing pieces of a puzzle. Now found it would ruin the picture to remove them. Without realizing how easy it had been, she'd made her decision.

"I and mine agree."

Uku smiled a wide smile and called for his master builders. It would take them a season to make the preparations. If they were alive after that they could begin work. If not, it gave them something to do until they were killed.

Watcher Urkel and King Gornd were walking through the stables. The Naradhama deisteeds had been in worse shape than they'd feared. Malnourished, poorly groomed and every one of them had a bad temper. Of course, eating crap and being either beaten or ignored would put anyone in a foul mood. The stable hands assured the Great Kings they were making good progress. The beasts took orders well enough and now, with hearty food and constant attention, they were calming down. Thirty turns, just to be safe, and they could be parsed out among the warrens.

The Great Kings shrugged. It wasn't a perfect answer but it was good enough. They had enough supplies within the walls to handle the extra burden for that long. Longer if need be. With that out of the way, they headed back to the palace.

When Gornd had first arrived he'd thought the retainers and servants to be so much frippery, a sign of weakness. But within five turns he'd been forced to appoint retainers of his own. The city was just too big and there were too many things that required his attention. Thousands of details he could easily ignore on the fringe, ranging from what food to serve when, to the deployment of troops, now occupied his time. There was no way an individual could do it all. He'd been impressed with how easy Urkel handled it and had said so when they were alone.

Now, having ridden with Urkel in battle, he was even more impressed. No dilettante he. When they were ambushed by the second Mayanoren squad, Urkel had rallied the troops before Gornd could respond, then he led a mad charge at the heart of their line allowing his troops the luxury of spreading mayhem from within. Not five epi-cliks later the squad was on fire, their weapons housed on Fierstan deisteeds and they were on their way again to the council.

But it was what happened right after the melee that had made Gornd realize he was in the presence of a truly great ruler. The troops were attending their wounds as they rode but Nak rode up to Urkel and, without saying a word, cut off his sleeve revealing a nasty wound Gornd had not noticed and began patching it up. Urkel had ridden silently along until it was bandaged and then, calm as calm could be, said: "Thank you Nak, now please return to your ranks so the troops don't break formation."

Nak had saluted and returned to his position without

comment.

There was much he could learn from Urkel if they lived through the season. There was some land west of the city that lay fallow. Gornd decided to ask Urkel if he and the BadgeBeth could purchase it after the war. It would make an ideal warren for them and allow him to remain close to his new friend and mentor.

Urkel seemed to be having similar thoughts.

"There is much we Fierstans could learn from your brand."

"I was thinking much the same about yours."

Urkel shrugged and continued. "Your brand has many fierce warriors."

"True, but not as disciplined as yours."

"Then, maybe so, but not now. As you have seen, discipline can be taught. No, your brand has many admirable qualities. More importantly, my soldiers seem to work well with yours. Not just on the field of battle either. I've seen them in the craft shops, and in the retainer ranks, as well and admired how easily one fits with the other."

The two Great Kings continued their trek towards the palace, each holding his own thoughts.

"Maybe," reflected Gornd," we can form some sort of formal alliance. I think we could all benefit from each other."

"You're thinking of the lands to the west?"

Gornd was shocked.

"Well, yes, actually, I was. How did you know?"

"I saw you ride out last even after everyone had gone to bed," he waved his hand dismissively before Gornd could interrupt, "and realized we were thinking the same thing. So, here's my decree, if we still live after the war, then those lands are yours free and clear. If not, who gives a damn?"

Gornd smiled. It was going to be good to learn from such as he. Assuming they lived, that is.

Unbeknownst to anyone, ten turns after the Succubi had arrived at the Pit, Elder Urnak and Queen A'lnuah had reached an agreement for the Succubi to stay. The upper reaches of the Pit were cavernous and vacant. They made an ideal roost for the Succubi and freed up barracks room for the Minotaurs. Additionally, the Succubi had built escape hatches in the roof. When they launched an attack, as they had on the Naradhama squads recently, they could leave without using any of the entrances. It allowed everyone to get out much more quickly and efficiently. It was an ideal arrangement.

It also helped that the two leaders had hit it off almost immediately. While normally reserved, in some ways they acted like young school smalls, always laughing and joking. Their relationship had rubbed off on the ranks and now everyone seemed to be getting along famously.

It also didn't hurt that Urnak's three wives absolutely loved the queen. They would go to the steam pits together and bathe or head over to the main shopping area and ogle the goods made by the craft-masters. Where they would go all of the other femmes of the Pit – no matter the brand –would follow, making this place or that fashionable for a while. It was all great fun.

For the regular folks, they removed the roof over the kick-ball field so the Succubi could play their version of the game, which required three dimensions instead of two. Matches were regularly scheduled so the Dwellers and the Succubi could each cheer for their heroes. One bonus was, as each side became familiar with the rules of the other, the crowds were now evenly mixed at each event. While the Minotaurs, by nature, favored the larger athletes, the Succubi preferred the leaner, more agile ones. This led to good natured heckling and betting. All in all the sporting events were much livelier than they'd been before and everyone seemed to like that.

Kronlk had made some minor advancements to the weapons devised by Hlaar and now the Minotaurs had bombs of their own they could launch at will. Their combined forces could create an acre of killing flame in less than an epi-clik.

It was Greko, however, who had devised the method of having five Succubi form a tight circle when they attacked and then to have one circle directly above another. That made them a much harder target to hit and helped focus their assault. While one bomb might miss, five aimed at the same target were sure to cause the damage required. The Succubi, not used to flying so close, had initially resisted. But, in an effort to keep things cordial, agreed to try. Although they only trained with the formation a few times, Queen A'lnuah had ordered it used when they attacked the Naradhama. Whatever reticence they may have had instantly vanished when they saw their targets obliterated in just one pass. By the time the even's raids were done several of the Succubi had kissed Greko passionately and told him to keep right on thinking those unusual thoughts.

He wasn't exactly sure how to take that.

He did know his dreams that even were full of images he'd rather not talk about.

But beneath the veneer of festive feelings lurked the real threat of what was to come. Maybe that was why the party continued. They knew, Minotaur and Succubus alike, that they could all be dead before the next Dark Sun came.

Three turns ago Geldish and his merry band of terrorists had left the confines of the trading post. They'd learned of the five hundred Naradhama rotating from garrison to garrison. Zrrm had given N'leah a radio so they could coordinate their attacks. Wherever the Naradhama weren't was exactly where the Brittle Riders were.

They'd also come up with a better plan than the one that had almost gotten them killed.

The riders, sans N'leah, would kill one set of sentries at even-split. While they were doing that N'leah would fly over the walls and drop bombs on the munitions depot. Then they would kill as many guards who came out to capture them as they could before they made their escape. Of the two garrisons, they'd attacked thus far that number was zero.

For some reason, some commanders thought it wiser to just leave well enough alone.

This even as they had headed south and east to attack the garrison just outside of Go-Chi. They were in a small thicket of trees looking down at a sight they'd never seen before. The outside of the garrison was lit up like it was a feast turn. Plus, there were clearly Naradhama patrols circling the perimeter.

N'leah was livid. She picked up the radio and keyed the main channel.

"Zrrm, wake up you piece of kgum dung."

"I am here N'leah, there's no need for insults."

"No need?!!?!," she hissed, "I'll give you 'no need' right up your bony little ... never mind. Listen, this place was supposed to be sleepy. It's crawling with Naradhama and they have lanterns every ten paces. You couldn't hide a skeeter bug near those walls."

"One epi-clik please."

It took longer than that but he did get back to them.

"According to my source, they are not there."

"Get a new source Zrrm, or would you like me to hand the radio to one of them so you can check for yourself?"

"Obviously not, N'leah, I have no wish to die this even nor any other. But my source is adamant all is well."

Geldish raised an eye ridge at N'leah while R'yune growled. She understood.

"Who's your source, Zrrm?"

While the Din-La, under normal circumstances, would rather die than divulge a trade secret, these were not normal circumstances.

"His name is Tnnq and he lives in the northern quadrant of Go-Chi."

He went on to give an exact location, made N'leah repeat it, and signed off. He knew what was about to happen and saw no need to listen in as it did.

They receded back into the copse and headed south to Go-Chi. They were just about to clear the woods when Geldish stopped them. They could hear the sounds of a patrol nearby. R'yune and Sland slipped off their nytsteeds and headed towards the noise. A few sepi-cliks later they heard a muffled yell, some scuffling and then silence. Sland and R'yune reappeared and R'yune held up four fingers and then slashed one across his throat.

The meaning was clear enough.

They slid around the western edge of the city limits and snuck in via a series of back alleys. Soon enough they could see Tnnq's home. The Din-La traditionally kept the exteriors of their homes modest, no matter how lavish the interiors, to remain inconspicuous. This home, however, looked like it had been vomited up by a jester. Announcing the presence of both a generator and wealth, the windows blazed with electric light, the exterior walls were covered in bright colors and the roof was a cavalcade of different materials all fitted together to give the place a garish air.

But the worst part, for the riders, was the unexpected accoutrement; there were four Naradhama, carrying only traditional weapons, by the front door. Geldish looked up and realized the sky was cloudy and the moons hid. He motioned to N'leah. She nodded, leapt off her nytsteed and arced into the darkling sky.

She returned quickly and held up four fingers. So they would have to kill eight guards to get at Tnnq. Maybe more since they didn't know if there were any inside. He doubted that though Tnnq would have had to give up the secret of his radio and that was worth more to a Din-La than most anything else. And if he had, Xhaknar would already be hailing his "new invention." Betraying Geldish was one thing, betraying the Din-La quite another. No matter what the actual situation was, they would have to make the kills quietly so as not to draw the attention of any reinforcements that may be nearby.

Geldish considered his options and then motioned for R'yune, N'leah, and Sland to go around to the rear. He held up five fingers to signify he wanted the attack to begin in five epi-cliks. They nodded, began counting, turned their nytsteeds, and disappeared up the alley.

BraarB and Geldish drew out their daggers and judged their weight. They would have to do. At the appointed time, Geldish dismounted and they strode out of the alley in front of the surprised guards. Before any of them could sound an alarm four daggers sliced through the air and then through their necks. All four were dead instantly.

Without hesitating they entered Tnnq's hideous home. A bell tinkled as the door opened.

"Hey, you guys know better than that," came a squeaky voice from the next room, "you know you can't come in here. That was my deal with your lord and maaaaa …"

Tnnq was staring directly at Geldish. He never saw BraarB beside him. Since all Geldish's questions had just been answered he merely reached out his hand and wrapped it around the Din-La's throat. Blue flame erupted around the tiny traitor's head and then the Din-La's eyes popped out and he was dead. N'leah came walking in from the back carrying Tnnq's radio. Geldish smiled, pleased to have such smart companions around him.

"Good work. I think we've left Xhaknar enough souvenirs this even. Let's meet back at the woods and figure out what we're going to do from there."

They nodded and left.

He and BraarB headed back to the alley where Geldish retrieved his nytsteed and began their journey back.

All of a sudden they heard shouts from about two streets over. Geldish cursed the vagaries of luck and they galloped towards the sound.

They turned the last corner just in time to see N'leah kick the head of a Naradhama into a trash can.

"Sorry for the commotion, boss," she said unapologetically, "it seems we got here at shift change."

Geldish and BraarB looked at the eight dead, and dismembered, Naradhama and smiled. Just then two haven lords appeared from the shadows.

"Please, you must go, Lord Xhaknar has placed squads of Mayanoren and Naradhama all over the city and they patrol constantly. Please, go, we'll clean up."

With no response readily available, the five riders nodded and headed for the city limits. Within epi-cliks they were in the woods and headed for camp.

After N'leah radioed in her final report Zrrm went to Bmmd's home and woke him. Then he told him about Tnnq. Neither could believe a Din-La had violated a clan contract. It had never happened. But the evidence was clear and Tnnq's final statement to Geldish was damning. Xhaknar had figured out a way to turn a Din-La.

They spoke into the even trying to figure out a way to see if there were any more traitors in their ranks.

By breaklight, they had a plan. Zrrm would ride to Geldish directly to inform him of it so there was no chance of it being leaked via radio. Then Bmmd would announce they'd needed a perfect target for the Brittle Riders and Geldish had offered one thousand goldens for the best. They would detail some specifics and see what came in.

Bmmd's and Zrrm's families would check each one. Every time they found a trap they would have the offending Din-La executed. They had a couple of specialists, on loan from the Fish-People, who did odd jobs for them who could handle that end of the deal.

Any targets that proved viable would be turned over to Geldish to do with as he wished. The Din-La would cover the reward money. They were too humiliated by Tnnq's actions to have it any other way.

By mid-break, Zrrm was gone.

Three slaves lay dead in the throne room. Xhaknar didn't even notice them. This petty insurrection had gone on long enough. The reports lay on the floor, spattered with blood, but he had no desire to read them again. One thousand Naradhama found rotting in the sun, their bones being picked clean by carrion birds.

Half a dozen garrisons burned and countless Mayanoren soldiers left along the roads or in guard houses with their throats cut or worse. Why the burning? Were they trying to make the bodies disappear? That seemed dumb if it were true.

Xhaknar may not have been the brightest candle in life's chandelier, but he wasn't stupid. It was all clear to him now.

Geldish had allied himself with these eastern demons and that was why the warrens were locking down. They didn't want war either. Well, that made sense. Why would they? After all, taxes were reasonably fair, he hadn't been forced to thin their ranks in many Suns and general executions were down since he'd imposed the curfew. Even the regular raiding parties had been too busy as of late to bother them. Yes, life was good in the warrens and they were afraid this crazy Rangka was going to ruin it all for them.

Maybe he could use that.

He still didn't know how Geldish had found out about Tnnq, but it was clear it was he who'd killed the little traitor. Xhaknar was going to do it himself soon enough, thus was the fate of all traitors, but that was beside the point. He'd had his Naradhama search the place after the bodies were found to see if they could find out how the Din-La got news to each other so quickly. They'd found no devices of any kind they couldn't explain and nothing more exciting than a chest of goldens in the basement. He let them keep half of those for no reason he could remember.

It didn't matter, he was sure it was a good one.

No, it was obvious to him now, being unable to rally the warrens in his lust for revenge, Geldish had found another power. One Xhaknar's spies had missed. And, while they were clearly deadly, they must not be that powerful. Otherwise, they would have marched on Anapsida and not bothered with these trivial raids.

Okay, then, that was fine. They might be a bother, but they weren't a threat. Not a real one anyway. He'd no longer play Geldish's game. He would recall all the Naradhama and begin preparing for his war on Südermann. He still had his Mayanoren red button brigade headed east and a spy following them. That should give him all the information he'd need on these miscreants and then he would deal with them mercilessly when the time came.

With that decided he began to calm down. He called for slaves to clean the throne room and sat down.

He was just about to enjoy a glass of ice wine when a question popped into his mind.

Whatever happened to those pestiferous monks?

G'rnk stood next to a Kgul in a grove of Jub Jub trees. While there hadn't been time to integrate their forces they had been learning to work together and, as far as G'rnk was concerned, work well at that. They read the latest reports from the scouts. The Mayanoren were in tight formation and headed directly for them. They should arrive right about even-fall. Behind them was a lone Naradhama hiding in grasses and behind trees. He was surely one of Xhaknar's spies sent to report on what was about to happen. They'd debated whether to let him live and deliver an honest report but eventually voted against it. The less Xhaknar knew, the better.

They each called their lieutenants, for lack of a better term, and reviewed the battle plan. It was straight forward enough. They would let the Mayanoren set up camp and then they would ambush them. It was the method of the ambush that was a little tricky considering they were going to be in the open. As to the spy, they'd drawn lots and a haven lord had won the honor of dispatching him. That would be done after even-fall as well. No need to take the risk of alerting the Mayanoren to their presence.

They made sure everyone was in position and waited. In a few cliks, it would be done, one way or the other.

The Mayanoren arrived at the incongruous meadow just as it was getting dark. The commander called for the camp to be made and posted sentries. Whether the commander wondered why there was a meadow where there should only be a wasteland, none will ever know.

Before the first campfires were lit the Kgul came charging out of the grove and firing their weapons. The commander had been told to look out for a surprise attack and was, therefore, not surprised by the surprise attack. He ordered his soldiers to form ranks and open fire. Bodies were falling around him but they were in formation quicker than most would have believed possible.

Just as the Kgul crashed, bodily, into the front lines of the Mayanoren, the Wolfen and their haven lord allies sprung from the rear. G'rnk was astounded with how disciplined the Mayanoren were. They'd never shown this level of skill previously. Oh well, then it was to be a battle and not a slaughter. That was fine with him as well. In fact, somehow, it was better.

The Wolfen and the haven lords sliced into the rear guard forcing half the troops to face away from the Kgul. The Mayanoren fired on their attackers in rotating ranks, with one line firing, then falling back while the next took their shots. It was a method of fighting no one had seen before. But, novel or not, they would overcome it.

The battle raged for a full clik, but finally, the Mayanoren were all dead. The Mantis Guard had been asked to stand by in case anything went wrong, but to otherwise just observe. That was nothing against the Royal Guard, but G'rnk needed to see his troops in action, not theirs. The guardsmen had agreed.

They began stripping the bodies of weapons, rounding up the deisteeds and clearing a space for the funeral pyre. Others quickly tended to the wounded, there were many, and counted up the dead, there were only a few. In the distance, a lone figure, hidden in the weeds, stood and made a final note in a little book. Out of nowhere he felt a stabbing pain and noticed an arrow protruding from his chest, a place where an arrow had no business being.

His final thought, as he lost his life, was to wonder if he'd also lost his mind. Had he really seen haven lords with weapons?

Südermann and Elaand reviewed the latest reports. They had already agreed to field the entire force of the Royal Mantis Guards, some twenty thousand strong, and the majority of the regular army as well, another one hundred thousand. There would be no half measures when dealing with Xhaknar. All five brands under his dominion would fight. Added to the four armies from the Plains, that numbered about fifty thousand each, they should match up well. All total, between the combined forces of the Naradhama and the Mayanoren, they were going to be outnumbered about two to one. He'd faced worse odds before and had come out victorious. And, though they would be outnumbered, they had a distinct technological and tactical edge over the troops from Anapsida.

They were pleased to note Geldish's mad plan was working as well. Xhaknar had been throwing forces, drib by drab, at shadows. Wonderfully lethal shadows, to be sure, but shadows nonetheless. Südermann idly added a spoonful of sugar to his brandy with his middle right hand and stirred. Elaand had served his lord for many Full Suns and was still amazed at the way all Südermenn casually did things like that.

They'd gone over G'rnk's report twice. The fact the Mayanoren might be competent had never occurred to them. That could make life more difficult.

A young cadet brought in a tray full of Minotaur pastries and set it beside Südermann, then he handed

Elaand a note, saluted and left. Elaand read the note and grimaced.

"Apparently, for all the wrong reasons, Xhaknar's finally done the right thing. He's recalled all of his Naradhama forces to Anapsida to begin his attack on us. According to this, he believes there's a new threat to the east which has been ransacking his troops and has no idea the warrens are involved. In fact, according to this, he's looking at options for giving the warrens a boon. It seems he believes they are locking down to avoid being tainted by Geldish's mad quest for revenge. Further, it seems he believes Geldish is aligned with this mysterious threat from the east. Since that threat has not directly assailed Anapsida, he's deemed it to be something he can deal with later. After he rules your lands."

"Overconfident son of a bug, isn't he?"

Elaand chuckled, "So what do we do, my lord"?

"First we notify the warrens, the temple, and Geldish. Second, he's going to have to align his troops outside the walls of Anapsida so they can march, in formation, from the first turn. Since we know he's paranoid and a stickler for details, let's assume he already has his provisions accounted for and the slaves he'll need to disburse them. Also, he'll make sure there are plenty of temp-slaves to entertain his troops. That's an affectation Yontar would never have condoned, but Xhaknar likes some pomp with his circumstance.

"If you add it all up, you're looking at a combined force of about one million warriors and attendants, two hundred thousand deisteeds, a hundred thousand kgums, and his royal self that have to be provided for over a long march. At least he thinks it's going to be a long march. I think we can help him get where he's going a little quicker.

"Anyway, to put all that together you're looking at thirty turns, at the least, before he's ready to march. Forty-five more realistically. But let's assume thirty so we don't get caught napping. Now, one thing we don't want to do is launch our assault anywhere near Anapsida. They'd just flee inside and we'd accomplish nothing. The first few turns worth of marching south of Anapsida is pretty open land, so that wouldn't work. My choice, and we can verify with the warrens, would be to meet him about one turn north of our border. The land is hilly and there is enough forest around to hide small armies in. If we're dug in within thirty-five turns, we can meet the monster and crush him."

Elaand considered this for a moment and then agreed. He went across the hall to the radio room and notified the warrens of the current situation and Lord Südermann's idea. There were concerns about marching so far in the open. Xhaknar would surely know they were on the move. It was decided they would march east, to the Gaping Canyon, then follow its edge south to the youngling pass, not used in millennia but still there, and then follow that west to the lands of Südermann. It was felt they could all be in place in twenty turns. That way they could let it be known the loyal warrens were going to deal with this threat from the east themselves. They would just forget to mention the minor fact they were that putative threat.

When Südermann heard the plan, he smiled, "This is the first time in my life where I can honestly say ignorance has its uses."

Geldish sat with Zrrm in a trading post about a hundred kays north of Anapsida. The Din-La plan had ferreted out two more traitors. Geldish didn't know how, but both had suffered fatal accidents. That was good enough. Of the legitimate options, Geldish had selected one and R'yune had demanded another. Given all they'd been through together, and since each target was within an easy distance of the other, they'd agreed to hit them both. Had they not been able to do so, Geldish was going to choose R'yune's target over his. It was the first time Geldish had ever seen R'yune smile.

Not that it mattered now, but Geldish had noted R'yune had a nice smile.

The first target was a Mayanoren training camp. According to the source, and confirmed by Zrrm's son, they had the barracks and the munitions all along one fence. While N'leah was dropping bombs from one end, the riders would come up the other shooting at anything that moved. Or didn't move. Either way, they would wreak havoc on the camp and rid the planet of a few more Mayanoren.

The second target was a Naradhama hunting lodge. There were currently the elders of twenty families of wealth there, including those of four generals. Whatever reason R'yune had for picking it was beyond Geldish's ken, but he knew its destruction would be a major embarrassment to Xhaknar.

They left the post at even-fall, headed south and west to their first target. Everything was exactly as they'd been told. They killed a sentry walking patrol and launched their offensive.

Within three epi-cliks they were riding into the even mists. They had no idea what was in the munitions depot, but when it blew, it blew sideways instead of up and set the whole barracks ablaze. With the other four riding by at full speed shooting round after round into the conflagration, the carnage was surely total. Not one Mayanoren had come out to chase them.

Less than two cliks later they were at the hunting lodge. As R'yune drew up an attack plan in the dirt Geldish realized he must have been here before. His plan included several key points in the interior their source had not known about. More correctly, could not have known about from her post outside the building.

They agreed that four of them would climb the building and enter through a rooftop garden. BraarB would guard the front door and anyone who came out whom she didn't know was hers to kill. There were two sentries by the gate. Those were quickly dispatched and then they were climbing the walls. When they reached the roof N'leah handed them each a few bombs and then loosed her weapon. R'yune popped the lock and they were in. Within sep-cliks explosions were rocking the top floor as they ran to the next floor down. They tore through the rooms and even Geldish was amazed at what they saw. Generals and their wives, generals and their mistresses and generals with both were only the beginning. He was sure he saw three mals in a bed in one room and a kgum in a harness in another. He didn't even want to guess what had happened to poor R'yune here.

When they reached the main floor they saw some haven lord servants huddled in the foyer. Geldish informed them leaving now would be a really good idea and they took him at his word.

They were just about to the main entrance when a huge Naradhama appeared with a weapon. He looked at the riders and immediately fixed his gaze on one.

"R'yune, you mangy sack of ..."

That was all he got out before R'yune put a nice size hole where a brain should be.

"Yeah," thought Geldish, "he's definitely been here before."

They escaped into the yard just as the roof fell in and flames leapt into the even sky.

R'yune looked at Geldish, his face a mass of glistening teeth and made a sound Geldish could only assume was laughter. N'leah looked at the grin, turned to watch the building implode, and smiled as well.

"Yeah partner, I'm pretty sure we got them all."

Yontar was still fuming all these turns later. Try as he might he couldn't come up with a way to cross the divide that kept him from corpulence. Since staying here wouldn't make any difference, he eased away from the home of his making and headed back towards Anapsida. Travel between geographic locations was easy enough. A journey that might have taken thirty turns below could be completed in a few epi-cliks. What that was worth was lost on Yontar since he couldn't actually touch any of the places he sailed over.

As he neared Anapsida he could feel Xhaknar's rage. His first thought was to smile, imagining the pain some poor slave was about to endure. But this didn't feel like one of his usual rages. This wasn't about food served cold, or a temp-slave not performing, this was wild seething hate. He'd never felt anything like it. It was vital, exhilarating, and fearsome all at once.

As he got closer he could make out some of the details of the rage. It was clearly aimed at Geldish. He wondered what that blighted Rangka had done now. He let his focus enter the throne room, one of the few interiors he could see in his current state, and could almost make out three Naradhama shapes, a couple of slave shapes, and Xhaknar. He wasn't sure but it looked like papers were tossed all over the floor.

Xhaknar's rage was palpable. It was trying to push Yontar out of the room. Actually, it was trying to push everyone and everything out of the room. It was a level of mental violence Yontar had never conceived could exist.

He let himself focus on Xhaknar alone. On the edges of his mind, he could make out flashes of images and reports. He was able to cull those flashes out of Xhaknar's memory and study them.

He was stunned.

Mayanoren being killed like prancing fowls, Naradhama dropping like kgums at a slaughterhouse, the warrens were all in seclusion and there was a new threat from the east? And that menace was aligned with Geldish?

That couldn't be right.

None of this was making any sense. He hadn't bothered with reports in over twenty Full Suns, but he'd kept his eyes on both the east and the west while he was still corporeal. There were no threats in either of those lands. Geldish was a thorn, Südermann was the enemy. There was nothing else that Xhaknar needed to worry about. And why would the warrens, always a problem, suddenly be helpful? Locking themselves away with the fringe was a wonderful boon, and the warrens did not give boons to Xhaknar.

No, this was all insane.

Xhaknar must have missed something. Some fact, some clue, something somewhere.

He calmed himself and concentrated. He needed to see what Xhaknar saw, needed to know what he knew. He found the small place where he could enter Xhaknar's mind when he was calm and hoped it would work now. For several epi-cliks, he has buffeted around like a twig in a wind storm, but eventually, he got in.

What he saw was chaos. He went through the reports in Xhaknar's memory and listened to the report from the young trooper. What he noticed, immediately, was none of them pointed directly to any eastern threat. That was innuendo and Xhaknar had seized it as the sole possibility. That was a mistake.

Every response after that was due to that mistake.

Okay, he couldn't fix what was, time to see what was coming.

He noted, with a special glee, Xhaknar was ready to march on that detestable Südermann. That was good. He also noted he'd stopped playing along with Geldish and was just leaving him his little terrors. Also good.

These were all good things, so what was causing his rage?

Then he felt it. Geldish had killed all of Xhaknar's Din-La spies. Yontar was impressed. He didn't know you could turn a Din-La. Rohta knew he'd killed enough of them trying. But how had Geldish ferreted out the plot? And, worse yet, dealt with them so quickly and finally? They were scattered all over the Plains as far as he could tell, there should have been no way that even a Rangka could have traversed such distances in so short a time.

Something was wrong here, Yontar was sure of it. Something was very, very, wrong.

"We are already too few," said the large Mayanoren sitting at a table with three others of rank, "we should never have let him go."

"We had no choice," opined the one next to him, "we are in no position to argue with Xhaknar. At least not yet."

After a pause, the first one poured a round of Whævin and spoke again.

"Is there any chance he'll survive?"

"I'd guess he's already dead," replied a third.

That brought another round of silence.

They called themselves the Named Ones. Not because they'd named themselves, that would be silly, but because they felt they were the ones who could save the name and reputation of the Mayanoren. They'd begun appearing about four generations ago. Smarter than their heirs, they'd soon realized they didn't fit in. They'd also realized, just as quickly ,there was nowhere for them to go. The leader of the red button brigade had been one of their compatriots. All total, they accounted for about five percent of the Mayanoren population.

"What do you think this mysterious threat is in the east?" asked the fourth.

"Nothing mysterious at all," the first considered, "probably just a warren or two who's set up an outpost they don't want our Great Lord Xhaknar to know about."

The others nodded, that made more sense than some imaginary beings who'd floated up out of the cavernous hole of the Gaping Canyon.

"I wish Yontar were still alive," said the first.

"Not that it helps," said the fourth, "but I know for a fact he's not dead. Not really, anyway. I was in the throne room several turns ago and heard Xhaknar mumbling. It seems Geldish trapped Yontar in some sort of nether realm. However, it was clear there's no way for him to get out."

They all chewed on that for a while.

"I wonder," cogitated the first, "if we could get him out."

That led to a lengthy discussion which accomplished nothing. They had no way to contact their former leader and, even if they did, not one of them was an astral warrior. They had no method to free him.

At the end of the circuitous debate, one of them had an idea. Truth be told, it was a pretty good one.

"A few of us should go back to the land of the makers. We can decant one of the others like Yontar and, as soon as he's sentient, ask him how to do it."

They had no idea how long that would take, but it was better than doing nothing. They argued briefly about who should go and it was decided it had to be some of the younger Named Ones since they wouldn't be missed by the Naradhama. If questioned they would all just say the poor warriors had been part of the red button brigade.

With that settled, they had another round of

Whævin.

Everything had to be explained satisfactorily, so it was. In every warren, and in every village, a pronouncement was posted.

Be it hereby proclaimed that the main warrens of the Great Lands of Xhaknar, long may he reign, have perceived a terrible threat coming from the east. As many of our beloved brands have noticed, this threat has forced the honored residents of the fringe to seek refuge in our warrens. Several turns ago, the leaders of the warrens and of the fringe – specifically; King Uku, Keeper of the Ice Realm, Watcher Urkel, Holder of the Great City of the Fierstans, Elder Urnak, Leader of the Council for the Dwellers of the Pit, King Gornd of the Revered House of BadgeBeth, Empress ClaalD of the Sacred Lairs of the Llamia and Queen A'lnuah of the Roosts of the Succubi – met in the Pit of the revered Dwellers.

There it was discussed what we are to do about this menace. There it was decided that we would meet it directly and, Great Rohta willing, defeat it.

There it was further agreed that each warren and each brand from the fringe would be honored with the privilege of doing battle against this deadly hazard since each has a meaningful stake in the outcome.

Brave scouts from every warren have reported back that the enemy has been camping along the Gaping Canyon, far to the south. We march this turn on them. We will meet at the edge of the Gaping Canyon, due east of the lands of the Fierstans and there we shall form ranks and take the battle to our foes.

We ask that you pray to the deities of your choice

that we are successful in this dangerous, yet necessary, venture.

Yours in Rohta,
(signed)
King Uku, Watcher Urkel, Elder Urnak, King Gornd, Empress ClaalD, Queen A'lnuah

While they'd all agreed it was risky even setting a generic location for the 'enemy,' no one thought Xhaknar would send troops to check. He was too preoccupied with his impending war with Südermann. And if he did? Well, then, there'd just be that many fewer Naradhama to deal with later.

They'd stored all of the new weapons and bombs on kgums and carried only traditional weapons as they marched. Xhaknar's spies would correctly report the warrens were on the move and headed east with nothing more dangerous than bows, swords, and lances.

To add substance to the story, large numbers of monks were seen fleeing the warrens a couple of turns before the great march. That made sense since everyone knew monks didn't fight and hated war. And if these monks rode steeds, that was just a quirk of their religion, nothing more.

The only thing that bothered anyone who thought about it was no one could seem to remember the monks arriving in the first place or seeing them in any of the warrens. Maybe the leaders had had them locked up for some reason and then decided to let them go once they had more pressing issues to deal with.

That rumor made sense and if it got a little help from the soldiers in the various warrens that didn't make it any less believable.

Four turns after the announcement was posted, the Se-Jeant and the Llamias met up with the combined allies of the Temple (who were hiding the Kgul in caravans), the Minotaurs and the Succubi and headed south.

Two turns later they met the Fierstans and the

BadgeBeth and combined ranks. One hundred and eighty-five thousand warriors and fifty thousand retainers began their journey to the youngling pass. Xhaknar's spies had followed them that far and then, having confirmed the pronouncement was true, returned to their network to inform their great leader all was well and the crazy brands of the warrens, and the lowlifes from the fringe, were going to solve his problem for him.

Two turns after the spies had left the combined forces of the warrens and the fringe were met by two thousand monks who, covered with weapons, looked less holy and more lethal than monks usually did. Even so, the assembled considered them a blessing. They were marching to war, not services, so they'd take all the divine intervention they could get.

They released the Kgul from the caravans, counted their new number at two hundred thousand and turned west on the youngling pass to meet whatever fates their gods would decree.

In the wilds of the western plains, Geldish strolled with BraarB under the blowing trees. There was a savage beauty to these lands. They'd been left alone after the Gen-O-Pod wars since there weren't enough brands to inhabit them then. Now, most were comfortable where they were and saw no reason to change. They'd only seen three hermits - one of whom was a Minotaur who'd insisted he was Rohta and demanded fealty - in the four turns since they'd left the trading post.

They'd readily agreed it would be suicide to cross the heart of Anapsida to meet the warrens by the Gaping Canyon. Instead, they'd headed further west and were now heading due south to the lands of Lord Südermann. The Din-La had insisted on bringing a kgum and a wagon for the journey. While it slowed them down, somewhat, they were still making good time and didn't have to worry about foraging. That was good because no one seemed to recognize half the fruits and vegetables that grew wild around here. They might be safe or they might not, better not to risk it until they were sure.

Zrrm and his cousin, Frrd, were cooking a breaklight repast and Sland was happily sampling the foods as they were completed. While Zrrm and Frrd were knocking Sland's hands away from the platters, BraarB knocked on N'leah's tent and was mildly bemused to see R'yune exit first.

After they were done eating, the Din-La were excellent cooks they all noted, they walked to a small lake nearby. They all, except Geldish, took advantage of it and rinsed the road dust off of their bodies. Geldish had gone into the back of the wagon and emerged a few epi-cliks later wearing a clean robe. No one wanted to know what was beneath, or what he had to do to keep it clean, so no one ever asked.

Once everyone was sparkling and refreshed they mounted up and continued south. Frrd worked the radio while Zrrm drove the kgum. They had all had a good laugh when Frrd had read them the proclamation that had been posted in the warrens. It was so absurd they all believed Xhaknar would accept it as true.

They listened to the alien sounds emanating from the forest but were otherwise unmolested. Sland had told them there had been a narkling sighted west of Anapsida but added no additional information. Nevertheless, they kept a wary eye on the borders of the forest.

When mid-break came they slowed to match the wagon but did not stop. Zrrm handed them each a small meal and a fresh canteen. As they had the first three turns, they would eat without stopping while the sun was up.

R'yune spotted a flock of gaily colored birds and pointed them out questioningly. No one was sure what they were, but they were gorgeous. A mixture of bright reds, greens, yellows and blues all arranged one beneath the other. Clearly, they were no threat so the riders watched them contentedly until they faded over the southern horizon.

Frrd had reported Xhaknar was continuing his troop buildup outside the walls of Anapsida. They were burning torches every even and had sentries posted every ten paces. Nothing was to be allowed to disrupt his plans. He also reported Bmmd had received an order for plastic parts not used for millennia. Geldish told him about the weapons that had stymied the Rangka so badly and asked Frrd to ask Bmmd to see if they would fit something like that.

A few epi-cliks later Bmmd confirmed his suspicions. Geldish was about to tell him to go ahead and fill the order and then paused. It was a large order and, as far as Xhaknar knew, there was only one Rangka. He had Frrd ask to find out if the weapons could be used, somehow, against the brands. It took another full clik to get an answer, but the answer was yes. The weapons could be altered to make the brands blind and nauseous. The range was severely limited, and the effect wasn't fatal, and would only last an epi-clik or so, but it could disorient a large group quickly.

Geldish told him to go ahead and fill the order, no reason to add any doubts to Xhaknar's increasing paranoia, and notify the Succubi they had another target when the war began.

That done, he nibbled on his meal and considered what was to come.

Oolnok had read the proclamation in the tavern with the rest of the villagers. About time the warrens stood up for themselves and quit relying on the charity of Lord Xhaknar, he thought. Do them some good to see how hard real battle could be.

Not that Oolnok had any experience on that front but he, like many of the villagers, had housed Naradhama when they were on patrol and needed a place to stay. Nice enough folks, those Naradhama, as long as you fed them quickly and hid your femmes. And, once sated, they would spin yarns about the battles they'd been in protecting the rights and sovereignty of the brands under Xhaknar.

The tales were too bloody for smalls of course, but Oolnok enjoyed them in his own way. Especially the ones where they would quash this rebellion or that and make the villages and warrens safe for good brands like Oolnok.

Oolnok knew it was bloody work, but it had to be done if the villagers were to be able to tend their farms and send their smalls to school. His smalls were at that age where they questioned everything so Oolnok kept them far away when the Naradhama were around. He didn't want them to think he was raising a family of rebels. When they were older they'd see how things were and not be so self-righteous.

While it was true all smalls he knew of went through this phase, he wasn't sure the same held true for the Naradhama and didn't want to take the risk. His one trip to the great city, taken with his wife one Full Sun after they were married, had driven that point home clearly. He'd seen Xhaknar's fountain and understood down to his bones that rebellion equaled death. After that, his wife's dreams had been troubled for many turns. But, as he told her, brutal brands need brutal lessons. That fountain's not for the likes of us.

He saw a few of his neighbors at the bar and walked over to talk. Everyone was excited about the festival of the

Warm Sun which was coming in just a couple of turns. They all agreed it was a shame the royals wouldn't be there this Sun but understood they had larger obligations. This new menace from the east had them baffled since they could think of nothing out there but the Gaping Canyon. Could some wild brands have formed some sort of society in that desolation? They all doubted it but stranger things had happened, even if they couldn't name one at the moment.

There was nothing to be done about it except to wait for the armies to return and show them who and what they'd killed.

With speculation behind them, they turned to important topics. Most of them had harvested larger than usual amounts of golden root. The Dark Sun staple had really flourished this season and all of them had held some back so as not to glut the market and drive down the price. Since they'd all gotten the best price on the market they'd agreed to empty their silos. If that drove the price down now, so be it, they'd already made more than they had in many Suns. This next trip to the warren would just be a bonus.

Some of his neighbors were going to go into the warren for the festival a turn early so they could stay at an inn. He thought that was a waste of goldens, but understood the allure. It was nice to sleep somewhere everything was taken care of for you. You didn't have to make your bed or pick up your towels after cleaning or anything. And, just like in the story books, the bathrooms were inside. All a visitor had to do was enjoy the sights. But Oolnok and his wife were saving for their retirement. Unlike many who worked until the turn they died, he and his wife wanted to enjoy their later years in peace.

Oolnok had already been approached by several families about mates for his smalls, but they were too young to consider for that and he didn't like the contracts that lasted years before the marriage could occur. Too many brands used them for loans and then had nothing to show for it when the turn arrived.

Nothing silly like that for Oolnok.

Especially not when life was sure and good.

Xhaknar held the proclamation in his hand and was agog. His spies were a bunch of worthless slugs. He should kill them all and start anew. Maybe even appoint that slave who'd found the dead spies in Go-Chi as their leader. How could they have not known the warrens and the fringe were under attack as well? With the Mayanoren red button brigade unheard from and his spy missing as well, Xhaknar added them to the many other casualties this eastern peril had caused. Of course, the fringe had been attacked, why else would they have come into the warrens? They hadn't been afraid of Xhaknar, well, he was sure they were but no more so than usual, they were afraid of these demons from the east. They'd actually fled towards Anapsida, that should have been his first clue. Only something more deadly than him would have made them do that.

Everything made perfect sense now.

When he considered the lost Mayanoren brigade, he briefly wondered how the enemy had gotten so far north when they were now reported so far to the south, and then he dismissed the thought. These terrors, who or whatever they were, seemed to move like Rangka. Not quite, but close enough. And, like the young trooper reported, some of them could fly. Maybe all of them. Let the warrens and the fringe bleed for a while. Perhaps he'd get lucky and they'd kill each other off. That would clear up a few problems.

At least his incompetent spies had finally found the

monks, albeit as they were fleeing for their lives. Still, it was one less thing to worry about. Plus, with the warrens unguarded he no longer needed to march on them. Their armies were too far away to cause him any problems. He was certain his army could crush each warren but was glad not to have to incur any losses needlessly. There would be enough blood violently shed when they reached Südermann's domain. Although confident Yontar's plan would defeat Südermann once and for all, it never paid to waste good warriors.

He glanced at the logistics reports a slave had brought him and smiled. They were slightly ahead of schedule. Another thirty turns and they should be on their way south. Xhaknar wished they could go sooner, but moving a million of anything, especially troops and their supplies, required extensive coordination and planning. This was going to be the largest killing force ever assembled. No reason to mess things up by hurrying pointlessly.

He walked over to his window and beamed as the troops, six abreast, continued their nonstop march through the gates to assume formations on the open plains. It was an impressive sight. A general saw him and had his troops execute a perfect salute without missing a step.

Yes, thought Xhaknar, Südermann will never know what hit him. When this is done the secrets of the bug-people will be his and the way will be clear for him to march on any who might oppose him. Since that would probably be everybody else, he knew he would have some work to do.

He returned to his throne and pulled out Yontar's projections. There were many items detailed that he had expected to find. Some seemed more like magic than anything else, like the mechanical eyes that could send an image anywhere you were, but Yontar had assured them they all were real. Maybe that's how the Din-La did it. They traded with everyone. Maybe they traded with

Südermann too. A little technology for imports he couldn't get? Yes, that made sense. Then that technology had allowed them to rule the trades.

For the first time in his long life, Xhaknar considered the Din-La. They had always struck him as weak, but now he wasn't so sure. They controlled almost all the trade and major banks and had done so without firing a shot or drawing a sword. When Xhaknar claimed Südermann's secrets he'd have to think about them some more. Maybe the Plains could use a change. Controlling all the trade and the banks would ensure Xhaknar of blind obedience from the masses. All the Plains' goldens would flow through him and all good things would come from him. He would make sure there was plenty of food, if not much else, for all.

People might not care if you raped their daughters, but steal food from their tables and they took up arms. And Xhaknar had enough to deal with for now.

Südermann was sitting, scanning the reports as they came in. Xhaknar had bought their ruse. That was abundantly clear now. And it looked like he was going to split the difference on Südermann's time estimate. That would give them ample time to settle in and prepare for the ambush. Although how over a quarter million troops could ambush anything was slightly beyond him. They couldn't just jump up from behind a rock and scream boogah boogah which was, essentially, what they were going to try and do.

The combined forces of the warren were still several turns off. He read the report about how a Mayanoren raiding party had stumbled onto them and attacked. Two hundred against two hundred thousand ended about as you'd expect. His allies, a novel concept now that he gave it form, had not suffered a single casualty in the raid. They had, however, been greatly amused at the attempt. In keeping with tradition, they'd looted the weapons, corralled the deisteeds and burned the bodies. If these victims were further west than they were supposed to be there was nothing that could be done about it. Let it be another mystery piled upon the many these inexplicable eastern terrors had already wrought.

Geldish was ahead of schedule and should be here in a few turns with his Brittle Riders. Südermann had enjoyed speaking with them. He hadn't been sure what to expect, but they'd struck him as acutely intelligent as well as lethal. Just the kind of brands you'd want as allies at times like these.

There was that word again. Well, there was no way around it, he had allies and now he had to deal with them. Their fates were tied together tighter than any braided mane the Llamia wore in battle. Besides, it felt good to know someone out there actually cared about what happened to you. They had been in seclusion for a long time. If they survived what was to come there'd be some unusual adjustments for them to make. Especially for the Ant-People. They were uncomfortable around similar brands, the inhabitants of the Plains would be anathema to them. Surely, though, there'd be some way to work things out.

Then again, after all this time, the Ant-People still refused to serve in the regular army and instead fielded their own militia. Granted, they'd agreed to fight in this war, but only after a litany of conditions had been met. After that Elaand, unsure whether to trust them or not, had assigned them Xhaknar's supply train as their primary target. While Südermann knew it to be silly, Elaand had made it sound as though they were being given the most important task of the war and they'd agreed.

However, the Ant-People were legendary for their

guerilla tactics. It would be like forcing Xhaknar to face the sixth army, if a small one, fighting through his rear. In retrospect, Elaand may have been more on target than he gave credit. Xhaknar was going to be far from home; it isn't like he could come over and ask Südermann for a cup of sugar.

Yes, cutting off his food and munitions supplies could cause him great harm and provide Südermann with some additional assurances. Südermann and his allies, to be correct about it.

One thing was for certain, a million hungry brands do not make good warriors.

His Südermann training had allowed for the possibility of allies. It was assumed they would be the Fish-People. And, in a way, they were. There was certainly no animosity between them, but no commonality either. He doubted if they'd go to war for him and his. Those stoic amphibians had no passion for anything but their privacy and the small crustaceans his brands pulled from the southern sea. And he felt sure that if he infringed on the former they would live without the latter.

G'rnk rode with Watcher Urkel and King Gornd. While he'd been in many battles, he'd never been to war. He asked them countless questions. If they were bothered they didn't let it show. In a way, it helped pass the time and they enjoyed G'rnk's company. The big Wolfen was smarter than he looked and a quick learner. As anyone who's served in an army knows, an officer who is afraid to ask questions is soon to be an officer with lots of dead soldiers. G'rnk was on his way to becoming a fine officer. Although the career path is seldom this public.

After the Mayanoren massacre, G'rnk had turned his troops over to the Mantis Guard for advanced training. Then he'd surprised everyone by deeming himself and all the other Wolfen to be recruits, nothing more, and joining in every drill with them. That wasn't too surprising to the Wolfen, they lived by a pack mentality and whatever benefitted the pack was what you did. If G'rnk felt the only way to learn the new tactics was to participate alongside everyone else, so be it. The Kgul had joined him the next turn and after that everyone was at the mercy of the Mantis Guards.

The Guardsmen, to their credit, took it all in stride, at least when facing their new "recruits." In private they were stunned and told Südermann so in a report. It was nothing an officer of rank would even remotely consider in their eyes. Yet there was no way to prevent it. So they taught, and they taught hard. Discipline was tight, commands were barked, and they treated every warrior as though they'd never seen a sharp object before in their lives. The Guard made it clear they would be amazed if they could tell foot one from foot two without a diagram.

It had been tough, but it had also been fair. The Guards, not knowing how else to handle things, simply treated everyone as equal and beneath them. G'rnk eschewed his officer's quarters for the duration of the training and slept when and where the troops did, often outside, on the ground, and in the cold.

When the Guard pronounced them fit to train amongst themselves again, G'rnk resumed his residency in his bunk.

A turn after they'd completed the training a Guard squad commander named Hlaat visited G'rnk.

"Sir, may I have a moment of your time?"

G'rnk motioned for him to sit.

"Sir, I just want to say your Wolfen, and to a larger degree than I'd hoped, the haven lords and the Kgul, have impressed me. Your ability to learn and assimilate on the go is nothing short of astounding. Your example, while certainly nothing any of my superiors would ever conceive or condone, seemed to tighten the bonds between the brands even more. It is going to be an honor to serve alongside you in what's coming."

G'rnk looked at him for a long time before commenting.

"This may come as a bit of a shock to you Commander, but we Wolfen do not like to fight. If we had our way, we would live quietly, raise our pups, and watch our muzzles go gently gray. Xhaknar has denied us that. Therefore, if fight we must, then we will do it to the best of our abilities. We will train in any style, any form, that makes us better, and then we will kill anything that crosses our path. And when we are done with the killing, it is my fondest wish to return to my ancestral home and raise a few pups of my own."

Hlaat considered it all and smiled.

"We are not as different as I feared after all. Good turn to you sir."

And with that, he was gone, leaving G'rnk with a smile he didn't even notice.

Now, all that training was about to be tested and G'rnk wanted to make sure nothing was forgotten. Empress ClaalD sauntered up beside them and, after listening for a few epi-cliks, put her hand on the big Wolfen's shoulder.

"G'rnk," she began sweetly, "you're just going to have to admit something to yourself. You don't know as much as we don't know. In fact, there's never been a leader in all history who's really had a clue what was going on. And while I know your kind doesn't normally have a leader, they have one now and that's you. Seeing you up here asking all these questions makes them think you don't know what you're doing. But I know you do. You trained your troops, better than any of us did according to the reports, you've given them all the tools they'll need to survive what comes if it can be survived at all that is, and you've shown yourself worthy on and off the field of battle. Return to your troops, act confident even if you have no reason to, and give them hope. That is all a leader can truly do."

G'rnk appeared angry, then insulted then something unclear and then laughed.

"You're right Empress. I guess, inside, I'm just as scared as everybody else but there's no need to let it show."

He quickly rejoined his troops and assumed the head of their lines.

Gornd turned and gave the empress a wry smile.

"Oh sure, give away all our secrets why don't you?"

The four, young, Named Ones rode past the southern wall of the Kordai Sanctuary and found the path indicated on their map. They still had many turns to go before they got where they were going but they didn't want to get lost at any juncture. Delays were entirely unacceptable.

They passed into a forest of hauntingly beautiful trees and noticed none of them. They saw some staggeringly gorgeous birds and ignored them. They had one goal, one mission, and it did not entail appreciating the local flora and fauna.

They may have had only one goal, but they had two tasks once they arrived at the facility. The first was straightforward enough; grab the instruction manuals in the makers' lab and then decant one of the super soldiers and bring it to sapience as soon as possible. The second was trickier. They were to see if they could find a way to use their, superior, DNA to make more Mayanoren like themselves.

They were smart, that wasn't the problem, it's just

the techniques used by the makers were lost when the Gen-O-Pod war erupted. The leaders who sent them on this mission didn't think that was entirely true. They said the makers kept meticulous records and, while Xhaknar and Yontar had killed them readily enough, they'd never bothered with any of the files. There simply hadn't been the need.

If the files were there then they would need to learn to use the machines that made everything work. While daunting at first, they soon realized they didn't need to know how to build the machines, or comprehend – at least not yet – precisely how they worked, they just needed to be able to turn them on and make sure they functioned according to whatever stated parameters there were.

Still a lot of work, true, but not impossible for four smart Mayanoren.

They rode on in silence. There wasn't really any need to say anything. They'd been briefed thoroughly on every aspect and warned they would still have to think on their own when they arrived. There were just too many variables to plan for every single one.

After a while, just to pass the time, they began quizzing each other on the language of the makers. What was a genome, what was a marker, what was mutable material, and what was not? They dissected the DNA strands down to their elemental parts and labeled each one. Their conversation was low and steady. If there was nothing around them for thousands of kays that didn't matter, they saw no reason to announce their presence.

If they were successful, Arreti would know of them soon enough.

N'leah, tired of either acting as a translator or listening to grunts, began teaching the riders the finger talk R'yune used. She explained it had been taught to him by the Din-La so they could, more easily, handle his accounts.

No one was sure which was more surprising, the fact they would soon be able to talk to R'yune, or that he had accounts with the Din-La.

Within a couple of turns, Geldish had, of course, mastered it, but the rest were coming well enough along that they could converse on basic subjects. What surprised everyone was how quickly Sland took to it. Although he had to make some unusual accommodations for his claws, he was understood well enough.

R'yune had joked when everyone could, at least, get his gist that watching Sland sign was like listening to someone with a lisp.

The Din-La, to no one's astonishment, already knew the language. They'd just kept that a secret because R'yune had never given them permission to share. To be fair, he'd never given it any thought whatsoever. He'd been getting along just fine the way things were.

As the turns wore on they'd spend long epi-cliks conversing amongst each other in this new language.

They were still two turns from the lands of Südermann when they saw the campfires in the distance. There were too many pillars of smoke just to be some lone traveler or even a small squad on patrol.

They quickly moved out of the grassland they'd been crossing and into a wooded glade. They waited for dark to come and then N'leah leapt into the sky and headed towards the fires. She returned a short while later and reported they were obviously soldiers from Kalindor. She recognized their uniforms easily enough; they opted for brightly colored ones and got close enough under a brief cloud cover to see their reptilian skin. She estimated their size at about twenty thousand plus the ubiquitous servants they employed.

Too much for them to handle.

Frrd contacted Südermann's palace and let him know the situation. After promising that they really, really, honest and truly, weren't kidding, the radio operator delivered the message to Lord Südermann. An epi-clik later, Lord Südermann himself responded.

"I am usually at my southern palace this time of the sun. They must be hoping to overrun my northern palace and gain a foothold in my lands in my absence. I'm impressed. They must have traveled far to the north and west to get around our border garrisons. Stay where you are for the even and let them march our way come breaklight. Our sentinels would have picked them up next turn anyway, but now we have some time to plan an even greater surprise for them.

"Don't worry, they won't be a problem. We'll see you in a few turns."

With nothing better to do, they made camp and waited for breaklight.

They all slept well, and when the sun broke across the horizon, treated themselves to a hearty meal made by the Din-La. When they were done they'd agreed to follow about a quarter turn behind the Kalindorian army. They were all headed in the same direction anyway and Geldish was curious what kind of surprise Lord Südermann had planned.

There were no scouts deployed to the rear of the army, so the riders had an easy time staying within reconnaissance distance. They marched the entire turn without incident and camped again for the even in a grove of trees the Din-La announced were once called Eucalyptus. They were pretty enough whatever they were.

The next breaklight saw them quicken their pace as the Kalindorian army went on a forced march for some reason. Unlike the last few turns, the skies this turn were cloudy and angry and the lands were leaner and harder. Geldish guessed they were due for some rain before mid-break.

As it worked out, that wasn't all that was due at the appointed time.

Just as they felt the first drops they all heard an unusual sound. It was like a piercing, distant, whistle. It was R'yune who placed it first, pointing for everyone to watch the skies. Uncountable, tiny, black winged tunnels came screaming out of the clouds. Small balls began preceding the tunnels and, suddenly the land in front of them erupted in waves of flame. The tunnels disbanded, revealing themselves to be Succubi, and disbursed back into the clouds.

The riders commented amongst themselves they'd never seen Succubi fly in such tight formations. They were all duly impressed.

The sounds of colossal amounts of weapons' fire could be heard as the rain increased to a torrent and Geldish motioned everyone to take cover in the nearby woods.

"They're going to be coming this way and I'll bet they're not going to be happy about it. We may as well stay safe and dry and watch the show."

Within a clik, the ragged remnants of the Kalindorian army were running past on foot while being hunted down by mounted Mantis Guards. Before they made the rise leading back to the prairie, the massacre was over. Not a single Kalindorian soldier was left standing.

Sland pointed at the returning Guardsmen and smiled.

"Well, dead one, what do you say? Shall we get a royal escort the rest of the way?"

They all laughed and agreed at the same time. Leaving the cover of the woods they were immediately soaked and spotted by the Guards. One of them let out a hearty whoop and rode over to them. It was Mnaas.

"Greetings Geldish, it is good to see you again. Did you enjoy our little surprise?"

"Indeed I did. I didn't know the Succubi had made

it to Lord Südermann's palace ahead of us."

"They didn't. Not really. The main body is still over a turn away. But when Lord Südermann got your message he asked for a small squad to fly ahead and have some target practice. They agreed and, well, here we are. Would you like to ride back with us?"

They did so they did.

Xhaknar finished reading his generals' reports and was pleased. They were ahead of schedule and could march in ten turns. Then he re-read Yontar's strategy. It was straightforward, just the way Xhaknar liked it. The Naradhama would march in fifty battle squares of ten thousand soldiers each and the Mayanoren would march in front. When they got to within one turn of Südermann's domain they were to stop and reform so the ten battle squares would align east to west, with gaps between them and the Mayanoren in the middle. With around fifty-three hundred troopers creating the first line, this would give him a battle front approximately three kays wide and completely mobile. The Mayanoren, of course, were there to catch the brunt of the violence so the Naradhama could march into Südermann's domain and crush anything and anyone in their path.

He knew, thanks to Geldish, he was going to be short a few Naradhama, so he'd arranged to have those squares at the rear. When they split out they would be the farthest away from the center of the battle so they should do fine against any straggling troops that Südermann may have.

With logistics out of the way, Xhaknar went to his northern window and looked at the scene below. It was awe inspiring. Most of the Naradhama had already formed squares and the Mayanoren were in position at the front. He absently noted the Mayanoren seemed to be in better formed ranks than he would have thought possible. Maybe training with the Naradhama had actually paid off. One more thing that had gone right.

The supply wagons to the rear were now getting settled into place. More ammunition would accompany this army than had been on the planet when the Gen-O-Pod war exploded. He was leaving nothing to chance.

Food and slaves were being expertly distributed amongst the battle squares by his generals. There was nothing to concern him there. He continued to watch the troops as every aspect of the plan came slowly together. Yes, they would ready and then, when they got to Südermann's domain, it would be like dropping an acre of stone on his head. That would squash the bug and free Xhaknar up, once and for all, to begin setting the planet right.

Everything was finally going according to plan.

It took the combined forces of the warren just over two more turns to make it to the borders of Südermann's lands. The storm that soaked Geldish and the rest after the Kalindor battle, if it could be called that, had hit the marchers like a hurricane. They were forced to make an emergency camp and just ride it out. They couldn't see five paces in front and they couldn't hear anything at all.

When they did arrive they were met by a contingent of Mantis Guards who led them on a half turn's jaunt to a staging area on the northern border. Once there they were greeted with tents full of freshly cooked food, portable toilets, and bathing facilities. For some, it was a better set up than any of the inns they'd been in. Others didn't even have that lofty comparison. By the time even-fall arrived they were all fed, clean, and happy. All across the camp were posters noting Xhaknar hadn't begun his march yet so they had a few turns to relax. Most of them took that command to mean sleep and they followed it as quickly as possible.

Come breaklight the food tents were operating at full capacity as the Mantis Guards and Lord Südermann's army had arrived just a clik before. More provisions were coming up from the south and soon there was a certain air of joviality permeating the camp. Some of the more creative troopers had included musical instruments in their gear and began leading the assembled in songs of valor and lore. When they tired of those, they switched to songs that would make a kgum blush.

All in all, the mood was festive.

N'leah stepped out of her tent, where R'yune lay napping, and wandered about randomly. If she hadn't known better, she would have thought she'd meandered into a feast turn in some foreign land. She stopped by one of the food tents, grabbed a snack, and then continued her aimless journey. She was completely lost in thought as she stepped around the two warriors, who looked like some insect that she couldn't quite place, and walked headfirst into P'marna.

They stood, motionless, staring at each other and then, as if by command, scooped each other up and kissed passionately. The other troops, who'd never seen two soldiers do that before, especially not before a battle, turned away politely. They remained like that for several epi-cliks until N'leah heard a gentle voice behind her.

"Ah," said the voice, "I see you two have found each other. Good."

P'marna opened her eyes as N'leah turned around and they were forced to meet the glittering gaze of Queen

A'lnuah. N'leah started to bow but the Queen stopped her. Then she started to stammer something, which may or may not have been an apology, but the Queen stopped her again. She tried to think of what else to do besides stand there with her jaw hanging open.

Unfortunately, she had to settle for that.

The Queen smiled wider.

"P'marna told me about your relationship before she was called into my service. There is no shame in love." She paused for a sepi-clik to gather her thoughts and then continued, "We have enough ugliness coming over the horizon. P'marna, take the rest of the turn off. Make sure to report to my caravan at breaklight."

P'marna managed to mumble something like an assent and the two lovers ran off, hand in hand, to be alone. Queen A'lnuah smiled as they disappeared and remembered some of her young trysts.

And some not so young.

Empress ClaalD walked up beside her, also smiling.

"If N'leah's as fierce in love as she is in battle, your young consort may not be able to walk come breaklight."

A'lnuah was going to make a cutting remark about rudeness but discovered she was laughing too hard to try.

The two leaders of the fringe then headed to the command tent to get the latest news.

Zrrm and Frrd would not be going to war. They were here strictly as observers. If this went wrong the Din-La had made plans to escape, en masse, to a distant land. And Zrrm and Frrd were the two to let everyone know which way the golens were finally falling. With nothing much to do at the moment, they were playing an idle game of Ti-Zam. The three dimensional strategy game was popular at officer training schools and amongst the Din-La.

Their wagon and its kgum were well off the staging area. Geldish had moved them there upon arriving at the camp for dual purposes; to keep them safe and out of the way.

They approved of both.

So they were caught off guard when there was a knock at the door. Frrd shrugged, got up and opened it. Surrounded, as they were, by a quarter million or more warriors, he doubted it was a burglar. But whatever he might have expected to greet him, it wasn't who was there.

"May I come in?," asked Lord Südermann.

Not knowing what else to do Frrd just opened the door wider and motioned him in.

Südermann took a seat next to the Ti-Zam game and poured himself a cup of Java. Then he laid a coin in the dish and turned to face them.

"Your citizens and mine have traded for many Suns. One reason I trusted you was my perception you were pacifists. Now I have seen Din-La at the Pit sharpening knives. Actually, nasty daggers, to be more precise. Then I heard from the Brittle Riders how and when those daggers were used. Now I ask you, was I wrong to trust you?"

They considered that for a few sepi-cliks and then Zrrm answered.

"No, your majesty, you were not. The Din-La had never been pacifists, just as we have never been warriors. When pushed, we have defended ourselves as best we can. For the most part that has been accomplished by strict adherence to our clan ties. But violence has had its place occasionally as well. What Kssp and Tffl, the two Din-La you are speaking of, did is out of the ordinary for us, but not unheard of. By slaying the fallen Mayanoren, they protected both themselves and our investment, which is considerable, in this war.

"We have chosen a side in this battle and have as

much to lose as anyone. While we cannot be warriors, mostly because we're really bad at it, we can do many other things, and those are what we'll do."

Südermann measured that response and laughed.

"So, I was right all along, the Din-La do have souls after all."

The three settled into a new, three-way, match and sipped Java. After a while, Südermann decided just to enjoy the turn. The planning was done, the pieces were in place, and they had scouts placed outside Anapsida. They would have plenty of warning when Xhaknar's mobile city of death began to move.

In the command tent, it should have been a bustle of activity. Instead, everyone was sitting around, sipping their favorite beverage, and looking bored. There really wasn't anything to do. Xhaknar's army was still turns away from being ready to march, the troops here were all well taken care of, and they had numerous safeguards in place to warn them when Xhaknar finally set forth.

It was G'rnk who finally suggested they have all the troops run through some basic training exercises together. Their lives were going to depend on each other, they may as well get to know each other before the battle.

That got everyone's attention and was rapidly agreed to. They would let everyone have the remainder of this turn off, they'd all marched hard to get here, and, come breaklight, begin running them through their paces.

Elaand was selected to oversee everything and each commander was given the role of supervising their troops and reporting any slackers. It was also decided to have a turn or two of war games. The winners would get some nominal prize to be determined later.

Mnaas couldn't stop laughing as everything was being arranged and, finally not able to take it anymore, Elaand snapped at him demanding an explanation.

As Mnaas explained what G'rnk had done at the last training camp and how he probably expected the officers here to follow his example …

He didn't have to finish. Elaand looked as though he'd swallowed a fish whole and everyone else was stunned. Mnaas had left out the fact G'rnk had deemed himself nothing but a recruit, and all the others followed suit, from his general report to the combined forces so only he and Südermann knew the whole story that had come in from the temple. He was afraid no one would believe him. Now that it was out every leader of the warrens looked at G'rnk with new respect. The officers of the Mantis Guard looked at him also, in horror.

G'rnk shrugged. "That was what needed to be done then, I would hope we don't need to do it now."

Soon the tent was awash in laughter.

Two Minotaurs, standing outside, paled. Nothing good ever came out of generals laughing, nothing at all.

Oolnok was standing in line to pay his taxes. He had all his receipts and his payment in a small purse tucked in his trousers. When it came his turn the Mayanoren seated there took the receipts, glanced at them, accepted the purse and, after counting it, handed Oolnok a receipt marked paid in full.

With his receipt in hand, he was free to do as he wished with the rest of the turn. He headed over to the tavern thinking there should be an updated news sheet by now. He wasn't disappointed. He read, with interest, the announcement that Lord Xhaknar was marching south to rid Arreti of the threat posed by Lord Südermann. Well, good for him, thought Oolnok, he'd always heard that Südermann character was a bad sort.

Then there was an update stating the brave warriors of the warrens had not been heard from since their march on the eastern horror and it was assumed some harm must have befallen them.

Oolnok was somewhat saddened by that news. Some of those warren leaders were okay in his book. It'd be a shame if they all died.

He was sure some would survive. After all, if no one lived who would tell the villagers about the battle?

Several of the villagers gathered around Oolnok and let him know there were buyers in the warren right now paying good goldens for prancing fowls and anything else a farm might have available. It seems they were stocking up for Xhaknar's march.

After some brief consideration four of them, including Oolnok, agreed to take what they could after next breaklight. He finished his flagon of skank and headed home. When he got there he brought his wife up to date on the news and gave her the tax receipt. This she filed away with the others just in case there was a problem with the warren's records in the future. They'd see for true that old Oolnok wasn't a cheater. He'd paid his taxes completely every Full Sun.

That even, as he and his wife sat on their porch, they saw several large wagons, drawn by kgums or rakyeens, go by. Each of them was lit with several lanterns so they guessed the drivers were going to push through the dark.

They were kind of attractive like that, thought Oolnok. He wondered what his wagon would look like if he added a couple of lanterns and decided to get some prices when he went to the warren next turn.

Every now and then they'd see a rider go by with his steed at a full gallop. Oolnok figured they had to be important messengers for Lord Xhaknar so he silently wished them well. After all, if something made Lord Xhaknar happy he was sure it made the Plains happy. And Oolnok saw no reason to mess with happiness.

Not his or anybody else's.

Yontar sensed something. Something wrong. Not, not wrong, that was the wrong word. He grimaced at his crushing destruction of common grammar and then returned to his thought. There was something new, yes, that was the right word. It was small and different and moving.

He let himself be pulled along by the thing, whatever it was. He had made out enough while at Anapsida to realize that, despite making almost every logical error possible, Xhaknar was about to do the right thing.

He slipped through the ether and passed, once again, the Kordai Sanctuary. This time he gave it nary a thought. The new thing was like some distant beacon, flickering far away. As he slid closer to it he felt it begin to resolve. It was like something he knew intimately and yet something completely unfamiliar.

This was the first new thing that had happened to Yontar since that crazy, half formed, BadgeBeth had visited. He wondered for a sepi-clik whatever happened to him but then refocused on what was in front of him.

It felt like something he should know, and know well, but it kept slipping around the edges, denying him clarity. Excited and confused, he focused harder and searched for the source.

Soon he found it. Four easily recognizable shapes riding through the forest. Mayanoren? Why would Mayanoren hold his attention? They were nothing but fodder.

But these weren't. There was something emanating from them, unlike anything he'd ever sensed from a lowly Mayanoren. It was intelligence, to be sure, but it was something more as well.

Since this was new and nothing else was happening, he decided to study it further. Why would intelligent Mayanoren be stealing through the dark forests? More importantly, why did it seem they were calling out to him? Maybe most important of all, where had intelligent Mayanoren come from in the first place?

He was able to make out some gross details and infer the rest. They were on deisteeds, they were uniformed, and they were carrying the new weapons. All right, that meant they were from Anapsida. Were they sent on a secret mission by Xhaknar? No, he would have found something that important when he was in his mind.

More facts, he needed more facts.

It was clear they were barely of warrior age, but that still meant they were there when he was alive. How had he missed them? He supposed that was easy. Anapsida was buried in tourists and new residents. Small mental noises like this would be lost in the general mish mash of it all. He was sensitive, not omniscient.

Enough of that then, there were four, intelligent, Mayanoren who seemed to have weak psychic abilities. They probably weren't even aware of them, just thought themselves lucky; always turning before the blade is pulled, always ducking before the arrow hits.

If that was clear enough, what wasn't was why they seemed to be calling him.

He let his thoughts get as close as they could to these new Mayanoren. Unlike Xhaknar, he couldn't get inside their minds, but he was able to get closer to them than any others he'd sensed since being here.

They weren't calling him, at least not intentionally, but they were focused on him. Their whole sense of being seemed wrapped around Yontar. As that became clear so did the concept they thought they could find him.

He was about to laugh until he realized that they knew, full well, where he was and weren't bothered by it at all. This new thing was now an interesting thing. They were headed to the facility of the makers, that much was evident by their direction now that he knew the underlying facts.

Had these smart Mayanoren figured how to do what he could not? Was there something at the facility they thought would bring him back?

Then came a sobering thought. Why in Rohta's name would they want to bring him back?

That required careful probing. He filtered out the flotsam about himself and pulled back shocked. They were convinced Xhaknar was going to lose his war with Südermann. They didn't believe in any eastern menace, they believed it was a ruse of some sorts by the warrens. And they believed it had worked.

They'd had access to the same basic facts as Xhaknar and had come to a radically different conclusion. More importantly to Yontar, since he hadn't been too concerned with what had transpired as with what was about to, their conclusions made perfect sense. Limiting their thoughts to what they could prove, they'd eliminated mystery demons and were left with a trap. Of what nature they didn't know, but a trap nonetheless.

And Yontar could see now the trap was working. The warrens were to be unmolested when Xhaknar marched on Südermann. There was no reason for him to waste the time or assets with their armies gone on some crazy kgum chase.

Yontar was awed. It was the kind of scheme he would have come up with had he been facing the wrath of

Anapsida. In one fell swoop, the warrens had been rendered as helpless as a small with a flower. And by their own volition.

So, if Yontar were on the other side, what would he do? Align with Südermann was the obvious answer, but the warrens were just as afraid of that bug monster as anyone else.

Or were they? Geldish seemed to be popping up a lot lately and he'd traveled extensively in his many Suns. Could he know Südermann, or at least know a way to contact him in a neutral manner?

That was possible. In fact, it was highly probable.

So what would they do if they garnered that alliance?

What would he do? He'd get every trooper he could and march to the lands of Südermann to meet Xhaknar.

Well, assuming what these Mayanoren believed was true, they'd just done that. They'd posted a proclamation, held a parade, waved their flags, tossed candies to the masses, and marched over one hundred and fifty thousand troops, along with enough caravans and wagons to support an army three times that size, to the Gaping Canyon, where they would easily enough turn west when they got to the youngling pass. They'd aligned themselves with Südermann right under Xhaknar's gaze. And he'd approved it.

He thought again about the caravans. Was there really an eastern menace, but one aligned with the warrens, they'd hidden in those many wagons? Possible, but dubious. More likely they oversupplied for the long, roundabout, trek to the domain of Südermann and his bug warriors.

Now, what could be done about it?

Absolutely nothing.

Even if he could get a coherent message to Xhaknar, he wouldn't be believed. And even if he was, Xhaknar would still march figuring he'd invested too much into the war and would lose too much face by backing out. Besides, if you add the combined might of the warrens with what they knew Südermann has, he'd still have an overwhelming advantage.

Realizing the Mayanoren had, at least, thirty more turns before they made it to the facility, and being as curious as he'd ever been in his life, he turned and headed for the home of Südermann.

It took him less than a clik to reach the northern border of Südermann's lands and he saw a lot of inchoate activity. At first, he thought Südermann was at war with someone else and then realized they were war games. He'd tried them for a while with the Naradhama when they were new, but they'd become too free thinking and he couldn't allow that.

He couldn't make out any specifics, but the general outlines showed these were all well trained troops and they had some tricks up their sleeves.

So this would be the war. Unending guile with considerable resources against an unstoppable army with unending resources.

Damn, thought Yontar, he really wished he could be there. It was going to be one Zanubi of a war.

"We must make this a battle and not a war," King Uku was addressing the commanders, "no matter how lavishly Lord Südermann supplies us, and no matter our technological advantages, the fact remains Xhaknar outnumbers us significantly and has unlimited resources. Or as close to that amount as need concern us.

"If this becomes protracted he could strip his garrisons and just overrun us with sheer numbers. At some point, we would simply run out of enough ammunition to kill them all, and then we would be done. We must be like assassins in the darkling even. We must strike fast, hard and be as lethal as we can from the beginning. Anything less than that and we're doomed."

There were murmurs of assent around the table as everyone looked at the latest reports. Elaand spoke next.

"We know enough now to know he's got around three hundred thousand Mayanoren set to lead the march and, as far as we can count, fifty battle squares of ten thousand troops each. Our guess is, since he's providing each square with their own supply wagons, he intends to spread those squares out into a three kay long front as he nears us. He'll probably leave the Mayanoren in the middle to absorb as much fire as possible.

"We need to attack before he can make the switch from the long column to the wide front. We would be too spread out to be of any value if that happens."

More murmurs of assent as Gornd stared at the map.

"Here then," he said stabbing the map with a claw, "two turns north of here, in the scrub mountains. This is the widest plain where he can make the change and then march on us. He'll have to make camp to make it happen. These aren't garrison soldiers with their cornicens and flags all marching in pretty shapes, they will need time and space to make the switch. We hit them there and we do it in the dark."

"How will we see in the dark?" asked Empress ClaalD.

"They'll have camp fires enough to warm and feed a million troops, they'll be lit up as pretty as you please. More worrying is how do we prevent them from seeing us? There is far less cover there than where Lord Südermann wanted to stage the ambush."

It took almost the remainder of the turn, but they were able to come up with a plan.

Since the Mayanoren always camped away from the

Naradhama, the Fierstan / BadgeBeth alliance would attack them as soon as the camp fires were lit. The Succubi would bomb the Naradhama randomly and cause as much damage as they could while the Ant-People would destroy as much as they could of munitions and supplies. The remaining forces would be split out behind the scrub mountains. With the best response time available it would still be half a clik before they could arrive. Until then, the others would be on their own.

"What worries me," Lord Südermann chose his words carefully, "is we are leaving those forces alone for a long time. Even in the chaos, you are planning, there's a good chance of them being overrun and annihilated."

Watcher Urkel laughed.

"Don't you fret Lord Südermann. We didn't bring any virgins with us and we aren't taking any home. We'll hold them until you arrive or you'll have easy targets when you get there since they'll all be huddled over us stripping our shiny new weapons."

With nothing more to be said, the conference broke up. Next breaklight the troops were informed of the strategy. Südermann was worried the Fierstans and BadgeBeth would feel as though they were sacrificial animals. Instead, they seemed to relish the thought. He heard one guardian, he thought his name was Nak, say to a BadgeBeth, "Did you hear that Zarn? We've got a whole half clik to ourselves and we're only outnumbered six to one. What will we do with the rest of our time?"

Südermann shook his head in wonder. As much as he loved them, he would never understand warriors.

By the time three Din-La wagons arrived three turns

later the camp had been turned upside down. They slept by light and drilled by dark. The wagons pulled up to the sentries and they announced who they were. Zrrm was sent for to verify their identities and they were finally let into the main site. It was near mid-break and the whole place was eerily silent.

They headed over to the command tent and found Lord Südermann sitting with Geldish.

"Greetings great rulers, I am called Tllw," he smiled, "I have brought your warriors a talisman for the coming war."

With that, he pulled out a patch and handed it to Südermann. It was a red diamond with a yellow lightning bolt slashing across it with a green letter 'R' in the middle.

"This is the original logo worn by the Great Rohta himself. It is the logo that once belonged to all our brands. We felt it was time, once again, this image tied us all together. We believe you have entered this war as many, but you will win as one."

Before they could say anything in response, he pulled an arm band out with an identical logo.

"For the Llamia and the Succubi."

Südermann thought for barely an instant.

"An excellent idea. We should have done something like this ourselves. Take them over to the quartermaster's tent and have him make the arrangements."

Tllw bowed and exited the tent.

Geldish chuckled humorlessly.

"Patches or no, I still wish the Rangka would ride with us. Combined we could defeat Xhaknar once and for all."

"Maybe so," deliberated Südermann, "but it is not to be and wishing cannot make it so. Besides, dead one, our original agreement was you would destroy Xhaknar's army, you said nothing about trying to kill Xhaknar himself."

Geldish actually laughed.

"So, my own words, like my forgotten flesh, come

back to haunt me. You're probably right. If his army is crushed we can imprison him. He's insanely strong, but steel walls should suffice."

It was Südermann's turn to be pensive.

"Have you thought what will happen? After this is done, I mean."

"With the Plains?" Südermann nodded and Geldish answered. "Assuming we survive, I imagine they'll put together their version of the old Elders' Council, but with a better military and improved responses to threats. They won't need us, that's for sure. Look at the alliances they've formed and what they've accomplished in such a short time. They deserve to work it out for themselves."

Südermann nodded again and went to get another snifter of brandy, with extra sugar.

Four turns after the Din-La arrived with their patches, word came in; Xhaknar was on the way.

It was as though an ancient city of the makers had decided to get up and walk, structures and all, to some new destination. The Mayanoren front line, three thousand across and one hundred deep, led the procession. Behind it, fifty battle squares with one hundred Naradhama across, an equal number deep marched two squares across and twenty-five deep. Between each row of squares followed food and supply wagons. Xhaknar had thought to have the temp-slaves there too but decided against it. He figured they would be too much of a distraction until after Südermann was crushed.

Behind the squares sat Lord Xhaknar in a palanquin carried by sixteen slaves. Behind him were countless wagons of munitions, spare supplies and, of course, the caravans of the temp-slaves.

The rhythmic staccato of the army's footsteps shook the ground and echoed for kays in all directions. That was fine with Xhaknar, let Südermann know they were coming. It would make it easier on him if they came out and met in the field instead of forcing him to slash through that damnable jungle.

Within a kay from the start of the march the slaves and supply workers had all fallen in step with the army, making the sound even louder and more terrifying. Another kay after that the sergeants had them all chanting in unison.

One glorious rhyme after another, extolling the greatness of their Lord Xhaknar and celebrating the victory which would soon be theirs.

Since Xhaknar had taken the time to align and provision his troops outside Anapsida he didn't have to wait for turns for them to form up. The sounds of the footsteps were like orgiastic thunder to Xhaknar. He let the essence wash over him. Nothing, absolutely nothing, was going to stop him now. Not with this army.

In ten turns he would be there. In twenty, the lands of Südermann would be his.

They would train for six more turns and on the seventh turn, they would march north to take their positions in and around the scrub mountains. They would arrive a turn or so ahead of Xhaknar, but it was felt that was better than arriving after.

Geldish was going over the latest reports from the spies and looking about as puzzled as a being with no skin can look.

"What troubles you, dead one," asked Elder Urnak,

"is there something amiss with our plans?"

"No, nothing important like that. Just something that is a bit of an enigma," he handed the reports to Urnak for review, "where are the steeds? He's marching almost eight hundred thousand soldiers on foot. Why in Rohta's name would he do that?"

Südermann chuckled. "That will be Yontar's doing, I'd imagine. The last two times they tried to attack us, many Suns ago, the Mantis Guard hung razor wire between the trees high enough to kill the rider but not low enough to harm the steed. We got a lot of free steeds those turns."

Geldish smiled, then nodded, "Then we've won. He's fighting the last battle, not the next one."

For the first time since the rumors of Geldish pilfering the repository had come to their attention, there was hope in the command tent. No longer just grim determination, although there was that in abundance, but now it was tempered with unforeseen optimism. Nothing crazy mind you, but enough for them to think there might be something to do the next Dark Sun other than hope someone mourned over their grave.

They looked over the rest of the reports and Queen A'lnuah smiled.

"He's coming in a straight line. It's almost tempting to let the Succubi get some target practice in before he arrives."

"Tempting, but foolish," said the Kgul, much to everyone's astonishment, "we would be giving away one of our greatest secrets before we had to. No, let them come and find out everything all at once. That is our best hope."

Once everyone got over their astonishment, they agreed. They would not toy with this army, they would kill it in one blow or die trying.

Let the monster come, they were as ready as they were going to be when he arrived.

Makish was tending to a small patch of garden when a Kgul walked up and stood. After an epi-clik, he finally stood up and looked at her.

"Yes, what can I do for you?"

"It has begun."

"We know."

"Will my mate return?"

"I don't know. I don't know if anyone of them will."

"Why did you not ride? Why did you leave them when they need you most?"

"When the Kgul needed me most, I found them a home. When they needed me most, I saved their brand. This they do not need me for. This is something they will, and must, do for themselves."

The Kgul pondered that for a moment and went back to her chores without showing any emotion. Elzish and Karrish came across the garden and stood near Makish watching the Kgul work.

"She is worried," stated Karrish," and probably scared. You know we did the right thing."

"Yes," replied Makish, "I know that, but that does not mean I have to like it. I fear for Geldish and his Brittle Riders. I fear for all the brands of the Plains. I fear for our future should Xhaknar win and return enraged. I know why we did not ride, I just feel ashamed we used logic to justify cowardice."

With that, he walked away from his brethren and headed into the kitchen of the temple.

The other two Rangka seemed lost in thought. They did not notice when a gentle rain began to fall. They did not notice when even-fall came and the skies grew dark. They did not notice when breaklight followed, as it always has.

They did notice that they were trying to reach Geldish, and he'd shut them out.

For the last turn as Rohta's Warriors – which is what they now called their alliance - assembled themselves in the scrub mountains, they could hear the growing, monotonous, sound of Xhaknar's army approaching. It was a sound to inspire dread, a sound to inspire fear, it was a sound designed to make blood turn blue and hearts turn yellow, it was a sound they patently ignored.

And when they did deign to notice it, to a one, they smiled a tight smile. The kind of smile that can only mean three little words; "Bring. It. On."

Watcher Urkel and King Gornd had stationed their troops near the south end of the valley between the scrub mountains. With the BadgeBeth leading the way, they dug deep trenches and shrouded them with wildwoods and branches. When they were done it looked like every other dying copse in the land.

Queen A'lnuah led her Succubi to the highest peak, which was only about three thousand feet or so up, and stationed them on the east side, away from prying eyes.

King Uku, Empress ClaalD, and Elder Urnak had positioned their troops behind the eastern peaks and picked a stretch of land that, though barren of hiding spots once they crossed the ridge, allowed them the fastest route to the Naradhama camps.

Lieutenant Elaand and G'rnk led their mixed troops of Wolfen, haven lords, Kgul and Mantis Guards up behind the western peaks and, like their counterparts across the valley, selected the quickest path down instead of the best camouflaged.

Lord Südermann and Geldish remained with Südermann's army and the Brittle Riders, who were set up on the northern end of the valley on the western side, hidden by a small forest. They would remain hidden until the others had completely engaged the Naradhama.

No one knew where the Ant-People were and everyone thought that was a good thing. After all, they were supposed to be hiding.

About mid-break the following turn the first of Xhaknar's scouts appeared. There were six of them , spread far apart, covering the whole valley in a moving crescent formation.

The furthest to the west was straggling behind, seemingly admiring the scenery. Suddenly an Ant-Person popped up from nowhere, drove a large, round, blade into the scout's back and let out a painful, shrieking noise as he disappeared to wherever it is he came from.

Geldish absently noted the Rangka could learn a trick or two from him.

The other scouts spun just in time to see their comrade fall and watch some rustling in the leaves. They drew exactly the right conclusion, at least as far as the Ant-Person was concerned.

"NARKLING! There are narklings here! Form up on center, weapons at the ready."

Everyone watched, mildly amused, as the five remaining scouts formed a back to back circle and eased out of the canyon, leaving their comrade behind.

Geldish turned to N'leah and smiled. "Let the others know they'll be in tight formation once they encamp. Much easier targets that way."

She giggled as she picked up the radio.

He realized she'd been in a much better mood as of late, although he wasn't sure why, and then turned to Lord Südermann.

"You know, rabid xenophobes or not, I could learn

to like those Ant-People."

Xhaknar listened to the reports about the narkling and laughed.

"Not to worry, that's good news. If there are narklings in those woods, that means there aren't any troops in there. We'd already be hearing the narkling hunting screams if there were. Just stay in a tight formation when we get to the valley and prepare to move the squares after camp is set.

"Oh, before I forget, when we get to the camp, send me a couple of slaves, mal or femme, I don't care. These last few turns have bored me and I need some excitement."

Even though they were now spread out to four squares wide and marching double time, it still took Xhaknar's army five cliks to completely enter the valley. Once there, however, they moved quickly. Within two cliks after even-fall they had the campfires burning and were passing out food to the troops.

About a clik after that, Xhaknar began getting the excitement he'd requested.

The sky was cloudy and the moons were hidden. The troops and their servants were laughing and joking and making rude suggestions, so they didn't hear the whistling noise from above until it was too late. No one knows who the Naradhama was who finally pointed up, but it was the last gesture of his or her life. He or she went to meet Rohta in an outburst of flame. The Succubi headed from east to west dropping bombs in tight formations and in rapid succession. Within an epi-clik, a third of the camp was on fire. Before the troopers could get their weapons aimed at the departing Succubi another wave came in from the south and was equally as deadly. The wave had disappeared to the west then reappeared from there and began another bombing run laying waste to the front of the lines this time as they headed east.

Some of the brighter Naradhama, not to be fooled again, aimed their weapons to the south to catch the return of the second wave. Unfortunately for them the second wave had circled east and approached from that direction.

Within five epi-cliks, the camp was in complete pandemonium.

While sharp shooters scanned the skies for any more incoming waves of Succubi, the Mayanoren lines simply exploded. Huge waves of dirt and debris smashed through their ranks and that dirt and debris were followed by twenty-thousand Fierstans on deisteeds firing volley after volley of cold, hard, steel.

The Mayanoren general was one of the Named Ones, but he could only work with what he had. And what he had was a bunch of freaked out Mayanoren soldiers who were trying their best to get the heck out of camp.

They ran straight into the Naradhama who were coming to investigate this new threat.

Actually, to be more accurate, they were pushed by fifteen thousand or so BadgeBeths who were not busy blowing up dirt. The fighting was so close in they ignored their swords and weapons and just started slicing through anyone not BadgeBeth with their claws. Appendages, limbs and, formerly internal, organs were tossed through the air as they continued their ruthless attack.

One of the Naradhama generals was able to rally not only his troops but enough Mayanoren to matter and begin a counter offensive. He was starting to make a steady advance when the whole north end of the valley went up in an explosion of apocalyptic proportions.

Xhaknar was thrown almost three hundred feet to the south and landed, rather unceremoniously, on a clump of bodies with his pants around his ankles and a dead temp-slave wrapped around his thighs.

Every single munitions wagon was gone as were about half the supply wagons and a third of the temp-slaves.

Geldish and Südermann looked at the destruction and smiled. Geldish reminded himself to meet an Ant-Person and say thank you when this was done.

But the Naradhama are the Naradhama, not some smalls playing with sticks. The generals issued orders and troops followed them. Sharp shooters were set up to scan the skies and other troops were sent to the front to crush the Fierstan and BadgeBeth attack.

Also true is the fact that numbers are numbers no matter what else you might wish them to be. As things stood right now Xhaknar's army still outnumbered its current attackers almost ten to one. Well, maybe, eight or nine to one when you factored in all the casualties caused thus far.

An entire battle square, somehow completely missed in the maelstrom, began advancing into the Fierstan and BadgeBeth lines and bodies started falling in their path. The Succubi, denied the element of surprise on their latest run, began falling from the skies as shots ripped through their wings and torsos.

Some were still clutching their bombs as they fell and exploded into the enemy ranks with a final, fiery, farewell as they died.

The Fierstans and BadgeBeth weren't done for yet. They split their formation and headed east and west towards the mountains. The Naradhama were forced to follow them into the harsh scrub bushes and were displeased to find a series of ditches which were filled with pointed spikes. As the Naradhama front lines fell to their deaths, the Fierstans and BadgeBeth turned and renewed their assault. They backed into a succession of crags that were fronted by a string of openings which allowed no more than fifty or so troopers through at any one time. It no longer mattered how many troopers the Naradhama had. They couldn't all fit through the entrances. Naradhama bodies were starting to pile up.

Each side had the other pinned down and it looked like it was going to be a long stalemate until the rest of the Naradhama arrived with explosives and crushed these interlopers.

One general, frustrated at the lack of progress, and unaware all of the munitions' wagons were gone, ordered grenades brought forward to kill the rebels.

Not that it mattered. The young trooper, Fifth class, who received the order, was killed a couple sepi-cliks later when the east and west walls of the canyon exploded with weapons fire and the remaining forces of Rohta's Warriors descended from above.

Nak, hiding behind a boulder in the crag, turned to Zarn and laughed.

"See, I told you we were having too much fun. They showed up ten epi-cliks early to join the party!"

Xhaknar was about to order the freeze guns broken out of munitions when he turned and noticed there were no munitions wagons. All he could do was watch helplessly as fifteen thousand Kgul slammed into the western edge of his army followed by thousands upon thousands of Wolfen and haven lords – haven lords? - and a large group of green skinned warriors with odd eyes he had to assume belonged to Südermann.

He turned just in time to see thousands more Llamia, being ridden by Se-Jeant warriors, descend on his eastern edge and they were flanked by thousands of additional Minotaurs.

One of his generals managed to make it back and give a report. Without hesitating Xhaknar ordered a small force to stay to the south and keep the Fierstans and BadgeBeth pinned down and every other available trooper to defend the east and west flanks.

The order had barely escaped his mouth when Geldish and the Brittle Riders, followed by one hundred thousand warriors from Südermann's army, came racing out of the north and smashed into Xhaknar's rear flank.

The fighting devolved quickly after that. Formations on both sides crumbled while fighting went from gun to gun, to sword to sword, to dagger to dagger, to, lastly, hand to hand or hand to claw as the case may be.

All through the even, past breaklight, and on past mid-break, the fighting wore on. The Fierstans and the BadgeBeth had broken out of the crags and rejoined the fray. Südermann's army held the northern front and slowly ground forward. The Mantis Guard mixed with the Kgul and turned into an unstoppable force. The Minotaurs aimed to meet with the Fierstans and began crushing anyone in their path. The Se-Jeants and the Llamias cut to the north to meet with Südermann's army and, slowly and painfully, began flanking the Naradhama.

Casualties were mounting and neither side was giving in.

Finally, it all began to wear down. Left with no other choice, Xhaknar called a retreat.

His generals began rounding up their troops and heading towards the north end of the canyon. The Succubi took that as an invitation and began bombing any formation featuring ten or more Mayanoren or Naradhama.

Xhaknar narrowly missed being hit by a bomb. He

picked himself off the ground and found himself staring at the point of a sword.

"I know you can't be killed, at least not easily," said Geldish calmly as his sword never wavered, "but it might be fun to try. Maybe cut you up every turn just to watch you grow pieces back so I can cut you up again. Maybe once a season we can schedule a public beheading just to raise goldens for the families you've ruined.

"Yes, that could be fun. Don't you agree?"

Xhaknar didn't speak. Instead, he looked slowly around and saw those four loathsome fringe dwellers, all with weapons pointed at him, covered in blood and gore, some of it was their own, and Südermann, the bug monster itself, sitting on a deisteed looking as though nothing special was going on. Beyond them, he saw his Naradhama surrendering and the few surviving Mayanoren escaping into the mountains without pursuit.

Ashes. It was all ashes. It had all been a Rangka trick. Well, he still could have one victory this turn. He quickly sprang to his right and drove his fist through Südermann's abdomen just as Geldish beheaded him.

They all dismounted as Geldish ordered Xhaknar's head and body to be burned immediately in separate fires and then knelt next to his new friend, the soon to be late, Lord Südermann.

"Ha," spat Südermann as blood coursed out of his mouth, "that's only two out of three. Let's see you bring water to Go-Chi."

And, with that, he died.

EPILOGUE

It took twenty turns to clear the battlefield. The bodies of the Mayanoren and the Naradhama were piled in the middle of the valley and, eventually, burned. Per the traditions of the Südermenn, Lord Südermann's body was transported to his homeland and buried, during a private ceremony for his family, in the grounds of the northern palace next to each of his predecessors. The deceased of Rohta's warriors were disbursed in accordance with the traditions of their brands. The wounded were tended to by the many medical experts Südermann had provided and the healers of the Plains. More survived than Geldish would have hoped but, even with that, a full third of the original warriors would not be returning to their families.

All of the royals had suffered one type of serious injury or another, but none more serious than Queen A'lnuah. She'd been lost near the end of the battle and was presumed dead. She was found, two turns later, buried under a pile of Naradhama corpses, covered with slash and bullet wounds. P'marna was called to administer the final rituals for the dead when A'lnuah spat a mouthful of blood and dirt on the ground and announced, weakly, she might need medical attention.

She was correct.

The Brittle Riders took a total of five hundred and eighty-seven stitches between the four of them, R'yune counted. The medicos were sure, within one Full Sun, there would hardly be any scars. As they noted, it was one advantage of being a brand. Due to the fact most brands were designed to do dangerous work, Rohta had added many embellishments to the standard immune system. And if some of those creatures were only, initially, for amusement, like the Succubi, it was still easier to leave the embellishments in rather than start over.

Geldish had managed to meet an Ant-Person before they took Lord Südermann's body back for burial. He told them how sorry he was Lord Südermann had died and how grateful he was for all of the Ant-People's support. The reply he got caught him off guard.

"Brands die, Lord Südermann lives forever. Nevertheless, you are," he seemed to be searching for a word he wouldn't offend himself with, "welcome." He'd then spun on his heel and faded into the camp.

At the end of twenty turns, Rohta's Warriors began to pack up their belongings and get ready to head home. The Din-La had reported the stunning news and agreed to set up trade emporiums in every warren. As Zrrm mentioned when he was tallying up the initial orders, which were coming in despite the fact there were no emporiums in place, the Din-La investment in the war was going to turn a tidy profit.

No one was sure whether to laugh or cry at that announcement, so they just left it alone.

While the battlefield was being cleansed and the wounded tended, the royals, minus A'lnuah who was still in the healers' tent, agreed to set up an Elders' Council, funded equally by the brands, to oversee governance. Gornd pointed out they should all decline seats on this new council so they could deal with the issues of their brands. Further, he felt they should appoint representatives who could be rotated every few Full Suns to prevent any one group from becoming entrenched. That idea was met with unanimous approval and the representatives were picked easily enough. They all waited for Queen A'lnuah to agree, before posting any formal announcement, which she did readily enough once she heard it.

The Fierstans would be represented by Guardian Teg, the BadgeBeth would be represented by Warrior Zarn, The Dwellers of the Pit would be represented by Greko, The Succubi would be represented by T'reena of Anara, the Se-Jeant would be represented by Ata, the Llamia would be represented by craft-master GnaalK, the Wolfen would be represented by Pack Leader T'rlp and the Kgul would be represented by a Kgul.

They didn't have any names, so they had to make do with that.

Geldish was offered a seat and politely declined. The Din-La declined as well because they didn't want to appear as though they were favoring one client over another. In addition, it was agreed a representative of Lord Südermann would have a seat but only have a vote on issues relating to his lands. They all hoped those would be few.

The final part of the agreement was the first council would serve for ten Full Suns. After that, each brand could pick a new representative and all future terms would be five Full Suns.

There were millions of other details to be dealt with, but they all felt this was a good start.

On the even of the twentieth turn, Elaand showed up with a small contingent of the Royal Mantis Guard. He announced the new Lord Südermann was prepared to honor any agreements between the warrens and her father, but she'd been unable to find any. When Geldish informed him that, since no one had realistically expected to survive this, there weren't any, Elaand looked stunned, and then laughed. Then, while looking around the command tent at all the slings and bandages and casts he started laughing so hard it took him a full five epi-cliks to stop. When he finally did manage to regain control he looked at Geldish hoping for an answer for his new, and young, lord.

"Lord Südermann wanted to open trade with the Plains. Start there. The Din-La can handle the arrangements and, if this Lord Südermann is anything like her father, she'll figure out the rest easily enough."

Elaand nodded soberly, made some notes in a small book he was carrying and sat down. All of the assembled took that moment to extend their condolences and share a short moment with Elaand. Elder Urnak left the tent briefly and returned with a sack, which he handed to him. He opened it and smiled. It was full of Minotaur pastries.

He'd felt Xhaknar die. That was another new experience. They seemed to be mounting up lately in this realm. He'd been over the battlefield when the ambush happened. There was nothing he could do, of course, so he'd watched in rapt fascination as the warrens and the forces of Südermann had delayed the second prong of their attack, allowing the Succubi and the two other brands to bear the brunt of the counter assault. He couldn't make out any details and Xhaknar's mind had been a raging torrent so there was no way in to get a better view.

But, he had to admit, that was the riskiest battlefield move he'd ever seen. Whoever thought of it would be a dangerous foe if he ever made it back.

The smart Mayanoren were still on their way to the facility, so there was naught there for him to see yet. He idly wondered what they were planning and decided to wait. At least it gave him something to look forward to. Suddenly, he sensed something else and eased over to see what it was.

He soon deduced it was another group of smart Mayanoren. They looked to be the only survivors from the battle. He couldn't make out their number, but it was easy enough to see they, too, were headed for the facility. They were on foot so it would take them longer to get there but, who knew? No matter what his immediate future promised to be interesting.

He wafted through his realm, which is how he thought of it now, and wondered what other surprises awaited. He was flabbergasted to get an answer so soon, but that did tend to be the nature of the concept of surprise.

"Hello Yontar," said the quiet voice of Geldish, "are you enjoying yourself?"

"Well, hello Geldish," he sneered as he whirled to face the Rangka, "did you come to gloat?"

"No, not at all. Things did not work out at all as I'd planned. I wanted Xhaknar imprisoned so I could swap his mind for yours and then know where you were at all times. Xhaknar, naturally, would have gone slowly insane here so I wouldn't have had to worry about him ever again. But, sadly, he made me kill him. And that means I have to come up with something else to do to you.

"You're already dead in the traditional sense, and nothing here can die any more, not even by my doing, so what do I do with you? You're a threat as long as you have consciousness, that much I know. I don't believe there's a way to escape the nether realm, but I believe if there is, you'll eventually find it.

"Now whether that's in five hundred Full Suns or five turns, I can't tell. But somehow, some way, you'll be a threat again."

"Are you asking me for advice? I'm probably not going to give you any, I hope you know that."

Geldish shrugged. "LA'KYEE Shhak, Yontar."

As Geldish faded from view, Yontar smiled.

"Oh, yeah, LA'KYEE Shhak Geldish, LA'KYEE Shhak."

Oolnok looked at his pretty wagon with the lanterns he'd added and smiled as he loaded his family up. They were going to the warren for the Warm Sun Festival. It had been one Full Sun since the village had heard about the death of Xhaknar and the destruction of his army. Oolnok had been worried the Südermann character was going to take over the Plains but was pleased to find out there was an Elders' Council like the one that was rumored to have been in place before Xhaknar.

The new council wasn't too bad either. They'd lowered taxes, outlawed slavers, cleaned up Anapsida and opened up a lot of new trade. It turned out those bug-people really liked na-porcine meat so Oolnok got over his initial revulsion and sold them as much as he could. He'd even gotten a loan from the Din-La to expand his farm and add a hundred more kgum and five hundred more na-porcines. The goldens were coming in nice and steady now.

He and his family were getting ready to head into the warren and spend an even at an inn when his neighbor rode up with some unbelievable news. And, though Oolnok didn't believe it, his family wanted to see. Well, they had some time, so he tossed some provisions in the wagon and they left with their neighbor, and about forty others Oolnok noted, and headed east.

When they passed the south gate of the warren Oolnok was shocked to see everyone pouring out to join them. He couldn't believe brands were that gullible. Then again he was going too, so who was he to say?

It took a full three turns to get to the Gaping Canyon. Along the way, brands were pointing at this or that, as they could see grasses and small flowers growing where there had been nothing but decay and cracked ground before. When they got to the canyon Oolnok looked and saw nothing but brands as far as the eye could see. It was as though every brand from every warren had emptied out on the edge.

Then he heard the sound. It was a mix of rumbling and whooshing he didn't recognize. It didn't seem threatening, but it bothered him he couldn't place it. He shaded his eyes to focus further east where it appeared the sound was coming from and saw the clouds. They weren't like any clouds he'd ever seen; they were dark and sinuous, about half way up the canyon walls and they covered the entire canyon from north to south. At least as far as he could tell.

Beneath them, he could finally make out the source of the whooshing sound. It was water cascading over the rocks and scrub bushes and filling the canyon.

"Well, will you look at that," murmured Oolnok, "if this keeps up in another Full Sun we can take the smalls here in the Good Sun and go swimming. I bet they'd like that."

His wife smiled at her wonderful husband and passed out prancing fowl sandwiches as they watched the canyon fill and the waters surge south towards Go-Chi.

The End of Book One

11000464R00199

Made in the USA
Lexington, KY
04 October 2018